Web of Deception

The Betrayal Continues

Book 2

By J.W. Hill

Web of Deception

The Betrayal Continues

Book 2

Copyright 2023

J.W. Hill

Editing by J. W. Hill

Chloe *D*

I dedicate this book to my wife, who has stood by me through thick and thin. She was there when I was at my lowest and ready to give up on life. She reached out her hand and helped me to my feet.

She picked me up and turned me in the right direction, giving me the guidance and the courage. I thank you, my Chole D.

Special Acknowledgement:

I want to acknowledge my brilliant daughter, Gabrielle Hill, who has encouraged me to live out my dream of becoming an author.

Thank you, Gabby, for standing with me I see your inspiration in continuing your education in nursing, and this has given me the desire to move forward with "A Betrayal Continues".

Congratulations on being chosen for the Bachelor of Nursing Program.

I also want to acknowledge my siblings for their support, and my aunts, cousins, and friends who have been supportive, thank you.

Most importantly, I want to thank God for his strength, guidance, and determination over my life.

~J.W. Hill

Chapter: 1

Lying on her back, listening to the quiet storm hour over the radio, Gloria closed her eyes to visualize being with Drew. Though it had been three days since they were together, Gloria continued to relive the moment. It was as perfect of an image as she could have fantasized. Gloria wasn't surprised by how their bodies reacted to each other, but what was surprising was how she continued to feel Drew's body movements pressing against her. Whether it was overactive nerves resulting from the intense orgasms she experienced or the way Drew etched his name into her heart, Gloria couldn't forget their magical morning by the lake. Their fairytale morning was causing Gloria to straddle the fence without knowing which side to land on. She had the utmost respect for Mason and how he treated her as his lady, but her heart stored too many memories of Drew to walk away so easily. Gloria didn't have to question Mason's love for her; he'd shown it many times. The problem she was facing with Mason; was how he made her feel when he made love to her. His balls-deep, rough sexual act was something she didn't enjoy. She often was left feeling as if she was some whore he'd picked up from the streets. But Drew, on the other hand, was totally different; he was caring, gentle and compassionate when it came to making love to her. Each time they made love, she felt Drew's love without him saying it. Drew was romantic and considerate when it came to her sexual needs. He made it his mission to satisfy her, and never had he disappointed her. But as perfect as Drew was, he wasn't without his problems. Gloria's turnoffs with Drew dealt with his inability to make things happen when it mattered most. Drew lacked the go-get-it attitude she wanted him to have. Drew's refusal to stand up to his mother in her defense was the main reason she sought comfort in other men's arms, and by doing so, she'd damaged their relationship. Gloria had a lot of work to do if she was going to win back Drew's heart, and if making love by the lake was any indication of what was to come, she was on her way to accomplishing her goal.

As Gloria looked over her life, she realized she had many options to choose from. There were several young interns who were itching for the chance to get into her panties, not to mention the married and well-established doctors who had asked her out for coffee. Gloria had everything going for her; she was smart, young, and beautiful, with a body to die for. She had it all, and though she had the pick of the litter, the man she wanted most was the man she threw away.

 Giving up on her relationship with Drew was the worst mistake Gloria had ever made but after sharing that beautiful Sunday morning together with him, she strongly believed she had a chance to regain what she walked away from.

For more than three days, Gloria waited for Drew to contact her, and after not hearing from him, Gloria decided to call him. It was late and she didn't think Drew would answer but to her amazement, he answered on the second ring.

"Hello," Drew answered.

"Hey, I hadn't heard from you, so I decided to call to check in with you. How are you?" Gloria asked.

"Doing well, you? Drew asked.

"I've been thinking about you," Gloria answered.

Gloria sensed Drew's hesitation to talk and asked if there were anything wrong. Not wanting to get into another shouting match, Drew answered by saying he was tired and had an early meeting the following morning.

"Drew, can you give me a minute," Gloria asked.

"Sure," Drew agreed.

"Sunday morning, did it mean anything to you?" Gloria inquired.

"Yes, it did, but," Drew replied.

"But, what?" Gloria asked while waiting to hear the bullshit excuse Drew was going to tell her.

"What happened Sunday shouldn't have happened. What we did was wrong." Drew announced.

"What we did was wrong?" Gloria repeated. "I don't understand, I mean, what are you saying? Gloria asked.

"I'm saying, it never should have happened, and it will never happen again," Drew was serious, and whether Gloria had taken him at his word was a question Drew couldn't immediately answer. Like Gloria, Drew thought about the consequences that could result from them being together. It wasn't that he didn't enjoy making love to Gloria; he just didn't want the drama that came with her.

"Drew Harrison, I believe you are afraid of Mason?" Gloria questioned.

"No, I'm not afraid of Mason; I'm afraid of what he will do to you," Drew answered. "Why can't you understand how dangerous that man is when he's provoked?"

Again, Gloria brushed Drew's concerns aside, while trying to convince him that Mason loved her too much to physically harm her. Gloria's denials left Drew astounded as to why she couldn't see the danger, she was in. She had no idea what she had gotten herself into. Maybe, it was because she'd been blinded by Mason's charm, but sooner or later, Mason was going to show his spots and when he does, Gloria will be in for a rude awakening.

Chapter: 2

Entering the board room, Drew greeted each member with a good morning before sitting. Today, their order of business consisted of increasing the production of their dairy products. Nancy was against the idea of stressing out her cows to meet the demand for their products, but the demand was too great to ignore. Nancy believed an increase in productivity would damage the quality of their products. It was an idea she wasn't ready to commit to until another solution was provided. After much debate, the decision was made to open the remaining one-hundred-and-fifty acres of unused fertile land for grazing. The board also agreed to purchase 300 additional head of Holstein cows to combat the demand for their milk and cheese products. The demand for Hillcrest's dairy products had increased 45 percent in a year, followed by their pork, chicken, organic fruits, and vegetable products, trailing at 20 percent. The company was on an upswing and Nancy had her neophyte crew to thank. Fresh out of the University of Virginia, Karyme was making deals that could rival any CEO of a Fortune 500 Company. Then there was Drew, whose savvy ability to outwit the witty made him the perfect piece of the puzzle that created what Nancy entitled "The Dynamic Duo." The final topic the board discussed involved filling the remaining vacancies for the new plant that was scheduled to open for business in four weeks. Drew was heading that task and happily reported that the vacancies were filled, and the training was scheduled to begin the following week. It was welcoming news that Drew and Karyme were able to fill more than one hundred fifty positions in three weeks. The popularity of the company had exceeded far beyond expectations, and with the new plant set to open, the chances of HillCrest Farms becoming a major factor in the food business increased significantly.

The meeting ended to everyone's satisfaction, and afterward, Drew and Karyme made their final walk of the afternoon through the plant before leaving for the day. It had been a walk they'd made for years, but today seemed different. Maybe it was because of how well the meeting went and how Drew and Karyme were recognized for their contributions to the company. After years of working beside each other, Drew noticed how beautiful Karyme was. Karyme no longer styled her hair in a bun or wore loose-fitting jeans to hide her body. She was allowing her natural curls to extend beyond her shoulders, but perhaps her most notable change was her business attire.

Drew was now seeing what his mother had been telling him for months. Karyme was not only smart but also beautiful, and man, was she ever sexy. Not wanting the evening to end, Drew invited Karyme to dinner. It was an invitation Karyme hadn't expected but welcomed with open arms. Drew hoped his invitation wasn't perceived as a date but a business dinner to continue their discussion regarding the company's future. But as the evening progressed, Drew found that he needed to be in Karyme's presence. He urgently needed a friend who wasn't afraid, to be honest. Drew couldn't say for certain if he was willing to pursue his relationship with Lynn after seeing her with Marshall. He needed time to consider if they had a future together. While at dinner, Drew presented Karyme with the questions he had circling his messy love life. Karyme wavered at the idea of having to answer Drew's question, knowing he was still in love with Lynn, but did so in the name of their friendship. Her answer was that he forgot the idea of being in a relationship with Lynn and concentrated on building his company. Drew nodded his head in agreement about concentrating on building his company but disagreed with Karyme about ending his relationship with Lynn. Drew felt he needed to give his relationship with Lynn one final chance before calling it quits.

It was late in the evening when Drew and Karyme returned home because, after dinner, they went for a walk in the park and continued their discussion about his relationship with Lynn. It was crucial that Drew cleared his mind before starting the final session of his classes. He wanted to make sure what he was about to do was right and knew only Karyme could help him make the right decision. Drew defended his decision of wanting to give his relationship with Lynn another try. He argued that he, too, had been deceitful and confessed his elusive affair with Lynn's sister. Karyme was rocked by Drew's confession but withheld judgment until he finished talking. They had long been friends, and Drew felt comfortable divulging his secrets to her. He knew she wouldn't judge him before knowing all of what had happened.

Though the news caught Karyme off guard, she never wavered. Never had she imagined; Drew would blatantly cross a line so taboo. Once hearing his story, Karyme strongly advised Drew not to pursue his relationship with Lynn. She was sure it was going to come back to hurt him when he least expected it.

Arriving home, the couple found Nancy sitting on the front porch, swinging in her favorite chair. When Drew and Karyme exited the car, Nancy quickly wiped her eyes. She often sat alone and cried because she missed her husband.

Andrew was the love of her life, and when he died, life as she knew it died with him. They were supposed to share a long life together, but cancer interfered, ruining everything she'd dreamed of. If there was ever a couple Nancy could compare to what she and Andrew had, it was Drew and Karyme. Nancy saw Karyme as the woman Drew needed in his life. Karyme was everything a woman should be. She was smart, strong-minded, and willing to go the extra mile to get the job done. She had a heart of gold, and Nancy wanted more than anything for Drew to accept the love Karyme wanted to give him. Karyme was beautiful, faithful, dedicated, and honest, but most importantly, she was in love with Drew. Seeing Drew and Karyme together motivated Nancy to convince Drew that Karyme would be the perfect wife. Nancy started by inquiring about their date. They both denied it was a date, but the way Karyme responded gave Nancy the hope she was looking for. It was no secret that Drew was going through a tough time, especially after going a couple of rounds with Lynn regarding her ex-boyfriend. Lynn's relationship with Marshall should have been enough for Drew not to dirty his hands again, but as he was with Gloria, Drew was finding it hard to tame a wild bronco who wanted to be on the open range. For some reason, Drew felt inclined to fix what was broken. Drew needed a simple turn in the right direction to realize the woman standing to his right was the woman who could make him happy. Nancy went on to compliment Drew and Karyme on how great they looked together. Nancy didn't stop there; she tried encouraging the couple to explore the idea of a relationship. It was a suggestion that left Karyme blushing and Drew wanting to run away and hide. But Drew couldn't entirely ignore his mother's suggestion. His attraction to Karyme was increasingly strengthening with each day that passed. His only problem was having to control his emotions while working beside her. He couldn't altogether overlook what his mother was trying to do, but Karyme was his best friend and the rock he could lean on when he needed advice.

Nancy sat and talked with the couple for more than an hour before leaving for the night. She had given her support regarding them being together. It was now up to them to work out the kinks to jump-start their relationship. Nancy left with the hope she had made enough of an impression for Drew to at least entertain the idea of giving Karyme a chance at loving him.

Her only prayer was that Drew would open his eyes and see the possibility of what Karyme could do for him.

She had no qualms with Lynn, and in all honesty, Lynn had made a good impression on her, but Lynn's lack of commitment to Drew made her just as dangerous as Gloria.

After receiving a call from Sophia, Karyme decided to end the night with Drew. She'd enjoyed time spent with Drew and hoped that he would take her advice regarding his relationship with Lynn.

"Thank you again for dinner," Karyme said, while unable to look Drew in the eyes.

"Maybe we can do this again sometime," Drew suggested.

"I would like that," Karyme responded.

Drew opened the door to Karyme's car for her to get in. Even though they had been in this position hundreds of times before, they both felt jittery. Drew fought his thoughts of wanting to pull Karyme into his arms to kiss her goodnight, but it wasn't time. Giving Karyme false hopes now could be devastating to their friendship. So instead, he did the next best thing, he embraced her and kissed her forehead, before wishing her goodnight.

Chapter: 3

Unlike her brother, Joanna loved training in the heat, especially during the hottest time of the day. She liked nothing better than to challenge the steep hills of the secondary roads to help build her endurance. Like Drew, track and field was Joanna's life. She'd worked hard to be recognized as one of the best female track athletes in the nation. Joanna was by far the fastest high school female in the nation, and though it could be debated that she was the best all-around female athlete in the world, there was no denying she was ranked in the top three. But to stay the best, Joanna had to maintain a strict regimen and train at least two to three times daily. Today, she was forced to change her training schedule after promising her mother she would accompany her to visit a sick relative in the hospital. In doing so, Joanna chose to run earlier than usual and made the mistake of leaving home without notifying anyone of her training route. At the time, she didn't see the importance of it and elected not to interrupt her mom or brother's busy schedules. Joanna was comfortable being on her own and believed she had no reason to think anything would happen to her, and then again, why should she because nothing ever happens in Jefferson County? Jefferson County was one of the safest places in the state. It was a county where everyone knew each other and everyone protected each other. So, Joanna had no reason to worry and left the house jogging at a slow pace. The heat was stifling and Joanna began sweating immediately. It was a sure indication that her two-mile run was going to be a long and grueling one. The temperatures should have been reason enough for concern but Joanna wasn't worried, she was accustomed to the high temperatures, and as she made her way up and down the hilly terrain, she found herself doing so without difficulty. Her punishing three miles run was a cakewalk compared to some of the workouts she was used to doing. As a driving force to surpass the legendary status of her brother, Joanna pushed herself even harder for the first half of her run. She wanted to feel the burn in her legs and pushed even harder as she approached the turning point in her run. Her desire to break her high school records inspired her to put in the needed work, but more than that, Joanna wanted to be held as a school hero just as Drew had. Reaching her stopping point, Joanna felt strong enough to add another mile to her workout but chose not to.

As an upcoming senior, Joanna had already submitted her letter of interest to attend Tennessee State University on a full athletic scholarship. It was where her idol, Miss Wilma Rudolph attended, and like Miss. Rudolph, Joanna's wanted to dominate the world in women's track and field. It was her ambition to become an Olympian and a World Champion, and she was more than determined to make it happen.

Reaching her turning point, Joanna made the turn for home. She was passed by a car with out-of-state tags that immediately stopped. It should have been a reason for concern but nothing ever happens in Jefferson County, especially in these parts. Turning around, the car drove slowly back towards Joanna. The passenger side window rolled down as it approached, and a white man in his twenties asked for directions. His sinister approach left Joanna with an eerie feeling but Joanna managed to keep her emotions intact. Suppressing her nerves, Joanna tried answering the gentleman's request without allowing them to see her shaken. Once giving them directions into town, the man thanked her, rolled up his window, and drove off. Joann carefully watched until the car was out of sight. Seeing the threat was over, she continued her run home but at a quicker pace. Her intuition was telling her danger was still present and at one point she thought about making a detour home through the woods but chose not to. Thankfully she chose not to because the car of men returned. It drove by her at a slow rate of speed before stopping to back up. The men began following Joanna as she continued jogging home. In the beginning, they were playful, only making harmless cat calls while encouraging Joanna to run faster but their playful cat calls transpired into a more serious situation. As the harassment continued, so did the derogatory remarks. The young men went as far as attempting to reach from the windows of their car to grope Joanna. Acting with a sense of urgency, Joanna began looking for avenues of escape. She was worried their playful antics were about to get out of hand and her analysis was proving to be correct. The attractive seventeen-year-old, standing five feet eleven inches tall was a target and it didn't take long for the men to make their move. Three of the four riders got out of the car and began running after Joanna while the driver followed close behind. The men were finding it difficult to keep up with Joanna as she raced to escape them.

Joanna believed she could outrun them and kept a steady pace to stay in front of them but her legs were getting heavy with each stride she made. At any other time, Joanna would have left the men in the dust but she didn't have the strength to do so today. Her energy had been depleted by her run and was too weak to lose the men entirely. Exhausted, Joanna barely had enough stamina to stay erect. The lactic acid buildup was wreaking havoc on her legs, and her would-be attackers were gaining ground. With her energy and speed gone, Joanna was fair game and was about to succumb to the men's assault. Though Joanna's efforts to escape the young men continued, she didn't have the strength to evade their pursuit. Hearing their footsteps gaining ground, Joanna felt a hand grabbing hold of her t-shirt, slowing her momentum even more. Her escape now depended on her will to fight. It wasn't long before she felt the second set of hands grabbed hold of her, followed by a third. Soon, she felt someone placing her in a bear hug and wrestled her to the ground. The men began tearing away at her t-shirt as Joanna fought to free herself. A hand covered her mouth to muffle her screams while two sets of hands grabbed hold of her legs.

Their intentions were to place her in the trunk of their car but Joanna was making things difficult by putting up a competitive fight. The men found themselves having to struggle to gain control of Joanna, causing the driver to have to get out of the car. Realizing what was about to happen, Joanna fought even harder. She was holding her own against the men who were ripping at her clothes like wild animals ripping flesh from their prey. Joann's shirt was ripped completely off and as the men fought to place her in the trunk of their car, they were able to remove Joanna's shorts. Slippery from the sweat covering her body, Joanna managed to break free. Wearing only a bra and panties, Joanna ran as fast as her legs could carry her. Once making it back to the main road, Joanna ran with urgency. She knew they were coming after her but she had to give it her all to escape. From a distance, she could hear a car approaching her direction. Desperately needing help, Joanna ran into the middle of the road, waving her hands frantically. Nearing the top of the hill, she looked back to see the men coming after her. Her first thought was to run through the woods to hide but they had seen her. Her only hope was to stop whoever was coming her way. Joanna elected to run in the middle of the road while waving her hands overhead. Hearing the car running at a high rate of speed, it was too late to evade the speeding car, Joanna braced herself for what she believed was going to be a collision. She closed her eyes, seeing her life flash before her.

"What the fuck." Mason screamed as he stomped his brakes, in an attempt to avoid the naked girl. In an effort to evade running into Joanna, Mason fought to maintain control of his vehicle. He veered off the side of the road onto the median; making a complete three-hundred-sixty-degree turn before coming to a complete stop. Getting out of his car, Mason realized the naked girl was Joanna. Grabbing hold of her arm, Mason rushed her to his car. Panicking, Joanna screamed for them to leave immediately but Mason had other ideas. Seeing the condition Joanna was in Mason became enraged, He pushed Joanna inside his car and removed Monkey's old shotgun from the back seat of his car. Distraught, Joanna tried talking but only confused Mason even more. With Joanna secured inside his car, Mason racked the forestock of his shot gun and aimed at the approaching car. Once in range, Mason squeezed off three rounds of slugs, hitting its target, before removing himself from harm's way. All three slugs struck their intended target causing the driver to lose control of his vehicle, flipping several times before coming to rest on its roof. Slowly the driver's side door opened and the driver struggled to free himself from the wreckage. Unfortunately for him, Mason was standing over him. Placing his foot on the driver's head, Mason applied pressure to stop his progress.

"Did they touch you?" Mason screamed at Joanna repeatedly while trying to get an answer. After hearing they hadn't raped her, Mason turned his anger back to the men inside the car. They may not have raped Joanna, but they surely violated her by tearing her clothes off.

"Tell me why shouldn't I splatter your fucking brains across the ground," Mason asked. "Answer me got dammit," Mason screamed, pointing the shotgun to the face of the driver.

"We're sorry sir; please don't kill us." The man pleaded.

From the car, Mason could hear Joanna screaming for him not to kill the men. Though Mason wanted desperately to blow all four men's heads off their shoulders, he couldn't because Monkey's cheap ass only had three shells in the chamber. Still, Mason felt the need to inflict more punishment on the men and did so, starting with the driver. Using the butt of his shotgun, Mason struck the driver in the back of his head, rendering him instantly unconscious. He next screamed for the remaining passengers to exit the vehicle and as each man slowly crawled their way out of the mangled car, he struck them in the back of their heads.

Once everyone was out of the car, Mason had them sit on the ground next to each other. The men pleaded for their lives, not knowing what was about to happen to them.

"Shut the fuck up," Mason screamed. "Why should I not kill every last one of you?"

The men screamed out, apologizing to Joanna for what they'd done to her. Mason's first instinct was to inflict more pain on them, but after seeing they were in such bad condition; he chose to use another method of punishment. He ordered each man to strip down to their underwear and took their clothes leaving them sitting on the side of the road. Mason may not have gotten the revenge he wanted for Joanna but it gave him satisfaction knowing the men hadn't gone unpunished for what they attempted to do to Joanna.

Driving away at a high rate of speed, Mason had Joanna to search through each man's wallet and take whatever money was inside. After doing so, he ordered her to tossed their clothes and empty wallets out the window.

"How much money we got?" Mason asked.

"One hundred, eighty-four dollars," Joanna replied.

"Good, stick it in my glove compartment," Mason instructed.

Mason was no more than a petty thief but even though he may have been, he'd come to Joanna's rescue in the nick of time. Wearing next to nothing, Joanna opened the glove compartment and placed the money inside. She closed it, feeling just as guilty as Mason was for stealing from the men. Yes, it was despicable what they tried doing to her and yes, they deserved the punishment Mason gave them but stealing from them wasn't something Joanna wanted to be a part of.

As Mason drove recklessly down the old secondary road, Joanna remained adamant, she didn't want to go to the police. She wanted to keep what happened; between them and to ensure Mason kept his word, she swore him to secrecy. Against his better judgment, Mason granted Joanna her wish but then again, he would have done anything to calm her. Not wanting to go home in her current condition, Joanna pleaded for Mason not to take her home. She didn't want Sophia to see her and asked if Mason knew of someplace to take her to get a change of clothes. Without having to think, Mason knew the right place to take her.

He had the keys to their grandfather's old farmhouse and was sure something was there for her to wear. He was also sure; Joanna would get herself together, before having to take her home. The old farmhouse was a place Mason usually brought his women, when he wanted to spend quality time with them. The house was always neat and tidy but, on the downside, it had a strong odor of mildew from being closed up for so long. It was a place Mason was certain Joanna could relax, before having to go home but if by chance she couldn't, he had just the remedy for her. There was plenty of cold beer and wine in the refrigerator, not to mention the four joints in his front pocket. On the way to the farm, Mason found it difficult to resist from staring at Joanna's semi-nude body. He tried keeping his focus on the road but found himself taking an occasional glimpse at Joanna's long silky legs, not to mention, her perky breast she tried hiding with her hands. For those who didn't know him would think he was a perverted bastard for lusting after his first cousin but Joanna wasn't his blood cousin. Unbeknownst to her, she had been adopted by his late uncle Andrew and Nancy, who raised her as their own. Joanna was only his cousin by name but in his distorted mind, he felt she was fair game, if she wanted to play.

"Got dammit, if only I had a couple more slugs, I swear, I would have killed them motherfuckers," Mason screamed out in frustration. He hated the thought of allowing the men to get away without being punished but knew he had done the right thing by letting them go. It also gave him an excuse to look across at Joanna, who was trying unsuccessfully to cover her body. Joanna remained quiet and continued staring out of the passenger's side window. She was relieved her ordeal was over and had Mason to thank but Mason's overzealous behavior was beginning to creep her out.

Arriving at Grandpa Harrison's old farmhouse, Joanna followed Mason to the front door. She was wearing only panties and was using her hands to cover her breast. Joanna reluctantly entered the house but found comfort in knowing there were clothes inside she could change into. Entering the house, Joanna was greeted by a suffocating heat and the smell of mildew dominating the hot thick air. She followed Mason down a narrow hallway that led to one of the rear bedrooms. Joanna watched from outside of the door as Mason opened the first drawer and removed a large green t-shirt. Seeing that Joanna was standing outside the bedroom door, Mason tossed the shirt to her.

17

He'd hoped Joanna would have caught it so he could get a free show but Joanna allowed the shirt to fall to the floor, ruining any chance of Mason seeing her breast. Joanna waited for Mason to turn his back before picking the shirt from the floor. Mason may not have seen her breast but Joanna couldn't hide the print of her camel toe protruding through her saturated panties. Mason felt awful, having sexual thoughts of his adopted cousin but he couldn't erase the fact that she was one sexy tall goddess.

Joanna remained outside the door and waited until Mason found a pair of shorts, he thought she could wear. Receiving the shorts, Joanna followed Mason to the hallway lining closet where he gave her a towel, wash cloth, and a bar of soap. From there Mason escorted Joanna to the single-family bathroom, to shower. Hesitant, Joanna slowly past Mason, avoiding any physical contact. Her tight little ass was too inviting not to stare but out of respect, Mason pretended not to have noticed. He listened, as Joanna locked the door behind her, and waited to hear the shower running before walking away. It was tough to overlook how grown-up Joanna had become. The once abnormally tall and skinny girl had grown into a beautiful and sexy goddess. Her small waist and firm ass, accented her tall slender body and the thought of his chocolate complexion meshing against Joanna's smooth caramel skin, excited Mason; to the point of him entertaining the idea of joining her in the shower. However, he thought better of his fantasy and chose to walk away. Mason couldn't argue that Joanna wasn't special in every sense of the word and though they weren't blood cousins, they were cousins nonetheless.

After showering, Joanna joined Mason at the kitchen table. She had calmed down some but was still tense. Needing to lighten the mood, Mason began by making small talk. He told a few corny jokes but it did nothing to lighten Joanna's mood. Joanna was finding it hard to accept what happened and knew, if it weren't for Mason's heroism, things may have ended differently.

Knowing he had to do something drastic, Mason reached into his front pocket and removed a plastic bag, containing marijuana joints. Lighting it, Mason took a few tokes before passing it to Joanna.

"Here; take a hit of this," Mason instructed. "It'll help you relax."

Fearful of the consequences, Joanna declined. She was unsure if Mason had a motive but trusted him enough to believe he had her best interest at heart.

"I can't," Joanna said. "I think I'm going to be drug tested next Friday before my meet."

"Damn, I didn't know they did drug tests in high school?" Mason said.

"Yeah, it started last year," Joanna replied.

Taking another hit from his joint, Mason got up and opened the refrigerator. He took out a bottle of Boone's Farm Apple Wine and got two glasses from the cabinet. Opening the wine, he poured Joanna a glass, followed by one for himself.

"Here, go ahead and take a swig, it'll help with your shakes," Mason suggested

Adamant it was the perfect potion to cure her ailments, Mason encouraged Joanna to drink. He needed her calm before taking her home and knew the wine would help ease her tension.

Agreeing with Mason, Joanna accepted the glass and took a drink. She was impressed by the smooth sweet taste of the chilled wine. It was the perfect remedy for her and it went down easy. It wasn't long before Joanna's tears transformed into a smile. She was now seeing the world from a comical perspective. For Mason, the wine had done what he expected. He had accomplished his goal; Joanna was calm enough to take home.

Looking at his watch, Mason knew Nancy was likely still at her office in town and Drew was at the plant. Now was the perfect time to take Joanna home without anyone having to question where she had been. Leaving the old farmhouse, Mason opted to take Joanna the long way home, instead of her having to revisit the scene. Nearing home, Joanna didn't want to draw attention to Mason bringing her home and suggested that he put her out at the edge of her driveway. She thanked Mason again, for his heroism but criticized the role he played with his involvement with Gloria. Joanna didn't condemn Mason for falling in love with Gloria but condemned him for his refusal to man up and approach Drew to admit the truth about his relationship with Gloria. As Joanna put it, Mason and Drew were like brothers, they should have been able to work things out between each other without a problem.

Surprised Joanna would take such a stance, Mason agreed with her. In all honesty, he hadn't handled the situation properly and, in a way, he owed Drew an apology and promised, he would undoubtedly rectify his mistake with Drew the first chance he got.

For the first time in months, Joanna saw Mason in a different light. He wasn't the selfish backstabbing bastard she once believed. He was more considerate and understanding than she gave him credit for. Maybe it was Gloria who helped revamp his negative image and if that was true, then maybe being with her was a good thing.

After saying their goodbyes, Joanna kissed Mason on his cheek. She got out of the car and waved a final time before turning to jog away. Her ordeal was over, she had finally made it home safely and she had Mason to thank.

Chapter: 4

With the start of the summer session beginning in two days, Drew arrived at his off-campus apartment with motivation. He was less than four weeks away from receiving his master's degree and he couldn't have been more excited. However, the thought of the possibility of Lynn attending made him nervous. Drew was uncertain as to how he would react if he saw her. Deep down inside, Drew still had strong feelings for Lynn but wanted them to go away. It was going to be a long first session now that he and Lynn were on the outs but it was his last session before having the credits, he needed to receive his Master's. Instead of soaking in his tears, Drew wanted to focus his attention on his future. He couldn't deny he didn't want Lynn to be a part of his future because he did. In spite of his feelings, Drew couldn't omit what was happening with Karyme. Mentally, something had happened between them over the two weeks he was home. He couldn't explain it but he found himself attracted to Karyme more than he had ever before. Like always, Karyme had been the ideal friend who was always willing to loan an ear when in need but this time she had become part of his feelings. After spending time with Karyme, Drew saw what his mother had seen in her. Karyme was an exceptionally beautiful woman who was highly intelligent and she cared deeply for him. Not only had Karyme stood by him throughout his troubled relationship with Gloria, she was also doing the same with Lynn. In addition to her ability to magically make his problems disappear, Karyme made him feel good about himself in the process. Karyme was more than a best friend; she was the major force that kept him on the straight and narrow. Karyme had contributed so much good to his life; it made him want to be an even better person. He was grateful to have such a woman by his side and he could see Karyme playing an important role in his life. It was no secret how she felt about him and the things she was willing to do for him but before he could explore the possibility of Karyme becoming a love interest, he first had to follow his path with Lynn to see where it took them.

Confining herself inside her dorm room, Lynn tried reading the beginning chapter of a romance novel for the fourth straight night but found herself reading the same paragraph repeatedly, without comprehending a single word. Her thoughts were of Drew and how much she missed him. She felt his pain with each message he left and though she wanted more than anything to talk to him, she wasn't prepared to answer any questions regarding Marshall.

What worried Lynn mostly was the fear of being pregnant. She had taken the morning-after pill but her period hadn't come. She'd even taken three pregnancy tests but each result was negative. But why hadn't she gotten her period? Lynn suspected being under too much stress may have been the contributing factor but couldn't say for certain. If by some chance she was pregnant she was clueless as to what to do. Lynn didn't believe in abortion but she didn't want to have Marshall's child either. Having to care for a baby she didn't want was causing Lynn to spiral toward another depression. Disappointing her parents was something Lynn feared the most. She couldn't give them another blackeye by getting pregnant by a man she called a rapist in front of everyone attending the party.

Feeling overly lonely, Lynn went to bed early. She turned off her overhead light and got into bed. She covered her shoulders with her blanket but couldn't sleep because her thoughts were of Drew and what he meant to her. Lynn twisted and turned, searching for a comfortable position to fall asleep but couldn't. She had too much on her mind to sleep. Her instincts were telling her to call Drew but she knew, it was in her best interest to wait until she knew for sure if she was pregnant

Chapter: 5

Drew stayed clear of the University's Student Commons because of his fear of running into Lynn. To stay clear of Lynn, Drew stayed mostly to himself, opting to study at home instead of the library. When he wasn't studying at home, he was with his coach, practicing twice daily. Once training was over, Drew returned to his apartment, usually feeling half dead. Often feeling too tired to eat, Drew would shower and go to bed. Though he missed Lynn, Drew tried focusing his attention on school and his upcoming track meet that was scheduled at the end of the month. With his track meet approaching, Drew's training intensified. This was to be his last hurrah before ending his collegiate career and he wanted to end it as a champion. His speed had returned, along with his desire to be competitive. His aspiration to become an Olympic and World champion was the driving force that got him up every morning at 4:30 am to train. To further motivate himself, Drew used his breakup with Lynn to push himself over his limit. His coach worried he was overtraining but not Drew, Drew wouldn't have it any other way. He was determined to accomplish his dreams, but first, he had to become the Big East Track meet, one- and two-hundred-meter champion.

Cutting his evening workout short, Drew left practice early to attend a meeting on campus. It was the meeting he was dreading because as one of the founding members, Lynn was scheduled to attend. Together, he, Lynn and fourteen other students representing the Greeks on campus, helped spearhead a community outreach program called "The Together Greeks" that assisted underprivileged children in the community. The group not only conducted food and toy drives but was well known for their work in addressing racial concerns. Racial tension nearly erupted after a black student was falsely accused and arrested for a home invasion after being seen walking through a mostly white neighborhood. It was later revealed that the student was returning back to campus after walking his girlfriend home. It was the work of "The Together Greeks" that kept tension at a minimum, saving not only the town but the university from what could have been a devastating incident. For their success, the organization and the town council got together and planned what was to be the town's first multi-fest event. As president of The Together Greeks, Drew couldn't have been prouder.

Lynn was the first to arrive at the auditorium. She sat in the dark and waited for everyone to arrive.

She'd contemplated skipping the meeting because she didn't want to face Drew. Though she missed him, Lynn feared having to answer questions pertaining to Marshall. It was absurd to think she could successfully avoid Drew the entire summer session and knew she would have to face him sooner or later. Looking at her watch, Lynn anticipated the moment Drew walked into the auditorium and became overly nervous knowing Drew could enter the room at any second. Fighting to contain herself, Lynn removed notes from her folder to read over, hoping it was enough to calm her. Seconds before the meeting was scheduled to begin, Drew and two other members entered through the doors, carrying boxes. Seeing Drew enter the room, Lynn nearly fell out of her seat. Drew was as handsome, as he'd always been and he looked to be in the best shape of his life. Drew's sweaty shirt, stuck to his body, giving him the look of Adonis. Lynn wanted more than anything to run up to him to tell him how much she loved and missed him but she needed to maintain her sanity.

Scanning the room, Drew saw Lynn sitting in the corner. He gave her a smile of assurance, before turning his attention on starting the meeting. Like Lynn, Drew had trouble containing his emotions. If only he could get over what happened with Marshall, he would tell her what was in his heart but he had to respect Lynn's wishes to give her the space and time she needed to clear her mind. Perspiring from head to toe, Drew took his position at the podium. Before opening the meeting, he apologized for his appearance and followed with the announcement that the meeting was going to be short. The fact that Drew had come at all was more than Lynn could have hoped for. Drew didn't have to apologize for his appearance, Lord knows, Lynn would have accepted him in any condition. Just seeing him standing at the podium had her heart beating a mile a minute. Watching Drew talking about the upcoming festival, felt like a dream. Lynn was so in love, she was willing to give her all, if she wasn't possibly carrying another man's child. When it was time for Lynn to give her report, she approached the podium, stopping short of allowing Drew to fully remove himself, before taking her rightful place. Her report was short but she reported she had gotten commitments from the groups performing the night of the festival. The room erupted in applause, as the groups were announced. It could be said the meeting was a success, and though seeing Drew was tough for Lynn to have to see, she was happy she had attended.

Just as Drew had promised, the meeting was short but everything that needed to be touched upon was covered. Before adjourning, Drew made an unexpected announcement that he would be stepping down immediately as chairman of the committee. It was no secret that this session would be his last but everyone expected him to stay on as president, at least until the beginning of the fall semester. To show their appreciation, all the members in attendance stood and applauded him, as Drew gave his final speech. He was proud of what they had created, and how well they had served the community they were a part of. By stepping down, Drew opened the floor for the members to appoint the next president to continue their work. The news was saddening to Lynn, she was faced with the reality that Drew was about to graduate and will be leaving her. If they were going to have a future together, Lynn had three weeks to solve their problems.

After the meeting adjourned, Drew stood at the door and shook each member's hand and thanked them for a job well done. Each member received a 3D crystal award and a certificate honoring them for their hard work and dedication. Drew was going to miss every member, especially Lynn. She was experiencing a dark period in her life when she first joined the group but after becoming a member, she began thriving; quickly taking the lead, and embracing the community, while implementing the importance of unity. Her hard work softened the friction that once exist between the college community and the locals. Lynn not only became an asset to the committee but she also became an asset to the surrounding community who instantly fell in love with her.

Lynn intentionally waited to be last to leave the conference room. She wanted to have a moment with Drew and as she approached him, she tried to remain calm but found herself too nervous to talk. She greeted Drew with a smile but found herself at a loss for words. Lynn wanted to express her feelings but was literally tongue-tied. She wanted nothing more than to tell Drew how much she loved him before falling into his arms but she was too nervous to say what was on her mind. In an attempt to break the ice, Drew extended his arms and gently embraced Lynn.

"I would love to give you a big old bear hug right now but I'm reeking of stink and sweat," Drew said with a smile.

Lynn didn't care how bad he smelled; or how wet he was, she wanted to feel his arms tightly around her and as Drew held her body against his, she melted into his arms. Locking her arms around his neck, Lynn pulled Drew's six feet four-inch body to her level and kissed his cheek.

"You taste like salt," Lynn responded with a smile. For a split second she narrowly allowed her wall to tumble but she quickly regrouped and released her embrace.

Unphased by her sudden withdrawal, Drew turned off the lights and locked the door behind them. Together they left the building and walked outside to the front of the building. Drew walked Lynn to her car which was parked on the street. He opened her door and waited for her to enter and secure herself into the car. Closing the door, Drew gave her one final smile before turning to walk away.

"Drew, I can drive you to your car if you like," Lynn suggested.

"Thanks, but I'm parked in the rear of the building." Drew responded.

"I hope to see you around," Lynn said.

"Me too," Drew responded.

After saying goodbye, Drew watched as Lynn drove away. It hurt having to see her leave without knowing what their future were going to be but he was hopeful that things would somehow work its way out.

Chapter: 6

On his drive to the train station, Mason could see that something was weighing heavy on Gloria's mind. When inquiring about it, he was met with resistance. Gloria was quick to say there was nothing wrong, except she was tired and couldn't wait to get on the train to go to sleep. It wasn't what she said that alarmed him but how she said it. It felt as if she was looking forward to getting away from him. Gloria's answer was creating doubt in Mason's already suspicious mind that she wasn't being honest with him. By her reaction, Mason was quick to believe it was more behind Gloria's behavior than what she was admitting. There was a storm brewing and Mason could feel a strong wind blowing in his direction. Something wasn't right about Gloria's sudden conference to Washington, D.C. How in God's name was she selected so quickly after just beginning her career as a nurse at General? Who in Sam Hill would have selected a nurse still in training to go on a conference? They were questions Mason needed answers to and it wouldn't be Gloria if she didn't have a comeback to Mason's concerns. Gloria answered his question by saying she was selected because she had been an employee of the hospital since being a student at Jefferson County High. Though Mason should have gone forward with checking with the hospital, he chose not to. He wanted to trust Gloria even though he felt something fishy was going on. For the past few days, Gloria had been distant when it came to him. Each day there was an excuse when it came to spending time with him. If she wasn't suffering from a massive headache, she was too exhausted. It was always something and quite frankly, Mason was getting tired of it but what was he going to do about it? He was too afraid to confront Gloria because of the fear she may leave him. So, he did what most pussy whipped bastards did, he kept his mouth shut and prayed everything would work itself out. In more ways than one, Mason felt Gloria's problems stemmed around Drew. He was uncertain to what extent but he was certain Drew had something to do with it. The thought of Gloria going back to Drew ran rapidly through Mason's mind but he couldn't allow it to dominate his thoughts. For half of his life, he'd been in love with Gloria and now that she was with him, Mason wasn't going to give up so easily on her. When overlooking his life, Mason felt the most important things had eluded him, including Gloria. He didn't believe God had given him a fair shake when it came to him and the life he was living. Compared to Drew, he'd struggled while trying to compete, especially when it came to the classroom and the athletic field. Lord knows, he graduated high school by the skin of his teeth but nonetheless, he graduated.

Drew on the other hand was not only highly intelligent, the son-of-a-bitch was a five-star athlete who was offered scholarships for football, basketball, and track and field. It's highly unlikely anyone who was offered a full scholarship to play sports in three different sports, would have turn them all down for an academic scholarship but Drew did just that. It was mindboggling how the motherfucker became so popular and so quickly but Drew did just that. Drew sat a standard Mason couldn't possibly reach and sadly for Mason, he was forced to have to hear about Drew's accomplishments from his mother. Flustered by the way life had pissed on him, Mason couldn't ignore the way Drew applied himself in preparation for his future. Still, it wasn't enough to stop him from arguing that Drew's success stemmed from him being born with a silver spoon in his mouth. Drew's financial situation was a problem that plagued Mason since childhood. It was another thing that Mason envied, along with Drew's achievements. Losing Gloria to Drew early in their childhood was another reason Mason hated Drew. Drew had beat him to the punch every time he competed against him and Mason envied him for it. But as time passed, Mason was presented with the opportunity to rip Drew's heart right out of his body and he took full advantage of it. Finally, after years of fighting for what he believed should have been his from the beginning, Mason had stolen Gloria away from Drew, and man, was it ever gratifying.

Mason continued to monitor Gloria closely on their drive to the train station. He listened carefully for her to make a mistake but she hadn't thus far. "Damn, she must be telling the truth," Mason said to himself. Though Gloria continued to be adamant about being tired and nothing more, Mason wasn't buying it. He felt strongly it had to do with Drew and though he couldn't prove it, he was correct in his assumption, Gloria was having second thoughts about him. Perhaps it was because of Drew's decision to go forth with his relationship with Lynn that brought on Gloria's jealousy, causing her to want him back. What actually triggered Gloria's mindset was stumbling upon a newspaper article listing the Harrisons and the Hillcrest

Cooperation's net worth as being twelve million dollars. Gloria now understood why her father pleaded so hard for her to stay in a relationship with Drew. He was looking out for her best interest but, like the rebellious young woman she was she, chose to follow the path leading to Mason.

It was a path she was now regretting and though she couldn't deny her love for Mason, staying with him would be a financial disaster. Financially, there couldn't be a future with Mason, his only asset was his Mustang. He wasn't educated and worked on a road construction crew as sign-turner. He was still living with his mother but most importantly, he was living paycheck to paycheck. In Gloria's mind, she needed a man capable of giving her the things in life she felt she deserved and that man was no other than Drew. It was up to her to make things right with Drew and she was doing so be taking a train to see him.

Chapter: 7

Just as he'd always done after track practice, Drew sprinted upstairs to his sixth-floor apartment. It had been a long and exhausting day but seeing Lynn today was inspirational. Their brief conversation left Drew with a feeling of confidence that they could salvage whatever was left of their relationship. Drew believed; with time they were going to work out their problems. He wasn't going to rush Lynn into doing something she wasn't ready for. Instead, Drew's plans were to give Lynn all the time she needed to decide if he was whom she wanted to be with. As soon as Drew entered his apartment, he considered calling Lynn but decided it wasn't the right moment to do so. He needed to fight his urges and stand down. Maybe in a day or two, when Lynn had a chance to think more clearly, he would call her then. Inside his apartment, Drew stripped down to his boxer briefs and carried his wet workout clothes to his laundry room. He placed his dirty laundry in the washer and began washing his clothes before making his way to the shower. Once in the shower, Drew allowed the water to bead against his face. The water felt great massaging his body and as he stood with his eyes closed, he visualized how tomorrow's track meet was going to play out in his mind. The training was over, the time had come to match his skills against the athletes competing to be crowned the fastest man on the East coast.

After showering, Drew went to the kitchen and made himself a turkey sandwich. He was too exhausted to cook or to stay up long enough to order takeout. Instead, he chose to eat a sandwich with chips, while sitting in front of the television. It would have been great if Lynn could have joined him but it was best, they spent time apart. The mere fact she refused to level with him, regarding what happened between her and Marshall continued to play out in his mind. In all sincerity, Marshall was to blame for them not being together. Something happened between them and Lynn nearly confessed to it before Ashley rudely interrupted them. Maybe someday Lynn may admit what occurred doing the three days she slept under the same roof with Marshall but until then, Drew knew, he had to be patient.

Overly exhausted, Drew had only eaten half of his sandwich before falling asleep on the couch. He was awakened minutes later by the sound of his phone. It was his mother who was calling to remind him that she and Joanna were driving up the following afternoon to attend his track meet. Sadly, Karyme wasn't coming.

She elected to work, citing that something important at the office had expectantly come up. It was fair to say that Drew was disappointed with her decision but understood the pressure she would have been under if she had chosen to come. Drew couldn't overlook the obvious, something was happening between him and Karyme. He couldn't say for certain how deep it went, but it was silly to think Karyme was only a friend. His attraction for her was tipping the scales and though he couldn't understand why, he couldn't omit his feelings. Ending his conversation with his mom, Drew drifted back to sleep, only to be disturbed minutes later but this time it was her doorbell. Approaching the door, Drew felt his heart rate increase. His adrenaline was pumping with the thought of Lynn standing outside of the door. Perhaps she was ready to talk and clear the air about his suspicions. Overly confident it was Lynn, Drew didn't bother to look through the peephole, instead, he opened the door, only to be shocked at the sight of Gloria standing with a smile as wide as Texas. Like always, Gloria knew how to make a grand entrance and tonight was no exception. Her short cotton dress clung tightly to her body while exposing her coke bottle shape. She stood arrogantly with her overnight bags in her hands; giving all indication that she was spending the night. One look at Gloria and Drew knew he was in trouble. If he allowed Gloria to spend the night, Drew knew, without a shadow of doubt that it was going to be a long, and miserable night.

"Surprise," Gloria said opening her arms to embrace Drew. "Well, aren't you going to invite me in?" She asked.

"Of course, please, come in," Drew replied. He led Gloria through the dark hallway into the opening of his living room. Puzzled by Gloria's means of travel to campus, Drew quickly inquired about her means of transportation.

"I caught the train," Gloria answered as she sat on the couch.

Without a doubt, trouble was brewing and Gloria's ulterior motive was becoming more transparent than ever. It was detrimental for Drew to get her out of his apartment as soon as possible if he was to salvage whatever was left of his relationship with Lynn. However, from the way things were looking, it wasn't going to be an easy job to put Gloria on the last train home. Drew was numb by the sudden appearance of Gloria's unexpected and unwelcoming arrival but he maintained a clear mind hoping to deal with the issue at hand.

31

"We need to talk," Gloria blurted out. "I know what you're about to say. We could have talked over the phone, but sometimes it's vital to sort things out in person. Don't'cha think?" Gloria asked.

Without getting into a pissing contest, Drew opted to find a solution. His main objective was to get Gloria out of his apartment before Lynn unexpectedly showed up but there was a problem. The last train had run for the night and the bus station was thirty miles away. By the time he got her there the last bus would have already left the station. Somehow Drew knew Gloria had planned it this way. In her twisted little mind, Gloria had amped up her game. The first train leaving out tomorrow morning was at 7:15 am, and Drew was willing to bet his last dollar that Gloria's sweet little ass was going to be leaving on that train headed for home. As far as tonight, well, I guess you could say, Gloria had Drew by the balls and there wasn't a damn thing he could do about it. Drew was so desperate to get Gloria out of his apartment, he thought about driving her home but doing so meant he wouldn't get the rest he needed for his afternoon track meet. Drew was fucked and he knew it. It would be morally wrong if he kicked Gloria out on the street. So, Drew was left with only one solution and that was to allow Gloria to spend the night with him. Somehow, he was going to make the best out of it and try to get through the night without crossing the line. But come hell or high water, Gloria was taking the early train back to Jefferson County the first thing the following morning.

Seeing, she had surpassed her first step; Gloria contemplated her next move. Her games not only alarmed Drew of her intentions but they reminded him of the impact it would bring if Mason found out about her spending the night with him. Gloria's unexpected move had Drew back paddling. Frankly, he didn't know what to do and his fidgety body told Gloria what she already suspected. Excusing himself from the room, Drew entered the security of the bathroom to call Lynn. As expected, her phone went to voicemail, leaving Drew in a near panic state of mind. He knew of the consequences if he was caught with Gloria inside his apartment. He also knew what would happen if Lynn showed up. Their strained relationship couldn't afford another bump in the road and Drew was going to do whatever to make sure this night ran smoothly. Returning to the room, Drew found Gloria sitting on the couch with her legs crossed. He didn't want to look but his eyes wouldn't allow him not to.

Gloria's beautiful yellow thighs were glistening in the dimly lit room reminding him of the times they were together. Drew tried his damndest not to stare but he couldn't help himself, Gloria was too damn sexy not to.

"Do Mason know you're here?" Drew asked.

"No, I told him I was going to a medical conference," Gloria responded with a cunning smirk. "He even drove me to the train station."

Gloria was playing Russian Roulette with her life. Somehow, she'd tricked Mason into believing she was at a medical conference when she was actually at his apartment. Drew couldn't imagine Mason not following up on Gloria and if he had, he would have found out the truth about her. It was crazy what Gloria was doing, she was overly confident of Mason's credulous behavior, but then again, Mason loved her so much he was willing to believe anything she told him.

Drew sat across the room from Gloria, trying to keep as much distance between them as possible. Gloria was as sweet as cotton candy but once you tasted her, your soul belonged to her. Drew knew what was in front of him, yet he found her too intriguing not to consider tasting a piece of her. Maybe, it was the way she looked at him that fascinated him so much. Gloria's hazel eyes were more than enough to melt him as if he was butter in a frying pan. Her ability to hypnotized you made it easy for her to bite your neck and once she injected you with her poison, you were hers for the long haul.

 Drew knew what was at stake and he wasn't about to test faith to have something he could never fully have. Everything was a challenge to Gloria, she didn't give, she only took but sooner or later, her luck was going to run out.

"Why are you sitting across the room from me?" Gloria asked. "You can sit next to me; I'm not going to bite, not hard anyway," Gloria said cynically. Her golden hair and hazel eyes glistened from the light of the television. She was as beautiful as queen Nefertiti and Drew found himself captivated by her and struggling to think of things to say. It felt as if he was seeing Gloria for the first time. Lord knows, Drew knew what Gloria was all about, just as he knew what she was after;

Drew's only problem was saying no and Gloria knew it.

It was her mission to get her way tonight and if playing dirty was going to get it, well, she was more than willing to do so. Drew pretended not to be fazed by Gloria's invitation and though he was as nervous as the first time they were together; he was going to do his best to fight his urges. To deter his thoughts, Drew concentrated on watching Sports Center. His hormones were ramping up but his mind continued to focus on the consequences he'll face if he chose to travel the path Gloria wanted him to travel. It was certainly going to be a difficult task for Drew to maintain but he had to do what was right if he wanted to be the man he wanted to be. Seeing he was seconds away from doing something ill-advised, Drew left the comfort of the couch and returned to the kitchen but this time to get a couple of bottles of water. He felt his mouth becoming dry and knew he needed water. Drew used his time in the kitchen to gather his thoughts and bury what he was considering doing. Again, he tried calling Lynn, and her phone went to voicemail. Unsure if he should leave a message, Drew opted not to. He grabbed two bottles of water from his refrigerator and reluctantly returned to where Gloria was waiting for him. Drew passed Gloria a bottle of water and as he did, Gloria used her free hand to grab hold of Drew's hand and guided him beside her. Her presence not only calmed him but reignited the fire burning inside him. Drew wanted Gloria but having her came with a price he wasn't prepared to pay.

Needing to keep his mind focused; Drew began thinking of Lynn and what it would do to her if she caught him in bed with Gloria. Lynn was most likely at the library studying and it was possible she would come by after leaving. Drew kept reminding himself not to get caught in an uncompromising position with Gloria and to do his best to fight off any advancements Gloria made toward him. To help his confused mind, Drew tried concentrating on the television but Gloria kept reminding him of what he was missing. Obviously, the water they were drinking, hadn't extinguish their fire and Lord knows Drew couldn't afford to allow his house to burn down. Gloria took a sip of her water before placing it on the nightstand. She continued to show Drew what she was interested in but Drew was fighting her every step of the way. If tonight was going to be the success Gloria was hoping to achieve, she needed to do something to tilt the scales in her direction. Without notice, Gloria got up and left the room. Drew's eyes zoomed in on her perfectly chiseled ass as she walked past. Gloria was a sight to behold and though Drew entertained the thought of getting back together with her; he knew doing so came with a steep price.

Drew couldn't omit the fact that Gloria was poison and though he was aware of it, he couldn't resist from wanting to drink the hemlock from her cup.

Gloria entered the bathroom, closing the door behind her. Searching through Drew's medicine cabinet, she looked for any signs of Lynn living with him but found none. Inquisitive, she left the bathroom and entered Drew's bedroom. There, Gloria searched for any signs of the "Rich Bitch" or his little senorita, keeping house with him. After finding nothing, Gloria saw her chances increasing. Now, more than ever, Gloria believed if she ever had a chance to get Drew back into her life, tonight was the golden opportunity to do so. Returning to the living room, Gloria was quick to inform Drew of where she had visited.

"I went to see where I was going to be sleeping tonight," Gloria teased as she sat beside Drew, crossing her legs. She was impressed by his queen size bed and was optimistic that she and Drew were going to be sleeping in it before the night ended. The thought of being rolled from side to side doing an uninterrupted night of lovemaking was exciting but first Gloria had to get Drew relaxed enough to accept the idea. The two spent the remainder of the evening watching television, laughing, and talking about old times. Drew had finally relaxed enough to discuss his spat with Lynn but stressed their breakup was only temporary.

The news was far greater than what Gloria had anticipated, which left her wanting to make a mad dash to Drew's heart yet again. It didn't take long for Drew and Gloria to begin horseplaying after watching wrestling. It was the opportunity Gloria needed to make her move. They wrestled from the couch falling to the floor. On the floor, Drew found himself in the uncompromising position he didn't to be in. He was on top of Gloria and before he knew what was happening, they were kissing. It felt like old times holding and kissing Gloria and it seemingly was making her visit worthwhile but Drew kept reminding himself not to fall into her trap again. He had done so at the lake just days earlier and he didn't want to make the same mistake again. Making love to Gloria by the lake left Drew feeling guilty for what he'd done to Mason. He knew how much Mason loved Gloria and the lengths he'll go through to keep her. It would undoubtedly crush him, if he ever found out about them but Gloria was making things difficult. She was too freaking sexy to resist but for Mason's sake, Drew had to try not to smash Gloria's brains out her head.

As the evening came to an end it was apparent sleeping arrangements had to be made. Like any gentleman, Drew was willing to give up his bed for the couch but Gloria wasn't having it. Gloria refused to allow Drew to sleep on the couch, knowing how important tomorrow's track and field competition was to him. Gloria left for the bathroom with her night bag. It was time to turn up the fire to get the night started and Gloria had the perfect night attire to do so. Opening her bag, Gloria removed a sheer short black nightgown with a matching thong. She also brought with her Drew's favorite perfume and body oils to apply after her shower.

Hearing the shower running, Drew removed the linens from the closet to prepare Gloria's bed for the night. It was hard to believe they were sleeping in separate rooms but as strange as it sounded, Drew didn't want it any other way. Well, at least that is what he wanted to believe. It was going to be hard having to resist Gloria when she came out of the bathroom because Drew could smell her perfume emanating from under the door. It was no surprise to Drew that he was going to be in for a long night but he had to at least give his best effort to resist the pressure Gloria was going to apply. She was most likely inside the bathroom plotting how she would seduce him but what was so sad about it was Drew knew what Gloria would do; he just didn't have an answer for it. While preparing the couch for Gloria, Drew realized he hadn't brought her pillow. He made his way back to his bedroom but stalled once seeing the bathroom light shining in the hallway. Drew approached the bathroom cautiously, hoping Gloria wasn't standing in the nude. He swallowed before walking pass the doorway and once, he did, he saw Gloria standing in front of the mirror combing her hair. She was wearing only a sheer black gown with a matching thong and man was she ever sexy. Just the sight of her sent nearly sent Drew into a frenzy. Her appearance mesmerized Drew, leaving him standing frozen with his mouth open.

"How do I look?" Gloria teased.

"Great as always." Drew answer. He didn't have to answer Gloria's question, his eyes had done it for him. Gloria was stunning and the sight of her left Drew with a million questions. Drew tried blocking images of Gloria from his mind but it was proving to be difficult. Like a spinning top, his mind was spinning out of control and to make matters worse, Gloria was following him to his bedroom. Once inside his room, Drew reached into his closet to get Gloria a pillow. Drew felt Gloria's hands rub his shoulders and he nearly panicked.

Seeing what was about to happen, Drew made a b-line from his bedroom down the hallway to the living room. It was nerve-racking to know his resistance was weak but Drew had to calm himself before his heart exploded. He wanted to erase his sinful thoughts but couldn't. Making love to Gloria was etched into of his mind and fighting his urges was useless. Drew needed to regain control of his mind and tried by reminding himself that it would be a mistake to sleep with Gloria but after seeing her on the couch Drew's resistance went haywire. He was captivated by the way Gloria's gown highlighted her smoot and silky yellow complexion. Gloria's body was flawless in every aspect of the word. She was sexier than he had ever seen her before and he found himself wanting her more. Drew was in trouble and there wasn't a damn thing he could do to escape it. He should have waved the white flag immediately but like a drug addict, he believed he could fight his cravings without help.

"Are you ok?" Gloria asked. She could tell Drew's mind was jacked up and she was the cause of it. It was exactly what she wanted and Gloria could see Drew's hard-on rising like the morning sun. Drew could best be described as a wounded animal that was waiting to be slaughtered but instead of putting him out of his misery, Gloria wanted him to suffer a while longer. Drew watched as Gloria spun her body from a sitting position into a supine position. Drew thought to himself how amorous it was to watch Gloria lower her body to adjust her head comfortably on the pillow. In doing so, her nightie rose, exposing her neatly trimmed vagina, seen through her sheer black panties. Drew tried everything to deter his thoughts from appealing to Gloria's attempts to seduce him but in his manic state of mind, he was unable to turn off his emotions. To salvage the dignity he had left, Drew decided to leave the scene. Saying goodnight, he turned and began walking down the hallway to his bedroom. He made it as far as the bathroom door before Gloria summoned him back. Dreading what may have been waiting for him, Drew reluctantly returned.

"Yes, Gloria, how can I help you?" Drew asked.

"Aren't you going to tuck me in?" Gloria asked while giggling like a little kid.

"Yeah, sure thing," Drew replied. He did his best to tuck the blanket under Gloria and after doing so, he again said goodnight and left the room, only to be called back a second time. Gloria was playing with his mind but Drew was doing his best to maintain his sanity.

"What now Gloria?" Drew asked.

"You forgot my goodnight kiss," Gloria said. She was taunting him and it was working. Whether Drew realized it or not he was going to be making love to Gloria within the hour, whether he wanted to or not, especially if Gloria had anything to do with it. Standing over Gloria, Drew leaned over and gently kissed Gloria on her lips. He followed, by whispering "goodnight" in her ear, before turning off the lamp. Drew left the room hoping it was for the last time but with each step he made, he anticipated hearing Gloria's voice calling him back. Surprisingly, Gloria didn't request his presence anymore. It was over; Drew's nightmare was finally over; at least that's what he initially believed, but little did he know, his nightmare was only beginning.

With her eyes wide open, Gloria looked into the darkness of the night. She thought about her past with Drew and the sweet intimate times they shared. There were good times and bad but throughout their relationship, Gloria never stopped loving him. Lord knows, she wasn't thinking when she made the decision to move on with Mason. It was a mistake she was now second-guessing and a mistake she wanted to rectify. It wasn't that she didn't love Mason because she did. The problem she faced was that she never stopped loving Drew and after seeing his reaction toward her tonight, Gloria now believed, Drew never stopped loving her either. In the beginning, Gloria believed, it was lust that fueled Drew but after seeing the glitter in his eyes, she now knew, it was true love Drew was feeling. After lying and fantasizing for more than thirty minutes, Gloria had, had enough; it was time to put her feelings into motion. Getting off the couch, she cautiously made her way down the long dark hallway toward Drew's bedroom.

Awake, Drew desperately tried falling asleep but couldn't. He twisted and turned while trying to bury his thoughts of Gloria. The thought that Gloria was sleeping a few feet away was driving him crazy and though he tried concentrating on other things, his hormones had taken over his thoughts. Drew wanted nothing more than to join Gloria in the next room but the voices inside of his head warned him not to fall prey to her again. Trying to get thoughts of Gloria out of his head, Drew squeezed his pillow around his head, hoping it was enough to repel the dirty thoughts from his mind but they refused to leave. Things got even more complicated, after hearing Gloria tip-toeing her way down the hallway toward his bedroom. Drew knew what was about to happen and even if he wanted to stop it, he didn't have the strength to do so.

He wanted Gloria just as much as she wanted him and after hearing her turning his door knob to enter his room; Drew knew without a doubt the evitable was only seconds away. Drew listened as Gloria opened the door and entered his room. Gloria had crossed the line and entered the lion's den and for making such a crucial mistake, he was about to pay the ultimate price.

"Are you awake?" Gloria asked.

"Yes," Drew responded.

"Mind, if I join you?" Gloria asked.

Without giving Gloria an answer, Drew pulled back his sheets, inviting her to join him. There wasn't any need to pretend anymore, Drew was ready for what was destined to happen, including the consequences that came with it. Once in bed, Gloria straddled Drew and instantly began teasing him, by kissing and biting on his ear. She rubbed her saturated vagina against his rock-hard penis, almost daring him to enter and with each attempt Drew made to enter, Gloria refrained him from doing so.

"Tell me you want me," Gloria instructed while continuing to tease Drew. "Tell me you love me and you want me back."

Reaching behind, Gloria grabbed hold of Drew's rock-hard, throbbing penis. She stroked it and rubbed it against her, intensifying their desire to have each other. Gloria's tireless teasing was taking Drew to the brink of a violent explosion. Drew had reached the point of no return and he was willing to do or say anything to receive the pleasure Gloria was restricting him from having. In order to have Gloria, Drew had to say and do exactly what she wanted and once nearing his breaking point, Drew said exactly what Gloria wanted him to.

"If you want this pussy to be yours again, you have to tell me, you want me back," Gloria said. "You want it, don't you?" Gloria teased.

"Yes, I want it," Drew replied.

"Then say it, say you love me and you want me back," Gloria instructed.

Gloria was driving Drew up a wall, by rubbing the head of his penis against the outer walls of her vagina. Drew wanted more than anything to enter those magical walls, to the point, he did the unthinkable.

"Yes, I love you, and I want you back in my life," Drew screamed out.

Finally, after what seemed like forever and a day, Gloria lowered her body over his, allowing his penis to enter her overly saturated vagina. Drew had made a big mistake by giving in to the pleasures of intimacy. Not only had he crossed the point of no return, he was also going to have to accept the penalties that came with making love to Gloria. There was no doubt he was going to regret this night, but he didn't want to think about it. He could only ask God to have mercy on his soul now that he had given in to Delilah.

Chapter: 8

Debating whether to surprise Drew with a visit, Lynn contemplated if it was the right time to do so. It was late and though her pregnancy tests were negative, Lynn couldn't relax until her period arrived. If it turned out she was pregnant, dreams of being with Drew would be over. Maybe she deserved to lose Drew after what she did to him but regardless of her mistake, Drew didn't deserve what she did to him. Accepting the blame would be easy if only she knew what happened that night. Lynn found it difficult to accept the story Marshall and Ashley gave her. She didn't remember talking to Ashley about wanting to sleep with Marshall. She was certain she hadn't consented to engage in unprotected intercourse with Marshall. There was no denying she was under the influence of prescribed medication and alcohol but she strongly believed she couldn't have been so irresponsible to risk her future for a quick roll in the hay. It should have been Drew, she had made love by the ocean, instead of Marshall. If by chance she was pregnant, Lynn knew she needed to place her ducks in a row by starting with informing Marshall, she was pregnant with his child. As the father, Marshall had legal rights; though it was highly unlikely he would exercise those rights. Chances were, he would try to convince her to terminate the pregnancy, because he wouldn't want the burden of being a father, and to be frank, Lynn wouldn't blame him if did. Lord knows, she didn't want to have to raise a child by a man whom she believed may have raped her a second time. But before jumping the gun, Lynn decided to call Marshall. She waited nervously for Marshall to pick up and wonder if he would pick up at all. There was no way to accurately predict the unexpected; all Lynn could do was hope for the best.

"Hello," Marshall answered.

"Marshall, this is Lynn. I want," Lynn tried explaining before she was interrupted.

"I know who this is. What the hell do you want?" Marshall said cutting Lynn off before she could apologize.

Lynn paused, before going forward with what she wanted to say. Her first thought was to abandon her plan by informing Marshall of her condition but felt she had a duty to uphold and went forward with what she wanted to say.

"First of all, I want to apologize for what I did to you. It was wrong, and I should have thought of a better way to handle the situation," Lynn said.

"You're right, you should have, but it's too fucking late now. So, thank you Lynn Boldmont, thank you for fucking up my life." Marshall replied angrily.

"Marshall, I know you are upset at me, and to some extent, I probably deserve it but can we talk civilly to each other just for one night?" Lynn asked.

"Well, ain't that a bitch, I can't fucking believe you. After you smashed a damn glass in my face that nearly cut my fucking nose off, you seriously think I would want to have anything to do with you?

"Marshall, don't be like that," Lynn said.

"Really, Lynn, you expect me to let go of the shit you did to me? If you do, you're fucking crazier than I thought.

"I didn't call you to be insulted," Lynn said.

"Why did you call me? Marshall asked. And one other thing, you got some fucking nerve to be calling me anyway, after you damn near destroyed fucking career. Thanks to you, my team is looking for a way to get rid of me. And all you gotta say to me is that you didn't call to get insulted," Marshall chuckled in disbelief.

Though it may not have been the most opportune time to share her diagnosis, Lynn went forward with informing Marshall about being possibly pregnant.

"Marshall, I may be pregnant,"

"Jesus Christ, I don't believe this shit. Are you fucking kidding me?" Marshall screamed out before going silent. He waited a few seconds to absorb the news before responding to Lynn. "How do you know it's my baby? You've fucked me and the farm boy," Marshall teased.

"I haven't slept with Drew; if I'm pregnant, it's your baby," Lynn responded.

"News flash, I want nothing to do with you or your baby. I'm going to do what the gangster niggers do, I'm going to leave you to raise the baby by your fucking self," Marshall replied with laughter.

Lynn expected a harsh reaction from Marshall but even for Marshall, it was a new low. After Marshall's explosion, Lynn felt it was in her best interest to end their conversation before anything else could be said. Marshall's attacks had brought tears to her eyes but her pride wouldn't allow him to benefit from it. Before ending their conversation, Marshall said a few more things that were on his mind.

"Lynn, don't you ever fucking call me again, you hear me? I don't give a fuck about you or the baby you may be carrying," Marshall screamed out, "It's over between us, I don't ever want to hear from you again, and another thing, if you are pregnant, I feel sorry for that baby, for having a crazy bitch for a mother. And by the way, your sister was a far better fuck than you." Marshall said before hanging up.

Though caught off guard, Lynn wasn't surprised at the allegations Marshall made. She had long suspected Marshall and Ashley were intimate, and thanks to Marshall's confession, he'd answered what she'd suspected all along. Marshall's reactions to Lynn's call left her in a horrible mood. She needed to talk to someone and called Ashley. It hadn't mattered that Ashley had slept with Marshall; Lynn needed to hear a familiar voice but Ashley's phone went to voicemail. Lynn then called her father. Harry answered but advised he was on an important overseas call. Acting on impulse, Lynn called Drew but got his voicemail. She suspected Drew was in bed for the night but she needed to talk to him. She knew she would have to come clean and tell him everything that happened and had decided to do so. Any other time she would have waited until morning to talk to him, but she was too upset to do so. Getting out of bed, Lynn removed her desk drawer and emptied all of its contents on her bed. She began assorting through the papers looking for a small envelope Drew had given her in case of an emergency. It didn't take long for her to find the key to Drew's apartment. Lynn could now enter without having to disturb him. She entertained the thought of wearing only a robe with nothing under it but realized she would worsen her situation if she did. In all honesty, making love with Drew wasn't as important as wanting to be held. Lynn wanted to feel Drew's arms around her. She needed Drew to tell her that he loved her and everything was going to be all right. Lynn left her dorm wearing a nightgown under her robe. She made the short drive to Drew's apartment, where she sat in her car for a few minutes before building the nerves to get out.

Chapter: 9

"Oh my God, we make love so beautifully," Gloria said while lying in Drew's arms. "God, I can't get enough of you." she went on to say.

Twice, Gloria had reached the summit and was hoping for a three-peat. Drew was the man that was giving her the feelings she needed and had been missing since leaving him for Mason. Though exhausted, Gloria wanted to feel Drew inside of her again but first, she had to regain her senses. While doing so, Gloria began asking questions pertaining to them getting back together. It was a subject Drew wasn't eager to share his feelings about and hesitated when having to answer Gloria's questions. He loved Gloria but his love fell short of wanting to come back to her. So much had transpired since their breakup; he had found another girl he wanted to share his future with. Frankly speaking, Drew didn't want the drama that came with Gloria and her cheating. She was currently involved with his cousin, who loved her to no end, and he wasn't going to be the one to ruin Mason's dreams. God knows he'd done enough damage by sleeping with Gloria, and there was no way he was going to do anymore.

"No man has ever made me feel the way you do. I love you, Drew Harrison, and I want us to wake up in each other's arms every morning. We can, you know; all you have to say is that you'll take me back," Gloria said.

Drew didn't respond to Gloria's comment. Though it felt good making love to the woman that had been his girl for more than six years, he didn't want her back. Going back to Gloria meant clashing with Mason, and he didn't want to have to do that. It wasn't that he was afraid of Mason; Drew didn't need the hassle that came with having a showdown with Mason. Gloria had made her decision, and because of it, it was too late to come back to him. Things had changed tremendously regarding his feelings; Gloria had ripped his heart out one too many times and because of it, he'd become numb to his feelings for her.

"You don't have to say you love me; the way you made love to me, told me everything I needed to know," Gloria said.

Drew listened to what Gloria was saying and nearly gave in to her, especially after hearing how much she wanted to feel him inside of her again.

By remounting Drew, Gloria gave an indication that she was ready for another round of intense lovemaking, and as her sex slave, he was more than eager to grant Gloria her wish. Gloria wanted this night to never end and though it felt like a fairytale, it was a sure bet that come tomorrow, she was going to be on the train heading home.

Out of condoms, Drew suggested that they end the night on a high note but was persuaded by Gloria to go forward with one final time. Gloria convinced him it was unnecessary to use condoms because she was on the pill. It wasn't that Drew didn't believe her, he felt it was important to protect himself. He was well aware that Gloria was on birth control and had been since the age of fifteen but Gloria was Mason's girl now and if by chance, she became pregnant, Drew wanted to know without a doubt he wouldn't be the father. Whatever Gloria had up her sleeve, Drew wasn't going to be hoodwinked by it. Needless to say, Drew fell victim to Gloria's mindset that he withdrew before orgasming. In doing so, Drew found himself fighting to break the grip from Gloria's legs held tightly around his waist. Feeling he was seconds before releasing a disaster, Drew managed to pull out in time. Gloria wasn't certain if she'd managed to hold him long enough to plant his semen inside of her but felt confident some of Drew's semen was released inside of her.

"What were you trying to do?" Drew screamed after realizing Gloria's attempt to possibly ruin his life.

Needing to put Drew's mind at ease, Gloria announced she was on the pill and had no reason to want to become pregnant. She was adamant she didn't want children but Drew didn't believe her. In his mind, Gloria wanted to get pregnant to trap him and he nearly fell victim to her.

Hearing Gloria speak didn't ease Drew's mind any; instead, it left him on full alert. Drew now suspected Gloria's motive was to get pregnant to trap him in a relationship he didn't want. Seeing what had happened, Drew now was regretting sleeping with Gloria.

He wished he had followed his first instincts and kicked her ass out of his apartment the moment she arrived, but it was too late to look back at what he should have done, he was in bed with Satan's bottom bitch and he needed her to get out. Drew could only pray; he hadn't impregnated her. Lord knows, if he had, he would have hell to pay, not only to Mason but to his mother, who was overwhelmed after hearing he had finally dumped the hazel-eyed devil.

Lying on her back, looking at the ceiling, Gloria arched her body, hoping to guide Drew's sperm inside of her. It was most likely her efforts were for nothing but this was perhaps her last opportunity to work her magic on him. For Gloria, having Drew's baby was important to her future. Carrying Drew's child meant he had to marry her to save face in the community. His mother was the mayor of the town, which meant Drew would have to do the right thing and marry her.

"Baby, I'm sorry about what happened. You felt so damn good inside of me, I didn't want to stop," Gloria explained.

In a last act of desperation, Gloria began kissing Drew again. She had apologized for her actions, blaming it on the way he made love to her. What was so strange was that Drew believed her and accepted her explanation without questioning her further. Seeing that Drew had fallen for her act, Gloria chose to pull another trick from her bag. She knew how much Drew enjoyed the pleasures of what her mouth had given him and kissed her way down his waist where his erect penis was standing at attention, waiting for her.

Chapter: 10

Standing outside of Drew's apartment, Lynn was in the position to knock but hesitated. She wasn't sure if she was sending the right message by wearing only a short gown under her robe. She didn't want to send the wrong message or get herself in a position she didn't want to be in, but Lynn wanted her man back and if having to make love to Drew was the answer to getting him back then she would strongly consider it. Again, Lynn raised her hand to knock but hesitated. She had a better idea; she was going to use her key instead. Once opening the door, her plans were to join Drew in bed. Reaching inside the pocket of her robe, Lynn removed her key but before inserting it into the lock, she contemplated if she was doing the right thing. Undecided about what to do, Lynn inserted the key into the lock. Turning the key, she slowly opened the door and stuck her head inside. It wasn't a surprise that the protected chain lock wasn't on the door because Drew never did so but what was surprising was how dark it was inside the apartment. Drew always left a light on because of his fear of total darkness. Stepping inside the apartment, Lynn could feel her heart pounding from nervousness, as she slowly made her way inside. She didn't know how Drew would take her coming by so late without calling first but chose to risk it anyway.

"Drew," Lynn called out softly.

Now inside, Lynn searched to find the light switch but tripped over Gloria's night bag on the floor and fell against the wall. Frightened by the idea that Drew may think she was a burglar, Lynn again, called out his name but this time louder. She continued to search for the overhead light and removed her iPhone to do so but before she could, her phone rang.

"Dammit;" Lynn said out loud, after seeing Ashley was face-timing her. Afraid to be seen inside Drew's apartment, Lynn ran out closing the door behind her and leaving it unlocked. Lynn ran down the stairs to her car before redialing her sister.

Hearing his door slam, Drew froze inside Gloria. He pushed Gloria off the top of him and placed his hand over her mouth.

"Shhh; somebody's in the house," Drew whispered. "Stay here and don't move."

With his legs shaking like an earthquake, Drew sat on the edge of his bed to put his pajama pants on. He quietly made his way to his bedroom door and cracked it enough to listen for any movement. Unable to hear anything other than his heart beating, Drew instantly knew it was Lynn. He was caught, and there wasn't a damn excuse he could make. Making his way from his bedroom down the hallway, Drew entered the living room but found no one present. He returned up the hall to the bathroom, thinking Lynn may have been hiding in either the bathroom or the kitchen, and carefully checked both rooms but found no sign of Lynn. Drew was sure he heard someone and checked the front door and found it unlocked. It was a sure sign that Lynn had been inside his apartment. Drew opened the front door and exited the apartment. He could hear someone running down the stairways and took it to be Lynn. Drew stood at the upstairs window and looked across the parking lot. Seconds later, he saw Lynn running to her car. She had indeed been inside his apartment but had she heard him making love to Gloria? Without knowing why Lynn left so abruptly, Drew could only watch the tail lights of her car leave the parking lot at a high rate of speed. His first reaction was to call her because he wasn't sure what she knew.

"Who was it?" Gloria asked; hoping it was Lynn who had entered the apartment.

"It was Lynn," Drew responded.

Gloria smiled; hoping Lynn had heard them making love and ran out in disgust. It was time for her to get the hell out of Drew's life anyway. Lord knows, he didn't need to be with no high sidity bitch, who was going to chew him up and spit him out like a piece of stale bubble gum. Drew needed a real woman, a woman who knew how to fulfill his every need. That woman was her, and she was glad the bitch had heard Drew squealing like a pig in his bedroom. Maybe now, the high-class bitch would learn to suck a good dick the way she knew how.

Locking the door behind him, Drew began making his way to his bedroom. He had fucked up by going against his better judgment. His nightmare had come true, Lynn had caught him and Gloria making love, and now it was over between them. It was fair to say Gloria was ready to celebrate and started by grabbing hold of Drew's hand to escort him back to bed. She was even hotter than before and was ready to do anything Drew wanted, but Drew wasn't in the mood and stopped Lynn's advancement.

Seeing what Gloria had in mind Drew pushed her hand away, he had more important things to do. He needed to call Lynn and find out exactly what she heard. Lynn's unexpected visit left Drew puzzled. He was uncertain if she had heard him and Gloria and needed to speak to her for answers. Drew called Lynn but only got her voicemail. Unable to reach Lynn only heightened Drew's already confused mind. With each passing minute, Drew became more paranoid; he again called but got the same response. Panicking at the thought of what must have been going through Lynn's mind, Drew began getting dressed to drive to her dorm. Seeing what Drew was about to do, Gloria tried intervening. She didn't see the urgency in him to rush so quickly over to Lynn's room without knowing the facts. But that didn't stop Drew. He was hell-bent on finding out what caused Lynn to abruptly leave his apartment. Drew left leaving Gloria to wonder if he would return for the night. His mind was focused on Lynn and the reason for her sudden departure. If by chance, Lynn heard him making love to Gloria, there was no way she would ever forgive him.

Once inside his car, Drew started his engine and began leaving the parking lot when his phone rang. It was Lynn, she was finally returning his call.

"Hello," Drew answered nervously.

"I saw you had called. I apologize for not returning your call earlier, but I was talking to Ashley," Lynn explained.

"That's ok, I was calling to see if you came by my apartment tonight?" Drew asked.

Lynn hesitated before admitting she had but explained she had used her key to enter but changed her mind. Lynn didn't seem upset nor did she ask questions. Something happened that caused her to change her mind but Drew had his lucky stars to thank that she didn't walk in on him making love to Gloria. In an element of surprise, Lynn asked if they could talk over breakfast. She admitted she had made a mistake by not revealing the truth about Marshall and wanted to talk more in-depth as to why she chose not to tell him. Lynn stressed the importance of wanting to discuss a possible future together but before doing so, she wanted to talk things out between them. Drew was more than willing to have breakfast with her. He was overwhelmed by her willingness to want fight for their relationship. God had answered his prayers and now it was time to straighten up his life by rectifying his wrongdoings.

In other words, his romantic night with Gloria was over and though it may have been too late to take her to a hotel for the night, it was going to be him sleeping alone on the couch.

Returning to his apartment, Drew closed and double-locked the door behind him. He even placed the chain over the door to eliminate any chance of Lynn breeching it again. As anticipated, Gloria was in bed waiting for his return. Entering the room, Drew placed his keys on his nightstand. He sat at the edge of the bed and began undressing.

"Everything all right?" Gloria asked.

"Yeah, thanks," Drew replied.

"Did she hear us?" Gloria asked, hoping Lynn had but to her disappointment, Lynn hadn't. "That fucking Bitch," Gloria said to herself. She couldn't believe Lynn would be so stupid to enter Drew's house, only to change her mind at the last minute. It felt like a scene from a soap opera but like a soap opera, the truth always reveals itself at the end.

In a last-ditch effort to get Drew back in bed with her, Gloria turned back the sheets for him to join her but this time, she was denied.

"You sleep here, I'm sleeping on the living room couch and Gloria, don't follow me," Drew instructed. "We've had a wonderful night but it's time to put an end to it." Drew turned off the lights and left the room. Gloria didn't ask why. She didn't have to; she could see the confusion on Drew's face. She saw the relief on his face that Lynn didn't know about them. Tonight, she was going to give Drew the space he needed but come tomorrow morning, Drew was fucking her before she left.

Chapter: 11

By seven-fifteen Gloria was seated on the train looking through the window, waving goodbye. Drew had fulfilled her sexual fantasies, and as she predicted, she'd gotten the fulfillment she sought with Mason. Now, Gloria was ready to go home to the man she'd made a commitment to; a commitment she no longer had any intension of keeping. Why couldn't Mason make her feel the way Drew could? And why couldn't he have the finances to compete with Drew? Needless to say, Mason had none of the qualities Drew possessed and it was frustrating. It would have made her decision a little harder if Mason had some of Drew's qualities. After spending the night with Drew, Gloria's decision was made and she was ready to move on from Mason. Some would argue, Gloria only wanted to be with Drew because of his family's wealth and to be honest, Gloria's decision had a lot to do with the Harrison's wealth, but it mostly had to do with Mason's inability to engage in an intellectual conversation with her friends. Mason's lack of education made it difficult for him to communicate with the elite. He sometimes embarrassed her with his corny lines and foul mouth while in the presence of her friends. It had gotten to the point where she stopped inviting him to events given by her friends. Gloria believed; Mason was only a fad she was experiencing. His bad boy image was what attracted her to him but after seeing the light, she now knew who she wanted to sleep beside at night and awake to in the mornings; the problem she faced was convincing Drew that she was over her obsession with other men.

Drew waved goodbye a final time as the train pulled away. It had been a night to remember but it was time to return to reality and work out his problems with Lynn. Drew had more than an hour before his was schedule to meet Lynn for breakfast. He was hopeful he and Lynn could reconcile before breakfast was over but Drew's first order of business was to return to his apartment and eliminate any signs of Gloria being there. More than anything, Drew wanted to have a relationship with Lynn and to make sure he did, he needed to cut ties with Gloria. Drew rushed home to clean and change his sheets, he didn't want any signs of another woman being there.

Drew arrived back on campus to find Lynn waiting outside the dining hall for him.

Like a teenager, Lynn's eyes lit up once seeing him. From her reaction, it was apparent she had missed him and Drew wasn't any different, he too was overjoyed at the sight of seeing Lynn. They were a couple in love and though they had challenges facing them, they were willing to face them together.

After breakfast, Lynn decided to go back to Drew's apartment and lucky for Drew; he had policed the entire apartment after taking Gloria to the train station. Lord knows, he couldn't afford for Lynn to discover any surprises waiting for her. Last night's unannounced visit from Lynn, nearly gave him a heart attack. Once at the apartment, Drew found himself overly frazzled from being up all night and fought to keep his eyes open. He was in desperate need of rest for this afternoon's track meet. Lynn saw that Drew was struggling to stay away and suggested they go into his bedroom to rest. Like Drew, Lynn had stayed awake for most of the night and was just as sleepy. Drew held Lynn's hand, leading her to his bedroom. He didn't have to worry about being caught with his pants down; his mother and sister weren't scheduled to arrive until four o'clock; giving him and Lynn plenty of time to do whatever they wanted to do. Inside Drew's bedroom, Lynn began undressing in front of him. It was the first time Lynn had ever undressed in his presence and her bold move had taken Drew completely by surprise. Though Lynn's actions were astonishing to say the least, Drew tried remaining calm. His heart rate increased with each item of clothing Lynn removed. Lynn was dressed in matching bra and panty set that accented her small frame. Though petite, Lynn's body was more athletic than he estimated and the sight of her urged Drew to lift her in his arms and placed her gently in bed.

 Drew was next to undress and he did so by stripping down to his boxer briefs. It had only been a few hours ago that he'd made love to Gloria, and he was about to make love to Lynn for the very first time. It felt unreal, almost dreamlike but this was a real-life event he was about to experience. With his focus on Lynn; Drew worried that he wouldn't be able to perform after pulling an all-nighter with Gloria. Not only that, his penis was sore from smashing Gloria throughout the night. Getting into bed, Drew reached for Lynn's hand and pulled her closer to him. He wasn't sure if anything was going to happen with them, he was hopeful it did. Drew was stimulated by seeing Lynn dressed in her bra and panties. His manhood stood at attention while waiting for its next command. Sadly, Drew's hope of a romantic morning was shot down.

"I'm sorry baby, the company came this morning. Maybe next time," Lynn teased.

"Awe, man, what a bummer," Drew replied.

For Lynn, she couldn't have been more relieved. She had dodged a bullet and was thankful that God was on her side.

Chapter: 12

Gloria's train arrived four hours behind schedule but you wouldn't have known it from the look in Mason's eyes. His angel had returned home to him and he couldn't have been happier. Mason could barely hold his excitement and greeted Gloria with a warm embrace and a welcoming kiss. It was surprising to see how much he'd missed her and Gloria found it hard not to resist. She hated the idea of having to play along with the game of being happy to see Mason but he'd made her homecoming a welcoming one. Still, she wished she was on WFU's campus with Drew to help root for him at his track meet. Instead, she was in the arms of a man she wasn't sure she wanted to be with anymore. Mason grabbed Gloria's bags to carry them to his car as Gloria followed closely behind him. She was nervous Mason was going to see the tags identifying where she'd been and needed to have a storyline if he noticed it. To get Mason's attention, Gloria began to talk to him about how much she missed him and couldn't wait to be with him. Of course, she was spitting him a bunch of bullshit lies but it was all she could do to get his attention. Seeing how happy Mason was Gloria felt guilty for having to lie but she needed to save her ass until she was sure what Drew wanted to do. Gloria wanted badly to tell Mason the truth that she didn't want to be with him anymore but she didn't have the heart. Mason had been there for her when she had no one else to rely on but she didn't love him the way he needed to be loved and now that she had a chance to reunite with Drew, she didn't want to blow it. Sure, she could tell Mason to fuck off but why? He didn't deserve the hurt she was about to place upon him but her hands were tied. If there was a bright side to this story, giving Mason one final night was it but before she broke things off, she wanted to give Mason the night of his life.

Last night with Drew was a night Gloria would never forget. Drew had given her the fuck of her life and after doing so, Gloria had no doubt he was about to sever ties with the "Rich Bitch." Gloria was very confident after last night. She strongly believed she'd done enough to persuade Drew to come back to her and why shouldn't she? Drew not only confessed his love for her, he openly admitted he wanted her back. But even though Gloria remained confident about the state their relationship, she continued to have concerns about the way Drew catered to Lynn. For now, she was going to keep Mason, at least until Drew close the door on Lynn.

By no means was Gloria stupid nor was she going to place all of her eggs in one basket. Her plans were to play things by ear and wait until she was sure Drew's intentions were honorable. She wasn't going to give up her good thing with Mason to end up with nothing. Yeah, she could pull the wool over the eyes of an old doctor at the hospital; Lord knows, she'd been propositioned many times but for Gloria, it was about being loved and pampered. All of the doctors at the hospital were married and couldn't give her the time she wanted to have. Sure, they could probably buy her anything she wanted but they couldn't give her the time she needed. The way Gloria looked at it, until she could get the things she wanted, she wasn't going to give up what she had.

Gloria stood by as Mason placed her luggage in the trunk of his car. She was relieved he hadn't notice anything and waited for him to open her door. Gloria understood the danger she had placed herself in and the first chance she got; she was going to get rid of the evidence. She wasn't ready for Mason to find out about Drew yet. For now, she was going to be the perfect girlfriend until she got the word from Drew that he was ready to resume their relationship.

"How was your trip?" Mason asked.

"I guess you can say I learned a lot. They conference only lasted a few hours and I was back on the train, but it was interesting," Gloria answered. Gloria displayed a fake smile when answering Mason's question. In reality, Gloria took a later train home to substitute for the time it would take to get home. She knew Mason wouldn't believe she had been at a conference for a few minutes and jump back on the train. So, to kill time, she got off the train in D.C. and waited for the late train for the town of Jefferson. her way back home, Gloria stopped over in D.C. and waited a few hours before taking a later train home.

"I'm sorry I didn't get the chance to bring you back anything," Gloria said.

"That's no problem baby," Mason replied. Frankly speaking, Mason hadn't expected Gloria to bring him anything because she'd never given him anything before.

Buckling her seat belts, Gloria waited for Mason to drive off. She continued to worry whether Mason noticed the claim tickets on her luggage but in all honesty, Mason didn't give a damn about checking a claim ticket, his mind was focused on taking Gloria to the hotel room he'd reserved.

He wanted to show her how much he'd missed her and to know for sure, if she had been involved with anyone while she was out of his sight. Mason continued to be suspicious of Gloria's sudden conference she had to attend for the job. No matter how he tried to factor her departure and return time, it didn't add up. If by chance she had taken the plane, he could've understood her early return home but to travel by train that stopped at every depot, it was highly unlikely she could return in the time she did. Mason suspected Gloria had spent the night with Drew and if she had, he would not only whip Drew's ass, Gloria wouldn't be spared.

"I got a surprise for you." Mason said as they continued their drive down the highway.

 It was no need for Gloria to get excited, she suspected Mason's plans included some cheap smelly motel to spend the night and Mason certified her suspicions by entering the parking lot of the Super 8 Motel.

"Well, I'll be damned," Gloria said to herself. "The broke motherfucker could have at least taken me to a Comfort Inn."

Seeing Mason's so-called surprise, Gloria's energy escaped her. She questioned her decision on whether she should break the news to him now, ending her charade instead of having to go through the same bullshit. Lord knows she wasn't in the mood for another night of fucking, especially after being smashed for most of last night. Then again, she should have suspected Mason to try his hand at wanting to be intimate. To be frank, Gloria wasn't sure if she could make it through the evening. Drew had done a number on her last night, as well as this morning and she was too tired to put forth any effort to be romantic. Just the thought of lying beside Mason after being with Drew gave Gloria the willies. She couldn't imagine how her body would respond once that time came and honestly, Gloria wanted nothing to do with Mason or his plans for a romantic night. Gloria was more interested in going home, rather than lying up in some flea-bag motel. Officially, she was still Mason's girl, at least until she dropped the bomb on his broke ass but as his girl it was her responsibility to satisfy him. Seeing where they were staying, Gloria made the decision to give Mason one final night of sex, before ending their relationship for good. Somehow, she was going to have to go through the evening and pretend to be the loving girlfriend Mason was expecting and with any luck, Mason was going to blow a gasket and end their night early as he always did.

Exiting the car, Gloria made her way to the door and waited for Mason to open it. Entering she tried keeping a positive attitude but found it hard to do. Much to her surprise, she found rose petals scattered about the room, a bottle of her favorite Italian Moscato chilling on ice, and two wine glasses. Mason spared no expense by purchasing a pepperoni and cheese tray with olives, surrounded by an abundant amount of fruit. From the looks of it, Mason had thought of everything; except for how she felt. On the bed was a pink On Gossamer Mesh nightie with Origami Pleats. Gloria was surprised to learn that Mason was aware of fashion but then again, he was willing to learn everything when it came to satisfying her.

Needing the comfort of soaking in a hot tub of water, Gloria convinced Mason to give her time to soak her acing body and to freshen up. He had no idea what she had gone through but was eager to grant her wish because of the reward he was about to receive. Inside the bathroom, Gloria sat on the toilet and contemplated how she was going to get through the evening. She was tired, sore, and a bit irritated from making love to Drew all night. Realistically, she wasn't in any condition to repeat another long night of lovemaking but for Mason's sake, she was willing to give him a final night of happiness before lowering the boom on him.

Gloria soaked for more than thirty minutes before getting out of the tub. Once doing so, she applied lotions and perfumes to her body, hoping it was going to be enough to give her the edge she needed to push Mason over the top and if that didn't work, Gloria had just the thing that did. She always carried a pack of vaginal moisturizer with her when she wasn't in the mood to make love to Mason. It was a trick taught to her by one of her co-workers who were juggling two lovers successfully at the same time. Gloria inserted the suppository into her vagina to help rejuvenate and prepare her for Mason. It was time to put the suppository to the test. Wearing her pink nightie, Gloria exited the bathroom and was greeted by Mason who was waiting for her with a glass of wine. Music from the radio was playing at a low tone to set the mood. Gloria pretended to be excited by Mason's attempt to be romantic and smiled as she fell into his awaiting arms. Gloria placed her head against his shoulder and began to sing the song playing over the radio.

"You have no idea, how much I've missed you," Mason said with sincerity. By no means was he a romantic but you wouldn't have known it by the way he was acting today. "I want to toast you and the love we have for each other. May this love last forever and no one come between us." Mason said.

After toasting, Mason led Gloria in a slow dance and gently kissed her before spinning her around to see how stunning she looked in her gown. Mason pulled Gloria back into his arms and slowly engaged her in a slow dance. Dancing at a slow pace, Mason danced his way toward the king-size bed. He laid Gloria on her back in the prone position and stood back to get a full view of her wearing the gown he'd given her. Kissing Gloria's moist lips, he kissed his way from Gloria's neck, down the side of her body to her pelvis. He was showing Gloria how much he loved her and what he was willing to do to satisfy her but Mason's inability to attend to Gloria's needs became an instant turn-off. Mason was failing the test to give Gloria the foreplay she wanted to prepare her for intercourse. Two minutes of foreplay wasn't nearly enough time to stimulate Gloria. For Gloria, the only way she could accommodate Mason's lack of compassion was to pretend she was making love to Drew. But in a surprising move, Mason turned Gloria on to her stomach and cautiously proceeded to spread her legs. He kissed his way from the heel of Gloria's foot to the crease of her buttocks. He had a surprise in store and couldn't wait to give it to her.

Using his tongue, Mason was unknowingly soothing the soreness of Gloria's inner and outer walls of her vagina. He could feel Gloria relaxing and knew he was doing his job correctly. The feeling was soothing enough to caused Gloria to release a high pitch moan. Mason was soothing Gloria's irritated and throbbing vagina. Mason's tongue caused Gloria to sink her teeth into her pillow while squeezing it tightly. The warmth and wetness of Mason's tongue was quickly causing Gloria's body to build towards a huge explosion. Feeling her orgasm on the horizon, Gloria released a loud moan. Not wanting it to end, she encouraged Mason to continue until she reached her peak. Gloria's intention to make her final night with Mason a success had gotten off to a good start. So much so, Mason was presenting a challenge for her not to end it. Tonight, Mason was showing his freaky side and Gloria was loving every minute of it. Mason was doing things to her body that he hadn't before and for that reason, Gloria began entertaining the idea of waiting before she ended their relationship. Mason continued his reckless behavior to satisfy Gloria. He licked her from the bottom of his feet to the top of her head. There were no restrictions when it came to providing Gloria with the pleasures she was seeking to receive. It was another sign that Mason was willing to do any and everything to make her happy.

To further please her, Mason placed Gloria's toes in his mouth and sucked them passionately as he inserted his penis inside of her. The feeling was electrifying that nearly caused

Gloria to nearly roll out of bed. Never had Gloria had her toes sucked before and before she realized what was happening, she was on her way towards another orgasm. Closing her eyes, Gloria continued to pretend it was Drew who was making love to her and as she did, she nearly screamed out his name. Once regaining her composure, Gloria began telling Mason how good he felt inside of her and how good he made her feel. She only wanted to speed up the process and did so by requesting that he explore deeper inside of her. She knew Mason wouldn't last if she took over their lovemaking session and she was correct with her assumption.

Hearing Gloria's request, Mason followed her instruction and in doing so, he lapsed into a frenzy and within seconds, it was over. Gloria's plan had worked to perfection; Mason had exploded like a mortar hitting its target.

"Yes," Gloria thought to herself. "I can get some sleep now," Gloria rolled over on her side and had nearly fallen asleep, when she felt Mason's erected penis pressing against her. She couldn't believe what was happening. Mason had always been a one and done man but not today, today he was ready to go another round.

Chapter: 13

The stadium was filled to capacity and the electricity was high. The anticipation of the sprint races was high and for the first time in his career, Drew was overly nervous. Nearly the entire town had come out to support of him and his bid to become the fastest man on the east coast. In the stands screaming his name were Nancy, Joanna, and Lynn. They'd witnessed Drew's victories in the two-hundred-meter run and had seen him victorious while anchoring the final leg of the 4x100-meter race. Finally, after sitting for nearly two hours, it was time for the main event. All three women cheered loudly, as the final race of the day was announced. Neither Nancy, Joanna nor Lynn chose to express an opinion on who would win the race but quietly they prayed Drew could at least finish in the top three. By doing so, Drew would qualify to compete at the prestigious Prefontaine Classic meet, held in Eugene Oregon in two weeks.

Setting his blocks. Drew felt ready. He believed his victory relied on him getting a good start but standing six feet, four inches in height; getting a great start was often difficult. However, earlier doing the qualifying rounds, Drew's reaction to the sound of the starter pistol had been excellent. He was confident in his ability and believed if he could stay close to the runners for the first sixty meters, his top-end speed would lead him to victory. Drew worried about this year's top sprinters; they were stronger than ever, not to mention Travis Britt who had dominated the track the entire season. Travis Britt was the favorite to win the race, but you couldn't tell Drew that. Drew strongly believed the race was his to win, but to do so, he had to get out of the blocks faster than normal to even have a chance. Drew had waited four years to prove his worth and with that being said, nothing was going to stop him from showing what he was capable of.

Crossing their fingers, Lynn watched nervously along with Nancy and Joanna as the runners were instructed to get into their blocks. Lynn said a quick prayer before joining hands with Nancy and Joanna. Together they stood with excitement as Drew positioned himself in the blocks. Once comfortable in the blocks, Drew concentrated on the sound of the starter pistol, hoping to get a strong start out of the blocks. More than anything Drew wanted to win this race; it was the race he'd dreamed of winning for more than three years and now the time had come for him to prove his worth to it. Pow, went the sound of the starter pistol. The entire field of runners broke out the blocks aggressively.

All eight racers got a clean start and was pushing to take the lead. Drew exploded from the blocks like a rocket and found himself in the mix of the leaders. It was the start he was hoping to get and man was he streaking like a bolt of lightning. Drew had taken the lead before his top-end speed kicked in at the sixty-meter mark, and because of it, his nearest competitive finished more than three strides behind him. To say it wasn't a contest would be an understatement, Drew had won by more than a half second. Lynn nearly jumped off the bleachers with Nancy and Joanna following suit. They were ecstatic by Drew's victory and rushed to the fence to greet Drew. He had accomplished another of his many goals; he had punched his ticket to Eugene Oregon to participate in the Prefontaine Classic.

Chapter: 14

Packing the last of his luggage, Drew was ready to leave for the airport. He was leaving two days early to have time to relax and train before the competition started. It was a successful tradition Drew followed since high school. Drew didn't have a coach, he trained the old-fashion way by using the routine he followed with his WFU coach, but with the twist of doing everything twice. Drew's odds of winning a place on the US Track and Field Team was slim to none but that didn't stop him from dreaming. He didn't have the sponsors representing him nor the backing from the top named coaches around the nation; all Drew had was himself. His mother and sister were going to miss his most important track meet of his life but that wasn't going to cause Drew to fold. He was motivated to face the impossible task that was standing in front of him and the fact he was doing it alone was an extra incentive to show what he was capable of doing.

Nancy, Joanna, and Karyme, all gathered around his car to see him off. Nancy was the first to embrace him and to wish him luck. She was saddened at the fact she wouldn't be attending, due to her obligation as mayor but comforted him by saying that she had full confidence in him. Joanna was next to speak with Drew. She spoke about being proud of him and his chances of winning a spot on the USA World Track Team. Last to wish Drew luck was Karyme; she embraced Drew and whispered in his ear. "Good luck to you, and when you come back a winner, I have a surprise instore for you," Karyme's comment was unexpected and gave Drew insight into what she was feeling. Sure, she may have been kidding but it was an intriguing thought nonetheless. Karyme, along with Nancy and Joanna, waved a final time as Drew drove away. His car hadn't reached the highway before Karyme found herself missing him. She wanted to tell Drew the truth about her feelings for him but chose not to. She understood his commitment to Lynn but it hadn't erased her love for him. It hurt knowing Drew didn't feel the same for her but it left her with the satisfaction that he cared enough not to take advantage of her.

While on his way to the airport, Drew's music may have been playing loud enough for everyone in the vicinity to hear but it hadn't disturbed his thoughts. Visions of Karyme were etched in his mind and for unknown reason, he couldn't erase them. Drew found himself wishing he had invited her to come along with him but knew she would never agree. It wasn't that he didn't believe Karyme would have rejected his offer but because her mother would have forbidden it.

You see, Sophia hated the idea of Karyme having romantic feelings for Drew and even warned her to avoid him at all costs. Karyme was twenty-one but you wouldn't have known it the way Sophia dictated her life. Yes, Sophia was her mother but more than that she was Karyme's guiding light who was determined, Karyme would have a better life than she.

Approaching Goodwyn's Convenience Store, Drew decided to gas up before heading to the airport. He entered the store yard and parked at the pumps. He was in a great mood and was looking forward to his upcoming trip to Oregon but his mood soon changed, after seeing Gloria. Gloria, along with Mason was interacting with their friends Gator Mack and his girlfriend Evelyn. The trepidation of seeing Gloria and knowing her imprudent ways left Drew with an uneasy feeling. Though Drew's instincts warned him to leave, he disregarded them. Instead, he got out of his car and began filling his tank. Out of his peripheral vision, he could see the group looking and pointing in his direction. Drew couldn't decipher what was being said but knew they were discussing him. Now, more than ever, Drew felt it was in his best interest to leave before Mason blew his top. Once filling his tank, Drew turned to the group of friends, and out of courtesy he acknowledged them by waving. In doing so, Drew locked eyes with Gloria. Instantly, Drew felt his heart sink. His biggest fear was about to come to fruition, Gloria was about to do something stupid that could expose the both of them. Seeing Gloria beginning to walk towards him, Drew entered the store. Without hesitation, Gloria followed Drew.

Seeing that Drew had entered the store to get away from her only intensified Gloria's desire to confront him. She understood the danger Mason presented but it wasn't enough to deter her from wanting to question Drew about fucking and dumping her, as if she was the town slut.

Gloria needed answers and she wasn't going to stand by and allow Drew to leave without getting them. Drew promised her he was going to give her an answer once he returned home and dammit, he was going to honor his word. It had been more than a week since he'd promised they would discuss getting back together and to think he'd returned home without notifying her, pissed Gloria off. Gloria believed, Drew was trying to take the bitch way out, by sneaking in and now out of town, without as much as saying hello. As much as she hated having to embarrass Mason in front of their friends, Gloria felt there was no other way but to confront Drew and expose him for the lying son-of-a-bitch he was. It was time to get the truth from

Drew, whether she had to pay with a tongue lashing or an old-fashion ass whipping from Mason, she was willing to take that chance. By avoiding Gloria, it was obvious, Drew had no intentions of getting back together with her but then again, why should he? He'd gotten what he wanted and instead of being a man about it, he reverted back to being the little pussy he'd always been.

The group watched Gloria walk across the store yard, following Drew inside. It was not only shocking for Mason but Gator and Evelyn stood dumbfounded in sheer disbelief. Gloria was doing the unthinkable, she was going to see her ex-boyfriend at the expense of her current man. It was funny, yet brazen that Gloria had the balls to pull off such a stunt, knowing the consequences she would face. Gloria had lost her freaking mind; she'd obviously forgotten who her man was. Lord knows, Mason wasn't going to take this shit sitting down and from the looks of things, he was about to take a stance to prove he was no push over. Seeing the mistake Gloria was making, Evelyn followed her inside the store. Evelyn didn't understand Gloria's mindset and couldn't sit by and allow her to make a fool out of Mason or herself for that matter. Evelyn felt she had to do something to stop Gloria before she went too far to turn back. Evelyn caught up with Gloria inside the store but was unsuccessful at convincing her to leave. Desperate to get Gloria out of the store, Evelyn grabbed hold of her hand.

"What the hell do you think you're doing? Evelyn asked. She was shocked by Gloria's actions and quickly reminded her how venomous Mason could be once he ever lost his temper.

"I'm not worried about what Mason might do to me. Right now, I have to talk to that lying cocksucking Drew," Gloria responded.

"Not today, you won't," Evelyn responded, pulling Gloria to the door of the store but before Evelyn could get Gloria out of the store, Drew appeared from behind one of the aisles. Seeing Gloria, Drew took a step backward. He couldn't believe Gloria had the audacity to follow him inside the store with Mason waiting on the outside.

"Well hello liar," Gloria said, referring to Drew.

"Hi Gloria, Evelyn, how are you guys doing?" Drew responded nervously.

64

"We doing fine. It's good to see you again, Drew. Come on, Gloria, we gotta go," Evelyn said, still holding a firm grip on Gloria's arm.

"Why haven't you called me?" Gloria asked as she pulled away from Evelyn

"I'm sorry, I've been really busy getting ready for my track meet, honestly, I didn't have the time," Drew responded.

"You promised me, we were going to discuss our relationship. What happened? What happened, Drew?"

"Can we talk about this when I come back? I'm running late to the airport," Drew explained.

"Bullshit, we're going to talk about this now," Gloria said, standing firmly while refusing to allow Drew to leave.

"Listen," Drew said, interrupting Gloria, "I know I promised that we were going to talk, and I'm going to keep my promise, just not now," Drew reiterated. He was not only becoming frustrated with Gloria; Drew was beginning to fear for his safety.

Mason was somewhere outside waiting for him to come out and frankly speaking, he didn't have time to square off with Mason. It wasn't that he was afraid of him, Drew had no problem bringing the smoke, now just wasn't the time. Gloria continued to press Drew for answers but Drew had nothing more to say. Drew's refusal to discuss having a future together, left Gloria believing he was stalling. Reluctant to engage further, Drew said farewell to the women and politely redirected Gloria to the side of him and left the store. Once outside, Drew remained vigilant of Mason's whereabouts. It was an uncomfortable feeling not knowing exactly where Mason was positioned, but Drew was certain Mason was someplace close. Drew got into his car and left the store as fast as he arrived. Leaving, Drew felt a sense of relief, knowing that he'd left without anything popping off. He may have dodged a bullet but he doubted very seriously if Gloria would.

Arriving at the airport, Drew called Lynn to inform her he was about to get on the plane but got her voicemail. Instead of leaving a message, Drew chose to text message Lynn. Inside the airport, Drew checked in his luggage and prepared to board his flight. Once in line, he placed his headphones on and began listening to music.

He felt a nudge in his back but paid it no attention to it, thinking it was accidental. Seconds later, Drew felt another nudge, followed by a hand touch to his ass. Now pissed that someone had intentionally violated him, Drew turned to face his accuser.

"Never let a woman to make reservations for you." Lynn laughed, "You may get the surprise of your life."

Chapter: 15

Two days passed since Drew and Lynn had checked into their hotel suite and as expected, Drew had been the perfect gentleman. He understood the morals Lynn was trying to display in regard to restricting intimacy but getting his libido on board with the idea was proving to be difficult. Lynn felt his frustration and wanted more than anything to alleviate his pain but her conscious wouldn't allow her to. With the pressure building increasingly heavy on Lynn's fragile mind, she was contemplating leveling with Drew. It was her way to bury her past, while hopefully moving on toward a successful future that included Drew. However, there was no way Drew would ever forgive her for what she did. Seeing what she was faced with, Lynn removed her bottle of prescribed Xanax from her purse and took two pills. She hoped it was enough to relax her to make love to Drew without having to deal with the guilt she was feeling. However, it was unlikely she would bring herself to tell Drew the truth because if she did, it would be over between them.

Not expecting a romantic night, Drew was the first to shower. After showering, he returned to their bedroom wrapped in a towel. Lynn was sitting on the edge of the bed, waiting on him. She surprised Drew with a pair of red silk pajamas with a matching robe she had brought while shopping in town. Lynn made it known; she had romantic plans for the night by greeting Drew with a kiss. Removing Drew's towel, Lynn began caressing his penis. It was an unexpected move on Lynn's behalf but what was unforeseen was Lynn's attempt to satisfy him orally. Though her performance could only be compared by that of a novice, Drew wasn't at all disappointed with her attempt. Lynn was doing her best to satisfy him and that alone was enough to please him. Lynn was giving him a sample of what their night together was going to be like and her attempt to please him orally was only a start. Lynn ended her tease and removed a bag containing her matching nightie and left for the bathroom to soak her body in preparation for giving it to the man she was in love with. Tonight, was going to be the night they make love for the first time and Lynn couldn't have been more excited. After months of waiting to be with the man she adored, Lynn was ready for it to happen.

Opening the balcony door, Drew brought out a bottle of Cabernet, submerged in a bucket of ice and placed it on the table. Next, he lit candles to give a romantic ambience. If tonight was anything he hoped it would be, he would need the sound of romantic music playing in the background.

Drew had the perfect music to play and used his playlist to play the best of Johnny Hartman, featuring John Coltrane. It was undoubtedly the most romantic music he could play doing their first sexual encounter together. Suddenly, the sound from Drew' phone interrupted him. Damn, it was Gloria, and Drew knew if he didn't answer, Gloria would continue calling until he did. Now was the perfect time to talk to her while Lynn was taking a bath. Answering, Drew pretended to be excited to hear from her, all the while waiting for the opportunity to get her off the phone. He was relieved that Mason hadn't beaten the hell out of her but now wasn't a good time to talk. But as expected, Gloria wanted to discuss the topic surrounding them getting back together. She again, confessed her undying love; while pleading for another chance to make things right between them.

"Drew, I made so many horrible mistakes in our relationship, but as God is my witness, I never stopped loving you. All I'm asking for is one last chance and I swear, I will never be unfaithful to you again." Gloria's pleas were genuine, she loved Drew and she wanted him back but Drew didn't want a relationship with her anymore, he was looking toward sharing his future with Lynn.

"I've heard that line thousand times and each time, you violate it by reaching out to another man. I don't want that anymore," Drew replied. "Being with you is too stressful." Drew didn't want Gloria to be a part of his life anymore. He was done with the games she constantly played, and knew, sooner or later, her games were going to cause someone to become physically hurt.

"Why can't you understand, I love you and I know you love me. Just give me the chance to prove to you that I can be the woman you want me to be," Gloria said. "I love you; I know you want to be married and so do I. Just give me the chance and I swear to you, I'll be the best wife you ever wanted."

"I'm sorry, I can't, I don't want to be with you anymore. Don't get me wrong, I believe you have good intentions, but I don't trust you," Drew said.

It was hard having to level with Gloria but it was the right time to do so. Drew never had the courage before but knew if he didn't do anything now, Gloria was going to ruin his relationship with Lynn. As strange as it may seemed, Drew was finally calling it quits. He was done with Gloria and her indecisiveness on whom she wanted. Yes, he loved Gloria and will always have strong feelings for her but he wasn't in love with her anymore.

He allowed his libido to think for him and it nearly got him in serious trouble with Mason. Mason could have made things difficult for him at the store but chose to stand down. Maybe, it was the one pass Mason was accustomed to giving people before he went all in on them but Drew believed, it was time to end things before it got out of hand. Unfortunately for Gloria, she was having trouble accepting the evitable. She continued doing her best to convince Drew to give her another chance to prove her love. Drew could hear the desperation in her voice but no matter how desperate Gloria had become, Drew refused to give in to her pleas.

Sensing Drew was about to end their conversation, Gloria tried everything to keep him on the phone. She suspected Lynn was with him and no matter how badly she wanted Drew to love her, he wasn't going to, not as long as he had Lynn whispering in his ear and telling him, she was no good for him. Hearing the water draining from the tub, Drew knew he had only minutes before Lynn would be making her grand entrance. His presumption was proven to be correct as Lynn emerged from the bathroom minutes later. She was wearing a sheer short white V-shaped nightie with thong panties to match. Her cleavage was exposed but only enough to tease his mind. Lynn's ripped abs glistened through the sheer silk material of her gown. Her flared nightie accented her long slender legs and with each step she made towards Drew, it felt as if he was in a dream. Lynn was breathtakingly beautiful and Drew couldn't wait to hold her in his arms. There was magic in the air and it was leading Drew to believe, tonight indeed was going to be the night they were going to make love.

Standing in the common area of their suite, Lynn made a complete turn to give Drew a comprehensive view of how she looked in her nightie. The mere presence of her nearly blew Drew away. He was mesmerized, not only by her beauty but the sexual persona she displayed. Lynn's eyes were frosted and she wore her hair on her shoulders. She illuminated the room and as she made her way toward Drew. Seeing Lynn approaching him, Drew reached out for her, securing her in his arms. Having Lynn in his arms, Drew nearly forgot he was on the phone with Gloria but his desire to hold Lynn prompted Drew to prematurely end his conversation with Gloria.

"I gotta go," Drew mumbled, as he disconnected their call and turned off his phone. He didn't want anyone disturbing him tonight. Tonight, was the night he concentrated on the lady of his life.

Lynn was as beautiful as a model in a magazine and man, was she ever sexy. The image of her was what fantasies were made of and making love to her was a dream Drew had fantasized about. Dropping his phone on the couch, Drew couldn't resist from kissing Lynn. He lowered his hands to clutch the cheeks of her buttocks to pull her closer to him. He wanted her unlike he'd ever wanted another woman but his quest to have her came with stipulations. Lynn was battling past demons that were causing her to have trust issues and though he had crossed the line with Gloria and Ashley, Drew decided to rededicate himself to make things right with Lynn. Drew knew whole heartedly that Lynn loved him because she'd shown it with her love and honesty. Her honesty was more than he'd shown her but being honest with Lynn about his affair with Ashley meant sabotaging their relationship.

Lifting Lynn in his arms, Drew aggressively positioned her against the wall. He passionately kissed her while removing the straps of her nightie from her shoulders. Drew placed Lynn's breast in his mouth and began nursing them. Applying the right amount of pressure to Lynn's breast, Drew could feel Lynn relaxing. This was the moment he'd waited for and now it was about to happen was a dream come true. But something was wrong, Drew felt a hesitation from Lynn and immediately stopped in the middle of undressing her.

"What's wrong babe?" Drew asked.

"Not here, I want you in our bedroom, Lynn explained.

In a lot of ways, Lynn's decision to make love in their bedroom made sense. Drew didn't want their first time to be a fuck against the wall; no matter how passionate it may had seemed. Like Lynn, he wanted their night together to be memorable, a memory they could forever reflect upon forever. Before retiring to their bedroom for the evening, Drew escorted Lynn outside on the balcony. There, he poured her a glass of wine and together they took a moment to look across the city and plan their future together. Drew was astonished by the way the lights from the candles enhanced Lynn's beauty. Lynn was more than his angel; she was the woman he'd chosen to be with.

"Here's to a beautiful beginning." Drew toasted, leaning over to kiss Lynn. He didn't have to tell her how in love he was with her, his eyes told his story and after their toast, Lynn took Drew by hand and led him to their bedroom.

Stopping short of the bed, they slow danced to the sweet baritone voice of Johnny Hartman, while kissing by candlelight. Drew whispered into Lynn's ears, telling her how much he loved her and how he was looking forward towards sharing his future with her. Drew followed with a solemn promise, to love, honor, and respect her, the way she deserved to be. His show of love was impressive enough to set the stage for what was to follow and as the evening continued, so had the buildup towards the inevitable. Hearing Drew's confession, sparked Lynn into questioning herself, if she could go forward with a relationship that was based on a lie. Drew was a great guy and though she loved every inch of him, she felt she wasn't good enough to be his girl. Although Lynn was ready for Drew to make love to her, she wasn't sure if she could go through with it without confessing what happened between, she and Marshall. Sure, things were over with Marshall and thank God she'd gotten her period but Lynn wasn't sure if she could pretend what happened with Marshall never happened. As it should, guilt was eating at her and it was interfering with what should have been a very special night together.

Taking the lead, Drew led Lynn to their bed. Once there, he gently kissed her and cautiously removed the straps from her gown over her shoulders, exposing her breast. He slowly and skillfully began kissing Lynn all over, heightening the sensation throughout her body. Drew's attention to detail nearly caused Lynn to forget what had been plaguing her, but what perhaps triggered Lynn's thoughts back to her problem was how Drew teased her body. It reminded her of how Marshall made her feel at the beach. It was safe to say Drew was making all the right moves, and Lynn found herself clinching her teeth to keep from screaming. Hearing Lynn's low moans of pleasure, Drew went all in to give her the sensation he was hoping she wanted. It was encouraging to know that Lynn was enjoying the pleasure he was giving her, so much so that it motivated Drew to continue his activity. Lynn was enjoying every second of what Drew was doing to her, but she was reminded of how she'd cheated on him. Lynn's hidden demons were resurfacing, bringing back vivid images of her awakening with Marshall on top of her. She desperately tried suppressing that night, but the guilt was too much for her to bury. Tonight, was supposed to be the first night they made beautiful love, but all Lynn could do was think of was how she cheated on Drew. Lynn couldn't erase from her mind what happened with Marshall. It wasn't because she still loved him or because of the way Marshall made love to her; it was because of the guilt she was carrying.

Drew didn't deserve what she did to him, and Lynn couldn't understand what happened or why she would want to sleep with Marshall without protection. Nevertheless, she did, and now, she was disgusted at herself for doing so. Lynn silently began tearing up, while Drew continued to think he was pleasing her. For weeks, Lynn hid her secret from Drew and now her guilt was beginning to boil over. More than anything Lynn wanted this night to happen but sadly, her inability to mask her guilt was too much for her to bear. Without warning, Lynn's silent cries gave way to a loud outburst; she pushed Drew off the top of her and curled up in a fetal position. Lynn had finally broken and after weeks of carrying the load of being unfaithful on her shoulders, the time had come for her to admit the truth of what happened with Marshall.

"Sweetheart, what's wrong?" Drew asked. He was stunned by what happened and his first thought was that Lynn may have had a flashback about her sexual assault and the way her body was coiled, gave all indication that it was.

Drew quickly learned; it was more than what he anticipated. Lynn's surprising act not only caught him with his pants down, but it hit him like a ton of bricks. Screaming to the top of her voice, Lynn was seemingly experiencing a panic attack.

"I'm sorry, I'm so sorry, I can't, I can't do this, I'm so sorry," Lynn kept repeating while keeping Drew at bay.

"Sweetheart, calm down; whatever it is, I'm sure we can fix it," Drew said while holding Lynn's hands.

"I don't deserve you," Lynn replied. She needed to tell Drew the truth but didn't know how. Telling Drew meant throwing away the best thing that had ever happened to her. Lynn's actions had Drew dumbfounded. He couldn't imagine what she was hiding that would cause him to leave her but was sure it had to do with Marshall.

"What is it?" Drew asked again.

Seeing the wreck Lynn was in, Drew began to speculate something more sinister happened between Lynn and Marshall. Lynn hadn't told him the entire story and Drew was afraid to ask, fearing the answer. Was Lynn trying to tell him she'd slept with Marshall and she may be pregnant.

Drew couldn't say for certain but the way Lynn was carrying on, it was the only thing that could have happened? Drew listened, as Lynn continued to be hysterical about whatever secret she'd been holding from him.

"I can't lose you; please Drew, you have to forgive me; I didn't know what I was doing," Lynn cried out.

Lynn's actions had Drew extremely concerned. She was distraught and becoming dangerous as each second passed. Whatever happened had Lynn convinced her future with Drew was in jeopardy. Not wanting to speculate, Drew needed more information to know what had happened.

"Lynn, listen to me, I need to know what's going on, so we can work at fixing it," Drew asked. He couldn't interpret what Lynn was trying to say. She wasn't making sense but the more she rattled on, the clearer it was becoming.

"Are you pregnant with Marshall's baby?" Drew asked.

"No," Lynn whimpered.

"Then what could be so bad, we can't work it out?" Drew asked.

"Baby, I mess up. I really mess up this time," Lynn repeated.

Drew tried assuring Lynn that he wasn't going to abandon her, no matter what she told him. In a way, he felt compelled to make that statement after his concerns heightened regarding Lynn's mental state. He didn't want Lynn to relapse, no matter how much he could be hurt by what she was about to tell him. Drew reminded Lynn of the promise he made to her regarding his promise to never hurt her. He also reminded Lynn that he was a man of his word, and no matter what she told him, he would never leave her without trying to fix what was broken. Drew's intention was to keep his word but he prayed.

Keeping his word didn't include Lynn sleeping with Marshall. If it proved she had done so, Drew didn't know if he could be a man of his word.

Too ashamed to look Drew in the eyes, Lynn looked to the floor. Her voice trembled as she began to confess her infidelity and how it came to be.

"Drew, I love you so much, but I did something really bad. The worst thing about it is I don't remember what or how it happened. Maybe, if I had done things differently, I wouldn't be in this situation, but I don't know, I can't explain it, but I take full responsibility for my actions.

Seeing that Lynn was about to lower the boom on him, Drew interrupted her. "What did you do?" Drew asked.

"I made the biggest mistake, I could ever make," Lynn replied.

"No baby, don't tell me you slept with Marshall?" Drew asked.

Though she wanted to say no, Lynn couldn't lie, she had to be honest and did so by nodding her head yes. Looking up, Lynn saw the hurt in Drew's eyes. Lynn once promised Drew, she would never hurt him if he gave her a chance to love him, but had done so, twice within a month. Lynn was following the path of Gloria, a path Drew wanted nothing to do with.

After learning your partner cheated, the most asked question is always why and in Drew's situation, it was no different. He couldn't understand why. Why had Lynn slept with the man she swore she wanted nothing to do with? Now mine you, this is the same man Lynn stood in front of the world and recanted allegations that Marshall never physically abused, sodomized or held her hostage after it was leaked. Lynn's excuse to him was because she wanted to help him get drafted into NBA, but she failed to mentioned, Marshall stayed an entire week under the same roof with her, until that too was leaked by her sister. This is also the same man Lynn accepted a ring from and promised to marry, in front of everyone and God, at the party she helped give in his honor, but swore it was a publicity stunt to improve Marshall's image to get a better contract. Lastly, this is the same man she slept with only hours before striking him in the face with a pair of her stilettos smashing a glass in his face, causing several lacerations. The question Drew wanted to know was why? Why had Lynn pretended to be in love with him, knowing good and damn well she was still in love with Marshall?

"Why Lynn, why did you sleep with Marshall if you love me so much?" Drew asked.

Lynn couldn't give Drew a straight answer because she didn't know what happened.

She was certain she hadn't invited Marshall into her bed, but she was told differently. What happened after she went to bed that night remains a mystery. The best she could do was tell Drew what she remembered and what was told to her by Ashley and Marshall. There was one thing Lynn remembered vividly, and that was what happened on the beach. Lynn intentionally omitted that part of her story was going to go with her to her grave. By no means was she going to incriminate herself from a mistake she knew was wrong.

"I don't remember much about that night," Lynn stated. "I remembered Marshall and I got into a heated argument earlier that evening because of you. I told him that you and I were together and that I was in love with you. Of course, Marshall wasn't happy with my decision, but it didn't stop him from wanting my help. The original deal the three of us agreed to was for me to give a press conference and lie about Marshall never physically harming me but unbeknownst to me, Marshall and Ashley concocted another scheme for Marshall and me to become engaged on camera to show that he was responsible and deserved the huge contract his agent was trying to secure for him. Then I began to get cold feet about the entire situation and when I told Marshall about it, he lost his temper and threw me to the ground and held me. He kept saying, that he needed my help and how imperative it was for me to do the interview. I was so afraid, I feared for my life. It wasn't until I screamed that something in him snapped and realized what he had done. He became humbled after that and tried to apologizing for what he'd done but it was too late. I ran back to the cottage and told Ashley what happened. But instead of her supporting me, she accused me of trying to sabotaged Marshall's chances to be selected for the NBA.

"Why didn't you just leave? Couldn't you see you were being set up?" Drew said.

"I don't know; Ashley kept bitchin about how I'm never there to help her after she stuck her neck on the line for me. So, to keep the peace, I did what she wanted," Lynn explained. "But Drew, as God is my witness, I never consented to sleep with Marshall."

"Why now Lynn, why couldn't you have told me this when it first happened?" Drew asked.

"Because I didn't want to lose you," Lynn answered.

It was obvious Ashley had sat Lynn up again but it still was no excuse for Lynn to allow herself to get in such a jam. In all reality, Lynn should have known better. Drew considered turning a blind eye to the fact that Lynn was a victim who was set up by her no-good sister and a two-bit hustler, who was only looking out for their interest. Lynn hadn't mentioned it but Drew was sure she may have mixed her prescribed psych medication with alcohol. In Drew's opinion, he saw Lynn as being a willing participant who was in a dangerous game that included staying under the same roof with a predator. Lynn should have known the consequences, yet chose to stay anyway. Whether she consented or not, Lynn placed herself in harm's way by trusting a man who'd raped her before. It wasn't surprising Drew wasn't shocked by what happened. In a way, he expected something sinister had happened by the way Ashley's behavior went well past disrespectful towards Lynn. Drew's first thought was that Ashley was going to spill the beans about their affair, but now realized she was aiming at her sister all the while.

Now knowing the truth, Drew left the room to go outside to sit on the balcony. He wanted to get some fresh air and to be away from Lynn until he could decide what he wanted to do. Sure, he promised Lynn he would try to work things out before saying it was over, but damn, what was she to expect after telling him she slept with her ex-boyfriend. Lynn waited a few minutes before following Drew outside. She sat in a chair positioned closer to the door, giving Drew the space, he needed. Lynn remained stared at Drew as he stared at the night sky. She didn't know what he was thinking but was sure it concerned her.

Lynn never intended to hurt Drew, her only desire was to love him and make him happy but relapsed and fell back into the arms of the man she once loved. Lynn understood what she did was wrong, and that was the reason she chose to confess. It was hard having to see Drew cry and when Lynn reached to wipe away Drew's tears but he pushed her hands away and ordered her to give him the space he needed. Considering what had happened, Drew could have been a total ass after finding out the woman he called his lady had cheated on him but Drew never broke form. Instead of lashing out, he did the opposite.

"Please, I need time to think," Drew said calmly.

Lynn couldn't much blame him for not wanting to be around her. She had failed him miserly, and even though she had failed him, Lynn was determined to regain his trust.

Drew stayed outside for more than an hour before returning to the common area of the hotel room. There, he found Lynn waiting for him. Like him, she was wide awake but unlike Drew, Lynn wanted to talk to work things out between them but Drew wasn't having it.

"I think it may be best if you leave tomorrow," Drew announced calmly.

Drew's announcement should have been shocking, but Lynn expected as much. Drew was acting out on emotions and though Lynn agreed she would leave; she had no intentions of doing so. Her intentions were to stay and fight for the man she loved.

(4:10 am) Gloria watched as Mason lie sleeping. Lying beside him, Gloria used her hand to lightly stroke his smooth-shaven face while trying to make sense of her life. Things hadn't worked out the way she wanted with Drew but thank her lucky stars she at least she had Mason to hold on to. Some would argue, Gloria wasn't being fair to Mason but in her defense, Gloria was making Mason happy by providing him with the love he wanted. Gloria didn't have to question Mason's love for her, he'd shown that he was willing to do whatever it took to make her happy but it wasn't enough. Gloria tried to love Mason the way he needed to be loved, but because of her undying love for Drew, she couldn't give her all. No one could say for certain if Mason knew how Gloria felt about him because he never spoke about it. Perhaps Mason was satisfied with the crumbs of love Gloria was giving him. Lord knows, Gloria hadn't done anything special to show him how much she loved him.

She was spending less and less time with him while spending more time trying to figure out how to get Drew back into her life. But Gloria's behavior never deterred Mason from waiting until she was ready to be with him. Mason should have known what was in Gloria's heart but he was blinded by his love for her. Without disturbing Mason, Gloria got out of bed with her phone and tip-toed down the hallway to the bathroom. She closed and locked the door behind her.

Sitting on the toilet, she called Drew and anxiously waited for him to answer and when his phone went directly to voicemail, Gloria became furious, knowing Drew was probably in bed with that Bitch. "Got dammit;" Gloria said in a low voice tone. "That motherfucker done turned off his phone."

Chapter: 16

Drew returned to his room to find Lynn's bags packed and placed near the door. It was only a matter of time before she was leaving and after seeing her bag, Drew began to have mixed emotions. He wanted to work things out but the thought of her sleeping with Marshall was too much for him to accept. This was supposed to have been their coming out party but instead, he was embarrassed.

"What time is your flight?" Drew asked.

"8:15 tonight," Lynn responded.

Lynn was hoping Drew would invite her to his track meet and once he didn't, she knew things were dire between them. Drew was pressed for time and needed to leave immediately if he was going to return in time for one of his qualifying rounds of the 200-meter race. Lynn's reckless behavior left Drew with a lot on his mind but if he was going to stand tall doing the meet, he needed to incorporate his pain into his races. Hopefully, it wouldn't come to that but if by chance it did, Drew needed to be prepared. This was the most important meet of his life. It was his chance not only to prove to the world who he was but to prove to himself that he deserved to be in the same category as some of track and field best runners of today.

"I have to go but I wanted to see you before I left," Drew said, before turning to leave.

"Drew wait," Lynn asked.

Drew stopped and turned to face Lynn before reaching the door. Lynn ran to Drew to embrace him. She placed her head on his chest before wrapping her arms around Drew's neck to pull him down to her level. From there Lynn kissed Drew on his cheek and whispered in his ear. "Good luck," Lynn said before releasing Drew to leave.

"Thank you," Drew replied. Saying nothing more, he left the room; closing the door behind him. His heart tried forgiving Lynn but his pride wouldn't allow him. He nearly asked Lynn to stay but again, his pride was too much to swallow. Drew wanted more than anything to turn around and back to the room. He wanted to ask Lynn to stay, but instead, he continued walking back to the track.

Drew's quick exit should have been a sign that it was over between them but Lynn didn't see things that way. Drew still had the spark in his eye; she not only saw it, she felt it in his embrace. Lynn knew the risk she was taking by confessing her indiscretion but she couldn't live with herself knowing what she had done. Yes, she was guilty by her own admission, but in doing so, she was given the harshest sentence. Lynn may have lost the man she truly loved but she wasn't giving up so easily, not when she believed there was still a chance, they could work things out. Lynn had seven hours before her plane was scheduled to leave and it was more than enough time to win back her man. Changing into her WFU shorts and t-shirt, Lynn left the hotel room en route to the stadium. She wanted to show support for her man, and nothing was going to stop her.

Lynn arrived at the stadium in time to see Drew qualify for tomorrow's finals. She was excited after witnessing Drew's second-place finish in the one-hundred-meter race. Drew was finally getting the media attention he deserved and his hard work and dedication to the sport was coming to light. The semi-final race for the two-hundred-meter run followed only minutes after the one-hundred and Lynn worried Drew wouldn't have enough time to re-energize himself. Nervous, Lynn stood to cheer with the rest of the stadium. At the sound of the gun, Drew sprinted from the blocks, getting a good start. As the runners made the turn into the home stretch Drew was in fourth place. Drew had to finish second to qualify in tomorrow's finals and at the final fifty meters, he made his move, passing two runners to finish the race in second place.

He was instantly predicted as one of the runners who could win it all in tomorrow's finals. Drew's determination had put him one step closer to achieving his dream of becoming a member of the US World, Track and Field Team and he had God to thank for it.

As the day ended, Drew was reminded of what he was about to be faced with in his hotel room. He remained undecided upon what to do about Lynn but felt now wasn't the time to make a decision. His love for Lynn was strong but loving her wasn't enough to forgive her for what she'd done. Before leaving the stadium, Drew heard his name called from the crowd; he looked into the stands and saw Lynn waving at him. Shielding a possible confrontation, Drew waved back before quietly leaving the stadium by way of the tunnel. It wasn't that he was avoiding Lynn; he needed time to think.

Making his way across town on foot, Drew had a lot to consider now that his relationship with Lynn was in jeopardy. He honestly was caught between a rock and a hard place and he didn't know which way to turn. His relationship was at a crossroads and for the first time, he was unsure of which direction to travel. Why had Lynn deliberately hidden her affair? Was it because she didn't want to lose him or because her conscious had gotten the best of her? Drew couldn't say for certain but suspected Lynn was more fascinated with the idea of having one last hurrah with Marshall before going forward with their relationship. If only she had come clean early, he may have found it in his heart to forgive her but she chose not to say anything until the weight became too much for her to bear. Drew walked for what seemed like hours before returning to his hotel room. He suspected Lynn had left for the airport by now, and he wouldn't have to face her until he returned to campus but entering the room, Drew found Lynn's bags still in the middle of the floor.

"Dammit," Drew said to himself. He wasn't happy with the idea of having to face Lynn and was silently upset at her decision not to leave as ordered. Drew's first priority was to shower and rub down his sore leg muscles. He didn't want to talk, he only wanted to go to bed. Tomorrow was the day he'd dreamed of since falling in love with track and field and he needed to be well prepared. Being prepared meant having to eat, though he wasn't hungry. There was some leftover food from the night before in the refrigeration and Drew thought he would eat what was left of it, before crawling into bed. Undressing, Drew got into the shower. He didn't know where Lynn was but suspected she was taking care of her travel arraignments. Tonight, wasn't the night she needed to leave. In a way, Drew wanted her to stay until he was finish and they could leave together. Drew was the first to admit he was an ass about what happened. If Lynn hadn't admitted what happened, he would have never known. He had to admire Lynn for being woman enough to admit her guilt. He on the other hand, was a pussy that didn't have the balls to tell Lynn what he'd done. Though wrong, Lynn had courage. Perhaps it was time for him to stand up for what he'd done but Drew wasn't going to do that; he was hoping to bury what he did forever. He also knew, Ashley wasn't going to say a word because she wouldn't want her parents to know how much of a slut she really was.

Lynn arrived back to the room minutes after Drew began to shower.

She'd brought home dinner with hopes of having their final meal together before leaving for the airport. Giving up on the man she was in love with was by far the hardest thing she had to do but Drew wanted it that way. To a certain extent, it was best she left because by staying, she could interfere with Drew's concentration. Drew had worked his ass off to be in this position and no matter how much she wanted to be with him, she wasn't going to jeopardize his chances of winning a spot on the U. S. Team.

After showering, Drew left the bathroom and was instantly overcome by the smell of Chinese food coming from the kitchen. The scent from it had Drew's stomach growling like a hungry lion. Drew made his way to the kitchen area and found Lynn sitting at the table waiting for him.

"Hey Sweetie, how are you?" Drew asked before kissing her on the cheek. He felt ashamed for avoiding Lynn at the stadium. To say he was wrong for what he did was an understatement and Drew realized the time had come for him to talk things out with Lynn.

"I'm good," Lynn replied. She too didn't have anything to say but it didn't have anything to do with Drew dodging her. Lynn had come to grips with their breakup and was ready to move on.

"Thank you for bringing dinner," Drew said.

"I wanted you to have energy for tomorrow. Lynn replied

"Thank you," Drew said.

It was only minutes ago that he contemplated eating the leftover pizza from last night and now he was about to eat fresh food for an unlikely source. Once again, Lynn had come through by thinking of him, without thinking of herself.

"You ran good races today," Lynn said.

"Thank you, and thank you for coming," Drew answered.

Seeing how Lynn had undertaken his standoffish ways by disregarding her feelings, Drew was having a change of heart. He didn't want Lynn to leave but his faint-hearted ways continued to play tricks on his mind.

The bottom line was Drew's heart held too much love for Lynn to allow her to leave. Drew felt if he stood by and allow Lynn to leave, any chance of loving her again would be over forever.

Asking the time her plane was scheduled to depart, Lynn was left with the thought that Drew still wanted her to leave. Lynn's first thought was to get up from the table and leave immediately but she swallowed her pride and stayed. She was willing to go without fighting for Drew, but something inside was trying to convince her not to. Lynn was going to return to campus without Drew, but you could bet your last dollar she wasn't going to give up on him without a fight. Drew meant too much to her to walk away without giving it the old girl scout try. Lynn answered Drew's question by saying her plane was schedule to leave at 2030 hours. Not knowing what to talk about, Lynn spoke very little after answering Drew's question. The lump in her throat held her at bay and she was seconds away from breaking down but somehow, she managed to hold form. Drew reached for Lynn's hand and led with blessing the food. When doing so, Drew squeezed Lynn's hands, as if he wanted to assure her things between them were going to be ok. After the blessing of the food Drew substantiated Lynn's suspicions by announcing what he was feeling inside of his heart.

"Listen, it's getting late and the both of us are tired. Why don't you cancel your flight for tonight," Drew asked. He honestly, didn't want Lynn to leave and she didn't want to leave. It was a win/win situation all the way around. For Lynn, she couldn't have been happier but she couldn't help but wonder was this only was for tonight.

"Do you want me to leave tomorrow instead?" Lynn asked.

"No, I want you to stay with me," Drew replied.

 Hot damn, Lynn had gotten the reprieve she'd been hoping for and she couldn't have been happier. Drew on the other hand was taking a chance at giving their relationship another chance but is love for Lynn was too much not to give them another chance. Hopefully this time, she would be honest and faithful to him and their relationship. Though Drew was optimistic he could forgive Lynn for what she did, he couldn't stop his pride was playing "Billy Badass" with him. Still, Drew's unanticipated decision to give their relationship another chance sent Lynn on a high.

It was an incredible decision, one which Lynn hadn't expected. Realistically, she understood what she did was unforgivable but she not only promised Drew she would forever be faithful, she promised to never again place their future in jeopardy. After swallowing his pride, Drew could now embrace Lynn with feelings.

He'd put his worries to rest and though they had a long road to travel, there was hope over the horizon. Come tomorrow, Lynn was going to be in attendance to cheer for her man as he attempts to achieve his dream of securing a spot on the US World Track and Field Team in both the 100-and-200-meter races. Lynn understood the magnitude of what tomorrow meant to Drew, as well as their future, and she had her lucky stars to thank for the opportunity Drew presented.

Taking Lynn by the hand, Drew led her outside on the balcony. There, they sit and talked about their future together. Drew was graduating in two weeks and he wanted to cement his plans on what he wanted for their future. Although he and Lynn had shared the same dreams, they'd never discussed their living arrangements once they were married. They both were in line to head their family's business but they were living in two different states while running two different companies. One of them would have to forgo their dream to head their family's company but who was going to make the sacrifice. Self-consciously, Lynn believed Drew should make the sacrifice to abdicate his appointed position because her family's business was more profitable. Drew on the other hand, believed as a man, it was his responsibility to be the head his household and take care for his family. Needless to say, a decision wasn't made but the debate did end admirably with a promise to revisit the conversation at a later date.

Assuming the two of them were going to be sleeping in the same bed, Lynn left the balcony to get ready for bed. Drew remained outside thinking about his upcoming graduation, as well as his future with Hillcrest Farms. Though he was the heir to his family's company, he wasn't sure if he wanted to run it. Truth be told, Karyme was doing a masterful job for Hillcrest

Farms and could easily run the company. As an interim president, she'd signally taken the company to new heights while studying for her degree at UVA. It wouldn't be fair to boot her out after she'd gotten the company several contracts with large retailers across the nation. It was a decision Drew needed to make and he had only weeks before having to do so. After setting on the balcony for more than an hour,

Drew re-entered the suite and found Lynn sitting in an Indian style, looking at wedding gowns on her iPad. Their talk had sparked Lynn to go forward with wanting to begin planning for their wedding. Though they hadn't set a date or given serious thought to a future together, teasing each other with the idea was all Lynn needed to reinstitute their initial plans.

"So, is it your intention to marry me?" Drew asked.

"Yes, yes, and then yes," Lynn answered jokingly.

Lynn was being funny because she was happy. Drew had given her reason to smile again and thanks to his decision to give them another chance at love, she could look toward spending the rest of her life with him.

Undressing, Drew joined Lynn in bed. Lynn was overjoyed to be sleeping beside Drew and immediately snuggled beside him. It felt great to be in Drew's arms and within minutes, they both drifted off to sleep. It wasn't long after Drew and Lynn were sleeping peacefully that Drew's phone began to vibrate. Awakened by the vibration Drew quickly turned off the sound. He glanced over at it and saw it was 12 am. Without having to look at the number, he knew it was Gloria calling him. Who else would be so inconsiderate to call so early in the morning? Drew also knew it was 3 am eastern standard time, and the time Gloria got up for work. Quietly getting out of bed, Drew went outside on the balcony. It took less than thirty seconds for Gloria to call a second time and after Drew answered, Gloria didn't dilly-dally around as to why she was calling. Her topic of choice was about them getting back together. Gloria demanded to know why Drew refused to give her another chance after promising to change her wicked ways. She admitted to having made a crucial mistake but promised she was sure of what she wanted and that she be allowed to rectify mistakes. Telling Gloria how and what he felt was like beating a dead horse. They'd just talked about this a couple of days earlier and his feelings hadn't changed, he was done and wanted no part of her anymore. It was hard to understand why it hadn't resonated with Gloria that it was over between them. But then again, throughout their relationship, this was the route Gloria took when she wanted to come back into his life after having an affair with someone. She would continue to pursue him until he gave in to her but not this time. For once and for all, it was over between them. As means of respect, Drew listened to what Gloria had to say before filtering her.

After spending the evening with Lynn and deciding to restart their relationship, Drew found the courage to tell Gloria what he hoped was for the last time.

"Gloria, I can't say this any clearer, I don't want to be with you anymore. I'm in love with Lynn, we're together now and there's nothing that's going to change that," Drew was as blatant as he knew how. He didn't care if what he said hurt Gloria's feelings; he was tired and frustrated by her antics and frankly, wouldn't have given a damn if she never spoke to him again.

"What did you say?" Gloria reacted shockingly to what Drew said. She couldn't believe Drew was talking to her in that tone of voice. It was "The Rich Bitch" who was talking in his ear. She was probably feeling his head up with all sorts of promises that she won't keep. It had only been two weeks ago that she and Drew had made the greatest love they'd ever made. He told her how much he wanted to be with her as well as how much he loved her. Now, all of a sudden, he'd made an about-face. Gloria found it difficult to accept Drew's answer and demanded an explanation. She wanted to know if Lynn played a role in his decision.

"Where's all of this coming from?" Gloria asked. "I bet your little rich girlfriend had something to do with you not wanting to get back with me."

"No, you were what caused our break up, Lynn had nothing to do with it. It was you who was sleeping with Tom, Dick, and Harry, and like the dumb ass I was, I took you back each time. But things are different now, I've found someone that will love only me." Drew had spread the mayo a little too thick and though he hated to have brought up Gloria's slutty past, he felt he had to do so to get through to her.

"Drew, I love you, and I know you love me. Listen, we can work this thing out, we've worked things out far more complicated than this." Gloria explained. Gloria could feel her grip on Drew loosening, she was becoming desperate and was looking for anything to hold on to Drew.

"Gloria, I don't know what I can say to make this any easier. Yes, you've played a vital role in me becoming a man. You were my first love and because I loved you so much, I turned a blind eye to your multiple affairs, but I can't do it anymore. I want a normal life and you can't give that to me," Drew said.

"I can, I know what I want, I want to be your wife and you, my husband. Please Drew, just give me one last chance," Gloria pleaded.

Pleading for a final chance was something Gloria was used to doing; she would shade a few tears and Drew would give in but this time things were different. Drew was putting up a fight by refusing to break, leading Gloria to realize she had played her games one too many times and because of it, she'd lost the man she loved. The phone went silent once Gloria realized it was over between them and Drew awaited to hear the onslaught of insults Gloria was known for but it never happened. Instead, Drew heard Gloria sobbed before regaining her composure. It was an understatement to say she was heartbroken but Gloria tried to maintain what pride she had left. Now wasn't the time for her to fight for what she wanted; Drew was nearly three-thousand-miles away with Lynn sleeping beside him. Gloria needed to have patience and wait until Drew return home. Only then she could be on even ground to fight and win for what she believed to be hers.

Chapter: 17

Drew's slow reaction to the sound of the starter pistol had him struggling to catch up with the leaders. At forty meters, Drew had moved up to third but was striding to catch up. With sixty meters left in the race, Drew didn't panic, he maintained his form and relied on his top-end speed to carry him to victory. But half-way through the race, Drew realized this wasn't the competition he was use to running down his competition, stealing the victory in a blaze of glory. He was behind and to win a spot on the team, he had to at least place in the top three. Drew needed to be on his A-game and he was far from being on it. Though he needed to finish in the top three to win a spot of the team, Drew didn't want to just finish in the top three, he wanted to win. By seventy meters Drew found himself in the mix of the leaders and now that his top end speed had kicked in, Drew was looking to run down his competitors but nobody had informed Travis Britt that he was supposed to bow down to Drew. Travis Britt, who was the fastest sprinter in the nation for the year, continued to maintain a half step lead over Drew as they approached the finish line. Drew tried his damndest not to look across at Travis, knowing if he had he would break stride and lose the race. Though tempted, Drew continued to focus on the finish line while maintaining his stride. Before reaching the finish line, a funny thing happened, Travis Britt made the vital mistake of seeing where Drew was positioned and lost his concentration, allowing Drew to out lean him across the finish line. It couldn't have been scripted any better but by no means was Drew satisfied with his victory. He had won by the skin of his teeth but it wasn't the race he was capable of running. Still, there was a bright side to his victory, he had secured a place on the US World Track and Field Team, achieving the first of two goals. In celebration, Drew climbed over the stadium wall to meet Lynn at the base of the stands and kissed her. It was his way of expressing the love he had for her. Drew didn't show out by doing some silly dance after being declaring the winner, or rip his shirt from his body while screaming to the top of his voice. He simply waved to the crowd and blew a few kisses before kissing his lady.

Drew returned to the track a little more than an hour later to run his final event, the 200-meter race. This time he left no doubt as to who was the fastest runner on the track. From the sound of the gun, Drew took an early lead and dominated the race from beginning to the end. In doing so, he set a new American record by posting the best time of the year.

Drew had solidified his presence as the man to beat, in the upcoming World's Championships, he'd kickstarted discussions as to who was the fastest man in the world.

Though showing his capabilities, Drew's mission wasn't completed. The world championships were being held in three weeks in Madrid, Spain, and if everything went accordingly, Drew was going into next year's Olympics as the man to beat.

The day concluded just as Drew had imagined. He'd made the US Track and Field Team and he couldn't have been happier. Rejuvenated, he and Lynn left the stadium hand and hand, unlike yesterday when they left separately. They could have gotten a shuttle ride to their hotel room but Drew wanted to walk. He wanted to share his special moment with his lady while sporting the town. It had only been a few hours ago, when Drew suggested Lynn catch the next plane back to WFU's campus but Thank God, they were able to work things out. It was Lynn's honesty and accountability that was monumental to Drew's decision to want to work things out. Lynn fought for what she believed in while disregarding the show-caused which nearly led to their breakup. Lynn made no excuses for what she did and was willing to accept the consequences that came with it. That in itself was enough to convince Drew of the type of woman she was. Sure, Lynn withheld information that could have made Drew's decision tougher to take her back but she at least was forthcoming with what was most important.

Anticipating a successful day, Drew made reservations at The Marché Restaurant, which was less than two blocks from their hotel. The Marche was an Italian Restaurant known for its good food and romantic atmosphere but before going to the dinner, Drew wanted to enjoy some of the sights before catching the plane the following morning.

Drew wanted the evening to be perfect because he wanted to further discuss his future with Lynn to iron out the small details about where they were going to reside once they were married.

Returning to their room, Drew was first to undress. He quickly got into the shower and was unexpectedly joined by Lynn. It was the first time he had ever seen Lynn completely nude and the sight of seeing her excited him. By joining him, Lynn was hoping to speed up the process for them to have time to window shop before arriving at the restaurant for dinner but joining Drew only derailed their plans.

89

There was unfinished business that needed to be completed and Lynn was more than willing to bypass window shopping before dinner. Their passionate kissing led to Drew lifting Lynn into his arms and placing her against the shower wall.

Using the wall as leverage, Drew patiently inserted his rock- hard penis inside of Lynn. Slowly and forbearingly, Drew inched his way through Lynn's tight and compressed vaginal walls, as the water from the shower beaded against their bodies. It was a feeling Lynn never experienced before and she wasn't sure if she was capable of accepting Drew's manhood. Relaxing, Lynn slowly managed to accept some of Drew's oversized manhood. Her screams of pleasure could be heard throughout the hallway of the hotel but it didn't stop her from wanting more. It was the way Drew made love to her that incited her screams. He was doing things to her that she had only read about, and now she was living it. This was the first time she'd ever made love to Drew but it was easy to predict she was going to become addicted to him.

"Oh, my God." Lynn kept repeating as Drew slowly made love to her. Lynn's voice became weaker as Drew continued making love to Lynn, causing her to slur her words. "Oh my God," Lynn uttered, releasing a weak scream. Her body went limp, causing Drew to fight to hold her in place. With his penis fitted firmly inside of her, Drew felt Lynn's hands lose grip from around his neck. Lynn's orgasm nearly caused him to drop her but Drew managed to hold her in place. It was the way Drew's penis massaged Lynn's G-spot that sent her into a frenzy. This was her first vaginal orgasm, and the sensation from it caused her to call out Drew's name. Overwhelmed by the feeling, Lynn began crying. She couldn't believe how lucky she was to be making love to the man she was deeply in love with. Drew himself felt an emotional rush, as he neared his orgasm. Like Lynn, he found it hard to believe they were making love after calling it quits just a day earlier.

Feeling his orgasm on the horizon, Drew fought to hold back the pressure that was building inside of him. They weren't using protection and he had to be careful not to ejaculate inside of Lynn. Unable to hold back, Drew quickly withdrew his penis from Lynn, allowing his semen to flow freely down the drain of the shower. Though intercourse had temporarily ended, their passion didn't stop there. They continued kissing, igniting Drew to become erect once more. Again, they began making love, and again, Lynn's passionate screams were heard outside the walls of their bathroom.

Once their shower was completed, an enfeebled Drew exited the tub and began drying himself. Lynn, on the other hand, didn't have the strength to get out of the tub and needed to be assisted out.

The couple exited the bathroom and returned to the bedroom to prepare for their evening out together. Stumbling, Lynn fell across the bed out of exhaustion.

"You ok," Drew asked.

"Never better," Lynn replied. She couldn't believe being made love to could feel so good. Never had she been made love to the way Drew made love to her. It was mindboggling, and if she had her way, she would elect to stay home and make love for the remainder of the night but their plans were to have dinner and celebrate Drew's victories today. Drew smiled while drying Lynn with his towel. He followed by rubbing Lynn's back with lotion. For months he'd dreamed what it would be like to make love to Lynn, and now that he had, it was more beautiful than he had ever imagined.

It was nearly six o'clock, and Lynn wasn't completely dressed for dinner. Her tardiness had Drew pacing anxiously in the common area of their hotel room.

Drew was hoping for a quiet dinner at a private table he'd reserved, but by missing their appointment, Drew had to cancel their reservation and eat locally with the rest of the patrons. It didn't matter that he had to dine with the public, in public, Drew was able to show how beautiful Lynn was.

"Sweetie, you need to put a move on it, our uber is waiting outside for us." Drew relayed.

"How do I look?" Lynn asked as she emerged from the bathroom. Drew was astonished by her beauty. He'd seen her many times before, but tonight was special. Standing before him was by far the most beautiful woman he'd ever seen. Lynn was dressed in a short silk red chiffon dress and she was breathtakingly beautiful. She was Drew's lady in red and he couldn't wait for the world to see them together. It was inconceivable for Drew to think, he could have ever fallen in love with anyone other than Gloria, but that was before Lynn had come into his life. Holding Lynn's hand, Drew led her into the elevator. Inside, he found it difficult to keep his eyes off of her and once their eyes met, he couldn't resist kissing.

"I love you, Ashlynn Renee' Boldmont," Drew whispered.

"Not as much as I love you," Lynn replied.

Exiting the elevator, the couple left the hotel lobby and got into the backseat of their Uber driver. Lynn was overwhelmed by the attention she was receiving and leaned over to kiss Drew once more, before leaning back into the seat.

"What a difference a day makes." Lynn thought to herself as she reminisced about what had occurred two nights ago. By choosing to own up to what happened, she not only gained Drew's respect, she was given another chance at love. Sure, it was going to take a while to regain Drew's trust fully but Lynn understood to win Drew's trust, she would need to dedicate herself to him.

During dinner, Drew began discussing their future plans. He'd confided to Lynn that he was contemplating rescinding his position at Hillcrest Farms and allowing Karyme to become full-time president. Lynn's dreams were about to come true; Drew was actually considering leaving his family's business to become part of Boldmont Enterprises. Before hearing more of Drew's plans, Lynn took a moment to congratulate him for his accomplishments and presented him with a gift. It was her way of congratulating him for making the US Team. In all sincerity, Drew hadn't expected a gift but was appreciative that Lynn thought enough of him to buy him something special. In all of his years of being with Gloria, he'd never received a gift for anything other than Christmas and that was only because she was expecting one in return. But with Lynn, everything was different, she would rather give than receive, and tonight was a prime example. Opening his gift, Drew was stunned by the sight of seeing the gold and black, Movado wristwatch. He hadn't expected such an elaborate gift and was astonished at the sight of it.

"You like it?" Lynn asked.

"I love it. Thank you." Drew responded, following with a kiss of appreciation.

"I wanted to buy you a Rolex but I couldn't afford it without maxing out my credit card," Lynn added.

It wouldn't have mattered if Lynn would have given him a Timex, Drew would have appreciated it nonetheless. It was the thought that counted and Lynn put a lot of thought into her gift to him.

Amazed by how lavished the gift was, Drew was speechless. He wasn't by no means a materialistic person but was taken by the amount of thought Lynn had put into it. The couple spent the remainder of dinner discussing their future together.

They were so into each other; they paid no attention to no one else. Drew and Lynn were enjoying what some would call called the perfect dinner. Life as Lynn once knew it could be compared to a morning mist being burned off by the heat of the morning sun. Lynn felt strongly that she had nothing to worry about, now that Drew was her man again.

If everything went accordingly to plan, they were going to become man and wife, whether her parents wanted it or not. Lynn had never been so deeply in love as she was with Drew, and no matter what her mother may have told her, Lynn knew, without a shadow of a doubt, she was ready to take the next step in her relationship with Drew. After dinner, Drew and Lynn waited outside the restaurant for their Uber driver to arrive. After waiting for more than twenty minutes, they decided to walk the two blocks back to their hotel room. It was a beautiful night and Drew wanted to strut and show off his lady dressed in red and Lynn didn't disappoint. The attention she was receiving was more than enough to convince Drew that he was the luckiest man alive. Not only had he found the woman of his dreams, he had also found a woman that loved him for him.

Tonight, couldn't have gone any better until Drew and Lynn came upon three men who they initially thought were homeless but soon learned they weren't. The men in question were athletes who were drinking after participating in today's track meet. Drew didn't recognize either of them but took them at their word. Frankly, Drew didn't give a shit who they were, his mindset was getting his lady back to their hotel room to continue their celebration but sadly, Drew's plan was temporarily derailed after the men felt disrespected.

"Good race today, Harrison," the short slender men man said. "Faith was on your side today." Drew didn't recognize him but assumed he ran the one-hundred-meter race since he had won the two-hundred by nearly a half second. Feeling uncomfortable, Drew only talked for a few seconds before refocusing his attention on getting Lynn to safety. It wasn't that he didn't want to be associated with the men, he only wanted a safe environment for Lynn after noticing they were being surrounded.

"Hey guys, it's been nice but my lady and I have an early flight tomorrow morning and we have to be leaving," Drew explained.

"Come on, let's go to the bar and have a few drinks," the first man asked.

"I would love to, but we have to be going," Drew said again.

"Come on champ, where's your sense of adventure?" the second man asked.

"Sorry fellows, we gotta go," Drew said.

"You too good to hang out with us? The third man asked. "Or your bitch won't let you?"

"Excuse me, what did you say?" Drew asked.

At that moment, Lynn grabbed hold of Drew's arm and began leading him up the street. She saw the fire in Drew's eyes and knew he wasn't going to take what the men said lightly. Seeing that Lynn and Drew were walking away the men began to follow them.

"You know one thing, you're one conceited motherfucker, you know that," the short sender man said.

"Dude, I don't know you guys, so why you trying me?" Drew asked.

"Because we don't like stuck up motherfuckers," the second of the three men replied.

"You don't know me," Drew responded.

The third and the largest man didn't say anything but tried intimidating Drew by using his fist to punch the inside of his hand. Not wanting to provoke the men any further, Drew apologized for any misunderstanding. He tried explaining his reason for wanting to go back to his hotel room but the men weren't hearing what he had to say. Seeing that he was outnumbered, Drew preceded to walk away but realized; his troubles had just begun.

Holding Lynn's hand, Drew walked at a slow and cautious pace but the crew continued to follow them.

Drew and Lynn got as close as a half block to their hotel before the second of the three men made a brazen move by grabbing hold of Drew's blazer

"Hey, motherfucker, I ain't finished with you yet," the second drunken man said while stopping Drew's forward progress.

"Get your hands off of me," Drew warned, snatching his arm away.

"What! What you wanna do? You gonna kick all three of our asses?" The first slender man asked.

"Naw, he ain't gone do that, because he too much of a pussy," the second man said, laughing out loud.

"Come on baby, let's go," Lynn instructed, pulling Drew by his arm. "Can't you see what they're trying to lure you into a fight."

Lynn was right, the gang were trying to incite Drew into fighting them. Why? No one could say for certain but Lynn believed it was because Drew turned them down to go drinking.

Hearing the possibility of an altercation about to take place, bystanders began to gather. It was the attention the men were seeking and they took full advantage of it by continuing to harass Drew. In the beginning, their insults were directed at Drew and when that didn't work, they turned their attention on Lynn.

"Yo, Harrison," the second man called out. "I always figured you for a pussy ass nigger, now I know you are, because you got your little half-white bitch, telling you what to do,"

"I bet she fucks him with a dildo too," the first man shouted out while laughing out loud.

They had the crowd behind them and because of it, they were ramping up Drew's temper. Needing to avoid a confrontation, Drew kept his feelings to himself; Lord knows he wanted to share a few choice words with the men but for Lynn's sake, he chose to keep quiet. What started as an awesome evening out on the town was turning into a disastrous night. Drew was doing everything in his power to protect Lynn while having to maintain his sanity, but the three drunk assholes were making things difficult.

But no matter how much Drew wanted to man up and kick some serious ass, he had to concentrate on getting Lynn out of harm's way. Against his better judgment, Drew chose to keep walking while overlooking the insults directed at him and Lynn. Lynn could see Drew's frustration building and tried her best to keep him calm but things were becoming unbearable.

"Can't you see what they're trying to do?" Lynn said. "They're a bunch of drunks who are trying to bait you into a fight, don't fall for it."

Lynn was right, Drew had worked too hard to piss his life away because three drunks chose them to harass. All it would take was for Drew to lose his cool, and his life could be ruined. Picking up his pace, Drew could see the top of their hotel and knew within minutes, their ordeal would be over, but little did he know, they weren't going to make it to their hotel unscathed. The shortest of the men took the gang's harassment to another level and did so by reaching under Lynn's dress and groping her buttocks. Feeling little Napoleon Bonaparte's hand cupping the cheek of her buttock was an assault that caused the commotion. Turning to face her accuser, Lynn took a swing at him but missed.

"Augh," Lynn shockingly screamed." You, short bastard." Lynn quickly responded by taking another anticipated swing at her attacker and missed a second time.

"Got damn, that little bitch got a soft ass," The short man said as he stepped back between his friends.

Realizing Lynn had been assaulted, Drew wasted no time defending her honor. Using his hand to remove Lynn from the line of fire, Drew prepared for battle. It was time to take matters into his own hands, vigilante style. For Drew, it was about honor and respect. Lynn had been disrespected and as her man, it was his responsibility to honor the promise he made to her as well as himself to protect her to the best of his ability, and if it meant having to fight three cock-strong motherfuckers, then so be it. With Lynn unassailable from further harm, Drew made his move. He unexpectedly made quick work of the little Napoleon. Pow, biff, bam were the sounds of Drew's fists, landing a stiff left, right, left to the jaw of little Napoleon, turning his lights out. Next, Drew turned his attention to the second man, who had already squared off and was waiting for his turn. The second man attempted to take a swing at Drew, but Drew's reaction was faster.

96

Pop, pop, bam was the sound of Drew's fists against his jaw that caught Drew's two lefts, and a right. Just as he'd done to little Napoleon, Drew had put his friend's lights out, knocking him directly across from his buddy. Whether it was out of fear or having the skills to take on all three men, Drew had made quick work of the first two.

If the onlookers hadn't seen it for themselves, they would have thought Mike Tyson himself was responsible for the first two knockouts, but Drew wasn't finished, two assholes were down, but he had one to go. Thank goodness he'd saved perhaps the best for last because this dude he was about to face was a different animal. Asshole number three stood every bit 6 feet 8 inches tall and weighed at least 350 pounds. His body was chiseled with muscles upon muscles, and from the look at him, he was as solid as granite, but as massive as he was, Drew didn't fear him. Hell no, not after making quick work of the first two, if Drew has anything to say about it, he would predict the John Henry lookalike was going night, night, just like his buddies had. Yup, Drew's confidence was on a high, so much so, he made the mistake of allowing the massive giant the chance to square up on him.

"Come on John Henry, let me see what you got?" Drew said with confidence. Perhaps Drew was feeling a bit too much confidence because he gave the man the chance to make the first move, and John Henry wasted no time by throwing the first of two haymakers. Drew ducked his first wild punch, and countered with a body blow. John Henry took a step back to catch his breath and came back with another. On the second haymaker, Drew was like Floyd Mayweather Jr. Not only was he accurate with his counter punches, he landed with power. Pow, biff, bam Drew landed directly to the chin of the much taller man. Though Drew hadn't expected Big John to be on the ground beside his two besties, he was surprised Big John hadn't wavered from any of the damage he inflicted upon him. Seeing that Big John was ready to make another move on him, Drew quickly went in with another combination, biff, bop, pow to the chin again, and again, Big John remained standing. Seeing this, Drew began to get worried. Big Bad John may have been the steel driving man because he had a jaw of granite and the wind from his swings could knock a bird out the sky. What was so frightening about Big John was the fact that he never had to shake the cob webs out of his head. The big motherfucker only looked at Drew and smiled.

"You hit like a bitch," Big John said to Drew as he laughed out loud.

Seeing what was about to happen the crowd waited anxiously for Drew's next move. In all likelihood, Drew should have taken the cowardly way out, and ran like a motherfucker, but he did the exact oppositive. Drew's dumb ass opted to stay and face the music, and why not? His lady was there routing for him, along with onlookers, who was impressed with him for standing up to the three bullies.

 They wanted Drew to kick ass and take names but Drew was finding it hard to kick Big John's ass. Drew had given Big John his all and it hadn't fazed the him. Drew watched in horror as the big man rushed toward him. Drew had no idea of what to do and it was at that moment, he realized he was in deep shit. Big John rushed and grabbed hold of Drew by his neck. Drew tried his damndest to break Big John's grip but couldn't. Breaking Big John's grip from around his neck could be best described as cutting down a Redwood tree by using a hand saw. Big John hands were at least 10 inches in length, expending nearly a foot, and with his hand tightly gripped around Drew's neck; Big John lifted Drew nearly nine feet in the air with one hand, and choked slammed him on the hood of an unoccupied car. The force from the impact was so great, it not only knocked the air out of Drew's lungs and numbed his entire body. Drew found himself in a battle of the fittest and he was literally getting crushed to death.

Though Drew temporally slipped free from Big John's grip, he was in no condition to escape and as his body slowly slid from the hood of the car, Big John managed to grab and lift him high in the air by the neck a second time for another choke slam. "Boom," was the sound of Drew's body being slammed on a second car that was parked behind the first damaged car. Drew tried unsuccessfully to break free but Big John's grip was too strong. Drew was slowly losing his battle of consciousness as Big John was choking him out. Seeing Drew struggling with the gigantic monster of a man, Lynn knew she had to do something if she was going to help Drew. Standing near a trash can, Lynn saw an empty .40 oz Steel Reserve glass bottle lying on top of the trash. Seizing it, Lynn rushed over to where Drew was being choked out and swung as hard as she could, striking her target directly across the rear of his head. The blow was so severe, it shattered upon impact, causing Big John to hit the ground with a thud. It's fair to say, Big John never knew what hit him. The blow not only rendered him unconscious, it cut caused several lacerations. Lynn wasn't left unscathed either, she received cuts to her fingers and hand.

The strike was so loud, it caused the crowd to immediately dispersed in every direction, after believing a gun had discharged. Lynn had done her job; she'd slayed goliath and rescued Drew from further injury. After realizing what she'd done, Lynn knew they had only seconds to leave the scene before the police arrived. Her risk of going to jail had increased after committing assault and battery. Being conscious minded, Lynn used every bit of strength she had to help Drew stand, while trying to get away from the scene before the police arrived.

She ran toward their hotel while holding on to Drew. Drew was doing is best to keep up but couldn't catch his breath and though Lynn wanted to stop to allow him time to gather himself, she couldn't.

Chapter: 18

Returning to their room the couple sit on their couch and tried to understand what happened and why? Drew tried everything in his power to avoid a confrontation but failed. He was placed in a position where he had no choice but to fight to protect his and Lynn's safety.

"You handled yourself well out there tonight baby," Lynn said; hoping it was enough to put Drew's mind at ease. Drew wasn't one for confrontation and hated the idea of having to fight but if placed in the same predicament, he wouldn't hesitate to do it over.

"Thank you for having my back out there, that dude was a monster," Drew said while laughing out loud. He was embarrassed for having to have his girlfriend come to his rescue but Drew was relieved that she had. He had no idea who the men were but the strength of the last guy was unbelievable. Drew had Lynn to thank, if it wasn't for her quick thinking, he would have gotten his ass handed to him. Unfortunately, by helping him, Lynn suffered lacerations to her hand and fingers. Thank God, it wasn't bad enough to need stitches. Drew apologized for his role in what happened but knew, the altercation couldn't be avoided. Drew cleaned Lynn's fingers and hand with an antiseptic cream before placing a band aide on it. Thank God, for her quick thinking. She was a beast out there and the way she carried him back to the hotel was bad ass.

"Do it hurt?" Drew asked.

"Just a little," Lynn responded.

"Will kissing it make it feel better?" Drew asked.

"Most diffidently, kissing it will make me feel good all over," Lynn replied, before busting into laughter.

"Get your mind out of the gutter," Drew chuckled.

As much as Drew wanted to get Lynn into bed to make mad passionate love to her, he couldn't, not until he said what was on his mind. Serious, Drew began to tell Lynn how much she meant to him. Though they hadn't known each other for no more than a year, he was ready to make a major commitment.

100

"Baby, I've been thinking about our future together," Drew said.

"What about it?" Lynn asked.

"I'm ready for us to start planning our lives together," Drew said. He didn't know how Lynn was going to react but hoped she felt the same as he.

"As in marriage?" Lynn asked.

"Yes," Drew answered. "Let's get married the minute we get back to campus."

Stunned by Drew's emotional request, Lynn was speechless. She was deeply in love with Drew and knew without a doubt she wanted to be his wife but getting married the minute they return to campus wasn't something she could agree on because of the unforeseen problems forthcoming that went by the names of Harold and Constance Boldmont. By no means would her parents accept the idea of her getting married while attending college, nonetheless getting married without an actual wedding. Yeah, she could defy their wishes but there would be a huge price to pay; a price she wasn't willing to sign for.

"Well, I'm waiting for an answer," Drew asked, after reminding Lynn it had been more than a minute since he'd suggested they get married.

"Drew, I'll marry you right now if it was possible but we have our parents to consider," Lynn replied. It wasn't that she didn't want to marry Drew; she was afraid of what it would do to her relationship with her parents if she did. Lynn didn't want to do anything that could jeopardize her chances to be appointed president of Boldmont Enterprises, including marrying Drew.

"Don't you want to marry me?" Drew asked.

"Of course, I do, more than anything but I feel we should discuss getting married with our parents. My parents want me to finish college and I can tell you now, they won't support us getting married so soon," Lynn replied.

Lynn could feel Drew's disappointment but knew it was the right decision to make. Drew didn't say much after that, even when Lynn tried resuming their conversation Drew chose not to participate. Though disappointed, he knew Lynn was right. Mentally, they weren't prepared to be married.

Sure, their families were wealthy and they could survive as a married couple but it was too much to consider at such a short time.

Drew himself were facing problems with Gloria that needed fixing along with how to tell his mother he was considering stepping down as president and CEO of Hillcrest to work for a company his girlfriend father owned. Then there was Lynn, and her affair with Marshall he had to deal with, not to mention Ashley, and her evil and cunning ways to contend. Lastly, there was Karyme, and his unexplained feelings for her. Drew wanted to get married to escape his problems but doing so would only create more problems.

Drew ended the conversation by saying he was going to shower. He was drained and after having an action-packed day and a rough night, he was ready for a hot shower and bed. Like Drew, Lynn too was exhausted, she was looking forward to climbing into bed and snuggling under him. Undressing, Lynn joined Drew in the shower. They didn't make love but shared an intimate moment when Lynn told Drew how much she loved him and that she would give serious consideration to his suggestion. It was enough to lead to a moment of passionate kissing and after getting out of the shower the couple again, dried and applied moisturizers to each other. It didn't take long before they were engulfed in one another. Unlike when they made love in the shower, Drew was cautious this time and wore a condom when making love to Lynn. They couldn't afford to continue taking chances without using some kind of protection because sooner or later, there luck was going to run out.

(12:00am)

Lynn was suddenly awakened by the constant non-stop vibration of Drew's phone. Looking at the clock and seeing it was 12am Lynn considered waking Drew but changed her mind after seeing the caller was Gloria. Thinking that Gloria would have gotten the message after her calls went unanswered, Lynn realized she hadn't. For more than forty minutes Drew's phone continued to vibrate. The constant calling became too annoying to ignore and it prompted Lynn to answer it. She had no right to invade on Drew's privacy by answering his phone but Gloria had ticked her last nerve. Before answering, Lynn's instincts warned her to wake Drew but she knew he was too exhausted to talk, so, she decided to be his secretary.

Lynn got out of bed with Drew's phone and went into the common area of their suite to have a seat on the couch.

"Hello," Lynn answered.

"Hello, who is this?" Gloria aggressively asked.

"Ashlynn Boldmont, and who might you be?" Lynn asked condescendingly.

"Awe, you're Drew's little Rich Bitch," Gloria teased.

Gloria was being disrespectful and Lynn's first instinct was to let Gloria know the type woman she could be but instead, she opted to kill her with kindness.

"I'm sorry, Drew is unavailable right now, can I take a message?" Lynn asked.

"Look, I don't know what kind of game you're playing but I don't have time to play with you, so, with that being said, could you put Drew on the got damn phone because you're beginning to piss me off," Gloria demanded.

"Did you just curse at me?" Lynn questioned. Gloria instantly sensed Lynn was becoming upset and decided to backtrack before it became an all-out shouting match. Instead of going all in on Lynn, Gloria lowered her tone.

"Look, maybe, we started off on the wrong foot and I may have prematurely raised my voice. If I did, I didn't mean to but its urgent that I speak to Drew, so if you would be a good little girl and wake him, I would greatly appreciate it," Gloria said in a much calmer voice. Gloria was hoping her change in attitude would persuade Lynn to wake Drew but she was wrong. Lynn wasn't going to allow Gloria to infringe on her relationship with Drew.

"I'm sorry, I can't wake him, you see, Drew had a rough day and he was really tired. I promise, I will tell him you called," Lynn said.

"So, you're his fucking secretary now? Gloria asked. She was becoming frustrated with Lynn's school girl antics and was close to giving Lynn a piece of her mind.

"As Drew's lady I have to look out for his wellbeing and I'm not going to wake him to talk to you. Now, let's try this again. Drew's sleeping after having a hard day and I'm not going to wake him. I will tell him you called when he wakes up," Lynn countered.

"Little girl, you seemed to forget; I've seen you before and you don't look like anything Drew would bring home to introduce to his family. How old are you anyway? Fifteen, sixteen, maybe seventeen years old?" Gloria teased.

"You're not enough woman for Drew, and believe me, he's going to get tire of you and come back home, where he belongs.

Gloria's disrespect of Lynn was beginning to get under Lynn's skin but instead of getting into a pissing contest inside the suite, Lynn decided to take their conversation outside on the balcony.

"Gloria, I'm not doing this tit for tat stuff with you, I will tell Drew you called," Lynn said again.

Lynn's refusal to wake Drew annoyed Gloria to the point that she lost her temper. "Look Bitch, I ain't got time for your shit. Now, put Drew on the phone and stop fucking with my time," Gloria screamed out.

Not surprised by Gloria's antics, Lynn stood her ground which irritated Gloria even more. Lynn's refusal to oblige Gloria's wishes became the straw that broke the camel's back. It was bad enough that Lynn was refusing to allow her to speak to Drew but the bitch had been sleeping with Drew since they'd landed in Eugene. Gloria wasn't in favor of reasoning with Lynn anymore and to substantiate it, she began cursing Lynn at the top of her voice. Now it was personal, Gloria didn't care about talking to Drew anymore, her focus was now on that twelve-year-old looking bitch of a girlfriend Drew was fucking. Instead of Lynn stooping to Gloria's level, she remained calm, which antagonized Gloria even more.

"Little girl, you don't know who you fucking with," Gloria shouted. Lynn had frustrated her to the point that Gloria decided it was time to put Lynn in her place but before doing so, Lynn struck a sore note that caused Gloria to reconsider what she wanted to hide.

"Now I understand why Drew got rid of your ghetto ass, I was told you were nothing more than a hood rat and you've proven that tonight," Lynn said; firing the shot that was heard around the world.

For a second Gloria went quiet; Lynn's "Hoodrat" jab had caught her by surprise. The "Rich Bitch" had drawn first blood and now it was Gloria's turn to throw the next stone. It wasn't surprising that Gloria would respond negatively about Lynn's

"Hoodrat" wisecrack. Drew's sister often used the term to describe her, she tolerated it because of Drew but she wasn't going to do so with this young bitch.

For that reason, only, Gloria decided to give Lynn a reason to wake Drew. She decided to tell Lynn about her illicit and steamy affair with Drew at his apartment, the night she showed up unexpectedly.

"You know, I wasn't going to say anything out of respect for Drew but you forced it out of me. You have no idea how badly I wanted you to come into Drew's bedroom the night you show up unexpectedly at his apartment. Because girl if you had, you would've seen me riding Drew's dick like a cowboy riding a bucking wild bull," Gloria laughed. "That's right, this ghetto hood rat had your man squealing like a pig, while you were fumbling around in the dark. Gloria's accusations left Lynn shaken. Hearing that Gloria was in bed having sex with Drew the night she visited him was shocking. Lynn struggled to swallow the news Gloria unlashed upon her, and to validate Gloria's story, she had to talk to Drew. To make matters worse, Gloria laughed when she told Lynn how Drew panicked when hearing her phone ring. Gloria had won the argument and like the bitch she was she continued to rub salt in Lynn's wounds by telling her that Drew made love to her before she left for home the next morning, while she was in her dorm room thinking about him.

"Now tell me this "Rich Bitch" how does it feel knowing that the hood rat was fucking your man, while your stupid young ass was standing outside of his bedroom? Like I said little girl, don't fuck with a real bitch when you don't have shit to fight with," Gloria laughed.

Gloria took great pride in sharing that information with Lynn and the shock of hearing what was said left Lynn speechless. She wanted to believe Gloria was lying but how would Gloria had known she came to Drew's apartment in the middle of the night? Nearly falling apart, Lynn tried to contain herself. She could see her heart beat from the outside of her nightie. The only thing she could think of was waking Drew to kick his ass. Lynn remembered finding perfume and body oils in Drew's bathroom but never questioned him about it because she believed it belonged to his mother or his sister. If Gloria was telling the truth, it was likely she was dealing with another lying, cheating motherfucker. She had fallen in love with Drew and was considering marrying him, now his ex-bitch was telling her, she was still fucking him. What if, she'd caught them in bed together?

How would she'd handle it? It was too much to think about right now, especially after hearing that two-dollar whore sniggering on the other end of the phone.

As much as Lynn hated to wake Drew, she felt she had no other choice. She needed to address this matter asap but before doing so, she first had to take care of that sniggering bitch.

"Gloria, if I was near you right now, I'll stomp your ass to China. But I'm not, so I can only do the next best thing, I'm going to stomp Drew's ass to China instead. So, don't fucking interrupt me by calling back," Lynn said. It was time to get to the bottom of Gloria's accusation and Lynn couldn't wait.

Knowing she had struck a nerve, Gloria laughed. She had won the battle and once Lynn confronts Drew and learns the truth; she'll win the war.

Furious, over what she had learned, Lynn opened the sliding glass doors of the balcony and stormed into the bedroom where Drew was sound asleep. She turned on the overhead lights and snatched the comforter and blankets from the bed; disturbing Drew's restful sleep. Standing above Drew with a look of rage, Lynn demanded answers.

"What the fuck's going on with you and that bitch Gloria?" Lynn screamed, throwing Drew's phone at him and striking him in the chest.

Covering his eyes from the glare of the overhead light, Drew tried fabricating a story to tell but it was too late; he'd been caught red-handed. He didn't know how much Gloria had revealed but assumed she'd told the complete story. How in God's name was he going to explain what happened without ruining their relationship? Drew was going to have to come up with something if he was going to keep Lynn.

Pissed and confused, Lynn was at a loss for words. Her eyes were full of tears as she stood over Drew with tightly clenched fist.

"You're going to tell me the truth and you're going to tell me right fucking now." Lynn demanded. Lynn was loud and she didn't care who heard what she had to say. Drew realized the state of their relationship depended upon him being truthful. He knew Lynn didn't want to hear any of his bullshit and he had no other option but to tell the truth about what happened.

The funny thing about it was that Drew didn't deny Gloria was there but did dress up the story to work in his favor. In other words, Drew lied his ass off by playing the victim to gain sympathy.

How could he get away with that? You ask, well, I guess you can say, Drew pulled a Donald Trump, and became the victim. He wanted Lynn to think he was set up, and did so with a lame ass excuse.

"I don't know what lie Gloria told you but here's the truth. The truth is, on the night in questioned, a knock came on the door, I ran to answer it because I thought it was you. Like a fool I opened the door, believing it was you and bam! it was Gloria standing there with that stupid ass smile on her face. She had taken the last train, which meant I couldn't send her home, so I had to let her stay until the next morning," Drew explained.

"Then you fucked her?" Lynn asked.

"No, hell no, I slept on the couch and gave her my bed. Lynn, I would never do anything to hurt you. I know what you're thinking but don't," Drew said.

"Why would you do something so stupid to sabotage our relationship? Why, Drew, why? You promised me you wouldn't hurt me. Got dammit, I trusted you." Lynn screamed out.

Drew tried holding Lynn, but she was too rallied up to allow him to touch her. "Baby let me explain." Drew pleaded while trying to embrace Lynn.

"Get your fucking hands off me Drew, I don't want you to touch me right now." Lynn shouted, pushing Drew away.

"Sweetie, it's not what you think, just calm down and let me explain. Nothing happened between Gloria and I," Drew said.

"The way she described it was the two of you were fucking like rabbits," Lynn said.

"She's lying, nothing happened between us," Drew reiterated. True to his word, Drew denied any knowledge of what Gloria was referring to. He was quick to deny any wrong doing but Lynn wasn't buying it. The story Gloria told was vivid and it was believable. Not knowing what all Gloria told, Drew could only play things by ear. He was sure Gloria admitted to them having sex but he needed an angle to discredit her. Stuttering, Drew continued to call Gloria a liar but it was quickly rebutted by Lynn who confronted him with the Gloria's story saying she was in bed with him when she entered his apartment.

"If you were sleeping on the couch in your living room, you should have heard me entering the apartment," Lynn questioned.

"Sweetie, I was so tired, I never heard the door open or close. I didn't know anything until Gloria woke me. Lynn, I swear, nothing happened, we were in separate rooms," Drew explained. The Good Lord knew he was lying his ass off but what else could he say? He had to do what he needed to do to keep the woman he wanted to be with.

"So why didn't you tell me about it? Why I had to hear it from that nasty bitch, huh? If it was as innocent as you say, then why couldn't you tell me? When I screwed up, I told you. I knew you would most likely leave me but I couldn't live with myself knowing what I had done. Why Drew, just tell me why?" Lynn asked.

"I didn't think it was important at the time because nothing happened between us," Drew responded.

"You didn't think it was important? Man, I should slap the shit out of you for saying some crap like that." Drew's response caused Lynn to become infuriated. So much so, she took out her frustration on everything made of glass, starting in their bath room. Lynn smashed a $400 a bottle OUD Ispahan perfume of hers on the bathroom ceramic tile floor.

"That's what I think of your dumb ass decision," Lynn said as she reached for a second bottle of perfume to smash. She reached and grabbed hold of her $300 bottle of Creed perfume and smashed it on the floor. "That's what I want to do to you right now Drew," Lynn screamed out, before smashing Drew's $300 bottle of cologne. "I hate that bitch and when I see her, I swear to God, I'm going to punch her and her motherfucking face."

Lynn was having a meltdown and Drew knew he had to intervene, before they got a visit from the hotel security. Drew calmly walked over to Lynn and guided her from the bathroom to the common area of the suite.

"It's alright, I'm going to fix it, I'm going to take care of Gloria and her lies, right now, ok," Drew said.

"You damn well better," Lynn responded.

Drew knew there was no way Lynn could ever know the truth about what happened with Gloria. He had to make a move to get Gloria out of his life for once and for all.

"I'm so sorry baby, I know I should have told you but things were going well between us, and after we got back together, I didn't want to ruin it. Please believe me." Drew responded. Lynn had calm down some, at least that's what Drew first believed until Lynn picked up her rant once more.

"You know one thing Drew Harrison, you're a got damn liar," Lynn screamed getting up from the couch. Lynn was loud and didn't give a damn who heard what was happening. It was crushing to know she had been deceived by the man she deeply respected and loved with all of her heart, only to find out he'd been two-timing her with a fucking whore. Seeing how quickly Lynn's anger escalated, Drew continued to try to calm her. He hated having to lie but stuck to his story. Relenting meant having his trust card suspended forever. Lynn wanted more than anything to be Drew's lady and only his lady. Regrettably, she was willing to accept his version of what happened, even though the truth was staring her in the face. God knew she didn't want another relationship like the one she had with Marshall but if she chose to let things go, she could possibly regret her mistake forever. Lynn cried out to Drew for the truth but Drew continued to stick to his story. He wanted to protect Lynn from another heartbreak and decided to put her mind to ease by taking steps to end all ties with Gloria.

Drew made the long-await decision to officially end all ties with Gloria. Calling her, Drew wasted no time with his mission and went forward as to why he was calling. He felt it was his responsibility to protect Lynn and he had no problem doing so. He told Gloria, he wanted no further association with her. He was breaking ties with her for good. Gloria had no right to tell Lynn about their affair and for doing so, she jeopardized his relationship with Lynn, something he didn't stand for. In front of Lynn, Drew had chosen who he wanted to be with and though Lynn was relieved, Gloria was devastated.

Chapter: 19

Lying in bed awake with Lynn in his arms, Drew realized how lucky he was to still have her after avoiding a near fiasco with Gloria. By no means had he been the ideal boyfriend, but after getting a reprieve, he was going to change his wicked ways. Drew couldn't deny he originally slept with Gloria out of spite to get back at Mason but never would he ever cross the line and cheat on Lynn again. From this moment on, he was going to love, support, and be as transparent as only he could be.

Looking at the clock and seeing he had an hour before they needed to get up to shower and catch the shuttle to the airport, Drew drifted back to sleep. Minutes later, he was startled by a loud banging on his door. Unsure as to who it was, Drew asked them to identify themselves.

"Who is it?" Drew asked.

"Police, open the door." The lead police officer instructed before banging on the door again.

"What's going on?" Lynn asked Drew, unsure as to what was happening.

"I don't know, stay here, I'll go see what's going on," Drew instructed.

Fearing the police were there to arrest him for his involvement with the earlier fight, Drew nervously made his way to the door. Once there, he looked through the peephole and saw that there were four police officers standing outside his door. Opening the door, Drew greeted the officers.

"How can I help you, officers?" Drew asked nervously.

The lead officer was the first to speak, he was abrasive and pushed Drew aside, entering the room without permission.

"How can I help you sir?" Drew again asked.

The officer entering didn't give an explanation, nor did he identify himself as he walk through the suite. Nervous that Lynn would be startled by the officer's unannounced appearance, Drew tried warning the officer that Lynn was in bed.

"Excuse me, officer, my girlfriends in bed, please identify yourself before you enter the room," Drew asked.

110

Irritated by what Drew was suggesting, the officer returned to where Drew was standing and shoved him against the wall. It wasn't hard to see that the officer was having a bad morning, and he was itching to inflict his authority on anyone who crossed him.

"Shut the fuck up, before I lock your black ass up," The officer said. I'm a fucking police officer and this badge gives me the authority to do what the fuck I want. You understand me, boy?" The officer shouted out.

Stunned by the officer's behavior, Drew did what was instructed. There was no need to argue his point across, the officer was going to win out every time. Now, feeling in control, the officer continued his investigation by exploring each room in the suite. He entered the bathroom and the smell of perfume was overwhelming.

"It fucking stinks in there?" the officer asked after being overcome by the strong smell of the perfume.

"I dropped my perfume bottle," Lynn answered.

"Smells like shit," the officer said.

The officer's antics were rubbing Lynn the wrong way, causing her to respond to his comment.

"That bottle of perfume costs more than what you make in a week, sir," Lynn said under her breath.

"What did you say to me?" the officer asked.

Lynn didn't repeat what she said, but you can best believe, it was on the tip of her tongue. The officer continued with his investigation by going through each and everything he thought was out of place. It was obvious he was looking to find something to make an arrest and after finding nothing, the officer began looking through the trash and found an empty wine bottle.

"How old are you, kid?" the officer asked. Without speaking, Lynn reached into her purse and passed the officer her driver's license. He looked at the year of her birth and began counting in his mind.

"Nineteen," Lynn answered. She was getting frustrated by what the officer was doing but tried keeping a level head.

"Have you been drinking?" The officer asked.

"That's not ours, some friends came by earlier in the evening," Lynn explained, shaking her head in disgust. It was an empty bottle and there was nothing he could do to her.

The officer continued to rummage through the suite while questioning Lynn regarding the earlier disturbance between her and Drew. Lynn tried explaining nothing happened but the officer wasn't hearing what she was saying. It was their belief a fight had taken place between the couple and they were determined to get to the bottom of it.

Standing outside the room, three officers were questioning Drew about the noise complaint involving him and Lynn. Drew explained, he and Lynn had a misunderstanding but was adamant no physical contact ever happened. Drew went on to say; he and Lynn had solved their misunderstanding and was about to leave for the airport within the hour. Though his explanation sounded believable, the officers had to clear up things before they could leave. The second of the three officers entered the room to assist with the investigation with Lynn, leaving two officers outside the door with Drew. Inside, Lynn remained sitting on the edge of the bed, waiting for the officers to finish their investigation. Once completed, the officers re-entered the bedroom where Lynn was still sitting. Again, they began interrogating Lynn, causing her to become uncomfortable.

"What happened to your fingers and hand?" The burley policeman asked.

"I accidentally cut it on a razor shaving my legs," Lynn responded.

"Yeah, right," The officer responded.

Lynn had lied; she now knew the officers weren't there to investigate the fight but her argument with Drew. Lynn became quiet after hearing the officer doubt her explanation. She gave serious thought to responding to his questions and became vague with her answers. The officer didn't ask any more questions, he walked around the room looking for anything to indicate a struggle had taken place.

After not seeing anything out of place, the officers returned outside the front door to where Drew was standing. Taking notice of the bruises on Drew's cheek and neck, the lead investigating officer began inquiring about it.

"What happened to your face and neck?" The officer asked.

"Awe that, I got into a scuffle with three guys outside a restaurant last night," Drew responded.

"Did you report the incident?" the officer asked.

"No, after the fight ended, Lynn and I returned to our room," Drew answered.

"Stay put," The lead officer said. The officers huddled and began talking amongst themselves. Drew had an eerie feeling that something bad was about to happen, and he and Lynn weren't going to like the results. Little did Drew know, he was right. After a brief meeting of the minds, the officers returned to join Drew by the door. The lead officer explained their finding and what was about to happen. It was just as Drew anticipated; the officers had gotten it wrong. Drew tried explaining his bruises came from the result of being attacked earlier in the evening but no one was listening. The police weren't buying Drew's story and denied his pleas to contact their dispatch to check if a call had been made regarding a report of a fight the prior evening. The police responded by asking Drew to assume the position and to place his hands behind his back. Drew couldn't believe he was about to be arrested for a crime of domestic violence. Drew stood in shock, as he watched the officer removed his cuffs from his pouch and locked them around his wrist. At the officer's directions, Drew was led into the common area and placed on the couch, until his warrant check was completed. Drew remained calm and was cooperative, hoping it was enough to straighten out the misunderstanding with the police, but Lynn on the other hand, wasn't as cooperative as Drew. She instantly began questioning why she was being arrested and why hadn't they called to check on the report about the fight from the previous evening. When asked to assume the position and place her hands behind her back, Lynn refused. She wasn't going to be arrested for something she didn't do.

"How can you arrest us for having an argument? These cuts are because I bust a bottle over a guy's head, not because I had a fight with Drew.

We were attacked by three guys, after leaving the restaurant last night. Look at our bruises, they're old," Lynn argued. Again, she displayed her cuts and bruises, and again, she was ignored.

Becoming frustrated with Lynn's refusal to adhere to his commands, the officer refused to listen to anything else Lynn had to say. He again instructed her to shut up and assume the position. The officer's mind was made, his fallacious investigation not only left Lynn frustrated, but it also led her to shout obscenities toward him.

"I guess because I'm black, I supposed to know what assuming the fucking position means? You're so eager to lock us up, you'll make up any excuse to do so." Lynn stated.

"You're black?" the burley officer joked.

Drew knew what this morning was leading to and asked Lynn not to say anymore. He pleaded that she follow the officer's instructions and allow them to take them to jail. Needless to say, Lynn wasn't on board with what Drew was asking her to do. She hadn't done anything to be arrested for, nor did she want an arrest on her record.

"Lynn, please, listen to me, let them cuff you, we'll straighten it out later," Drew said from the common area.

"Why should I allow him to arrest me when I did nothing wrong? It's obvious, they're a bunch of racist ass cops, especially this fat, donut-eating Barney Fife here," Lynn yelled out, referring to the burley officer who was trying to arrest her. Lynn's derision of the burly police officer, left him enraged. It was time to take control of the situation and the officer was too eager to do so. He'd heard enough of Lynn's criticism of him and decided to impose his will. The officer used his authority by grabbing hold of Lynn's arm, forcefully pulling her up from the bed and constraining her against the wall face first.

"You, fat fuck," Lynn screamed.

"Shut the fuck up." The policeman yelled out, shut your fucking mouth, "I've heard just enough from you. Hey, Moretti, here's another from the Mo'Nig tribe," The burly officer laughed as he reached to remove the cuffs from his pouch.

"You, racist fat cracker, you don't know who my father is?" Lynn warned.

"I don't give a damn who your father is, and if he walked through those doors, I'll take his ass to jail right with yours," the officer responded.

Using his weight to restrict Lynn from moving, the officer was intentionally pressing her face against the wall to prevent her from talking. By using his body, the officer was free to twist Lynn's arms behind her back to cuff her. Lynn screamed from the pain as the officer inflicted unnecessary pain on her arm. Drew felt helpless having to hear Lynn screaming but there was nothing he could do; because he, too, was cuffed from behind. Drew listened in horror as Lynn screamed from the pain being inflicted upon her. It was obvious she was being punished for refusing to adhere to the officer's original order. Lynn tried to fight against the officer's overly aggressive nature but she was no match for a man weighing nearly two-hundred pounds more than she but it hadn't stopped Lynn from verbally insulting him.

"I bet you feel like a real man now? Yeah, you're getting your rocks off by rough handling a one-hundred-ten pounds lady, don't you?" Lynn questioned.

"Shut the hell up, you ain't no lady, you're a smart mouth little bitch, whose parents should have whipped your little ass when you were a child," the burly officer responded.

"I bet you're the type of father who beats their kid for eating the last biscuit," Lynn stated.

"Lynn, stop antagonizing him, that's what he wants you to do," Drew screamed out from the couch in the common area.

"You better listen to your little boyfriend in the other room," the officer said to Lynn.

"Kiss my ass," Lynn shouted out at the officer.

Lynn's rude behavior caused the officer to press her face tighter against the wall. It was no doubt that he was trying to hurt Lynn with the brutal way he was handling her. By using his hand to push Lynn's face against the wall was uncalled for. His brutal behavior against Lynn caused her nose to bleed profusely.

"I can't breathe," Lynn mumbled. "Stop, you're hurting me." Lynn managed to get out.

Blood was running from her nose and trickling down the wall as she tried screaming for help. The sound of hearing Lynn being manhandled was too much for Drew to bear. He had to do something and do so before she was seriously injured. Using the couch to steady himself, Drew slid his hands from behind his back, to the front of him. His goal was only to prevent Lynn from further harm and nothing more. With his hands in front of him, Drew rushed by the officers, who were caught off guard and ran into the bedroom where Lynn was being held. Using the momentum generated from the speed he accumulated, Drew used his shoulder to football tackle the officer, knocking him across the room to the floor. Drew never considered the consequences he would face, and quite frankly, he didn't give a damn. His only concern was to alleviate the pain the officer was applying to Lynn. After realizing what he'd done, Drew did what he thought was the safest thing to do. He dropped to his knees and raised his cuffed hands over his head, surrendering to the police. It should have been over, at least, that's what Drew thought anyway. He had no idea what was about to happen to him. Yeah, he was sure he was going to be roughed up before being taken off to jail because he had assaulted a police officer, but at least he wouldn't be shot dead. Nervously, Drew waited for the officer's approach but instead of being approached, Drew felt a pinch to the back of his neck, as well as his shoulders. Seconds later, he felt a second pinch to his waist, and without warning, he felt a jolt of electricity through his body.

Drew fell to the floor and began shaking uncontrollably. He'd just been hit with 50,000 volts of electricity, and his body shook uncontrollably. Drew could hear the burley officer screaming, "Stop resisting," as they entertained themselves taking turns activating the stun gun. To make matters worse, the officers began striking Drew with their metal ASP batons in between shocks. They'd neglected the proper techniques in striking a combative prisoner. Instead, their only concerns were eliminating what they considered a threat, and between each strike, the officers yelled for Drew to stop being combative.

It was a technique used by the officers to continue beating the hell out of Drew without repercussion. Seeing Drew's motionless body stretched out across the floor, Lynn pleaded for them to stop. Drew was being beaten to death and it was her fault.

116

"Stop, beating him," Lynn screamed. "Please, God, make them stop," Lynn cried out. "I give up, I won't resist anymore,"

The beating of Drew was not only inhuman, but it was also downright unnecessary. There was no need to tase Drew or beat the hell out of him the way they had because he'd fallen to his knees and raised his hand in surrender. It was all about getting even, and to think Drew was only trying to save Lynn from further injury. Finally, after nearly beating Drew unconscious, the officers removed the prongs from his body and reapplied the cuffs from the front of him to his rear, but this time they used leg iron to hogtie him. Lying face down on the floor, Drew couldn't believe he was living such a nightmare. Just hours ago, he was being crowned U.S. fastest man in both the one- and two-hundred-meter races, and now he was about to go to jail. It was a nightmare he wouldn't wish for anyone.

The burley officer resumed his arrest of Lynn by lifting her from the floor. He again placed her face to the wall but didn't apply as much pressure as before. Lynn's nose continued to bleed, but it didn't matter to the officer. In a way, he enjoyed what he was doing to Lynn, and to further humiliate her, he began a thorough search of her. It hadn't mattered Lynn was wearing only a sheer robe covering a sheer nightie with matching panties. The officer positioned himself close behind Lynn and used his gloved hand to frisk her. In doing so, he fondled not only her breast and buttocks. To make things more difficult, he made an attempt to insert his finger into her vagina. Disgusted by what the officer was trying to do, Lynn used the back of her head to strike him in his face. She narrowly missed striking his nose but was tall enough to make direct contact to his chin. Bam, was the sound of Lynn's head hitting the officer's chin. The officer stumbled, nearly losing conscious before falling against Lynn, who had been placed against the wall. Once regaining his senses, the burley officer returned to his aggressive tactics.

"Aaaah; shit! This fucking bitch just head-butted me in my damn nose," The officer shouted out.

After being stunned by Lynn's head butt, the officer used his aggression to forcefully throw Lynn to the floor face first. Luckily for Lynn, she barely missed the glass and metal frame lamp stand in the room. Lynn laid motionless, after getting the breath knocked out of her.

Before she could catch her breath, the burley officer picked her up by her cuffs and escorted her to the common area where he shoved her toward the couch.

"You, fucking Bitch; I should whip your little ass like I did your boyfriend." The burly officer said. It was tough to witness but hotel security did their job by filming the entire situation. Seeing what happened, one of the hotel security officers helped Lynn to her feet and assisted her on the couch. They were dumbfounded at what they were seeing. The officers were on a rampage and didn't seem to give a damn about the repercussions, their mindset was simply to kick ass and take names.

After having been unjustly treated, Lynn sat and cried. She didn't make any further threats because she feared retaliation, if not to herself, then to Drew. Drew was hurt badly and Lynn could only pray that he was going to be ok. He had absorbed so much unnecessary punishment and the police still weren't finished with him. From the couch, Lynn watched as two officers dragged Drew across the floor, outside into the hallway. On their way outside, they accidentally dropped him on his face, then, to further humiliate him, the police intentionally strike his head against the door jamb while taking him out. Drew and Lynn were on their way to jail with several charges, stemming from their run-in with the police, but what perhaps was their most serious charge was the assault of a police officer. It was a sure bet; they wouldn't receive a bond, meaning they were going to be stuck in jail until their bond hearing Monday morning. What was most concerning for both of them was the fact that they were going to have to call their parents to come to their rescue.

Lynn could only imagine how her parents were going to react, after she tell them she had been arrested. Lynn would rather take another beating from the police rather than having to call her parents but she had no other alternative.

In an effort to hide the barbarity inflicted on Drew, the decision was made to carry his limp body down the back stairs to the awaiting paddy wagon that was waiting to transport him to county lockup. Lynn's arrest hadn't resulted much better and though she wasn't beaten to a pulp, she suffered a bloody nose and several scratches and bruises on her face. But unlike Drew, Lynn wasn't taken down the back stairs, she was marched through the lobby wearing only her sheer white night gown and robe. It was the policemen's way of embarrassing her but in doing so, they covered her face with a towel to hide the bruises and bloody nose she sustained by their hands.

Unfortunately for Lynn, hiding her face wasn't enough to conceal who she was. Her name had been out there since her altercation with Marshall and now she was back in the news again for domestic violence.

Lynn wanted to escape the onslaught of reporters who was surrounding the police cruiser trying to get a picture. Though Lynn didn't expect the officers to show her any sympathy, she pleaded for them to remove her from the scene nonetheless. After learning who Lynn was the officers made the decision to leave the scene. They laughed and joked about her knocking Marshall over the railings doing their engagement party.

"That's one good right hook you got there, little lady." One officer joked.

"So, the guy you were fighting, was he your boyfriend?" The second officer asked.

"No, the guy you nearly killed, is my boyfriend;" Lynn replied.

Lynn didn't care that they were poking fun at her, her mindset was on Drew and what he must be going through. She didn't know how bad Drew was hurt and it was unlikely anyone was going to tell her. Lynn was even uncertain if they were going to be booked at the same jail but she suspected they would. Whether she got the chance to talk to Drew remained to be seen but after this was all over, she was certain, she was going to marry Drew the moment they got back to campus.

Dazed, confused, and bleeding from his mouth and ear, Drew laid in the rear of the paddy wagon's floor. He hadn't been secured and was at the mercy of the wagon master as he was being taken to jail. Drew could hear the officer's bragging at the way they manhandled him but was too weak to respond. To further humiliate him, Drew could hear them reenacting the way he shook after being tased. Needing to cover their tracks the officers had contacted two EMT friends and had them to meet at an undisclosed location to examine Drew before taking them to jail. They had thought of everything, including muting the hotel security officers who filmed the incident. As luck would have it, one of the security officers wanted to be a policeman and promised not to implicate any of them for what happened. After getting a clearance on Drew, the officers drove him to the county jail.

Chapter: 20

After working at his office for eighty plus hours for the third consecutive week, Harry was hoping to sleep in this Sunday morning but unfortunately for him, the home phone rang, awakening him from a deep sleep. Harry's first instinct was to ignore it but he thought better of doing so with two daughters out of the house for the summer.

"Hello;" Harry answered. He was barely awake until hearing the news. Suddenly, he set up in bed and with a deep morning base in his voice, and shouted; "You what? What the hell are you doing in jail?" Harry asked.

Constance also sat up in bed, "What's going on?" she asked. Constance listened as Harry tried making sense of what was being said to him. Constance didn't know what was actually happening but was certain it involved Lynn. Wanting to know more, Constance leaned over her husband's shoulder and placed her ear against Harry's. It was becoming a constant occurrence for Lynn and frankly she was getting tired of it.

"We'll be on the next plane out," Harry said before hanging up.

"What did Lynn do now?" Constance asked, following Harry out of bed.

"She flew her little fast ass to Oregon, and got arrested," Harry responded

 "What is she doing in Oregon, she supposed to be at school?" Constance said.

"Following that damn boy, I bet," Harry responded.

"Oh God, are you for real?" Constance replied, reacting to the news.

It was hard to believe Lynn could have been so irresponsible while betraying their trust. It was their understanding, she had ceased all communications with Drew and now, she was sitting in jail on a slew of charges including assaulting a police officer.

"We should just let her rot in jail," Constance said as she began packing for their trip. They had no idea as to how long they would to be in Eugene Oregon and needed to play it safe. Harry was livid that his daughter had disobeyed his wishes and he let it be known by his abusive language describing his feelings.

He couldn't believe he was spending a Sunday on a plane, having to fly across the nation to bail his youngest daughter out of jail. Lynn was making it easy for him to appoint Ashley as president with the stunts she was pulling. Harry packed his bags and called his lawyer to find and hire an attorney that could handle Lynn's case. After talking with his lawyer, Harry and Constance made the necessary arrangements for their trip and left for the airport.

After talking to her father, Lynn passed the phone to the jail officer standing beside her. She couldn't say for certain if her parents were flying out today but even if they did, she wasn't getting a bail hearing until tomorrow morning. The thought of being assigned a cell was an awakening experience for Lynn. It was beginning to sink in that she was going to stay in jail until Monday morning. The thought of it scared her shitless but Lynn knew she couldn't show fear. If she was going to survive, she was going to have to put her big girl panties on and face the music. However, Lynn wasn't concern about her fear as much as she was for Drew. She worried about Drew and because she hadn't seen him, she began to wonder if he was in the hospital. She'd witnessed the beating he'd received and was worried sick about the state of his health. Lynn followed the female jail officer back to her cell where she was given a cup of shampoo and led to the shower.

"You need to saturate your body with this stuff, everywhere you have hair." The jail officer instructed.

"What kind of shampoo is this?" Lynn asked naively before smelling it.

The jail officer snickered before divulging the purpose of the shampoo. "Honey, I can see this is your first time being locked up. Just think of it as being the Phillip B. shampoo you're used to using. But to answer your question, this shampoo is used to kill crabs."

Now wasn't a time for jokes, but Lynn knew she had to keep her nose clean if she was to make it until her parents arrive to bail her out. Having to undress in front of the female officer was degrading, but having to use a shampoo of such enormity was even more humiliating. Having to be strip searched under the watchful eyes of the female officer left Lynn feeling violated all over again. Removing the jumpsuit, she was given to call her parents, Lynn stood naked as the officer had her to run her hands through her hair. Lynn hid her tears and cried silently when instructed to squat and cough.

121

"Why is this necessary?" Lynn asked.

"We can't have you people bringing drugs into our jail." The officer responded.

Biting her tongue, Lynn remained quiet. She wanted desperately to tell the officer to go straight to hell but knew it was her mouth that got her and Drew taken to jail in the first place. After the strip search was completed, Lynn was issued another jumpsuit, a pair of jail shoes, and a pair of inmate panties. It was time for her to enter the shower, and as Lynn did, her body shivered from the cold water coming from the shower. To make matters worse, the pressure from the water wreaked havoc on her skin. Lynn cried throughout her four-minute shower. Why had this happened to she and Drew after they'd finally patched up their differences? Lynn couldn't answer with certainty but began believing it was a sign that she and Drew shouldn't be a couple. It was a silly analogy, to say the least, but so many things had blocked their paths throughout their relationship. After showering, Lynn dressed in her issued green jumpsuit and orange plastic flops. Her hair was a mess and the effects from the shampoo were already taking a toll on her skin. Lynn was then taken to a cell filled with ten other women who had gone through what she had. The funny thing about it, they weren't fazed by being in jail. It was a norm for them but for Lynn, it was horror. She sat on the bench nearest to the window, staying clear of everyone, hoping to stay out of trouble. The other women hadn't noticed her and were in deep conversation amongst themselves. They didn't seem to care that Lynn was being antisocial, to them, she was just another half-white bitch who got hung up in some dumb shit with her nigger boyfriend. Searching through the lobby, Lynn searched for any signs of Drew but there were none. She never got the chance to see Drew after the police took him away, and she couldn't imagine what he must be going through. Her fears that Drew didn't survive the beating heightened after not seeing him. Lynn's inquisitive nature prompted her to ask several jailers about Drew and his condition but no one would relinquish any information to her. Lynn was able to gather some information concerning Drew being at the jail. She was advised Drew was there but a keep separate order was implemented and she couldn't have any contact with him. A keep separate list was a policy implemented by the jail to prevent parties of domestic abuse from having any contact. It was a policy Lynn wasn't in favor of because it restricted her from knowing anything about Drew or his health. Fighting sleep, Lynn was determined to see him.

Drew was owed a phone call and she felt sooner or later he would be granted his right. It was nearly 7 am when Drew was escorted from his cell to the phone. He was being escorted by two officers who seem to be holding him up. Lynn was horrified by Drew's condition and watched helplessly as he struggled to make his way to the phone. Once there, Drew couldn't see the numbers he was dialing. Both eyes were closed and he looked confused while trying to comprehend the questions the officers were asking him. Seeing what Drew was going through, Lynn attempted to get the officer's attention by knocking on her cell door. When that didn't work, she started kicking the door to get anyone's attention. By kicking the door, Lynn hadn't gotten Drew's attention but had gotten the attention of the jailer assigned to her section. Rushing over to her cell, the jailer had a look of seriousness on her face.

It was obvious she meant business and expressed her intentions with threats of strapping Lynn into the jail's restraint chair. Faced with threats of being restrained, Lynn ended her attempts to contact Drew. She had seen firsthand what the chair was capable of doing to a person strapped into it and wanted no part of it. Lynn felt helpless and could only sit and watch as Drew stood clueless by the phone, unable to remember his home phone number. Something was wrong; Drew needed help but Lynn didn't know how to help him. Lynn waited for an officer to make their required 15-minute round and pleaded for her to help Drew but the officer denied her request. After witnessing how Drew was struggling to process questions asked to him by the jail officers escorting him, the officer promised Lynn, she would allow her to contact his mother, the first chance she got.

Feeling the effects of the beating he sustained at the hands of the police, Drew laid face-first on the cold concrete floor to help soothe his aching body. While on the floor, he began drifting in and out of consciousness. Moments later, he violently began coughing up blood. Seeing what was happening, the inmates in the holding cell began screaming for help. Hearing the commotion, officers quickly responded to the holding cell. Entering, they found Drew lying face down in his own vomit of blood. Drew was unconscious and he was barely breathing. A medical alert was issued over the radio and within seconds, medical staff arrived on scene and began administering assistance. Drew was taken by stretcher from booking to the medical unit for additional assistance. After determining his condition was critical, the decision was made to contact EMS to transport him to Oregon State Hospital.

Unhinged at the sight of seeing Drew lying motionless on the stretcher, Lynn began screaming and banging on her cell door, as hard as she could. She was deeply disturbed by what she saw and wanted desperately to be there for Drew. Fed with up Lynn's antics, four jail officers responded to her cell. Opening the door, they placed Lynn face first against the wall and cuffed her hands from behind. Removing her from her cell, they escorted her to where their restraint chair was positioned and strapped her in tightly. Screaming for help, Lynn cried out for Drew as she feared the worst. She pleaded for information on his condition but her cries were ignored. Adjuring for anyone to listen, Lynn's implore for leniency fell on deaf ears. Her behavior had warranted punishment and though the officers sympathized for her, she had broken their rules and needed to pay for doing so. Strapped in the chair the officers placed the helmet over Lynn's head. The smell of stale sweat, and rotten caucus reeked from the padding of the helmet and as scent engulfed Lynn nasal passage, she began dry-heaving. Her screams of being claustrophobic fell on deaf ears but lucky for her, the watch commander entered booking and made the decision to remove her helmet. The watch commander did however, warned Lynn that her behavior warranted whether the helmet would be placed back over her head.

Strapped in the chair, Lynn asked the watch commander if she would loan an ear to hear her story. She wanted to tell what happened and why she and Drew were arrested. Their incarceration had nothing to do with a domestic disturbance but violence resulting from the police. Lynn argued it was a classic case of being arrested while being black. In a surprising change of events, the Lieutenant chose to hear Lynn's story and after hearing it, she was obliterated by the events that had allegedly taken place. It was now all making sense; the way Lynn was brought in wearing only her night clothes and Drew being beaten to an inch of his life. The trauma he sustained hadn't warranted his crime and it gave the Lieutenant a different perspective of what may have occurred. Hearing Lynn's story had gained much needed sympathy. She and Drew had endured an unimaginable experience no one should have to encounter and after hearing Lynn's story; the watch commander removed her from the restraint chair. She also allowed Lynn to call Drew's mother to inform her about what had happened to them and about Drew's condition. Regrettably, Lynn had to inform Nancy about what happened to Drew, and after doing so, she was lead back and placed into her cell without incident. Lynn thanked the watch commander for being kind and understanding.

As promised, the watch commander kept Lynn informed with updates on Drew and did so hourly, until her shift ended at 11am. Before leaving, she returned to Lynn's cell to wish her luck. She saw Lynn as possibly being her daughter, who had gone out of town and was targeted by the police. She passed Lynn her card and informed her to contact her if she could ever be of any assistance. Lynn thanked her and promised to call her once everything was settled.

Chapter: 21

The news of Drew's arrest spread across Jefferson County like the plague. Gloria learned of Drew's arrest from the radio while riding to work with her father. Though it was shocking to find out about Drew's arrest, Gloria felt a sense of vindication for the way he treated her.

"Serves his ass right." Gloria thought to herself before getting stuck in the ass by one of many springs from the front passenger seat of her father's truck. Whether Gloria deserved what she got for thinking that way of Drew was debatable but it felt good to get payback. As far as Gloria was concerned, Drew had gotten what he deserved. He had dumped her for the "Rich Bitch" and for doing so, he'd gotten burned. Gloria suspected she was the reason Drew got into a tussle with the police. It was she who opened Pandora's box by telling his little child girlfriend she was fucking her man.

"I wonder what caused Drew to fight the police?" Pistol asked.

"Because he's a dumb ass," Gloria answered while pretending she didn't care.

Pistol hated hearing the news about Drew being in jail. Lord knows if there was such a thing as a Drew Harrison fan club, her father would be president. He didn't believe Drew's shit stunk. If he had his way, she would be married to Drew right now. In a way, Gloria wished her father did have his way because she would give anything to be Drew's wife. If Drew was married to her, he wouldn't be in jail in some fucked up state; he'll be at home with her. Hopefully, now that he's free from his little young girlfriend, her chances will increase for him to come back to her. Lord knows if it happens, her father would be the happiest man in the world. In his mind, Drew was the only man he felt was good enough for her and in a way, she understood why. For one, Drew was by far, one of the most respectable men she'd ever known; he would give you the shirt off his back and to be honest, Drew gave her some of the happiest times in her life but he had some bad points also with one of them being he loved working more than he enjoyed having fun or spending money. Drew is a twenty-year-old man with a fifty-year-old mindset. He believed in not wasting money and did so by giving himself a weekly salary of $100 dollars. Who does that? But what stands out mostly about Drew is the fact that he and his family are wealthy and being wealthy meant they could provide her with the life she felt she deserved.

Gloria was quiet the remainder of her ride to work. She had a lot to think about now that Drew and "The Rich Bitch" was probably over. Their breakup may benefit her and if it comes to fruition, her next challenge would be what to do with Mason. However, Gloria didn't want to count her chickens before they hatched; at least not until she knew for sure it was over between them. Gloria's mind remained on Drew for the remainder of her twelve hours shift at the hospital. Though she wanted to hate Drew for the way he treated her, she couldn't because she was still in love with him.

After hearing the news that Drew had been hurt from his altercation with the police, Gloria became concerned and after Mason called to tell her that Nancy had flown out to Eugene, Gloria's anxiety heightened. Believing Drew's injuries were severe, Gloria called all of her contacts to find out anything about Drew's health. She didn't learn much but did however, learn Karyme had flown out with Nancy. It wasn't until later in the evening that Gloria learned Drew had been beaten up severely by the police and was in the hospital. It was hard to understand what happened for Drew to want to fight the police? Hell, Drew would run from a fight instead of having to engage in one. He would have never resisted an arrest; nonetheless fight an officer. Drew was too much of a pussy to go against anything that would stain the Harrison's precious name. But regardless of what happen and how it happened, Drew was in the hospital and the little "Wetback" ass was where she was supposed to be. In other words, Karyme had infringed on what should have been her seat on the plane. Like every other time in her relationship with Drew, Karyme was always somewhere near by to reap the benefits. Personally, Gloria didn't hate Karyme; she envied her. Maybe it was the way Drew gravitated to Karyme that caused Gloria to envy Karyme so much. Whatever it was, Gloria knew it had to be more than a friendship they were pretending to have.

It had been a long day but finally it was over. Gloria had completed the last of her four, twelve-hour shifts and she was ready for her long weekend. Tomorrow, she and Mason was driving to Richmond for a day of shopping but Gloria weren't looking forward to it. She wanted to stay near home to get updated news pertaining to Drew. It seemed funny that she would rather hang around home, instead of spending Mason's money. Gloria left the hospital and walked to the parking lot where Mason was supposed to meet her but like always, he was late. After talking to Mason on the phone, Gloria decided to wait for him at Larry's.

There, she could sit and wait, while calling around for news about Drew. Gloria waited for more than twenty minutes for Mason to arrive. She wasn't sure if he would make a big issue out of what happened to Drew but as soon as she entered the car, she was met with all the negative news she expected would happen.

"Did you hear about your boy?" Mason asked.

"Who?" Gloria replied.

"Drew," Mason responded.

"Yeah, one of the nurses said she heard he got arrested for something," Gloria replied. She knew all about what happened but pretended not to.

"The shit's deeper than that," Mason said. "Momma said the stupid motherfucker tried to fight four white cops and they beat the fuck out of him. Momma also said they even locked that pretty red bitch of his up too." Mason laughed. He found joy in hearing about Drew's unfortunate run-in with the police. For years, Drew had been the so-called model, he was supposed to imitate and Mason found it impossible to live up to the second coming but as it turned out, he didn't have to live up to Drew anymore, the golden child had finally fucked up. The golden child was in jail without the bail and Mason couldn't have been happier.

"Thank God, I don't have to worry about the motherfucker being around you anymore." Mason said.

"What are you talking about?" Gloria replied.

"Drew, I don't have to worry about him trying to steal you back, because the stupid motherfucker tried to fight four white cops and mark my word, his ass ain't getting out of jail, no time soon," Mason said with confidence.

Having to listen to all the negative talk about Drew reminded Gloria of why she didn't want to spend the night with Mason because she was going to have hear about Drew all night.

Chapter: 22

Monday morning at 0900 hours; Harry and Constance sit nervously in the courtroom waiting impatiently for Lynn to be arraigned. They were devastated at the sight of her being led into the courtroom by two deputies who escorted her to her awaiting lawyer. Before talking to her lawyer, Lynn turned to see if her parents were sitting in the courtroom. Seeing them, she smiled and gave a half-wave before turning her attention back to her lawyer. Both, Harry and Constance were aghast by the number of bruises covering Lynn's face. They barely recognized her because of her swollen face and the number of bruises covering it. Seeing Lynn left no doubt an injustice had taken place and Harry nearly lost it once seeing the abuse Lynn had suffered. He stood up and demanded to know who was responsible for his daughter's injuries. If not for Constance and the quick thinking of Lynn's lawyer, Harry would have joined his daughter in jail. The judge was quick to take control of his courtroom and threatened jail time if Harry didn't restrain himself. It was safe to say Harry's outburst pissed the judge off and he took it out on Lynn the moment her case was called.

Acting on the advice of her attorney, Lynn submitted a not-guilty plea. Maybe it was the way the judge stared at her that gave Lynn all indication that he was about to lower the boom on her. Having no criminal record and having never been in any trouble; Lynn's lawyer believed she was going to be released on her own recognizance but Lynn soon learned how wrong he was. As the judge read off her charges, he raised his eyebrow in disgust.

"Miss Boldmont, I see you've been charged with resisting arrest, domestic assault, assault and battery against an officer, assault of an officer, times two, and disorderly conduct. Are these charges true?" The judge asked.

"No sir," Lynn answered.

"So, what you're saying, the police lied?" The judge countered.

"Yes sir," Lynn answered.

"Miss Boldmont, where are you from?" The judge asked.

"Annapolis Maryland sir," Lynn answered.

"Miss Boldmont, these are serious charges against you," the judge said.

"Yes sir, they are," Lynn whispered, shaking her head in agreement.

"I'm setting your bail at $300 thousand dollars," the judge ordered.

Speaking out against the judge's ruling, Lynn's l lawyer argued. "But sir, my client has never been in trouble before. She's a college student and a model citizen, from a very prominent family."

"I don't care if her father is the President of the United States, that's my ruling," The judge said.

"But sir," The lawyer countered.

"You want me to increase it." The judge asked.

"No sir;" The lawyer said, before realizing the judge wasn't in a good mood. The entire courtroom was shocked by the judge's harsh punishment but no one complained not to the judge anyway. $300 thousand dollars was a lot of money but Harry was willing to pay it to get his daughter released. After hearing Lynn's trial date, Harry and Constance exited the courtroom. They took a short walk to the clerk's office and paid the thirty thousand dollars to have Lynn released.

Once the bond was secured, Lynn was taken back to the holding cell to be transported to booking to be processed out. She had a two to three-hour wait before being officially released but Lynn didn't care, she was going home. It should have been a joyous occasion for Lynn but her mind continued to be on Drew and his health.

The Sheriff's transport van didn't return to the jail until 1:00 pm. Lynn, along with twelve other women prisoners were taken to the holding cells and locked in. Out of the twelve women who went for arraignment, only Lynn was being released. While being processed out, Lynn turned to the women and waved goodbye. It was a bittersweet moment to know she was going home but she was leaving Drew. Unable to wear the sheer robe home she came into jail wearing, an officer issued Lynn sweats, and a pair of sneakers to wear home. Once dressed, Lynn was escorted through the exit door that led to the sally port. Seeing she was only a door away from freedom, Lynn didn't know whether to jump for joy or to cry.

Walking through the final exit door, Lynn felt a sense of relief. The heat from the sun burned her face, but she didn't care, she was going home. Lynn saw her mother standing in the parking lot waving her arms back and forth to get her attention. As Lynn made her way over to where her parents were, she realized she had taken freedom for granted; going to jail and having your freedom taken was the worst thing that could happen to anyone. As she approached her parents, Lynn suspected her punishment for getting in trouble would be swift and severe, she just didn't know how severe. Constance, who had been a thorn in her side her entire life, surprised Lynn by greeting her with an embrace but her father chose not to celebrate her homecoming, instead, he looked away. Unlike Constance, he showed no emotions. Constance on the other hand were very concerned about Lynn's facial bruises.

"What did they do to you in there?" Constance asked; while softly touching Lynn's face with a paper napkin.

"It was the police; they did this when they arrested us." Lynn said, getting into the rear of the car. Her body hurt from head to toe but she didn't care, she was going home.

"What happened?" Constance questioned.

"Mom, it's a long story but you have to believe me when I tell you, we didn't do any of the stuff we're being accused of," Lynn explained.

"Thank God, you're safe. Where are your clothes?" Constance asked.

"At the hotel," Lynn responded.

"What hotel?" Constance asked.

"The Best Western, near the campus," Lynn answered.

"Harold, take us to the hotel, Lynn needs a shower, she stinks." Constance asked.

Any other time, Lynn would have been offended by her mother's choice of words but not today, today she was in agreement with her mom. Harry never spoke a word; he continued looking forward. His reception towards Lynn hadn't gone as she had hoped, she knew he would be disappointed in her but his refusal to show any kind of emotions, was alarming.

The thought of her possibly ruining her relationship with her dad made her cringe. Her father meant the world to her and disappointing him was something she never wanted to do. Lynn sat quietly as Harry drove to the hotel. Harry never spoke a word or asked questions pertaining to the hotel. Instead of having to talk to Lynn, he followed the direction of the navigation system in the car. Whatever thoughts he had, he kept them to himself. It wasn't until they arrived at the hotel that Harry said anything and Lynn wasn't surprised to hear that it wasn't pleasant. Driving into the parking lot, Harry turned off the car's engine. He used his rear-view mirror to look at Lynn and he spoke low, yet stern.

"You got twenty-minutes to shower, pack or do whatever you have to do and if you're not back by then, you'll have to find your own way home." Harry's emotional threat was one to believe and Lynn displayed it with an immediate dismissal from the backseat of the car. It may had been the tone in her father's voice that prompted Lynn to act so expeditiously but she didn't have to be a genius to understand the seriousness in it. To hurry her along, Constance left with her. She too comprehended the seriousness in Harry's voice to know he was serious.

Taking the elevator to Lynn's suite, neither woman spoke a word. Inside the room, Lynn began stripping, and quickly entered the shower. To make the twenty-minute deadline, Constance helped her pack. In doing so, she took the opportunity to invade upon Lynn's privacy by searching through her luggage. In doing so, she discovered several revealing gowns and nighties. Not stopping there, Constance continued her search by rummaging through Lynn's purse and discovered an unopened box, containing a Plan B pill in a secret compartment. Alarmed by what she uncovered; Constance didn't want to prematurely jump to conclusions before learning the facts. Instead, she tried remaining calm, trusting that Lynn was responsible enough not to get pregnant. Still, Constance couldn't omit Lynn's weakness towards men when it came to satisfying their desires. Surely, they were going to have to talk but as a mother, it was her responsibility to ensure that Lynn wouldn't make a life altering mistake. Removing the box from Lynn's purse, Constance placed it on the dresser. She removed a bottle of water from the mini refrigerator in the room, and waited for Lynn to return from the shower.

Returning from the bathroom wrapped in a towel, Lynn was shocked to see her mother had ventured into her purse and found her pill.

"Were you and Drew intimate?" Constance asked with a look of concern on her face.

"Mother," Lynn replied; embarrassed Constance had questioned her about intimacy. It was also embarrassing Constance had rummaged through her purse but Lynn wasn't going to complain, not after her mother had been so understanding. Though Lynn was of age, she felt uncomfortable talking about sex with her mother. They'd never had the conversation about sex and doing so now felt awkward.

"Here, take this?" Constance instructed; passing Lynn the open pack containing the pill and a bottle of water. Constance's tranquil approach had transitioned into mother mode. She had an obligation to protect her daughter's future and she was beginning by eliminating any chance of her being pregnant. As embarrassing it was for Lynn, she hadn't taken precaution to protect herself the first time she and Drew were intimate. It was Lynn's belief that Drew's withdraw method in the shower was effective but to be safe she followed her mother's instructions. Expecting Constance to discipline her, Lynn prepared for the worst but instead of being chastised, Constance embraced her. She gave Lynn the boost of confidence she wasn't expecting to receive. It was a far different outcome than what she was expecting but Lynn welcomed her mother's soft approach.

Pressed for time, Lynn searched through Drew's luggage to locate his medals and the watch she gave him. Once doing so, she placed the items in her bag for keepsake. She wasn't sure if he would make bail or if his personal belongings would be there when he came for them, so she took what she felt was valuable.

"What are you doing? Come on, we have to get a move on it before your father leaves us," Constance warned.

Lynn and her mother returned to the front desk to check out. They brought Drew's bags and ask that they be stored until he returned to retrieve them. It was the least Constance could do for the man she believed was too toxic to be with her daughter. Constance and Lynn returned to the car way past the time prearranged by Harry but their return was early enough to make it to the airport without having to rush. It was time to leave Oregon behind, along with the bad memories that came with it.

While on their way to the airport, Harry understood how paramount it was to infringe upon his daughter's relationship with Drew before it became too late. Lynn was vulnerable which could lead to another mental breakdown. It was time to intervene before things got out of hand but before doing so, he first had to discuss it with his wife.

Boarding the plane, Lynn quietly sandwiched herself between her parents and reclined in her seat. She could finally sleep without having to worry about being violated in some way. Lynn slept in her mother's arms for most of the flight without getting as much as a stare from her father. Harry refused to look in her direction or share a civil conversation with her. He was so disappointed in Lynn; he nearly cried. He knew he'd raised her better than she was acting and it was heartbreaking to know she could do something against their will.

The flight landed at BWI Airport late in the night after a short layover in Dallas. Harry continued his silence while still refusing to engage in conversation with his daughter. Once home, Lynn ran upstairs to her room. She closed and locked the door behind her to have time alone. It was humiliating to know she had tarnished the Boldmont name yet again but this time by being arrested. She came up to her room because she didn't want to have to hear her parents bitch about how disappointed they were with her; at least until she learned the state of Drew's health. In spite of the likelihood of being forbidden from seeing Drew again, Lynn continued to plan her future. She was prepared to fly out to Vegas to get married once Drew healed from his injuries. Though it was late, Lynn made the decision to call Nancy to inquire about Drew's health. To her surprise, Nancy was very cordial and updated her on Drew's progress. Thank God, he was going to make a full recovery. Nancy stated, Drew was released on bond and once he was released from the hospital, they were flying home. It was great news to hear, so much so, Lynn began planning their wedding. She was hoping to return to campus no later than this upcoming Wednesday. She wasn't sure when Drew would return but assumed it was the following week. If everything turns out the way she expected, they will become man and wife no later than the weekend following Drew's return.

Chapter: 23

Drew remained in the hospital for two additional days, before being released in the custody of his mother. He returned home long enough to recover and against his mother's advice, he returned to WFU to complete the final week of college. He had a lot to catch up on but believed he could do so. Drew remained optimistic that the Whiteman-Fitzgerald University's community wouldn't pre-judge him for what occurred in Oregon but he soon learned how wrong he was. He'd been portrayed negatively by the media, which had poisoned the minds of many against him. Drew returned to mixed reactions among the community with most being negative. He never dreamed the community he loved would turn a blind eye to him. The reception he received was hurtful. He was ridiculed for the allegation of domestic violence and violence against the police. In the minds of many, Drew hadn't been the victim of police brutality as he proclaimed but an offender who had beaten and mauled his girlfriend, before attacking the police officers who were there to protect and serve. Under no circumstances did the town want Drew to represent their community or the university in the upcoming World Championships. He wasn't the role model they once believed and some went as far as applying pressure to university officials for his immediate expulsion.

After days of campaigning, enough support had been generated for the university to go forward with having Drew expelled. For Drew, it was the beginning of his fall from grace. The University's premature dismissal of him was not only wrong, it was another slap in Drew's face. In their defense, the university couldn't risk losing millions of dollars in donations from boosters and private donors. Although it was a difficult decision because Drew hadn't been found guilty, and was a brilliant student, the board unanimously agreed to rescind the remainder of his scholarship and officially expel him from school.

Drew was in his morning class when he was approached by five university police officers to escort him off campus. Not wanting to make a scene, Drew complied with the officer's commands and left class without incident. He was then escorted off campus and officially given a letter, banning him from returning to campus without written permission. The letter was a mere formality the university had turned their backs on him. Being forbidden meant Drew wouldn't be allowed to finish the final week of the summer session to graduate. Now with an uncertain future, Drew returned to his apartment to gather his thoughts.

He could consult a lawyer to fight his expulsion but doing so would be a waste. The university had the upper hand and Drew hadn't a leg to stand on. You see, Drew fell under the student standard of conduct rule which stated; as long as he was a part of the University or representing it in some compacity, he had a duty to conduct himself professionally at all times. Drew unfortunately hadn't done that, leaving his future to hinder upon his upcoming verdict. Until then, Drew could only hunker down and wait.

Lost, Drew reached out for his mother to share the somber news. He was nearly in tears when they spoke but tried to remain strong. Nancy continued to be the rock he needed. She wasn't one to shy away from her children; she was great at listening before giving advice. Once listening, Nancy suggested Drew return home. She told him, now wasn't the time to fight, he needed to regroup and create a strategy. As Nancy put it, the truth was going to be revealed but advised Drew, it may take some time. She believed once the truth was revealed, he and Lynn were going to be exonerated but first, he had to maintain a clear head and not bring trouble to himself. Taking his mother's advice, Drew packed some of his belongings and left the University for home. He used his drive home to reflect on his future and what he was going to do with the rest of his life. Everything he'd worked for had vanished before his eyes and reclaiming it was going to be an uphill battle. It was fair to say, after receiving the news he was going to be disqualified from the US Track Team, Drew's career as a professional track and field athlete was over before it even began. He had no time to think about his problems with the US Track and Field Team, his freedom was more important.

Drew returned home to a hero's reception that consisted of only his mother, sister and Karyme. It wasn't the reception he wanted from his university's community but it was a reception nonetheless.

Without question, Drew's family was his rock and without them, surviving his ordeal would be impossible. The family wanted to show support and did so by showing Drew how proud they were of him and what he accomplished. They gave him the time he needed to unwind before gathering around the table to talk. Like a well-oiled machine, the trio brainstormed a strategy that would place Drew back at the top. Life as Drew knew it may have temporarily changed for the moment but hopefully it wouldn't stay this way for long.

Chapter: 24

Along with the rest of the nation, Lynn learned of Drew's dismissal from the US World Track and Field Team, as well as from the university, by listening to the radio. She was stunned by the swift action taken against Drew and wished she could be there to support him but unfortunately for Lynn, her parents had intervened and were now dictating her life the way they wanted it to go. They'd taken total control of her and were making decisions for her whether she wanted them to or not. Lynn was forced to withdraw from school. Not only that, she was forced to turn over the keys to her car, her credit cards, her cell phone, her apple watch, and most disturbing, her bank account was frozen. What followed was the most damning, Lynn was forced to call Drew to sever all ties with him. Lynn resisted at first but after being threatened by being removed as her father's successor to run Boldmont Enterprises, Lynn relented and did exactly what she was ordered to do. It was a decision she was totally against but to win back her father's trust, she felt she had no other choice.

To keep Lynn on schedule to graduate, her parents suggested she take online classes instead of returning to school. It was their way of keeping her from Drew or anyone else that could bring confusion into her life. In reality, online classes were what Lynn wanted. She didn't want to have to return to college without Drew being there. Taking online classes meant, Lynn could continue training at the office while studying for her degree. It should have been a slam-dunk situation but Lynn's love for Drew got in the way of her plans.

As the days passed, Lynn fell into a depression. The fact that she was being trained by her father to take over the multi-million-dollar company he built from his garage, should have been enough for her to forget about Drew but Lynn couldn't. She loved Drew too much to pick up and go on with her life without him. To cope with his absence, Lynn increased the dosage of her medication to help her sleep but even that didn't work. Building a new life without Drew was more than Lynn could handle and though she fought her urges to contact Drew, she kept her word not to. Harry and Constance noticed a change in Lynn after forcing her to end her relationship with Drew. For Constance, it was heartbreaking having to see Lynn struggling to live without Drew but Constance and Harry knew it was for the best. Constance wanted to do something to help Lynn but was uncertain as to what to do.

Lynn was hurting and there were warning telling Constance Lynn was about to do something unconscionable. Constance recognized Lynn had lost interest in hanging out with her friends and family. After work, she drove straight home, complained about being tired and go to her room for the night. Because of her lack of an appetite, Lynn's weight began to suffer. Lynn was showing signs of relapsing into another mental health crisis. Concerned, Constance approached Harry with her observations, and suggested they restore Lynn's privileges but Harry declined to loosen the grip he had on Lynn. He did, however, came up with his theory of how to help Lynn, and it included allowing her to resume her relationship with Drew. In order for Lynn to get back the life she enjoyed, she had to self-admit herself into the Serenity Gardens for an evaluation. It was what Lynn wasn't certain it was something she would agree to.

Lynn's intervention began later that afternoon when the family left the office together. Lynn sensed something was about to happen because her father had never ridden to work with them but suggested they should on this peculiar morning. The man lived at the office and often stayed late into the evening hours before coming home. Recognizing this, Lynn felt something was coming down the pike, she just didn't know what. Harry devoted the entire day to Lynn, including her into meetings as well as his private conversations with clients. Her father was personally training her, instead of his vice president but what was so bizarre about the day was once 3:00 arrived, they all left the office without bringing any of their work home. Yes, something was about to blast off, Lynn just didn't know what. Their drive home went smoothly; her parents were in great spirits and even poked fun at each other. Her father told the story of how he met her mother for the millionth time. It was a romantic story, to say the least, but each time her dad told the story, there was a reason behind it and today was no different. It wasn't until they reached home that her father admitted his reason for coming home early. He knew Lynn was going straight to her room for the night and wanted to talk to her before she did. They escorted Lynn into the parlor where they had her to sit. Constance was the first to speak. Her conversation was short but powerful.

Constance began by saying, she and Harry agreed, her punishment was too harsh and they were considering reinstating her privileges, including her prized 66 GTO convertible. Lynn was more than ecstatic but wondered if her parents were including Drew as a part of the deal.

Now, it was Harry's time to speak. He opened by informing Lynn of his evaluation of her on her job performance. Harry didn't hold back any criticism when informing Lynn of her shortcomings and what she needed to improve on. However, her overall evaluation was excellent. Harry explained he needed her attention to be only on the company because he was considering promoting her to Chief Administrative Officer of Boldmont Enterprises. It was a position Lynn hadn't considered being appointed so early in her career but was willing to embrace it. What followed nearly blow Lynn's head off her shoulders. Her father gave his approval for her to resume her relationship with Drew. The news nearly caused Lynn to jump on the coffee table and do the jig but as expected, his approval came with a catch. In order to resume her relationship with Drew, Lynn had to agree to self-admit herself into Serenity Gardens. As Harry would explain, he didn't believe Lynn's mind was strong enough to take charge of a multi-million-dollar company, along with a serious relationship simultaneously. He wanted her to have a sound mind, as well as being tough enough to run Boldmont Enterprises without a hitch. He stressed the importance of Lynn getting the early help she needed because of his retirement plans. Within two years Harry was planning to retire. Lynn was overwhelmed at the thought of being once step closer to running the company but having the man she loved more by her side was more than she could have ever hope for. The only foreseen problem was the idea of having to self-admit herself into a mental hospital. Lynn didn't know how long her so-called evaluation would last but was well aware of having the right to leave (AMA) Against Medical Advice if the time expanded beyond the summer. It was a decision Lynn wanted to sleep on before rendering her decision.

The intervention went about as well as expected; so much so, that Lynn ate dinner with her parents for the first time in weeks. Having Lynn to join them for dinner was an encouraging sign but Harry couldn't say for certain if Lynn would agree to their terms. Harry expressed his desire that Lynn wait to contact Drew. It was an idea Lynn was in agreement with. There was no way she was going to contact Drew to tell him, she could be with him once returning from an insane asylum. No, Lynn was willing to wait until this bullshit was over. She was aware of what her parents were doing, the problem was she didn't have an answer for solving it.

Once their intervention was completed, Constance and Harry felt confident Lynn would accept their proposal but couldn't say for certain.

Sure, it was a juvenile way of controlling Lynn and though it was an illogical request, Lynn was left feeling it was in her best interest to take advantage of it. Lynn wasn't naïve about what her parent's intentions were and knew it was their way of controlling her to keep her on a short enough leash from Drew. Whether it was worth it remains to be seen but it wasn't enough to stop Lynn from considering it. Lynn wanted to think about it overnight and render her decision over lunch tomorrow afternoon.

As planned, Lynn left her office and took the short walk across the hall to her father's office. Harry immediately informed her, Constance wouldn't be joining them because of an unexpected problem came up in accounting minutes ago. Lynn had gotten her wish; she didn't want her mother to join them because she wanted to spend some quality time with her father alone. Since her debacle in Eugene, Lynn and her father hadn't spent any time together outside of work but Lynn was hoping today would be a start of a new beginning with her father.

Pressed for time, Lynn and her father walked downtown to have lunch at a local delicatessen; rather than have lunch at one of the fancy restaurants. They shared a chicken salad sandwich and a pickle while sitting at an outside table. For Harry, it was hard to believe his baby girl had grown up so quickly before his eyes. His beautiful little angel with ponytails was now a gorgeous young lady who was still the apple of his eye.

It's true that Lynn had made a few hiccups on her way to adulthood but her mistakes only reminded him of mistakes he'd made at her age. Harry understood there were going to be bumps in the road for Lynn and as her father, it was his responsibility to be there, not only for Lynn but for Ashley. As an adult, Lynn needed to learn how to solve her problems without having to involve him or Constance, and for that reason, Harry strongly believed, Lynn needed help, other than what he could provide for her. Yes, he could protect her but Lynn needed to be stronger mentally, and to get the help she so deservingly needed, she had to self-admit herself into Serenity Gardens. Still, the decision was Lynn's to make and Harry prayed she chose the right decision. Lynn spent most of the night thinking about how she could best serve not only herself but her family. She realized she needed a clear her head before assuming her rightful position at her father's company. Not only did Lynn want to resume her relationship with Drew, but she wanted to have a strong and sound mind to run the company effectively.

140

It was because of those reasons Lynn announced to her father, she'd decided to self-admit herself into the hospital to seek help. Though pleased with Lynn's decision, it wasn't a moment to jump for joy. His baby girl was returning to a mental institution to seek help. By checking into Serenity Gardens, Lynn was giving up her freedom for the remainder of the summer months. Yes, it was only a temporary separation from Drew but hopefully, it was enough time to give her the time she needed to break free of the hold Drew had on her.

Looking at his watch, Harry realized he was running late for a meeting. For having to abruptly leave, Harry kissed Lynn on her forehead before removing his wallet. From his wallet, Harry removed his credit card and placed it in Lynn's hands. He wanted her to get the things she needed for her stay in the hospital. With the credit card, Harry gave Lynn the remainder of the day off to get her affairs in order. He was happy with her decision and knew it was the best decision to make. It was Lynn's first step towards her future and Harry knew it was the right step.

Kissing her father goodbye, Lynn remained downtown. She immediately began shopping at some of her favorite boutiques. Like most women, Lynn shared a passion for purses and wanted to add another to her collection. Entering a small boutique located on a corner street, Lynn entered and began browsing. She hadn't been in the store more than a minute, when she felt the presence of being watched, Lynn quickly turned to face who was following her and was floored by who it was. The shock of seeing Mia standing only a few steps behind her, nearly caused Lynn knees to buckle. Lynn instantly put space between them and was standing at arm's length away. Seeing Mia brought back disturbing memories she wanted to bury.

"Hi Lynn, I thought that was you?" Mia said.

Lynn stood speechless; she could only stare after being shocked by seeing her ex-best friend. She hadn't seen Mia since dropping the charges against her but swore if she had she would get her revenge.

"It's been a long time," Lynn replied.

"Yeah, it has. It's beautiful, isn't it? It's the purse I was going to buy once I get paid." Mia said.

Taking a deep breath, Lynn acknowledged Mia, by giving her a fake smile. Lynn's first instinct was to shine the floor with Mia but knew she couldn't afford to be arrested again. Lynn was curious to know why Mia chose to deceive her after being her best friend since grade school. It was a question only Mia could answer and to get the answers she wanted; Lynn needed to discuss it more in-depth with her. Sensing Lynn was uncomfortable in her presence, Mia took heed to her feelings, believing it was time to leave.

"It was good seeing you again Lynn; and for what it's worth, I'm sorry," Mia said before turning to walk away. It was hard having to see Mia again but Lynn wasn't ready to let her go; not yet, and not before knowing why she chose to sabotage their friendship while helping Marshall rape her.

"Hey Mia wait," Lynn asked; slightly touching Mia's arm to redirect her attention back to her. "Could I have a minute of your time?"

Unable to look Lynn in her eyes, Mia agreed to talk. It was obvious Mia was remorseful for the role she played in causing Lynn's mental meltdown. She was haunted by what she'd done and wanted to get it off her chest. Finally, after many sleepless nights, Mia had gotten the opportunity to face Lynn and not only to formally apologize to her but to clear her closet of why she chose to do what she did. Mia wanted to be fully exonerated for her part in Lynn's assault but to do so she had to stand up to face Lynn before asking for forgiveness.

"Sure, I have a few minutes. Donna, could you hold it down, while I take a quick break," Mia asked her fellow worker. The co-worker nodded her head yes. Mia led Lynn quietly behind the counter and down a narrow hallway that led to a storage room where her small office was. Mia invited Lynn to sit as she prepared herself to answer any and all questions Lynn had. By agreeing to talk, Mia was giving Lynn the key to opening Pandora's Box. At first, Mia hesitated, she wanted to keep the entire incident buried, just as Lynn had but quickly relented after believing Lynn had a right to know why she was assaulted. Before answering Lynn's questions, Mia felt the need to apologize for the hell she'd put her through and after doing so, she went forward with the role she played in the attack. Mia admitted their intention wasn't to harm Lynn but to introduce her to something they believed, she wanted and was ready for. Unfortunately, their plan spiraled out of control which led to Lynn to being sexually assaulted.

142

Mia exploded into tears, pleading for forgiveness and though Mia's sincerity left Lynn feeling the pain she had been carrying inside, it hadn't changed the fact to what Mia had done to her nor had it changed her mind about forgiving Mia.

Lynn watched as Mia's tears fell from her cheeks. She even held back her own, especially during Mia's confession about the love and respect she had for her. Mia spoke about missing their friendship and how much it meant to have Lynn as a best friend. Mia also confessed to being bi-sexual and had fantasized for years about being with her. Mia stated; it wasn't until she began sleeping with Marshall that she allowed her fantasy to take control of her. Mia admitted while in bed one night with Marshall, the discussion of having a threesome came up and she fell all in with the idea. The plan was to spike her drink with the drug GHB doing dinner to loosen her up, and following that they were going to introduce her to their world. Mia was unequivocal in her explanation that she and Marshall never planned to rape her but only to seduce her into participating but she accidently poured too much of the drug into her tea, causing her to drift in and out of consciousness. Now knowing the truth, Lynn didn't know whether to smash Mia's face with the large stapler on her desk or to simply walk out. Mia was supposed to have been her best friend, it was her job to protect her from harm but instead of doing so, she participated in Marshall's devious plan to live out one of his fantasies.

At the completion of Mia's heart wrenching confession, she again asked for forgiveness but it was something Lynn wasn't prepared to do but relayed she would consider it. Lynn did however, thank Mia for her honesty and before leaving, Lynn embraced Mia, knowing she finally gotten the truth as to what happened and why. Lynn hadn't self-consciously wanted to engage in a threesome nor was she attractive to the idea. For months, she'd believed she was at fault for what happened to her but thanks to Mia, Lynn now knew the truth. It was time to let go of the self-hate and anger that consumed he life. She was grateful for having seen Mia and finally learning the truth but she wasn't ready to forgive her for what she did to her.

Lynn spent the remainder of the evening shopping for all she thought she would been needing doing her stay at Serenity Gardens. Her plans were only to stay two to three weeks believing this would be the last time she was going to ever have to visit a mental hospital again.

Chapter: 25

Mason was excited over the lavish dinner he had prepared for the night. The steaks were in the oven at a low temperature and he was ready to pick up Gloria. Tonight, was going to be the night of all nights and if everything went accordingly, it was guaranteed that Mason was going to be the talk of the town. For this special occasion, Mason wished he could have taken Gloria somewhere special to celebrate but his bank account had taken a direct hit from overindulging in hotel rentals and dining at upscale restaurants. He'd blown his entire savings to impress Gloria and now he was flat broke. From the sound of Gloria's voice, she was expecting more than a romantic dinner. She was expecting Mason to take her to Richmond to dine at the Lemaire, as well as spend the night at the Jefferson. The mere fact that he barely had enough money to cover the cost of gas to get there was an indication that tonight could be a bust. Though broke, Mason had a plan and that plan was to prove his undying love and his willingness to be the man Gloria wanted him to be. In an effort to show a more creative side while hiding his financial situation, Mason's plans were to present a more positive and romantic image of himself. He was hoping Gloria would see that he was as qualified and mature as any other man. Mason wasn't a fool by no means, he was fully aware of Gloria's expectations of him but his willingness to oblige her wishes was unparallel. It was his desire to become Gloria's husband and if he could somehow accomplish it, it would be a dream come true. Until Gloria came into his life, Mason had never considered marriage. He was immature and his immature ways led him to sleep with an unknown number of women. It was a feat he was proud of and often bragged about it. But after Gloria entered his life, things changed. He understood the life he led wasn't as glamorous as first believed nor was it exciting anymore. Gloria had given him a different perspective on life. She had shown him how to love and what it meant to be loved. Without a doubt, Mason believed the time had come to make Gloria his wife.

Reaching inside his front jacket pocket, Mason removed his grandmother's ring. He wished he could afford a more expensive one; because it was what Gloria would want but the meaning behind it was far greater than its value. Unlike Drew, Mason couldn't afford to give the lavish gifts Gloria was accustomed to receiving but when it came to loving her, there was no comparison. Staring at his ring, Mason imagined what his grandmother must have felt when his grandfather first proposed to her. Her legs must have buckled after being overwhelmed by becoming his wife.

It was a feeling he was hoping Gloria would feel when he falls to one knee and ask her to marry him. To set the mood, Mason got out his collection of romantic CDs' and began playing them. He lit the scented candles throughout the house to relax the mood. Lastly, he brought out his mother's best China to celebrate the evening. Seeing that everything was in place, Mason was ready to begin their romantic evening. All he needed was to have Gloria setting at the table and his night would be complete. Checking the time, Mason realized he was running behind schedule. He grabbed his keys he left the house enroute to pick up his date for the night. He arrived at Gloria's house minutes later but before getting out his car, he paused. Mason was unsure what his presence would bring and after saying a quick prayer, he made his way to the front door. Ringing the doorbell, Mason waited nervously. Knowing both Pistol and Mattie were home, he was extremely nervous, but as a man, this was something he had to do. The chances of Pistol accepting him as Gloria's equal were highly unlikely but for Gloria's sake, he was going to at least try to be sociable. Like her father, Gloria's little sister Kelly, hated the ground Mason walked on. She too was a Drew Harrison fan and made no bones about being one, but lucky for Mason, Gloria's mother had long accepted the idea of them being together. In a lot of ways, Mason was hoping to get the opportunity to engage in conversation with the family.

He wanted the chance they'd given Drew, and if they did, without a doubt, they would love him, just as Gloria has. Realistically, Mason knew he was fooling himself. Pistol and Kelley would never accept him. They hated the ground he walked on but it wasn't going to dampen his soul. Regardless of how they felt about him, he wasn't going to stop loving Gloria. Knocking a second time, Mason heard footsteps approaching the door. His heartbeat could be seen beating outside of his shirt, but he had to keep his cool. There was no way he was going to allow anyone to see him sweat, especially Pistol. Hearing the footsteps coming closer, Mason took two deep breaths before the door opened, and as the door opened, he was relieved it was only Gloria's younger sister, Kelley.

Kelley was sixteen years old and by looking at her, you wouldn't know it; she was built like her older sister but Kelley had a pissy attitude, especially when it came to him. Blocking the doorway, Kelley stared Mason up and down with a look of disgust on her face.

"Oh, it's you," Kelley responded. "Why are you here?"

145

"What do you think I'm here for?" Mason answered.

Without a further response, Mason brushed past Kelley and began making his way down the hallway. He wasn't in the mood to take any shit from a little spoiled brat, who was in need of an old fashion country ass whipping. Mason followed the narrow hallway that led to the family room and as he entered the room, he saw Pistol sitting with his face buried in the newspaper. As a show of respect, Mason greeted him.

"Good evening," Mason said.

Without saying a word, Pistol lowered his newspaper and gave Mason a mean look, before covering his face again.

"Stupid motherfucker." Mason thought to himself while sitting on the couch by the open door. Any other time, Mason would have been troubled by Pistol's refusal to acknowledge his presence but he found it funny seeing Pistol with a newspaper up to his face. Everybody who knew him knew damn well, he couldn't read a single word printed on the paper and to top that, the section he was supposedly reading was upside down. To get even, Mason contemplated informing Pistol that he was reading the paper upside down but opted not to. It didn't matter how Pistol felt about him, he was going to marry Gloria, whether Pistol wanted him to or not. The best news about it was the mere fact that Pistol, Kelley, or that punk-ass Drew could do about it. Drew may have been Pistol's choice for Gloria but within a few months, it was going to be him calling Pistol "Dad," not Drew.

Mason sat for a few minutes before deciding to try once more to break the ice with Pistol. He knew how much Pistol loved attending baseball games and made an attempt to bait him into a conversation.

"You think the Tigers are going to win it all this year?" Mason asked.

"I don't know, they might," Pistol answered with the paper still covering his face.

"At least the simple bastard had the decency to respond to me this time. "Mason thought to himself. Mason quit talking after that. He had given it his best but Pistol avoided him as if he was a homeless man begging for money. It wasn't long before Gloria entered the room and it wasn't a surprise that she entered in a grand fashion. The sight of her nearly took Mason's breath, and as he stood to greet her.

Mason felt himself wanting to tell Gloria how much he loved her. Gloria was by far the most beautiful woman he'd ever seen, and to think she was his was a feeling to behold. As Gloria approached Mason, he felt the urge to cry. He couldn't believe that Gloria could love someone like him. Throughout his life, Mason had always been the underdog but finally, the underdog had gotten the upper hand and accomplished the impossible. Wiping the tear beginning to format in his eye, Mason reached out to embrace Gloria. Holding Gloria in his arms, Mason could smell her sweet perfume emanating from her body. It reminded him of the first time he first kissed her. It was a night in which he would never forget and he prayed tonight would fare just as well. Releasing his embrace, Mason attempted to kiss Gloria but was spurned away. Embarrassed, Mason convinced himself Gloria's rejection was only because she didn't want him to smear the ruby red lipstick she was wearing. Like always, when it came to Gloria, Mason had an excuse to justify the means and tonight was no exception.

Saying his goodbye to the family, Mason followed Gloria from the house to his car. Mimicking what he felt Drew would do, Mason gentlemanly opened the car door for Gloria and waited until she was comfortably sitting before closing her door. He looked to see if anyone was looking and saw that Mattie was standing at the front door.

Mason smiled to himself as he walked around the rear of his car to get in. Gloria's family was seeing him for the first time in a different light. He was showing them a part of him they never knew existed. More than anything Mason wanted to impress Gloria's parents and did so by showing he could be as romantic as Drew. Before getting into his car, Mason jokingly promised Mattie to have Gloria home before midnight. Now, more than ever, Mason was convinced he had a chance to win over the family; well, at least he'd gained favor with Mattie.

Leaving the house, Gloria was excited about the night and immediately began asking questions pertaining to where they were going. Her hopes were that Mason was taking her to the Lemaire for dinner and the way he was dressed gave her every indication he was. Turning on the main road, Gloria's anticipation was getting the best of her. She was dying to know where they were dining but Mason was refusing to give her any hints. Gloria had bragged to her friends about tonight and had even gone out on a limb to predict where she thought they were going.

147

It was just a matter of time before she would know for sure but Mason wasn't making it easy for her.

"Baby, where you taking me tonight?" Gloria asked inquisitively.

"It's a surprise," Mason responded.

"I hope it's the Lemaire? I've heard so much about it. My co-workers have said the food is so delicious and we will enjoy the ambiance of it. That bitch Missy Thompson and her husband went last week. She came back bragging about how much money they spent and how they stayed the night at the Jefferson. Can we spend the night at the Jefferson?" Gloria asked. Gloria was seeing a side of Mason she didn't know existed. He was more attentive and his romantic side had overshadowed his shortcomings. He was beginning to rival Drew when it came to winning her affection and he had done so by showing how much he loved her. Mason had no problem going out on a limb when it came to making her happy. Drew, on the other hand, stuck to basics and often declined to take the extra steps to make her happy. But with Mason, things were different, Mason was willing to do whatever it took to make her happy and didn't mind spending his last penny to do so. Tonight, things were no different, Mason was doing it again, he was showing his romantic side and Gloria was enjoying every second of it. Mason had taken another giant leap to make Gloria happy and his efforts were seemingly working. The look on Gloria's face was priceless, she appreciated everything Mason was doing for her. It was only days ago that she contemplated breaking things off with him but after Drew wanted nothing to do with her, she had the good sense to stay with the man that loved her unconditionally.

Driving in circles, Mason droved for more than ten minutes before Gloria realized her surprise drive to Richmond was a sham. They weren't going to be dining at the Lemaire, nor were they spending the night at the Jefferson. Mason's so-called surprise was nothing but a bunch of lies, and it not only pissed her off. Gloria was left her debating if she should demand that he take her home rather than go along with his bullshit game. She had gotten dolled up for nothing; Mason was only intending to take her to Funky Broadway's juke joint. Gloria was overly pissed because of how Mason had played her. Frankly, she was getting tired of being used and would rather spend time by herself than be used and abused, like some whore.

Why on God's green earth would that stupid son-of-a-bitch think she would want to go to a freaking juke joint dressed the way she was? Seeing Gloria's disappointment, Mason knew he needed to do something. If tonight was going to go as planned, he needed to make a move asap. Mason assured Gloria, he had something special planned for the night and that he needed her to be opened minded. Having an open mind wasn't something Gloria was accustomed to doing but she was going to give it her best shot. She was banking on the fact that Mason had never disappointed her before and wanted to believe he had something special in store for her. Sure, he wasn't taking her to an upscale restaurant or spending the night at a five-star hotel but Gloria felt confident enough to know, Mason had done his best to plan something special.

Circling the neighborhood, a second time, Mason pulled into his driveway. His tactics caused Gloria's suspicions to resurface and though she wasn't sure what the hell Mason was planning, she was sure it hadn't involved dining. Gloria was starving and would have been happier eating at the Golden Corral but instead of having something of dinner, Mason was most likely going to give her a plate of cheese, olives, and pepperoni he'd made and will think it was enough to please her. It had only been two nights ago that he had decorated his bedroom to have a night of boring sex that was so disappointing, she'd nearly fallen asleep. Disenchanted by the thought of what she believed was going to be another disastrous evening, Gloria tried hiding her emotions but Mason easily read her facial expression. What he hoped would be a success was starting off as a bust. Still, Mason went forward with his plans, and to make things more interesting, he asked Gloria to close her eyes. Doing so, Mason led her inside the house and set her at the dining room table. With her eyes closed, Gloria could smell the steaks simmering in the oven.

The smell alone was enough to cause her empty stomach to growl. Gloria only hoped the food taste was as good as it smelled and though she wasn't going to be eating at "The Lemaire", at least she was going to eating something. Gloria opened her eyes and noticed how well the house was decorated. She was impressed by Mason's effort to make the night a success but she was still disappointed about not dining in Richmond. Mason poured Gloria a glass of red wine and made a toast to a long-lasting life together. Gloria was uncertain as to how long their life together was going to be because Mason broke ass couldn't afford to give her the life she wanted to have. Still, she was going to try and enjoy the evening.

Looking around, Gloria tried finding something good in what Mason tried doing but couldn't. His decorations were that of a novice and though the food smelled good, it wasn't enough to give her any hope about how the night was going to end. Gloria struggled to differentiate her past relationship with Drew from her present relationship with Mason. The relationships were like night and day and the more Gloria tried accepting Mason for the man he was she couldn't omit the man she wanted him to be. Mason was far from being an intelligent man or an overly attractive one for that matter; but what made him special was the way he treated her. He gave his all to make her happy but he wasn't doing the job she needed him to do. There was times Gloria was too embarrassed to introduce him as her man, because Mason didn't have what it took to be the man she needed to associate with her friends. He couldn't relate to the issues her friends would talk about or what to say if he was asked a question. Still, Mason tried and out of obligation, she had to at least, give him a chance.

As the night progressed, Mason's romantic ways continued to confuse Gloria. He wasn't by any means Drew but he unknowingly was making an impact on her. Dinner was amazing and the wine accentuated it even more. Mason's transformation, transitioned Gloria from a melancholy mood, into a more exuberant one. Seeing Gloria's mood change, Mason moved into position to take advantage of the moment. He began by informing her about his job promotion. His new position afforded him the opportunity to spoil her even more. Mason even discussed the possibility of moving out of his mother's house and he asked if Gloria would move in with him. Now, having Gloria's attention, Mason built up the nerves to fall to one knee. His hands shook as he nervously reached inside his blazer's pocket and removed the box containing his grandmother's engagement ring.

"Gloria, I've been in love with you since the first day I laid eyes on you. When we got together, it was like a dream come true and I want this dream to continue. So, with that being said, Gloria, will you marry me?" Mason asked.

Shocked by Mason's proposal, Gloria nearly spat out the wine she was drinking but managed to swallow it before embarrassing herself and humiliating Mason. Holding his breath, Mason waited nervously for Gloria's decision. He explained how his grandfather worked and saved for three years to buy his grandmother the ring because he wanted so desperately for her to be his wife.

Mason's story may have been romantic but Gloria couldn't see herself wearing a seventy-year-old ring with a diamond too small to see with the naked eye. Mason's sentiments were touching but his ring was nothing she wanted to wear.

"Damn," Gloria thought to herself after realizing she was stuck in the mud and only had Mason to pull, her out. She had no idea how she going to tell Mason she didn't want to marry him. Like always, Mason found a way to screw up her plans.

Gloria couldn't deny she enjoyed spending time with Mason but not enough to want to marry him. Now that her chances with Drew was over, Gloria was considering hooking up with one of the young interns at the hospital or one of the old geezers who constantly asked her to marry them, though they were days away from croaking. If the truth be told, Gloria was only holding on to Mason, until some better came along. She didn't want a broke ass man; she wanted a man that could give her the world.

"Think Gloria, think, got dammit," Gloria said to herself as she searched for the right words to say. Gloria needed to think of something and do so fast because Mason was looking mighty silly rocking back and forth on one knee. There was no way Gloria could tell Mason she didn't want to marry him because she was aware of his temper and knew what he was capable of doing to her. Gloria's only choice was to accept Mason's ring, while pretending to be ecstatic about marrying him. For Gloria, accepting Mason's proposal wasn't the worst thing she could do because she could always delay the proceedings. What was most disheartening was the idea of having to wear his grandmother's ring in the presence of her friends and co-workers. The ring was too embarrassing to wear. For one, the diamond was too small for the naked eye to see and secondly, it was no inconceivable way she could be caught dead wearing something so generic. Still, she couldn't disappoint the man that had given her everything. Without saying a single word, Gloria lifted her hand from her lap and spread her fingers for

Mason to place his ring on it. As Mason did, chills raced through her body. Gloria asked God help her because she was saying yes when she wanted to say no. Lord knows, Gloria wanted to tell Mason to take his grandmother's cheap ass cracker jack ring and go fuck himself with it, but instead, she accepted his ring without saying a single word.

Mason gently kissed Gloria on her lips while promising her, she wouldn't regret her decision to marry him, but Gloria already had. Mason also made a promise to give her everything her heart desire and then some but that too was bullshit. Mason was living a pipe dream, a dream that could never come true. Truth be told, Mason's only recognition was the financial support he provided her doing college and nothing more. She couldn't deny he hadn't been there for her when she needed him because she had, and she appreciated his generosity. However, his lack of goals in life was a turn off to her. The fact that he was uneducated and too damn dumb to compile a future was proof enough that he wasn't the man for her.

Chapter: 26

Drew arrived at the office early than usual. It was the first time in months he'd arrived before Karyme and in a way, he needed time to reflect upon his future. He debated whether he had a desire to run the company and was considering stepping away. Karyme knew the company like the back of her hand and quietly kept; she was more effective running it than he. Drew's only reason for not leaving was because of the sacrifice his father made to ensure a legacy was left for them to carry on. His father dedicated his life to building Hillcrest Farms and opted not to refinance it to get the chemotherapy he needed to help prolonged his life. He knew he was going to die but he refused to be selfish and give up everything he wanted to leave his family. The mere fact that he heroically sacrificed his life for his family was more than enough to warrant Drew to continue fighting for the legacy his father worked to preserve. Like his father, Drew was on the verge of seeing the success of his hard work, only to have it taken away from him before achieving it. But unlike his father, Drew had a second chance at life, he still could get his degree, just not from WFU. Thinking of what his father would have done if placed in his situation, Drew revisited the incident in his mind. Having to see Lynn in distress while being manhandled by the overly aggressive police officer led Drew to believe his father would have done the exact same thing. Drew understood what he did was wrong, however, he knew if he hadn't interfered with the officer's aggressive behavior toward Lynn, she may not be living today. As a man, he chose to do what he felt was right, even though his decision may cause him to be sentenced to jail time.

Karyme arrived at the office an hour later. She was surprised to see Drew was there so early and she welcomed him with a friendly embrace. Wearing three-inch heels, Karyme still found it difficult to lock her arms around Drew's neck. Her five feet three-inch body was no match for his massive six feet four-inch frame. To accommodate her, Drew had to lift her in his arms but in doing so, he was captivated by the sweet scent of her hair shampoo. Closing his eyes, Drew became lost in the moment, temporarily forgetting his thoughts of Lynn. Karyme was the picture of beauty and holding her in his arms gave him the feeling of comfort he was in need of. It was a gratifying to be around someone who cared about him, especially after receiving a black eye to his spotless reputation. Sitting at his desk, Drew watched as Karyme filed the company's invoice hard copies. It was difficult having to concentrate on his work after seeing how beautiful his best friend was.

Drew wasn't sure if he was paying attention to Karyme because of his breakup with Lynn or if his feelings for Karyme were becoming stronger. One thing for sure, he knew Karyme would never desert him as did Lynn. Lynn's refusal to accept his calls weighed heavy on his heart and he was beginning to worry if he would ever talk to her again. Drew suspected Lynn's parents were the reason for their breakup but what he didn't expect was Lynn not even trying to find a way to contact him. Lynn was four months away from her twentieth birthday but you wouldn't have known it by the way her parents dictated her life. Her father knew it was Lynn's life-long dream to run the family business and he dangled the idea that if she walked the straight and narrow path he carved for her, the company would be hers to run. Drew had a decision to make, though premature, he knew he had to move on with his life. He couldn't afford to wait for a miracle to happen; his heart wouldn't allow it. Whether he wanted to or not, he had to go on.

As Interim-President, Karyme made an executive decision to close the office early to officially welcome Drew home. She surprised him with a basket of food that was delivered to the office before noon. Today, they were having lunch by the lake and it was because Karyme wanted to brighten Drew's spirits. After being told about Lynn's missing in action routine, Karyme knew Drew was down in the dumps and felt having lunch by the lake was the key to putting a smile on his face.

It was a perfect sunny afternoon with the temperatures in the high eighties. The late-summer breezes were blowing gently across the lake, setting the stage for a beautiful afternoon. For the first time in weeks, Drew smiled. It was nothing to brag about and chances was it was only temporary but Karyme had somehow managed to do what his mother and sister couldn't. Her kind gesture set the mood for an unexpected event that even caught her by surprise. Drew was ready to talk about what happened doing his trip to Oregon and what led to his injuries, and incarceration.

Drew held back nothing when telling his story. He had previously withheld details surrounding the excessive force he received from the city and university police departments because he didn't want his mother to know the trauma he sustained. As Drew told his story, Karyme got a lump in her throat. It was heartbreaking to know what Drew had gone through. Karyme cried along with Drew, as he explained how it felt being tased twice before getting the hell beat out of him.

154

She felt each blow Drew received and having to see the tears in Drew's eyes was more than enough for Karyme to reach and pull him in her arms. She wanted him to know, everything would be alright. As his best friend, Karyme promised to always be there for him no matter what the situation was. Mentally, Drew was a wreck, he'd lost his girlfriend, got kicked out of school and was released from the U.S. Track and Field Team. Drew's world may have been a disaster but thanks to Karyme, the afternoon had made things better, even though it was only temporary.

Drew and Karyme, spent the remainder of the afternoon together before deciding to return to the plant to make a final walk through the coolers to record the temperature gauges to the company's older milk coolers. In doing so, Drew found himself fixated on Karyme. She was as beautiful as he had ever seen her. Karyme wasn't wearing her hair in a ponytail anymore, nor was she wearing the loose-fitting clothes to hide the shape of her body. She was dressing like an executive would for a fortune 500 company and man, was she ever gorgeous. Drew now understood what his mother had been telling him for years. Karyme was gorgeous; she wasn't the same little girl who was self-conscious about her overbite, or her vampire teeth that protruded through her upper gums. Her overbite was corrected with braces and her vampire teeth had been removed. Gone were the pop bottle glasses she was often teased about as a teen. They'd been replaced by contacts giving her the look of the beauty queen she was. Karyme had transformed herself from an ugly duckling to the most beautiful swan ever but there was only one problem, Drew had deemed her as his sister and by doing so, she was untouchable.

At the completion of their inspection, the couple returned to the office to close out the day. Though the weekend was coming upon them, neither had plans. They dismissed the idea of reporting to the office the following morning for the exception of making a round in the warehouse to check the temperatures of the old coolers. Having no plans of his own for the night, Drew invited Karyme to dinner. His decision to ask Karyme came on a whim but he couldn't let her go after finding himself wanting to spend more time with her. It was a moment Karyme had dreamed of and jumped at the invitation. Leaving the office, Drew escorted Karyme to her car. Once there, they embraced and he thanked her again for showing him an unforgettable afternoon. Before releasing his embrace; Drew kissed Karyme's forehead and reminded her how much he was looking forward to their dinner date. Karyme smiled and as she did so, her eyes sparkled from the afternoon sun.

She too was looking forward to tonight and could barely wait for it to begin. Seeing Karyme leave, Drew couldn't ignore the butterflies floating inside of his stomach. It was a feeling he couldn't explain, yet it was a feeling he'd been missing. Karyme somehow had managed to help him relax and forget the problems he was facing. Shaking the cobwebs from his head, Drew smiled to himself before opening the door to his car. Reaching in his pocket for his car keys, he was quickly reminded, he'd left his car keys on his desk. Excited about tonight, Drew returned to his office to get his keys. Grabbing them from his desk, Drew turned to find Gloria standing unexpectedly standing in the doorway.

"Hello, lover," Gloria said as she made her way inside the office, closing the door behind her.

Gloria made her way over to Drew's desk to sit. She positioned herself provocatively and faced Drew, who had the good sense to go stand by the door. Dressed in a mini-skirt, Gloria intentionally revealed the black lace panties she was wearing, while facing Drew. Drew tried to look away but couldn't and his reluctance to do so gave Gloria the assurance she needed to push forward with her desire to seduce him. Drew's perturbation had him wanting to run for dear life but instead, he remained frozen in place. Seeing that Drew was potentially under her spell, Gloria spread her legs apart even wider. Now, that she'd gotten Drew's attention, it was time to reel him in. Realizing he was about to walk down another beaten path to an irresistible moment of sex; Drew didn't feel the need to fight his urges. He knew it was a battle he wasn't going to win and sadly, there wasn't a damn thing he could do to fight it.

It was going to happen whether he wanted it or not because it was what Gloria wanted and like Gloria always said; "Whatever Gloria wants, Gloria gets." Yes, Gloria was undoubtedly going to get what she wanted but not today. This evening, Drew had plans with Karyme and those plans consisted of dinner and a night out on the town and no one, not even sexy ass Gloria, was going to interfere with that.

"You driving your father's car?" Drew asked.

"No, I'm driving Mason's car?" Gloria answered.

"What! have you gone mad?" Drew disturbingly responded, knowing the consequences the both of them would face if Mason ever found out about what Gloria had done.

"Whoa, don't be such a wuss, Mason is at work. I'm going to pick him up at 5pm. Now, where were we?" Gloria asked, placing her arms around Drew's neck

"I'm not going down this road with you again," Drew said, removing Gloria's arms from around his neck.

"Are you going to be a pussy all your life? Where's your sense of adventure?" Gloria asked.

"Gloria, you need to leave," Drew said with authority.

"I see you back to lusting after the little "Wet Back," now that the "Rich Bitch" haven't been around in a while." Gloria said teasingly. She placed her arms back around Drew's neck and tried kissing him but Drew turned away. "Now come on and give me that fat dick of yours." Gloria said, kissing Drew on his neck. Whispering in Drew's ear, Gloria reminded him of the dangers he'll face if he slept with Karyme. "Word of advice, don't go raw dog in your little Mexican princess because if you do, I'm willing to bet the farm; you're going to have a house full of those little taco eating bastards to take care of."

"Gloria, get out my office." Drew demanded, while removing Gloria's arms from around his neck again.

Gloria's prejudicial comments caused Drew to quickly come to Karyme's defense. He wasn't going to allow Gloria to continually make negative comments towards Karyme in his presence. As Karyme's best friend, it was his responsibility to stand up and protect her honor.

"Touchy aren't we," Gloria teased as she rubbed Drew's chin. She kissed him gently on his lips and whispered. "Is that better?" Gloria was hoping it was enough to deter Drew from wanting to bite her head off and to test her theory, Gloria continued with her antics.

"Now enough talk about your little Taco, I want to talk about us." Gloria said, while blocking the office door, preventing Drew from leaving.

"I'm getting that dick before I leave here today," Gloria said.

Using an aggressive approached Gloria pushed Drew onto the office couch and began to wrestle with him.

She began kissing Drew and tried speeding up the process by kicking off her shoes. She knew Drew's weakness and began unbuckling his pants. Gloria knew what he wanted and she could barely wait to oblige him. Gloria's aggressive behavior turned Drew on but his obligation to Karyme was enough to force him to resist. Drew wasn't going to stand Karyme up, not for a woman he had chosen to put in his past.

"What's wrong baby? I know you want me." Gloria said; setting up on the couch.

Drew hesitated, he wanted Gloria but not in the manner she was expecting. It was time to tie up all loose ends but before doing so, Drew had to make sure he was clear about his relationship with her and where it was going.

For years, their relationship was the envy of many but as time passed, so had his feelings for Gloria. Drew was trying to move on and it was time Gloria done the same. But Gloria was refusing to do so, her persistence to have Drew in her life again had taken precedence over reality. In a simpler world, Drew would fall prey to her if she chose to strip down naked but surprisingly, her tactics didn't work this time around; Drew was refusing to take the bait. Having had enough, Drew grabbed hold of Gloria's arm and guided her gently to the front door. It was time he showed how serious he was.

"Gloria, I've told you for the last time, I don't want to be with you anymore. How simple can I say it," Drew admitted. He knew the news was going to be crushing but there was no other way to say it.

"What!" Gloria reacted shockingly. "But you're still in love with me. I know you are."

"No, I'm not, I'm not in love with you, not anymore," Drew explained.

"But we made love," Gloria replied.

"No, we had sex, I made love to Lynn, because I'm in love with her," Drew said convincingly.

"What the fuck." Gloria thought to herself, as she made the painful decision to get dressed. She couldn't believe that son-of-a-bitch had turned his back on her. Why did he not want her anymore? The "Rich Bitch" had wised up and left his stupid ass. What the hell could she do to get this man back?" Gloria thought to herself. "I don't understand you man, Lynn dumped you because she realized you're a stupid ass.

I was willing to give you another chance but you're too fucking stupid to take it. Awe, shit, it's the Wetback."

"Gloria, it's time for you to leave," Drew announced as he opened the door. Drew didn't deny Gloria's accusation but then again, it wasn't any of her business if she was correct.

Drew followed Gloria from the office downstairs to the ground floor without as much as a single word said between them. They both had a lot on their mind with Gloria faring more. It was hard for Gloria to fathom that Drew had chosen not to have any further affiliation with her. For years, she dominated him by pussy whipping him into doing what she wanted but whether it was his involvement with the "Rich Bitch" or his little Senorita, one or both of them had fucked things up for her.

Following Gloria to the parking lot, Drew felt a sense of relief knowing he had made the right decision to kick Gloria out of his office. By resisting Gloria, Drew had broken the spell she once held over him. It felt great being a free man and thank God, he could finally close the book on a woman who had so much negative influence on him.

Chapter: 27

The Harrison family, all gathered in their family room to watch the ABC News Special, detailing police racial profiling and excessive force. Renewed interest had generated across the nation after the news broke about Drew and Lynn's encounters with the Eugene and University Police Departments. As promised, an investigative reporter from KVAC 13 had delivered. Somehow, he had obtained copies of the police and hotel tapes and was broadcasting them across the nation. By doing so, it was changing the opinions of millions who chose to tuned to tonight's special. The man who allegedly assaulted four innocent police officers and two security guards who was only doing their jobs; was indeed a victim. Fortunately for Drew and Lynn, the footage clearly showed the actions the police took against them. The police lied in their reports, as well as the statements they released to the public. The tapes clearly showed Drew hadn't been the aggressor, nor was it clear that Lynn refused to be arrested. The tape showed Lynn being physically assaulted, doing her arrest. As for Drew, the tape showed him being brutally beaten and tased, after raising his hands in surrender.

He hadn't been a threat nor had it been warranted for him to receive repeated blows to his head and neck by the police who used departmental issued steal ASP batons to subdue him. After being tased countless times, Drew was restrained, beaten, and dragged like a wild animal across the floor as he was being mauled. It was shocking to see what Drew and Lynn had experienced and the nation was reacting to it. The allegations that Drew and Lynn were under the influence of drugs were false and the nation was seeing a firsthand account of the horrific experience the couple endured and was outraged by it. When interviewing one of the hotel security guards on their accounts of what happened; his version of what occurred didn't corresponded to what the police reported. The hotel security guards admitted, they hadn't been assaulted during the altercation and footage from the tapes substantiated it. Their story collaborated with Drew and Lynn's account of what happened, but what was most damaging was what the tapes showed. It was clear Lynn was being suffocated from her own blood after her face was slammed against the wall several times before Drew intervened. But before intervening, you could hear Drew screaming to the police for mercy; pleading for the officer to allow her to breathe.

It left a sickening feeling inside the stomachs of those who watched but more than that, it kicked off public perception of how the police covered up their shady dealings.

Once the public viewed the actual incident of what happened, they formed a more favorable opinion of Drew and Lynn. Drew's statue of sacrificing his health and well-being, elevated him to a heroic nature, while the integrity of the police departments was compromised by the officer's dirty tactics. An outcry seeking justice for Drew and Lynn had begun and plans to take it to the streets were in in place. Even those who were tuning in for the first time were outraged at the punishment the decorated track star and his girlfriend endured by the hands of the police. The story not only left the city of Eugene in turmoil, it educated the nation in what could happen to a black All-American boy and girl, who crossed paths with bad police officers.

Feeling the pressure from the nation's outcry, the state's prosecutor decided to drop all charges against Drew and Lynn, as well as; terminated the officers involved. The officers' behavior was not only unprofessional but violated the civil rights of Lynn and Drew. The police unprovoked beating of Drew, left him nearly unrecognizable, and hospitalized for nearly a week. Drew had lost everything he'd achieved. Not only had he lost the chance to obtain his Master's Degree after being suspended from school, he lost his spot on the US Track and Field Team. His integrity was challenged, after the town he'd worked so hard to unite had turned their backs to him. But finally, after weeks of waiting, Drew and Lynn were vindicated for the injustice they'd received at the hands of the police. Drew felt a great sense of relief knowing the truth had finally been revealed. The release of his medical records showed no signs of any drugs and alcohol in his system nor had his actions from the tapes lead anyone to believe he was under the influence. The truth of the matter was simple; Drew and Lynn were stereotyped because of the color of their skin and for that reason, they were perceived to be hostile and violent. The policemen's actions not only damaged Drew physically, it damaged him financially. Drew lost potential large sums of money on pending commercials, magazine advertisements, personal appearances, and other endorsements. No one could predict the amount of money he could have earned if he had won the one and two-hundred-meter-races; at the upcoming Track and Field World's Championship, but to say it was millions of dollars would be accurate.

Unfortunately for Drew, he wasn't given the opportunity to cash in on his victories, at the Prefontaine Invitational Meet and he had the City of Eugene, and University Police Departments to thank. As for the WFU community, who spearheaded the campaign that forced Drew's expulsion; the television special didn't exempt them from criticism either. They too were left scrambling how to rectify their mistakes. The University robbed Drew of his remaining track scholarship along with perhaps his most prized accomplishment; his master's degree. Drew had been scheduled to receive his degree at the end of the first summer session but the university chose not to wait for the final results of the investigation before it took action. There were many stories written after Drew's arrest. Some went as far as accusing him of being everything from a drug-addicted and woman-beater to being an all-out thug. Now, faced with the truth, no one was willing to step up to write a rebuttal. Most opted to pretend the incident never occurred, while others hoped the story would just go away. Yup, everything had worked out, just as his mother had promised. Drew's reputation was damaged but he was now able to walk with his head high. He knew there would be some who believed what the police said but he didn't care, nor did he care that he was labeled as a hero for saving Lynn from further injury. Drew couldn't have scripted what happened to him any better. He was about to get his life back, and thanks to the television special, the truth had finally come out. Drew would have given his last penny to have Lynn beside him to help celebrate being vindicated but it wasn't to be. The mere fact that he hadn't heard from her in over a month had given all indication, she had happily gone forward without him. In an effort to contact her, Drew was informed, Lynn didn't want to be contacted. As Ashley put it, Lynn wanted him to forget about her.

The show of support for Drew and Lynn received from people across the nation was astonishing, and thanks to Karyme and his family, he didn't have to go through it alone. Karyme was there to pull him forward when he wanted to give up. She refused to allow him to go through his horrific ordeal alone, and for her love and support, he would forever be grateful. is what brought him through his storm.

At the conclusion of the television special, Karyme said goodnight to everyone. Drew wanted to extend their night together, but Karyme couldn't because her mother was expecting her home by 10:30 pm, and to ensure she was there, Sophia was waiting up for her. Holding Karyme's hand, Drew escorted her to her car.

Once outside, Drew did the gentlemanly thing and opened the door for Karyme, but before she got inside, Drew took a chance that she was feeling the same as him, and tightly embraced her. Receiving what she believed was going to be another of Drew Harrison's customary embrace and kiss on the forehead, before saying goodnight, Karyme waited. To her surprise, Drew kissed her on her lips. It wasn't the closed-mouth kiss she'd received on their prom night but a kiss of passion. To say Karyme was shocked beyond belief was an understatement. It took Karyme a few seconds to adjust to Drew's tongue inside of her mouth, but once she did, she left no doubt it was something she wanted. It had been her dream to be given a real kiss by the man she'd adored for years, and like an overwhelmed teenager who was kissed by their first crush, Karyme melted in Drew's arms. Following their kiss, Karyme placed her face against Drew's chest to silently grasp what had just happened. Drew was finally holding her the way she wanted to be held and he wasn't showing any signs of wanting to let go. Perhaps, they were sharing a moment they would reflect upon for years to come and if it was the case, her dreams were coming true. Karyme continued to bury her face into Drew's chest. She couldn't get over how good he smelled. She wished Drew could hold her all night but knew in reality, it was impossible. For now, she was going to soak up every second Drew was giving her to store in her memory to reflect upon for years to come. Karyme knew she had to get a grasp on her over-active mind. She wanted to believe that Drew wanted her as his girl but in reality, she knew he was only acting on his emotions, after seeing the news broadcast.

Karyme had no idea Drew feelings had crossed the threshold of a friendship. For weeks he'd battled with his feelings toward her. Drew too wanted to believe they could be no more than friends but his mind was leading him to push the envelope. In the beginning, Drew thought his feelings were lust but as time passed, his desire to be with Karyme had nothing to do with lust, he was falling in love with her. However, Drew remained uncertain as to how he was going to take their friendship to the next level. What was going to happen if their relationship didn't work out? There was so much at stake to the point that Drew didn't want to chance losing is best friend.

Seeing where their night was heading toward, Drew released his grip on Karyme.

"I apologize, if took things too far," Drew said.

Karyme giggled, "I enjoyed it, really I did," Feeling more confident than ever, Karyme locked her arms around Drew's neck; pulling him down to her level and began kissing him once more. Drew didn't have to apologize about anything, it was what she wanted. Now more convince then before, Karyme could feel where Drew's heart was heading; after years of dreaming, her dreams were finally coming true. Drew was showing interest in her and his touch was just as she'd hoped. In a bold move; Drew lifted Karyme in his arms and placed her on the hood of her car. He positioned himself between her legs as he continued kissing her passionately. Karyme wanted to pinch herself to see if she was dreaming but was too afraid to do so, if by chance she was. She was making out with the man she was deeply in love with and it felt so surreal. Wearing a flare cut mini skirt, Karyme could feel Drew's manhood pressing against the outer layer of her panties. It was the first time she'd ever been so close to a man and because it was Drew, she felt herself wanting to open her legs wider to feel the full force of Drew's manhood to press against the outer layers of her panties. Karyme's body was sending all the wrong messages but her mind was refusing to persuade her to stop. Instead of pushing Drew away, Karyme wrapped her legs around his waist, while kissing him more passionately. She couldn't understand what was happening. Why was she teasing Drew, knowing she wasn't in any position to make love to him?

"What am I doing?" Karyme questioned.

It was shocking to imagine she was pushing the envelope towards the unthinkable but Karyme was doing just that. In the heat of passion, she pulled Drew's shirt from his pants and placed her hands under it to caress his body. By doing so, Karyme had given Drew an open invitation to do the same to her. She wanted to feel Drew's bare body against hers and as she did, their passionate kissing led them to explore each other even deeper. Karyme could feel Drew's throbbing penis pressing against her. It was knocking on the door of her protected wall, begging for the chance to enter. Without considering the consequences, Karyme capitalized on the moment. She was sure, she wanted to invite Drew inside of her but knew it wasn't a moral thing to do. She had never been with a man before but always dreamed her first lover was Drew and now that she had been presented with the opportunity, she was strongly considering it. Karyme wasn't going to be making love in a tropical paradise in the Caribbeans or some dingy mold-infested motel on the outskirts of town, for that matter.

164

In Karyme's case, she was about to make love to the man she was madly in love with on the hood of her car. Unfastening Drew's pants, Karyme removed his rock-hard penis and began fondling it. It was the first time she'd ever held a penis, and had no idea what followed next. She'd been told, her instincts would guide her in the right direction but Karyme now realized, her friends were wrong. She was sitting on the hood of her car with Drew's penis in her hand and had no freaking idea what to do with it. However, she felt a positive reaction from Drew as she slowly stroked it. Drew released a slight grunt, while kissing Karyme deeper, giving her the knowledge that she was doing something right. It felt great, knowing she was pleasuring Drew, but like her, he wanted more. Kissing more passionately, Drew placed his hand under Karyme's skirt and slid her panties to the side. He began using his fingers to tease her with clitoral stimulation. Drew's finger moments were not only inviting, but they also had Karyme pleading to feel more. Taking control of his penis, Drew used it to caress the outer layers of Karyme's vagina. He wanted Karyme familiar with the size of him as well as the feeling she was going to receive from him. Karyme's low moans were all Drew needed to hear to know she was nearly ready for the next step. His patience to take his time was not only stimulating to Karyme, but it also gave her the direction he was going.

"I want to feel you inside of me," Karyme whispered in between deep breaths.

With her panties fully removed, Drew used his finger to further stimulate Karyme's clitoris. He followed by inserting his finger inside her. Feeling Drew's finger inside of her, Karyme instinctively moved her body with the motion of Drew's finger. Now, more than ever, Karyme was sure what she wanted. Tonight, she was ready to make love to Drew. Removing his finger, Drew carefully guided his penis inside Karyme's vagina.

Although Karyme's vagina was dripping wet and ready for entry, penetrating her was proving to be difficult. In doing so, Drew felt Karyme's body tense up. He sensed Karyme's discomfort but her thirst to sexually appease him, overruled any thought of ruining their beautiful moment together. Unfortunately for Karyme, making love for the first time was very uncomfortable; so much so, Drew wanted to stop. He was well aware they were rushing into something they should have discussed. Drew wasn't going to allow his selfishness to ruin Karyme's first experience, nor did he want her first time to be on the hood of a car.

"I don't want to do this here," Drew admitted.

"But I want you," Karyme replied.

"And I want you too, but I want our first time together to be romantic, someplace we can forever have memories of. I don't want it to be on the hood of your car," Drew admitted.

Realizing their night together was abruptly ending, Karyme began to tear up. She feared she had blown her only chance to have Drew. Karyme wanted to be the woman Drew was expecting and the woman he was needing. Seeing how shaken Karyme became, Drew comforted her by alluding to the outcome of their night. He explained, this was only the first of many steps toward their future together. It was unexpected, but inviting news to help soothe Karyme's damaged ego. Drew's announcement of wanting to go forward with a relationship was more than Karyme anticipated. Her dreams had finally come true, Drew was looking to have a future with her and he solidified it with a kiss.

Tonight's botched attempt to make love hadn't affected Drew's feelings toward wanting to go forth with a relationship with Karyme. It only gave him more respect for her because of lengths she was willing to go through to satisfy him. Drew lifted Karyme from the hood of the car and placed her feet back to the ground. He held her in his arms, kissing her again, before re-opening the door for her to get inside her car. Once inside; Drew secured her door, he leaned inside and kissed Karyme a final time before saying good night.

"Good night my love," Drew said.

"Good night," Karyme responded. It had been a good night indeed and though their attempts to make love was foiled by her inability to go through with her first time, the night was amazing nonetheless.

 Drew stood on his front porch and watched the tail lights from Karyme's care disappear in the night. He reflected upon how beautiful their first passionate moment shared together were and realized his mother had been correct.

Chapter: 28

Lynn remained deeply troubled by the way her relationship with Drew ended. Her fight to salvage what was left had ended at the urgency of her parents. They knew her desire to someday run the company would convince her to do what they wanted and they used that knowledge against her. Not only did they flaunt the idea of her being the chosen one but sweetened the pot by adding that her father was considering retirement in two years. That was enough time for her to fully learn the company. But what became the game changer was the idea that her parents were allowing her to resume her relationship with Drew. Their well calculated plan was for her to commit herself into Serenity Gardens for therapy. As they so eloquently put it; they wanted her to strengthen her mind to take on the pack of wolves that she'll be facing when running the company. It seemed like a win/win situation at the time and after weighing her options, Lynn saw the benefits that came with it. To be with Drew, she was willing to admit herself to the private mental institution that was located on the outskirts of Virginia, while going on the belief that she was going to be sharing a future with Drew. After careful consideration, Lynn agreed to self-admit herself for a three-week evaluation. It was a small price to pay to be with the man she was going to marry.

Despite being described as the model patient, Lynn cheeked most of her medications and flushed them once returning to her room. Her determination to maintain a clear mind to focus her attention on Drew was the driving force to get her through the hell she was battling. She wasn't suffering from a mental disorder; nor did she need medication to help cope with her everyday problems. Lynn's only mistake was loving Drew and wanting to spend a lifetime with him. For nearly a month, she sat dormant inside her assigned ward; waiting patiently for the day her doctors decided to release her and when they refused to do so, she decided to exercise her right to leave AMA. Armed with the knowledge that she could sign herself out of the hospital because she was a voluntary admit, Lynn opted to enforce that right. In doing so, she was shocked to learn her parents had gone behind her back and obtained a Temporary Detention Order that forced her to stay against her will. Lynn was devastated her parents had betrayed her and became irate and combative because of it. She unsuccessfully tried escaping the ward twice; getting as far as the parking lot, before staff safely detained and returned her to the ward.

There, Lynn was restrained to her bed and medicated. Lynn fought valiantly but proved to be no match for the Depakote administered by needle to her. She quickly fell asleep, forgetting everything she'd planned to do against her parents. Lynn woke hours later soaked in her own urine and still restrained to her bed. Her sitter, who was sitting in the hallway and monitoring her every move saw that Lynn was fully awake and summoned her nurse. Within minutes, Lynn's nurse arrived with additional medication in the instant she needed to be further medicated. Lynn was still heavily medicated and presented no threat. The decision was made to remove her restraints and allow her to shower. While being escorted to the bathroom, Lynn cried from embarrassment after wetting the plastic mattress she was secured against. It was humiliating by the barbaric way she was treated after self-admitting herself. Her admittance to Serenity Gardens wasn't supposed to be this way. Her parents promised, she was only going to stay for three weeks to condition her mind, before tackling the wrath of the cooperate world but they'd lied. They made it sound so tropical but instead, she was suffering into her second month of torture. What was supposed to have been a self-admittance had emerged into a Temporary Detention Order. Lynn humbling experience to learn her parents had double-crossed her was more than she could ever anticipate. She trusted her parents, especially her father, whom she placed high on a pedestal. Her parents had always had her best interest at heart but to learn they had gone behind her back to seek and obtained a Temporary Detention Order to keep her at a mental hospital against her wishes was devastating. It was hard to come to grips after she'd been misled into thinking she was only there for a short stay. It was a strategy her parents used to get her away from Drew and it worked.

After showering, Lynn cleaned her room and waited for her parents to visit. She was in need of an explanation as to why they chose to take her over state lines to take advantage of Virginia Code 37.2-809 to hold her against her will, rather than allow her to make her own decision. Sadly, Lynn would never get the chance to ask any questions because after learning she was going home, she decided not to confront her parents; fearing they would change their minds about her relationship with Drew.

Once home, Lynn went to her room to unpack. Her phone hadn't been returned to her as of yet and calling Drew would have to wait for now but as soon as she was free to do so, Drew was going to be the first person she contacted.

Still feeling the effects from the Depakote administered to her the night before, Lynn wouldn't get the chance to unpack. She fell asleep as fast as soon as she laid across her bed, and after sleeping for more than three hours, she was awakened by the sound of her intercom in her room. It was her mother informing her to get dressed for dinner. They were expecting guests and Constance instructed Lynn to dress appropriately. Still groggy, Lynn got out of bed and staggered into her bathroom shower. She was unaware who their dinner guests were but if she had to guess, her guess would be friends of her parents. Once showering, Lynn got dressed and made her way downstairs. It was perhaps the fastest she'd gotten dressed in years and though she was dressed appropriate, she hadn't looked anywhere near capable of what she was accustom to looking. There was no reason for her to get all dolled up, especially knowing she wasn't going to be seeing Drew. Making her way downstairs, Lynn joined her parents in the parlor.

"You look, beautiful dear," Harry complimented as he kissed Lynn on her forehead.

"Thank you, daddy," Lynn replied.

Constance agreed with Harry by giving her nod of approval. Lynn should have suspected something was wrong after her father chose to have a drink before dinner. It was something he almost never did unless something was weighing heavy on his mind. Harry was nervous but Lynn chalked it up by thinking it may have been because he wasn't comfortable with her mother's choice of dinner guests. Lord knows, her mother was no stranger to inviting friends to dinner her dad wasn't particularly fond of. Still, Lynn hadn't foreseen it being much of a problem until their front doorbell rang. Her father nearly dropped his drink but quickly caught it before any spilled. They all stood to greet their guest as their housekeeper opened the door to invite them inside. To say Lynn was surprised who their guest was, was an understatement, and to conceal her disappointment, she looked at the floor. Their guest was no other than the Hutchinson's. Mr. and Mrs. Hutchinson were old friends of Lynn's parents. She and Ashley grew up with Austin but Lynn hadn't seen Austin since graduating high school. Seeing Austin left no doubt in Lynn's mind that her parents invited the Hutchinson family for dinner for one reason only. They were hoping sparks would ignite between she and Austin. Needless to say, Austin was attractive, a little too pretty for her. Austin could outdress any male model on the strip.

It's fair to say, Austin was as gay as Liberace, but what was so extraordinary about it was the fact that his parents were too wrapped up in each other to even notice.

Dinner went on as planned and after dinner, the families returned to the parlor for drinks. Lynn and Austin shared a friendly connection but that was as far as it went. Both, Constance and Harry, realized their mistake and decided to threw in their hand. After the Hutchinson's departed, Lynn began questioning her parents motivates. It was at that moment she learned of their intentions. They were against her pursuing a relationship with Drew and they both agreed being with Drew was detrimental to her future. Lynn didn't take her parents comments well and became highly upset.

"You lied to me, you said if I self-admit myself into that looney bin, you would support my relationship with Drew," Lynn said. She paced the floor in anger after realizing her parents had lied to her. "Oh my God, I can't believe the both of you deliberately lied to me."

"We had all intention of honoring our word but we came to recognize that Drew is no good for you," Harry replied. "Pumpkin, you're about to inherit a major company, a company I started from my parent's garage before turning it into a multi-million-dollar business.

"No matter how you try to dress it up daddy, you lied to me," Lynn said.

"Oh my God, Lynn, the man caused you to jail," Constance interrupted.

"Mom, I'm the reason we went to jail. It was me who caused Drew to put his life on the line to save me from getting the shit beat out of me. I'm the reason hotel security had to call the cops in the first place. My God, Drew was nearly killed because of me," Lynn explained.

"Regardless of who caused the police to respond; Drew placed you in harm's way, when he took you to Oregon with him. Now, for your sake and ours, just be the good daughter you are and listen to your father and me."

"No, I'm going to call Drew and explain to him why I broke it off, and I'm going to beg him to take me back," Lynn ranted.

"You would do no such thing," Constance said.

"Drew and I will get married the first chance we are together. You can't bet on that," Lynn confessed.

Lynn had dug her heels deep into the ground and she wasn't about to budge an inch. More than anything, she wanted a life with Drew and if it meant she had to stand up to her parents to do so, she was willing. Hearing what Lynn was considering, Constance knew they had to make an unpopular decision if they were going to keep her from Drew. Lynn had lost focus of the life they painted for her but more than that, they had lost the influence they once had over her. Yes, they'd lied to her but it was for her own good. Lynn's extended stay at Serenity Gardens hadn't helped the way they had expected and they would have to come up with another plan. Maybe, it was because they'd miscalculated how deep her love was for Drew but as sure as the sun rises in the east, they were going to end Lynn's relationship with Drew. To ensure Lynn would stay in line, her parents started by announcing they were keeping the keys to her car, keeping her bank account frozen, as well as her credit cards. Until Lynn refocused her life on the blueprint they set for her, she was going to be held in captivity.

After crying for most of the night, Lynn suddenly sat up in bed. She remembered the stashed money she'd hidden in her shoe box in the event of a rainy day. Well, the rainy day was now and Lynn could stop crying because she had an ace in the hole. Getting out of bed, Lynn opened her closet and began dismantling the stacked boxes of shoes that were neatly stored. She nearly opened her entire shoe collection before finding what she'd been searching for. Inside a box, containing a pair of boots was five- thousand dollars. It wasn't enough money to fly around the world but it was enough to buy a ticket to see Drew. Lynn packed a few items and began planning her getaway. Her first thought was to call Ashley to inform her what she was about to do but had a last-minute change of heart. Lynn waited until 3am to make her getaway. She quietly made her way down the back stairs to the kitchen and without disturbing her parents, Lynn disengaged the alarm system and quietly exited the house undetected. From the backyard, she made her way to the rear gate. She entered her pass code and exited the gate without sounding the alarm. Lynn didn't care that her parents would likely see her on camera leaving, her only concern was getting away from the life they expected her to live.

Leaving the compound, Lynn disappeared in the night. She walked nearly a mile before arriving at an all-night diner.

There, she called Uber, who arrived minutes later and drove her to the bus station. Lynn's decision to take the bus instead of the quicker train ride was something she was already regretting. The bus was crowded with nearly every seat filled. Lucky for her, she found a seat next to an elderly lady who was on her way to see her daughter in South Carolina.

The elderly woman was a very charming but reeked of body order from being on the bus for so long. Still, the elderly lady's body odor was no match to the dictatorship she was under at home.

Chapter: 29

Karyme arrived to work later than usual and as she entered the office, it was obvious she had suffered from a lack of sleep. Her eyes were swollen and she was wearing glasses, instead of her contacts. Entering the office, she greeted Drew with a soft kiss on his lips and set down at her desk. Karyme wasn't her cheerful self; she was distant and didn't want to talk. Something heavy was weighing on her mind and it wasn't hard to figure out what it was. It was a sure bet that she'd had gotten into another argument with her mother. Sophia had never hidden her feelings about where she stood with her relationship with their employer. Feeling a need to learn what Karyme problem was Drew began probing for answers.

"Rough night huh?" Drew asked.

Karyme pretended not to hear him and continued to open her e-mails. Karyme wasn't in the mood to talk about her agreement with her mother. She didn't want to have to tell Drew the real reason she was so upset but Drew wasn't going to be satisfied until he knew the truth.

"Sweetheart, what's wrong?" Drew asked again.

Karyme turned to Drew, she didn't want to share her dilemma but knew she would have to because it affected both of them. There was no right way to say what she was dealing with but he had a right to know. The state of their relationship was at stake and Karyme needed to make a decision within the next two hours. She should have told Drew last night about her shocking call but after sharing their special moment together, it wasn't the right time.

"Karyme, do you trust me?" Drew asked.

"Yes;" Karyme replied.

"Is it your mother tripping about our relationship again?" Drew asked.

"No, mama isn't the problem," Karyme answered.

"Then what is? Drew asked.

Unable to find the right words to say, Karyme was direct. She loved Drew and hoped their relationship could survive the distance that would be between them.

"Drew, there's no good way to say this but before I graduated from UVA, I submitted my resume to the company, Aircraft America. Aircraft America design Learjets for clients across the world and, well, when I got home last night, I got a message to call them and when I did, I was offered a lucrative position, and I want to take it," Karyme said.

"Just like that, without first talking to me," Drew replied.

"It's my dream job and to be honest, when I applied, I didn't think they would offer it to me. So, you can well imagine how surprised I was," Karyme said.

Drew didn't respond, nor did he show any emotions about how he felt. He suspected the job was out of state but had no idea were.

"Where's the company?" Drew asked.

"Merced California," Karyme answered.

"California," Drew reacted surprisingly.

 "I'm flying out today to meet with them on Monday." Karyme could see the disappointment on Drew's face but this was a once-in-a-lifetime opportunity for her to have the life she'd worked so hard for. Taken by surprise, Drew was at a loss for words. It was hard to believe Karyme would even consider accepting a job so far away. Never, did he think she would ever leave him, yet she was about to choose the path Gloria and Lynn had. Karyme's punch to the gut hurt like a motherfucker but Drew tried to hide his feelings. How could Karyme step on his heart after telling him she loved him, but then again, that was the story of his life. Karyme was not only leaving him; she was leaving the company she helped build. Drew couldn't deny Karyme was the driving force behind the company's upswing. She'd played a vital role in helping Hillcrest Farms to branch out across the east coast. Not only that, Karyme played a major role in helping Drew regain his life. He'd fallen in love with her and now she was leaving him. Throughout his ups and downs, Karyme was there to balance the scales. She'd always stirred him in the right direction and Drew found himself depending on her. But why now? Why had Karyme decided to leave? Drew wanted to blame her mother for the sudden change in her. He also wanted to blame the pressure of them being together but he ultimately knew, neither had anything to do with the other.

The fact was that Hillcrest Farms didn't hold Karyme's attention anymore, nor did he. Karyme was after something more challenging and the thought of it was upsetting. It was fair to say Drew was being selfish for wanting to hold on to someone that wanted to spread their wings, but after losing two women, he didn't want to lose another. It was hard for Drew to accept why Karyme wanted to move across the country, even though he knew the reason. Still, it didn't make him feel any better. Karyme's announcement had cut deeper than she anticipated. Drew's unsympathetic behavior towards her was unexpected. Sadly, Karyme felt Drew's pain and wished she could have shield him more from her unexpected blow but there was no other way to tell him.

Now that Karyme had opened up about her decision, Drew shut down like an old hooptie. He barricaded the remainder of his feelings inside, while refusing to discuss their conversation any further. He'd undergone a long-distance relationship with Gloria and knew the stress that came with it. As far as he was concerned, it was in his best interest to salvage whatever pieces of his heart that were left and move on. Drew believed, he had again, been jacked by love and promised himself from this moment on, to never allow his heart to be crushed again. Drew vowed to look after himself, and himself only. Sure, it was a silly thing to consider, but reportingly having his heart broken was becoming too much to bear. Karyme was quick to judge Drew and compared his behavior to that of an egocentric. She had taken his fragile heart into consideration because she knew what he had gone through with Gloria and Lynn but she reminded him of how much she loved him and her beliefs that they could make their long-distance relationship work. Karyme didn't want it to be about her, but she wanted Drew to understand this was the job she wanted and needed to boost her career.

Taking as much as he could absorb, Drew got his briefcase and made his way to the door. By deciding to accept Aircraft American's offer, Karyme had made her decision; she was leaving the company and trashing their relationship before it had gotten off the ground. Seeing Drew attempting to make his way out the office, Karyme called out for him to stop.

"Drew please, don't go," Karyme pleaded as she rushed from her desk to grab hold of Drew's arm. She placed her head against his chest and wrapped her arms around him. Karyme couldn't deny her desire to challenge her abilities for a job more challenging and believed, she had met her goals at Hillcrest Farms.

175

Sadly, it was time to move on. Karyme, along with Drew, help build the small family company into a powerhouse. Hillcrest was outselling some of the best name-brand companies in the nation and after fulfilling her goals, it was time to move on. It wasn't that she didn't believe Hillcrest had reached its peak but the opposite. There was plenty of room for expansion but with Drew returning and eager to assume full duties as president and CEO of the company, Karyme felt there was no room for her to grow.

Holding a strong grip on Drew, Karyme spoke candidly as she went forward with weighing the pros and cons of accepting the job. It was obvious she was torn on what to do because Drew was the love of her life, and other than her mother, the Harrison family had been the only family she had ever known. Karyme tried explaining her reasons as to why she needed to accept the position but in doing so, she was challenged by Drew's beliefs that she didn't want a relationship with him.

"Drew, I want this job but I want to be with you," Karyme said. "If you're not willing to commit to our relationship, then I won't accept the position, I will stay here with you."

They were words Drew wanted to hear but as a man, he couldn't allow Karyme to walk away from her dream. Yes, he would miss her, and yes, the probability of their long-distance relationship would end in a breakup but he wasn't going to be responsible for her having to give up her dreams. Drew placed his brief case on the floor and held Karyme tightly in his arms. It was his way of giving his approval as well as to show Karyme, how much he loved her.

"I think you should take the job," Drew said to Karyme. "I'm not going anywhere; you got me to the end of time."

Chapter: 30

Harry lightly knocked on Lynn's door but didn't get a response. Waiting a few seconds, he knocked again but louder. Still, there was no answer. After not getting a response, Harry sensed something was wrong. He entered the room and found it in disarray. There were no signs of Lynn and the scene gave indication that she was gone. Harry rushed to her closet, he found it as cluttered as her room. Harry couldn't say for certain, if any of her luggage from yesterday was missing but assumed it was. Panicking, he screamed for his wife as he frantically searched through the house for any signs of Lynn. Fearing the worse, Harry ran downstairs to the garage. There, he found Lynn's car parked just as she'd left it. His search extended throughout the grounds of their property but there were no signs of her. It didn't take long for Constance to locate Lynn on camera. She'd left the property by way of the rear gate, and she was on foot. Constance believed Lynn had taken a train to see Drew. Using the process of elimination, Harry contacted Ashley to see if Lynn had made contact with her, and after learning she hadn't, Harry knew there was only one other place she could be. Harry needed to get in contact with Drew and lucky for him, Ashley had Drew's number. Whether Lynn wanted it or not, Harry was going to protect her from ever being hurt again, and if it meant he had to travel across kingdom come to find her, he was willing to do so. Unfortunately for Harry, Constance didn't share his ideas, she had a different take when it came to Lynn. She believed as parents, they'd done everything humanly possible to keep Lynn out of harm's way but she refused to obey their wishes. As far as Constance was concerned, Lynn was going to do what Lynn wanted to whether they approve of it or not. But conveying her beliefs to Harry didn't set well. Lynn was his baby girl and his choice to take over the family business.

Determined to find Lynn and bring her home safely, Harry called Drew but only got his voice mail. Drew's voicemail only left Harry more frustrated but it didn't deter his pursuit to locate the whereabouts of his daughter. Harry made more than thirty-seven calls to Drew before reaching him. He was shock by the fact that Drew hadn't heard from Lynn but refused to become discourage from it. Instead, Harry deputized Drew as a part of his posse to seek and locate Lynn. Like Harry, Drew became overly concerned about Lynn's disappearance. He was searching blind to find her after having no idea where to start. Both Harry and Drew agreed to contact each other if they found out any news regarding Lynn's disappearance.

Relaxing for the first time since her travel began, Lynn saw a highway sign notifying her that she was forty-five miles away from the town of Jefferson. It was time to contact Drew and inform him of her unexpected arrival. Lynn needed Drew to meet her at the bus station but had no way of contacting him. Seeing that her newly made friend was in possession of a phone; Lynn asked to use it to contact her ride. The thought of hearing Drew's voice again after nearly two and a half months was overwhelming. Lynn had dream of this moment, since flying out of Eugene and it was seconds away from it becoming reality.

Drew returned to the office and flopped down on his couch. It had been an unforeseen morning, one in which he won't forget. After thinking he and Karyme had a chance to make things work, she decided to follow her career path to California. To make things worse, Karyme declined his offer to take her and Sophia to the airport and took an Uber instead. Whether it was her idea to decline his offer or her mother's, Drew couldn't say for certain, but knowing Karyme was gone, left him with an empty feeling. Deciding to call it a day, Drew shut down his computer. He was ready to take his walk through the plant but found himself stirring at Karyme's desk. Today was perhaps the last day, Karyme would set there and after realizing it, Drew nearly broke down. He'd lost another love but this was a special love, Karyme was his best friend. Not wanting to take any work home, Drew placed his brief case beside his desk and began to leave, but before he did, his cell phone rang. Drew's first thought was to let it ring, but felt it may be Karyme calling before getting on the plane.

"Hello," Drew answered.

"Drew, oooh, thank God, it's you," Lynn said.

Relieved it was Lynn; Drew could now stop worrying about her. "Are you ok?" Drew asked.

"Yeah, I'm fine. I'm calling because I need you to pick me up at the bus station in Jefferson." Lynn explained.

Lynn didn't have time to answer any questions but told Drew she would explain everything to him once he got there. Her bus was less than thirty-miles from the station and Lynn stressed the importance of him being there to meet her.

Drew knew he needed to call Mr. Boldmont but felt the need to wait until he grasps what was happening with the family. Drew's conversation with Lynn was short and he quickly left the office for his car. On his way to the airport, Drew called his mother to inform her of their unexpected house guest. He couldn't say for certain how Nancy was going to react to the news but knew she would never deny anyone help. Any other time Nancy most likely would have welcomed Lynn with open arms but this time was different, he was in new relationship with the woman she approved of and fully supported. Lynn's arrival certainly could put his relationship with Karyme in jeopardy but Drew felt he had no other choice but to help Lynn, until she worked whatever problems she was experiencing with her parents. Lord knows, staying under the same roof with Lynn wasn't going to be an easy thing for Drew. He still had feelings for her and he didn't know what would happen once they were together. Calling his mother, Drew explained what transpired and what he wanted to do. Without questioning his logic, Nancy respectfully accepted his decision but with a twist. She expressed the importance of him being truthful to Karyme in order to avoid a controversy. It was too late to stop Lynn from coming, she was on a bus and less than thirty miles away but it wasn't too late to inform Karyme about Lynn. Certainly, Karyme was going to have a negative opinion about Lynn being there but it was Drew's responsibility to comfort her and do so by expressing his desire to love her and only her. Drew was all in with relaying the truth to Karyme but it had to be later in the afternoon. Karyme was on her way to California and wouldn't arrive until late in the night. In a way, Drew had his lucky stars to thank because Karyme wasn't due back until Tuesday afternoon and thank God, Sophia decided to travel with her.

Drew arrived minutes before the bus and nervously waited at the terminal for Lynn to arrive. As the bus pulled into the depot, Drew found himself excited. Feelings he thought were gone, suddenly reappeared. Once again, his demons were resurfacing to make his life a living hell. Seeing Lynn running towards him felt like a dream but if it was a dream, Drew wanted to wake up before it was too late. He wasn't supposed to have butterflies inside of his stomach for Lynn. Karyme was his lady now; he'd given her his heart but what Drew failed to realize; Lynn still had a part of it. Once again, Lynn had clouded Drew's thoughts, placing Karyme back to playing backup.

Running in a full sprint, Lynn jumped into Drew's arms, locking her arms and legs around him. For a second, Drew temporarily forgot that he was in a relationship with Karyme.

Seeing Lynn again brought back so many memories and Drew found himself wanting to forgive her for abandoning him doing his tough times. He was left hypnotized with the idea of allowing Lynn to kiss him as he welcomed her. Realizing what he was doing, Drew broke away, hoping it was enough to break the spell he was under.

"How was your trip?" Drew asked, retrieving Lynn's luggage from the bus driver.

"It wasn't the best but I made the best of it knowing I was going to see you," Lynn replied.

Lynn held on to Drew's arm as they walked to his car. She had a lot of explaining to do and promised to do so the minute they had time alone.

Once home, Drew carried Lynn's bag upstairs to her room. Once more he was reminded, he needed to level with both women but felt it wasn't the appropriate time to do so. In all honesty, Drew didn't have the heart to hurt either woman nor did he want to destroy what he had built. In a bizarre way, Drew wanted his cake and eat it too. He wanted Lynn but his heart told him Karyme was his choice.

"Is everything okay?" Lynn asked.

"Yes, everything is fine," Drew replied. He smiled and placed Lynn's luggage on the floor. Feeling the need to leave the room, Drew turned to leave but Lynn stopped him before he left. She could see something was wrong and believed it was because of her.

"Are you sure?" Lynn asked again.

"I'm positive," Drew replied.

But Lynn knew he wasn't, she knew what he was feeling was the result of her, after promising she would treat him better than Gloria. In reality, she hadn't treated him any better. If she was going to satisfy him, she had to do better. Before leaving the room, Drew embraced Lynn. He kissed her forehead and quietly turn to leave the room. He got as far as the door before Lynn again stopped him.

"Drew, don't leave," Lynn pleaded.

"I think it would be best if I did. I don't want any regrets," Drew replied.

"There wouldn't be any regrets on my part," Lynn responded, hoping it was enough to convince Drew to stay.

The mere fact they were home alone was inspiring enough to want to accept Lynn's invitation but it wasn't the moral thing to do in his mother's house. Drew needed to consider Karyme and what it'll do to her if he did. Karyme didn't deserve the heartache it would bring to her but Drew found it hard blocking out the vivid memories of their magical time in Eugene, before all hell broke loose. More than anything Drew wanted to relive that moment but things had changed since he was in a relationship with Karyme. Being with Karyme should have been enough for Drew but there was something about Lynn that he couldn't kick. Yes, he loved Karyme and he wanted his future to include her but his feelings for Lynn were stronger than he anticipated. Drew was sure he'd made the right choice by choosing to be with Karyme but seeing Lynn again was causing his mind to cloud. Like most love stories, something always ruined the happy couple, and in this case, the villain was Lynn.

Drew was faced with multiple obstacles with his first being Gloria. Gloria possessed the ability to convince him to do just about anything she wanted. Then there was Lynn. It's fair to say, Drew loved her but their history together was like the stock market, one day it was high above the clouds and the next, it crashes like an ocean wave against giant volcanic rocks. Drew couldn't blame Lynn's past mental condition for their problems, instead, he blamed her parents. Drew understood why her parents were concerned about Lynn's safety, her relationship with Marshall was a disaster and they felt it was too early for Lynn to get into another serious relationship. But what her parents didn't know was the extent he was willing to go to ensure that Lynn was happy. They only saw the negative side of what their relationship could be. Drew believed he and Lynn could have had a beautiful relationship but it wasn't meant to be. Karyme had thrown him a lifeline, and saved him from drowning. It should be a no brainer when it came to Karyme being his best choice but Lynn's sudden emergence had clouded Drew's mind.

Drew found himself standing at a crossroad and though his heart was telling him to take a right that led to Karyme, Lynn's presence was convincing him to take a left. Drew had to make a choice; he could only pray it was the right choice.

It was after dinner when Drew and Lynn got the chance to talk. They took a golf cart drive to the lake and once arriving, they sat on the pier. Lynn was the first to speak. Before going into her story, she wanted to clear up any misconceptions pertaining to why she broke things off with him. Lynn explained, after their arrest, her parents was adamant Drew was no good for her and demanded she break things off with him. Lynn went on to tell how her parents suspended her privileges and confiscated her car. It wasn't a surprising that Lynn's parents would do such a thing, but what was shocking, was the lengths they went through to keep them apart. It was shocking to learn how Lynn was tricked into self-admitting herself into a mental institution only to deceive her by obtaining a TDO to forced her to be committed longer. Lynn stated, she had, had enough of her parents bullying her and had no intentions of ever returning to live under their roof.

After hearing Lynn's story, Drew was more convince than ever that now wasn't the time to inform Lynn about his relationship with Karyme. Lynn had gone through hell and back and there was no way he was going to give her a one-way ticket back to hell, but this time covered in gasoline. Drew didn't know the lengths to where his relationship with Lynn would go or if it'll go anywhere but he was going to do his best to give her a relaxing weekend.

Leaving the lake, the couple returned home. Drew found it disturbing the way Lynn was treated by her parents and was strongly considering not contacting Harry to inform him that Lynn was with him. However, he'd promised Harry, he would contact him the minute he heard from Lynn and being a man of his word, Drew removed his phone from his pocket and handed it to Lynn. Drew explained, Harry had called looking for her earlier and wanted Lynn to call him. At first, Lynn refused but after Drew said how devastated Harry sounded, Lynn made the decision to call him. She had done enough damage to her family and didn't want to do anymore, especially knowing about her father's weak heart. As Lynn made the call to her father, Drew went inside to give her the privacy he felt she needed but while inside, he used the allotted time to attempted to contact Karyme by using their landline but was unable to reach her. Hating to leave messages, Drew felt obligated to do so. He hadn't heard from Karyme and began to get worried.

Seconds later, Karyme returned Drew's call. She informed him that they were at Dallas Fort Worth Airport and they were about to board for Merced. Missing each other, the couple exchanged I love you's before ending their conversation.

Though relieved Karyme and her mother was safe, but Drew's heart continued to ache. His life was complicated and he didn't know what to do to fix it. Drew rejoined Lynn on the front porch to listened to the last of her conversation with her father. Harry and Lynn had managed to solved their problem and Lynn had agreed for him to drive down tomorrow evening to get her. They had a lot to work out and hopefully, they could do so on their long drive home. Frankly, Drew would have preferred Lynn would give up on trying to please her parents rather than having to suffer through the hell they were putting her through. She'd shown, she was willing to do anything to be with him yet for her parents, it wasn't enough.

Sitting in his mother's swing chair, Drew used his hands to cupped Lynn's faced before kissing her.

"What was that for?" Lynn asked.

"For the sacrifice you made on my behalf," Drew replied.

It was the perfect night for being outside. Though it was mid-autumn, you wouldn't have known by how comfortable it was. Drew found himself fighting to resist Lynn's touch but her persistence was proving to be difficult. Before Drew realized what was happening, he and Lynn had taken things to the extreme. Wearing only a pair shorts and a t-shirt, Drew had no difficulty touching all of Lynn's hot spots. Tonight, should have been the night Drew became a man and stood up for his morals but he couldn't. Lynn was leaving tomorrow afternoon and he wanted to give her the carefree night she deserved. While kissing Drew, Lynn unzipped his pants and removed his penis. Lynn wanted to show Drew how much she loved him but making love on the front porch wasn't the most auspicious place. Acting on impulse, Lynn leaned forward and buried her face into Drew lap. Drew's jaw nearly popped out of socket from the jolt Lynn's moist mouth brought to him. Not only was it unexpected, it was exciting and daring.

The thought that his mother or sister could come outside and catch them in the act gave Drew a rush. But the fear of being caught became too much for Drew to bear.

As great as it felt, Drew wasn't accustomed to making love in the open, not when he could be caught at any time. Hungry enough to tear into each other, the couple took their act to the garage. There, they made love on Drew's work desk located in the rear corner of the building.

Chapter: 31

Drew arrived at the office at 6:15 am. He'd considered not working today but changed his mind after having to check and log the coolers of milk stored in the warehouse. Climbing the stairs to his office, Drew saw what he thought was a light coming from his office. He cautiously made his way up the stairs to the second floor. Standing outside his office, Drew put his ear to the door to listen for any movement. He couldn't remember if he had turned off the lights and after not hearing anything, he opened the door. Drew was shocked by what he saw. Never, in his wildest dreams would he have imagined Karyme would be setting at her desk.

"Good morning baby." Karyme said, greeting him with enthusiasm.

"Karyme," Drew said shockingly. "What are you doing here?" Drew responded, trying not to look guilty.

Karyme got up from her desk and wrapped her arms around Drew's neck, greeting him with a kiss.

"You know one thing, I love you." Karyme said to Drew.

"I love you too," Drew replied. "I thought you was in California?"

"I got as far as the Dallas Fort Worth airport and changed my mind about the job. I'm not going to allow a job to come between the man I love and want to spend the rest of my life with," Karyme responded. Karyme was happy to see Drew and she showed it in her kiss. Drew was as nervous as a defendant standing in front of a judge waiting to hear his verdict. Drew was putting on a brave face but he was breaking fast. Again, his reckless behavior had put him into a beleaguered situation that was bound to cause the demise of their relationship.

"You look as if you're not happy to see me," Karyme said, seeing the look of surprise on Drew's face.

"Of course, I'm happy to see you. I'm shocked because I wasn't expecting to see you until Tuesday afternoon," Drew replied.

It was shocking to think Lynn was probably up and getting dress to come over. Drew hands were shaking like a leaf on a windy day but to hide his nervousness, he had to gain control of himself.

Drew hoped Lynn hadn't noticed him sweating because if she had, she'll know something was wrong. Drew went around to his desk to sit. What the hell was he thinking to believe he could get away with Lynn being at his house. He was going to have to tell Karyme, but how? How in God's name was he going to tell his current girlfriend that his ex-girlfriend was staying with him for the weekend? In an effort to hold on to his relationship with Karyme, Drew knew it was in his best interest to level with Karyme. Now more than ever, it was vital that he confess the truth but Drew couldn't bring himself to do so. It wasn't that he was a coward, he didn't want to drop this in Karyme's lap so early in the morning. Maybe after church, when he had prayed for forgiveness and asked for guidance, he would have the nerves to level with both women.

"You must be exhausted? When did you get home." Drew asked.

"Around 3:45 am," Karyme answered.

Karyme got up to pour herself a cup of coffee as well as a cup for Drew. The cup was piping hot and Drew couldn't wait to take a sip.

"Thank you. You must have known I needed a pick me up to help me started this morning," Drew said, leaning back in his chair.

"You look tense, you, ok?" Karyme asked.

"Yeah, I'm fine, I'm just surprise to see you, is all," Drew responded.

Drew's adrenalin was pumping and Karyme was picking up on his unusual behavior. Drew was relieved Lynn chose to sleep in instead of coming to the office with him this morning. He couldn't imagine what he would do if the two women would have bumped heads before he got the chance to explain. Perhaps, it was in his best interest to admit the truth to Karyme this morning but Drew was afraid. He didn't know how Karyme would react to Lynn staying under his roof. There was no way Karyme would forgive him for what he'd done and that thought alone caused him to freeze up. Drew had barely taken two sips from his coffee when Karyme suggested they make their mid-morning rounds through the plant. It was an unusual request for Karyme to want to conduct their property checks so early in the morning but nonetheless, Drew didn't object. Grabbing his cup of coffee, Drew followed Karyme out of the office and down the flight of steps to where the coolers were stored.

186

They walked halfway through the plant before Drew reached for Karyme's hand. He wasn't sure how Karyme was going to react after being such an ass to her the day before, but to his surprise, Karyme was willing to overlook his behavior.

"I apologize for the way I acted yesterday," Drew said.

"No, yesterday was my fault; I shouldn't have sprung my job offer on you so quickly," Karyme responded.

Karyme's act of forgiveness should have inspired Drew to be honest with her but needless to say it didn't. Instead of being the man he should have been, Drew opted to remain quiet. He realized what he was doing could potentially come back to bite him in the ass but he was willing to roll the dice. More than anything, Drew wanted to come clean with Karyme but his heart wouldn't allow him. To hide his guilty conscious; Drew grabbed Karyme and held her tightly in his arms. He kissed her and attempted to tell her what happened but bitched out at the last second.

"What is going on with you?" Karyme asked.

"What do you mean?" Drew replied.

"You're acting as if you're guilty of something," Karyme said.

"What are you talking about? Drew questioned. "I'm excited about you being home, is all," Drew responded.

Karyme felt something was wrong and before the morning was over, she was going to find out. Needing a reason for hiding his guilt, Drew blamed yesterday as the reason for his behavior. Drew didn't want to be the reason for Lynn's decision to turn down the job and asked that she make arrangements to reschedule her meeting on Monday.

"I feel so bad you gave up your dream job for me," Drew added.

"You would have done the same for me," Karyme said. She was sure if Drew was in her position, he wouldn't have hesitated to turn down a position to preserve their relationship. Walking hand and hand, Drew and Karyme continued their inspection of the older coolers, and once finished, they returned to the office to complete the remaining paperwork, before leaving for the morning. Both Drew and Karyme were attending their respective church this morning.

187

Karyme was driving into town to worship at The Sacred Heart Catholic Church and Drew, well, he was attending their family's church just minutes down the road from his house. Still at the office, Drew remained on pins and needles and continued to glimpse at Karyme. He tried building the nerves to tell Karyme about Lynn but he couldn't. He loved Karyme too much to break her heart but ultimately knew, it was in his best interest to do so. Throughout their friendship, Karyme had always been his biggest supporter and the only woman, other than his mother that loved him unconditionally. Telling Karyme now, not only would be devastating to their relationship, but he would lose her trust. Drew continued to look over at Karyme when she wasn't looking. He wanted so much to be satisfied with only Karyme but the feelings he had for Lynn wouldn't allow him. Drew never doubted his love for Karyme, he just couldn't resist helping Lynn in her time of need. Lynn could best be described as his damsel in distress, and for some unexplained reason, Drew couldn't resist from helping Lynn.

Karyme was giving him everything he needed in a successful relationship but like a fool, he found a way to destroy it. The controversy that came with Lynn should have been more than enough to ignore but Drew couldn't, it was as if he was addicted to wanting to be on hand to help Lynn whenever she needed him. Was he crazy, or just plain stupid? Drew couldn't answer that question honestly, but was certain he didn't want to lose either woman.

Seeing that Drew was constantly staring at her, Karyme took it upon herself to level with her decision to turn down the job offer. She wanted Drew to know, he had nothing to do with her decision, it was her decision and she chose to make it alone.

"Drew, there's something you need to know," Karyme said, interrupting Drew's train of thought.

"What is it dear?" Drew responded.

"Your actions yesterday had nothing to do with me changing my mind. I made the decision because I realized you mean more to me than working for Aircraft America. I love you and I know you feel the same for me. Our discussion yesterday about someday getting married resonated with me as mother and I was on the plane yesterday. I couldn't take the job knowing how much I want to be your wife. Leaving now wouldn't be fair to either of us. I want to stay and work on what I believed to be an everlasting love," Karyme said.

It was Lynn's way of telling Drew, she wanted to share the rest of her life with him. Whether it was a risk she was taking remained to be seen but Karyme wasn't ready to leave her one and only love.

"I love you more than you would ever know," Karyme confessed. "And I can see us together forever."

Karyme's confession was more than Drew could take. It was time to level with her, time to tell the truth about Lynn and what happened between them last night.

"Karyme, there's something I need to tell you," Drew said.

Finally, after much deliberation, Drew had taken his first steps to confess his indiscretions by manning up to his fuck up with hopes of getting a reprieve. Lord knows, he didn't want to lose Karyme, not after being sure she was whom he wanted to spend the rest of his life with. It was a bittersweet moment to know Karyme wanted to share her life with him but Drew couldn't help but be reminded of his responsibility to come clean. It wasn't going to be easy to explain what happened but Drew knew he had to somehow maintain the courage to be honest. He understood the consequences he faced; he also knew the problems it would bring between them but he was about to be truthful for the first time in his life. Without debating his decision further, Drew set at the end of his desk. He reached for Karyme's hand and pulled her into his arms. Before saying anything, he kissed her which led to another and another. Before long, their kisses become passionate. It felt so right kissing and holding Karyme in his arms. Father God, knew how much he loved her but Drew had to face reality. He was about to break Karyme's heart this morning and there was no easy way to do it. How fucking stupid could he have been to commit to two women, knowing the shit it would cause.

Drew had to know, sooner or later, the shit was going to hit the fan and he questioned himself as to why he would intentionally destroy the life of the woman he truly adored. To sum it up, Drew came to the conclusion that he was a self-centered bastard who only thought about his wants. It was the reason he couldn't admit the truth because admitting the truth meant he would lose Karyme. In hindsight, Drew was no better than Gloria, he was a liar, and a egotistical bastard but most importantly, he was a coward. He was using the excuse of not wanting to be responsible for causing Lynn to have another mental breakdown but in reality, he didn't want to lose either woman.

The fact remained that Drew shouldn't have become physically involved with Karyme until he was sure things with Lynn were over but like always, he somehow found a way to hurt the person he loved the most. But why Karyme? She was his best friend. Fuck! he was supposed to spend the rest of his life with her but because of his inability to do the right thing, he wasn't going to get that chance.

"Stop being a coward, and tell her." Drew said to himself. He wished there was another way without having to hurt Karyme but it wasn't. He was going to have to man up and admit his infidelities. Once building his nerves, Drew released his hold of Karyme.

"Sweetheart, we need to talk," Drew said.

From the look on his face, Karyme knew something was wrong. She was uncertain as to what Drew was about to say but was sure it involved Lynn. Like Gloria, Lynn had Drew wrapped around her finger. Since being with her, Drew had only experienced trouble. Within the year of them being together, Drew had been arrested, beaten within inches of his life, and had endured two, gut-punching breakups with her, but with Karyme's help, Drew had reclaimed the stable life he once had. For the first time in months, he was happy and now his face was showing the tell-tale signs of a guilty man, who was about to confess his involvement of some kind with Lynn. Drew was by far the most loving and caring man Karyme had ever known and to see that Lynn taking advantage of him was heartbreaking. Each time Drew had gotten involved with her, she managed to break his heart, leaving her to help pick up the pieces. But not this time, Karyme wasn't going to allow Lynn to destroy what she had built with Drew. She was going to do everything in her power to show Drew, he deserved better. Standing at her desk, Karyme did the unexpected. She wasn't going to allow Drew to get away from her, not this time.

"I love you, Andrew Christopher Harrison. You have made me the happiest woman in the world and Friday night was just the tip of the iceberg for us," Karyme said. She assured Drew, she wanted to be with only him.

Drew couldn't deny his feelings, he loved Karyme but he was sure things ended for them last night when he slept with Lynn. Once telling Karyme what he'd done, Drew was sure they would part ways for the last time. The sad thing about it, Karyme was everything rolled up into one.

She was his best friend, his lover, his confidant, and the woman he wanted to share the rest of his life with but his obligation to Lynn will undoubtedly prevent him from achieving that dream. Drew's heart belonged to Karyme but realistically, his mind belonged to Lynn.

Dressed in a short floral print wrap dress that barely covered her upper thighs, Karyme untied her dress and removed it from her shoulders allowing it to fall freely to the floor. The office wasn't the most auspicious place to celebrate something so secrete but it was romantic nonetheless. Karyme walked to the office and locked it. Once doing so, she made her way back across the office, stopping at the couch. Wearing only her sexy butterfly print bra and matching panties set, Karyme stood by the couch, waiting for Drew. Karyme was stunning, nearly causing Drew to jump out of his skin. Karyme was seducing him without laying a finger on him. She slowly removing her bra allowing her perky sized 38 breasts to stand at attention. If that wasn't enough, Karyme followed by stepping out of her panties. Completely naked, Karyme motioned for Drew to join her. For the first time in her life, Karyme was willing to fight for the man she loved and if it meant she had to step up her game and fight dirty, she was willing.

"Come here," Karyme signaled with her finger. "I want you now."

Drew wanted her as much as she wanted him and though making love to her was tempting, Drew was going to have to decline her offer. He had to tell Karyme about Lynn.

"Why are you standing over there staring at me?" Karyme asked. "Come here," she instructed again.

It was obvious what was about to happen and to be frank, seeing Karyme completely naked had taken all of Drew's energy. Karyme was second to none when it came to turning Drew on. The sight of her hypnotized him causing him to temporarily forget his objective. Drew forgot about the consequences he was facing and did just as Karyme instructed. Approaching Karyme, Drew lifted her into his arms before gently lying her on the couch. He was as nervous as the first time they were together but knowing Karyme was going to be his wife, prompt Drew to relaxed. Somehow, he was going to get over this obstacle he was facing, and once his did, he would never go outside of his relationship ever again.

Drew looked down at Karyme before locking eyes. From there they touched foreheads followed by kissing softly. They took time to reflect about their feelings towards each other. Drew wanted Karyme not only to see the love he had for her; Drew wanted her to feel it. Drew said a silent prayer and asked God to comfort Karyme, once the truth was revealed. He knew there was no way he could prevent from telling her the truth, but he wanted this moment as much as Karyme did. For his mistake, Drew was willing to accept whatever punishment, as long as it didn't involve losing Karyme. Drew didn't care about himself nor was he going to make any excuses, he was going to be a man and accept his punishment, but telling Karyme was going to have to wait for now. Drew continued to kiss Karyme passionately but had a change of heart. He again, wanted to man up but was too afraid.

Deciding not to let things get out of control, Drew set up and leaned back on the couch. He hadn't altogether worked out the kinks of what he was going to say but prepared himself to begin talking and face the consequences that were sure to follow. Attempting to speak, Karyme interrupted him. She locked her arms around his neck and resumed kissing and undressing him. Pulling away, Drew was determined to talk, before wussing out but each time he attempted, Karyme countered. Her aggressive behavior to persuade Drew to make love to her was beginning to work. Karyme had his pants unbuckled and was holding his rock-hard penis in her hand. Drew knew, if he was to follow through with his intentions, he had to think logically with his mind, instead of his penis. He had become embellished in the thought of making love to Karyme but knew he had to fight his desires. Drew had Karyme's feelings to consider, instead of his own. He could no longer continue to make a fool out of her, he had to do the right thing.

"Baby stop," Drew asked, as he gently removed Karyme's hand from around his penis, placing it back into his boxer briefs but as soon as he did, Karyme grab hold of it and removed it again.

"Come on now, you're killing me," Drew pleaded, pushing Karyme's hands away a second time. He was fighting his urges as well as Karyme's and if he didn't stop her, he was going to give in to his desires. Karyme wanted him and she was going all out to get what she wanted. There was no way she was going to lose Drew, not when she was so close to having him.

"Sweetie please, stop, before I forget what I have to tell you. We really need to talk. Baby please, this is important," Drew said as he moaned from the way Karyme was caressing his penis.

"Don't you want me?" Karyme asked. She locked her arms again around Drew's neck. "Listen to me. I want you; I want you right now," Karyme reiterated how much she wanted Drew. She further enticed him, by whispering into his ear and telling him how badly she wanted to feel his cock inside of her. Eager to have Drew, Karyme once again began caressing his penis while kissing him passionately.

"Baby no, we can't do this today; we have church." Drew said as he tried breaking away.

"We have plenty of time," Karyme responded.

Drew's words of needing to talk fell on deaf ears, Karyme was on a quest to seduce him and it was working.

"Make love to me," Karyme whispered, as she reclined on the couch pulling Drew on top of her.

Damn, Drew had fucked up, he allowed Karyme to place his penis inside of her. By doing so, his so-called confession would be the most unethical thing he could do, especially after being inside of her.

"How the fuck did I allowed myself to get into such an uncompromising position?" Drew thought to himself. He had only one job, and that was to tell Karyme about Lynn and for some inexplicable reason, he couldn't even do that right. It's fair to say, Drew wanted to make love to Karyme more than telling her about his fuck up. He wasn't happy about having to break her heart but he was doing it nonetheless. Karyme was his world; she was the positive influence he needed in his life and hurting her was the last thing he wanted to do but it was too late.

Drew felt Karyme's discomfort and patiently penetrated his way deeper inside her. Karyme's body had responded far better than he expected. Being patient had worked in Drew's favor and though he wanted to explore deeper, his first responsibility was to Karyme. He wanted her to enjoy the passion they were sharing and from the look in her eyes, and the way she was holding him, she was enjoying being made love to.

Their lovemaking was as beautiful as a bride and groom on a honeymoon but sadly, their honeymoon was about to come to an end. By making love to Karyme, Drew had made the situation far worse. It was going to be even harder for him not to break her heart and though Drew never claimed to be a perfect man, he never intentionally wanted to hurt Karyme.

As their lovemaking progressed, Karyme's passionate screams could be heard beyond the walls of the office and lucky for them, the plant was closed on the weekends.

"Oh my God, I feel you in of my stomach." Karyme grimaced. Drew was in unfamiliar territory but Karyme didn't want him to stop. Stopping now would be a devastating blow to her effort to win his heart. Sensing he had ventured too deep, Drew became motionless, choosing to wait until Karyme was comfortable enough to continue. Drew remained cautious and waited until he believed it was time to proceed. Making love to Karyme felt so right, Drew nearly cried. He should have been the happiest man in the world but instead, it was looking as if it was going to be the worst day of his life. He was misleading Karyme and if he didn't stop now, he was going to regret it. But telling Karyme the truth could destroy her. The state of their friendship for life was at stake, Drew couldn't afford to lose the woman he planned to live out his life with. Consumed with guilt, Drew believed he had to do the right thing before it was too late. He hadn't ejaculated and believed the time had come for him to withdraw. Seeing what Drew was about to do, Karyme went into action. She wasn't having it and continued with her efforts to keep his motor running. She wanted Drew and was willing to do anything to convince him not to stop.

"Don't stop, I need you," Karyme pleaded.

Obligated to finish what was started, Drew was denying Karyme of what she desired and though it was under false circumstances, Drew wanted to share what he believed was their final time together.

"I love you so much," Karyme confessed, as her tears began to fall from her eyes. It was all she could do to show her love. She had given her all, including her virginity to the man she wanted to spend the rest of her life with. Satisfying Drew became a must for Karyme and she was determined to accept every inch of his hard thick penis inside of her. To do so, Karyme synchronized her body movements with his, giving Drew access to explore deeper inside of her. Drew's burning desire to satisfy

Karyme out weighted the guilt he was feeling. His willingness to please her, had taken precedence over wanting to stop making love to her. His methods of stimulation coerced Karyme into becoming even more receptive to him. Although she was relaxed and was accepting most of his manhood, Drew preceded with caution. The gratification of hearing Karyme's moans of pleasure enhanced Drew's feeling. It was a moment in time he wanted to freeze but the noise from the office phone brought him back to reality.

Chapter: 32

Lynn was awakened by the sun's rays shining through her upstairs bedroom window. She greeted the morning with a smile as she thought of Drew and the life, she was looking to share with him. She'd had an unforgettable night, one in which she would never forget and for the first time in months, she was stress free. Lynn couldn't say for certain how long her happiness would last because her father was due to arrive to take her home late afternoon. But as for now, she was going to enjoy every second she had with Drew. Lynn set at the edge of her bed and stretched before getting up. She tied her robe around her and with her clothes in hand, she made her way down the hallway to the shared bathroom. It was hard to believe that she and Drew had worked things out so easily, after spending months apart. What was so ironic, was the way they made love after working things out. It was by far the most intense lovemaking she'd ever experienced, to the point that she could still feel Drew's body movements against her. Just the thought of last night was enough to give her the courage to risk joining Drew in bed for an early morning surprise. Before reaching the bathroom, Lynn stopped at Drew's bedroom and lightly knocked on the door. She had no idea if his mother was home but from the smell of bacon and freshly brewed coffee coming from downstairs; it was obvious, Ms. Harrison was downstairs cooking breakfast. As for Joanna, Lynn wasn't sure where she was but from her door being closed, it was obvious she was still sleeping. After not getting an answer, Lynn knocked again, still, there was no answer. Slowly she opened the door to Drew's bedroom.

"Hello," Lynn acknowledged before entering the room.

Now inside, Lynn closed the door behind her. Drew's absence had given her the perfect opportunity to see if he was hiding any secrets. Lynn searched for anything to prove if Drew was involved with anyone. It wasn't something Lynn was accustomed to doing but since her unexpected arrival yesterday, Drew hadn't been himself. He was edgy and seemed to be on high alert the entire evening. Needless to say, Drew's odd behavior triggered Lynn's suspicions. Like his apartment, Drew's room was as neat as a five-star hotel. There was nothing out of place, not even a coating of dust had settled on his furniture. Seeing a framed picture of Karyme on his nightstand should have been a red flag but Lynn was well aware of Drew's close childhood ties to her.

It was Gloria that she was most concerned about and from the look of things, Lynn hadn't seen anything remotely displaying his involvement with her. Not finding any evidence linking Drew to Gloria, Lynn felt a sense of relief. Her female intuition was sounding off and it was telling her to look further but she had been in Drew's bedroom long enough. Maybe she was overreacting but Drew's behavior yesterday warranted her to want to dot all of her I's and cross her T's. From the way the room looked, Gloria was yesterday's news. There wasn't a single item that could tie Drew to her. He was Gloria free, but to satisfy her curiosity, Lynn continued to search. Opening the drawer to Drew's nightstand caused Lynn's anxiety to heighten. Inside the drawer was Drew's cell phone.

 Normally, she wouldn't have dared invaded his privacy but his bizarre behavior was enough to do so. Removing Drew's phone from the drawer, Lynn pushed the button to power it up. If her memory served her correct, Drew had never applied a pass code to his phone. Lynn's rapid heartbeat increased as Drew's phone powered up. She didn't know what she was going to find but prayed it wasn't anything to cause her to relapse into a depression. She loved Drew more than she had ever loved anyone. So much so, she was considering forgoing her inheritance. Searching through Drew's text messages, Lynn saw that most were from Gloria, who pleaded for Drew to take her back. It was relieving to know; Drew refused her pleas. It should have been enough for Lynn to end her madness but she continued her search. It wasn't until she came upon a text from Karyme that she became alarmed. It had to do with Friday night's 20/20 special which involved their encounter with police in Eugene Oregon. Karyme texted about being surprised by the way the night had gone. She didn't elaborate on what happened but Lynn was floored at the thought of Drew moving on so quickly. Her heart dropped to the pit of her stomach as she read on. Never in her wildest dreams did she ever think, Drew would venture outside of their relationship so quickly. Though crushed by what Drew may have done, Lynn chose to read on. She felt some sense of relief after reading only a kiss materialized between them. Drew's celebration that the charges had been dropped, may have been his reason for kissing Karyme.

Any other time Lynn would have been devastated that her man had kissed another woman but after reading the entire text messages between them; she was relieved Drew not only apologize for what happened, he promised to never cross the line again. Though the evidence wasn't there, Lynn questioned if it was possible that

Drew and Karyme shared an underline relationship. She couldn't say for certain but she was going to find out and hopefully soon. Lynn searched Drew's phone for further incriminating texts or pictures but there were none. Though Drew had crossed the line by kissing Karyme, nothing seriously had materialized between them. Satisfied, she had found all she was going to find, Lynn left Drew's room for the bathroom. Lynn hadn't much time before her father was scheduled to arrive to pick her up. Though returning home wasn't something she was looking forward to doing, Lynn felt she had proven her point by standing up for what she believed. Her father promised to hear her out and come to a compromise that was beneficial for everyone. Her only worry was that her parents wouldn't keep their end of the bargain but if they didn't, her plans were to leave for good.

Once dressed, Lynn went downstairs and joined Nancy in the kitchen for a morning cup of coffee. Drew's absence was a sure indication that he was at the office and Lynn was anxious to join him. It was silly to think Drew wouldn't go to work this morning. He was a carbon copy of her father who was determined to do what it took to maintain a successful company. Going into the office on the weekend wasn't anything odd for Drew to do, and like her father, Drew never missed a Sunday service. As a family, Lynn was joining the Harrisons for church services, and she couldn't wait to see Gloria's face when they arrived. Though she hadn't brought anything appropriate to wear, Nancy was gracious enough to loan her a dress. It fit a little loose but it was appropriate for church. After enjoying a conversation with Nancy over a cup of coffee, Lynn was eager to join Drew at the office. She wanted to learn more about the company now that her chances to join the Harrison family had increased. Running a food processing company wasn't what Lynn had envisioned in her future but now that she was faced with the possibility of being shut out of her family, she welcomed the challenge. Following Nancy's directions, Lynn took the narrow path that led to the rear gate of the building. Once there, her instructions were to go to the front of the building and ring the bell for Drew to come down to let her inside.

Chapter: 33

"Don't answer it," Karyme pleaded. She held on to Drew for dear life while trying to prevent him from getting off of her. She was on the verge of an orgasm and not even the ringing of the office phone was going to interfere with that. Releasing a high pitch squeal, Karyme was experiencing what she believed to be her first ever orgasm. She tried holding on to Drew's sweaty body but was too weak to maintain a firm grip. Her body shook uncontrollably as her eyes temporarily went blurry while rolling in the back of her head. It happened; Karyme had experienced her first orgasm. The feeling was far greater than she imagined and to have experienced it with Drew was even more gratifying. Drew remained erect while inside Karyme. He hadn't orgasmed and as the phone began ringing a second time, he felt obligated to answer it. If his instincts were correct, it was Lynn calling to greet him a good morning. As much as he wanted to ignore it, Drew knew he couldn't. He got up and rushed to his desk to answer.

"Hillcrest Farms, how may I help you? Drew asked. Thank God, it wasn't Lynn, but his mother was calling to inform him that Lynn was on her way over. Knowing the front door had been left unlocked, it was crucial that he and Karyme got dressed as soon as possible.

"Get up, we need to get dress." Drew instructed as he searched for his clothes. His body was sweaty and he was looking for anything to wipe the perspiration from him. Using his shirt, Drew wiped his face and chest before putting it on. He searched urgently for his underwear and located them inside his pants that was lying on the left side of the couch. Drew struggled to get dress. He was in panic mode and he was dressing as fast as he could. "You need to get dress asap," Drew warned.

"Why, what's going on?" Karyme asked, dubious to Drew's urgent need to get dress.

Drew realized the possibility of Lynn coming to the plant to see him was high but took the chance to make love to Karyme. Again, he'd made a vital decision of allowing his penis to think for him, instead of following his mind. Now it was too late, he was about to be caught red handed and neither Karyme or Lynn was aware of the position he'd placed them in. Once getting dressed, Drew rushed to neat up the office, knowing he had only minutes to do so before Lynn arrived. He sprayed the office with an air refresher and repositioned the couch.

199

"Drew, what is going on?" Karyme asked again. She watched the urgency in Drew's actions as well as the mortal fear he displayed while prepping the room. "What the hell is going on?" Karyme asked again, while clueless to what was about to happen. Karyme's first thoughts were that her mother had found out about them and was on her way over to confront them. If this was the case, she needed to expedite her effort in getting dress.

"Is mami on her way here?" Karyme asked.

"No, much worse." Drew replied.

"What could be worse than getting caught by my mami?" Karyme asked.

Facing Karyme with a ridiculous look on his face, Drew fumbled over the words to explain what was happening.

"Sweetie, I don't know how to tell you this, but before I do, I want you to know that I love you with all my heart, and I pray that you will forgive me."

Karyme stood silent as she prepared herself for the worse. She could see it was more than an unexpected visit from her mother or Drew's mother for that matter. Something heavy was about to be dropped on her that could potentially cause their breakup. Had Drew slept with Gloria? Karyme had no idea what was about to happen that caused Drew to lose his composure.

Do this have anything to with Gloria?" Karyme asked.

"No." Drew replied.

"Then what?" Karyme asked.

Seeing the fear in Drew's face, Karyme realized what he was about to tell her would change their lives forever. What had begun as the happiest moment in her life was quickly becoming a nightmare. Something was coming down the pike, Karyme just didn't know what. Drew wanted to hold Karyme before confessing the truth. He placed his arms around her and squeezed her tightly before releasing his grip. Drew wanted Karyme to feel the sincerity of his heart when he told her the truth. It's true that his callous behavior was not only insensitive but unbecoming of the morals and values he'd set for himself.

Drew had been a coward and a cheater and he was about to pay for his misgivings by losing the one woman who stood by him through thick and thin.

"It's about Lynn, isn't it?" Karyme asked.

"Yes," Drew responded. "Sweetheart, I neglected to tell you that Lynn caught the bus here yesterday. She's on her way over from the house now." Drew confessed. It was one of the hardest things he ever had to do but if he had done so earlier, things wouldn't have been so hectic.

"Lynn spent the night at your house and you're just telling me," Karyme shockingly asked. "Oh my God, oh my God."

"Sweetie, I tried telling you but you wouldn't let me," Drew replied.

"That's bullshit, and you know it," Karyme said. Karyme was angrier at Drew than she was shock. She couldn't believe Drew would do this to her.

Too ashamed to look Karyme in the eye, Drew tried reaching to hold her but was pushed away.

"Get your fucking hands off of me. You done fucked me and now you're telling me your little bitch stayed with you last night. How could you do this to me?" Karyme screamed.

It was the first time Drew had ever heard Karyme curse and rightfully so; she was devastated by the news and responded the only way she knew how. Karyme slapped Drew's face with such force, it nearly knocked him against the office wall. "You motherfucker; you literally fuck me in every sense of the word,"

"Karyme please, let me explain." Drew pleaded but it was too late to tell the truth because the truth were minutes away from entering the office.

"Tell me this Drew, did you sleep with Lynn last night?" Karyme asked.

With a straight face Drew answered no. There was still a chance he could fix things with Karyme and if he had admitted the truth, it would have been impossible to ever get her back.

Incapacitated by the jolt her heart had just endured, Karyme could only lash out. Drew's attempt to console her once more was met with resistance.

201

Snatching her purse from the file cabinet, Karyme rushed to leave but collapsed in tears before reaching the office door. Drew rushed by her side to aid her but his assistance was denied.

"Don't fuckling touch me," Karyme screamed out. "Don't you ever, fucking touch me again,"

 It was devastating to learn the only man she'd ever loved and trusted had betrayed her. Karyme loved Drew with all of her heart. She loved him so much; she gave him her most prized possession. Gloria had been right when she anointed her as being Drew's side-piece.

Gloria had forewarned her that Drew would never introduce her as his lady because she was the help. It was true, Drew had no intentions to make her his lady and Lynn resurfacing proved it. How could she had been so stupid to believe Drew could ever love someone like her. It was a time Drew made her believed they would be the ideal couple but like everything else, Drew proved her dreams to be false. Though hurt, Karyme felt she needed to be strong and with every ounce of strength she had left, Karyme lifted herself up from the floor and opened the door. Not wanting her to leave, Drew tightly wrapped his arms around Karyme's waist from the rear and buried his face in her hair. He pleaded for forgiveness, hoping not to lose the woman he truly loved but it was too late, Lynn was fed up with his bullshit.

 Seeing his future spiral downward, Drew continued to reiterate the love he felt for Karyme. He pleaded his case for Karyme not to give up on them but his pleas went unanswered. He'd lost Karyme and sadly, there wasn't a damn thing he could do about it. Still refusing to give up, Drew tried explaining what was in his heart but Karyme wanted no parts of it. She'd heard enough and was ready to close the book on their short-lived relationship for good. In an effort to free herself from Drew's grip, Karyme screamed for him to release her.

"Drew please, let me go," Karyme pleaded. She didn't want to hear anything else Drew had to say, and told him as much.

Sensing it was the only thing to do, Drew obliged. His last-ditch effort to convince Karyme to hear him out hadn't work and though he hated to release her; he had to accept the inevitable. Drew stood at the door and watched Karyme leave the office.

But before walking away, Karyme turned and shoved Drew from the threshold of the door and pulled the door shut before making her way downstairs. Karyme wiped the tears from her eyes as she made her way down the two flights of stairs. She prayed she wouldn't come face to face with Lynn because she didn't know how she would react if she did. Once on the ground floor, Karyme rushed to the exit door that led out of the building to the parking lot where her car was parked. She opened the door, only to see Lynn making her way up the stairs. Karyme hands began shaking as Lynn walked towards her. She was seconds away from facing the woman that stole her life and though she wanted to confront her about her intentions for Drew, Karyme thought it would be best if she said nothing. Drew had made his choice and Lynn was who he wanted to be with. It was an easy comparison between Lynn to Gloria and in Karyme's opinion, Lynn was a carbon copy of Gloria, who for years had taken advantage of Drew before he saw the light. Karyme could only pray that Drew would see Lynn for what she was before she ruined his life. Though it was over between them, it hadn't stopped Karyme from caring about the man she still loved. She understood getting over Drew was going to be difficult but Karyme knew she had to go on with her life. The only problem was that she'd decline her position at Aircraft America and getting another window of opportunity would be impossible.

Standing face-to-face with Lynn, Karyme stood with her head high. She wasn't going to bow down to Lynn and though she didn't know what to say, Karyme did the next best thing, she smiled. Lynn was the first to speak and in doing so, she extended her hand to greet Karyme.

"Good morning, I don't believe we've ever met, I'm Ashlynn Boldmont," Lynn said.

"I'm Karyme Rios-Gonzales," Karyme replied. Karyme was doing everything in her power not to break down but knew she had to leave before she did.

"Drew has told me so much about you, it's great to finally meet you," Lynn said.

"Thank you, and it's great finally meeting you," Karyme responded.

Karyme continued to smile but Lynn easily picked up on it as being fake. It was easy to see that Karyme had been crying. Why? Lynn hadn't to foggiest idea but she was going to find out when she saw Drew.

203

"Is that man of mine still in the office?" Lynn asked with assurance.

"Yeah, he's waiting for you," Karyme responded. Hearing that Lynn was referring to Drew as her man, Karyme couldn't handle being around her anymore. She was uncertain if Lynn was intentionally rubbing salt in her wounds but felt it was time to leave before she lost her emotions.

"I would love to talk to you longer but I'm running late for church. Maybe we'll get together and talk soon. It was great meeting you," Karyme responded as she began making her way towards her car. Karyme was left with a sickening feeling inside of her stomach for having to shake the hand of the woman who stole her man and even though she wanted to punch Lynn's lights out, Karyme managed to maintained her dignity.

Lynn watched as Karyme walked to her car. It was obvious she was over-run with emotions and her face exhibited the hurt and pain of a broken heart. Once again Lynn's interest peaked at the idea that Drew was somehow involved with his so-called best friend. It wouldn't have been a surprise if Drew had fallen for the Latina beauty because Karyme was gorgeous and her personality alone was captivating. Karyme was like the girl next door but now that she was back into Drew's life, Lynn was going to do everything in her power to shield him from the beautiful Karyme, along with Gloria, who was still trying to get Drew into her bed. It was going to be a near impossible task to keep Karyme from Drew because they worked together, but Lynn had a plan.

Climbing the stairs, Lynn recognized if she was going to recapture Drew's heart fully, she was going to have to step up her game. She entered the office to find Drew placing folders in his cabinet.

"Good morning baby," Lynn said, greeting Drew with a kiss.

Touching his cheek, Lynn was quick to inquire about his bruise.

"What happened to your cheek?" Lynn asked.

"It's nothing," Drew responded.

Drew didn't want to go into what happened, but it didn't stop Lynn from wanting to know. Drew was her man, and if Karyme laid hands on Drew, she was going to make it her problem. Lynn first thought was to run downstairs to confront Karyme.

"Oh, hell Naw," Lynn said, as she turned to leave the office.

Drew grabbed hold of Lynn's arm, preventing her from leaving. It wasn't going to be any fighting on his behalf today. He was the culprit of what happened this morning and whether Lynn like the idea of him getting the taste smacked from his mouth, the fact remained that he deserved it.

"What do you think you're going? Drew asked.

"I'm going to smack the shit out of Karyme, like she did to you," Lynn answered.

"Let it go, Karyme and I have these fights all the time," Drew explained.

"What are you talking about?" Lynn asked.

"It has to do with business. She's acting president and I went against her wishes and closed a deal without her consent," Drew explained. Once again, Drew was lying his ass off, but he wasn't about to tell the truth of what actually happened, not after leading Lynn to think they had a future together.

"You need to fire her ass," Lynn said.

Lynn was aware of the closeness Karyme shared with the Harrison's. They grew up together, and though Drew may have closed a deal with her consent, it didn't justify slapping the soon to be owner of the company.

 Without adding insult to injury, Lynn chose not to pry further. Her goal was to repair their relationship, not damage it any more than she had already had. Seeing that Drew was in need of a friend, Lynn wanted to do something to help ease the tension Drew was feeling. She was certain Drew and Karyme were having some type of a close relationship but remained uncertain as to how far it had gone. Lynn knew, if she was to regain Drew's heart fully it was detrimental, she reacted immediately.

"I met Karyme downstairs," Lynn said. "She's way more beautiful than her pictures. It's hard to believe, she doesn't have a man."

"Karyme is all about building her career," Drew said. He waited for an onslaught of questions but got none. It was as if Lynn trusted and believed him, when he said, he and Karyme were no more than friends. Logging the last of his information into his computer, Drew logged off, ending his morning shift. It was nearing the time they would have to leave to get ready for church and he didn't want to be late.

"It must be hard working in an enclosed area with such a pretty girl?" Lynn asked. Her questions were the start of an interrogation to learn more about Drew's association with Karyme. Lynn was on track to dig for the information she needed.

She wanted to be sure if Drew was involved with Karyme and if so, how deep was their involvement. To divert Lynn's question to a more tranquil conversation, Drew changed the subject.

"Did you sleep well last night?" Drew asked, hoping it was enough to deter Lynn from asking additional questions pertaining to Karyme.

"I slept like a baby, thanks to you," Lynn responded with a smile.

It wasn't hard to figure out what Drew was trying to do but for now, Lynn decided to back off before she ruined the surprise, she had in store for him. It had been a stimulating experience to spend the weekend with Drew and his family and after spending another night on the farm, Lynn could see herself living the quit life. Since arriving, she hadn't suffered any headaches or had to take medication to help combat her anxiety. This was partly because she was with the man, she wanted to spend the rest of life with. But before she could even think about relaxing, Lynn first had to make sure Drew was on board with them having a future together. Lynn was willing to give up her inheritance if she could marry Drew and have his children. Lynn stood behind Drew, who was still sitting at his desk. She placed her hands on his shoulders, and without warning, she pulled his chair from behind his desk and spun it around to face her. Wearing a sundress, Lynn straddled Drew and locked her arms around his neck. It was the perfect way to greet him to say good morning.

"Can you imagine us being together like this every day?" Lynn asked.

"If we were, I wouldn't get any work done for sure," Drew laughed.

Drew was blown away by Lynn's aggression but it wasn't Lynn he saw straddling him; it was Karyme. He couldn't help but imagine what she was going through.

Drew didn't know how he was going to get Karyme back into his life but he had to find a way. Karyme was the woman he loved but Lynn was the woman he wanted. Standing, Lynn untied the shoulder straps to her sun dress, allowing it to fall freely to the floor. Standing in only her panties, she quickly removed them.

"Here's what you didn't see last night." Lynn said, giving Drew full access to her body. Lynn had regained most of the weight she'd lost and she had filled out in all the right places. Her breast had grown larger and so had her hips and buttocks. Lynn had grown into her own, so much so, it stimulated Drew to want to continue from last night.

"Like what you see?" Lynn asked.

"I love with what I see." Drew responded.

A sense of urgency raced through Drew's body as his desire to have Lynn increased. Her light tanned skin tone was enough to spark his desire, but it hadn't erased his visions of he and Karyme. Again, Drew was allowing his penis to think for him and thanks to Lynn standing naked in front of him, his conscious began playing tricks on him. With his penis now throbbing like a toothache, Drew's morals and values were being put to the test. His thoughts now consisted with only making love to Lynn, relieving the pressure he had built with Karyme. Unbuttoning Drew's shirt, Lynn pulled him from his chair and unbuckle his pants. Lynn guided Drew's trousers to his ankles, before untying his shoe laces. She guided him back into his desk chair and removed his shoes and trousers. Lynn wanted Drew to know how much she love him and what she was willing to do to keep him. Doing her absence, Karyme may have become her rival but after today, Karyme was going to be just another girl, who crossed Drew's path. After today, Drew was going to be off-limits and Lynn was sure of that. The excitement of making love to Lynn had become overpowering, Drew couldn't think of anything else he wanted to do more. So much so, he'd forgotten what was most important to him. His morning had gotten off to a terrific start, a start Drew hadn't expected but welcomed. Karyme had shocked him with an early morning surprise but then, Lynn abruptly interrupted them. Now she had taken the same route as Karyme, and things were headed in the same direction.

Lynn took control, by straddling Drew in his desk chair. Lynn used the arm rest to slowly lower her body over Drew's. She had no plans to tease Drew, she wanted to feel him inside of her.

"I love you," Lynn whispered. She looked into Drew's eyes to see what he was feeling and though his eyes showed his feelings, his mouth never parted. "You love me?" Lynn asked.

Drew answered; "Yes, I love you very much."

Lynn lowered her body more, giving Drew more access to her. She could feel him penetrating deeper, giving her the pleasure, she was craving. Lynn's moans transformed into screams of passion. She was enticed by the way Drew was penetrating her and asked that he stand.

"Lift me up," Lynn instructed. She wanted Drew to stand, while holding her to feel the depths of his penis penetrating deeper inside of her. Lynn interlocked her fingers around Drew's neck as he stood from his chair. Lynn could feel Drew's penis exploring deeper inside of her as he lifted her up and down on his penis, and as he did so, Lynn pleaded for him not to stop.

"Oh my God, oh my God," Lynn repeated as her body shook uncontrollably. "I'm coming already," Lynn cried out.

Drew had robbed her of her strength by giving her an intense orgasm and though her body continued to shake out of control, Lynn wanted more. Her body belonged to Drew and it was his to do as he pleased. Drew's desire to please Lynn prompted him to change their setting. With Lynn held secured in his arms, Drew continued to make love to her as he walked across the room to the awaiting couch. With each step he made, he found himself exploring deeper inside Lynn. The sensation from his throbbing penis was more than Lynn could withstand. She was seconds away from another orgasm that made holding on to Drew difficult. Drew and Lynn were playing a dangerous game of Russian roulette with their future. All it would take was one slip-up and their lives would forever change. But Drew believed, he was a master of the withdrawal method and why wouldn't he; after being successful many times before? However, now wasn't the time to evaluate the consequences they were facing. They were two consenting adults whose attraction for each other overpowered the danger they were facing.

Once on the couch, Drew gently positioned Lynn on her back. He used his hand to remove the hair from her face and kissed her. Staring down at Lynn, Drew could hardly believe what was happening.

It had only been a few weeks ago when their relationship seemed over and now, he was making love to her on the couch in his office, after doing the same with Karyme. Making love to two women minutes apart wasn't anything Drew wanted to boast about. In fact, he was ashamed of what he was doing. It was troubling to know he had hurt Karyme, after years of being the best of friends but now was the time to think about it.

"I love you, Drew Harrison," Lynn whispered again.

Hearing Lynn say I love you, stimulated Drew to want her even more. No one had ever made him feel the way Lynn had and because of it, the pressure began building inside of him for an explosion that was sure to come. Sensing Drew was nearing an orgasm, Lynn took it upon herself to make a demand, without first discussing it with Drew. She whispered the words; no responsible man would ever want to partake in.

"I want to feel your juices inside of me." Lynn requested.

For Lynn, it was her way to complete their reunification but Drew saw things differently. He saw it as being an irrational decision they will later regret. It was an invitation Drew wanted nothing to do with. So much so, he contemplated abruptly ending his morning surprise. However, Lynn was overly persuasive; she had the upper hand and she was using it to her advantage. Maybe, it was the way she made love to him that had Drew wanting to oblige her wishes. Whatever the reason, Drew was left undecided, if ejaculating inside of Lynn was what he wanted. He wanted to pull out but by doing so, he would not only disappoint Lynn, it would ruin their morning together. For Lynn, it wasn't about her becoming his woman, she wanted to give Drew the pleasure of ejaculating inside of her, without having to use the withdrawal method or wearing a condom.

"Baby, are you sure this is what you want?" Drew questioned.

Again, Lynn requested he not withdraw from her and again, Drew reminded her of the consequences they faced. Drew had gone out on a limb by painting a picture of what could happen if they chose to cross the line, but his warnings hadn't been enough to deter Lynn. Her mind was made, it was what she wanted and nothing was going to change it. Throwing caution to the wind while forfeiting his morals and values, Drew chose to accommodate Lynn's wishes.

Although he remained apprehensive regarding the depths of his love for her, his decision was made; he was going through with it. It was a decision he knew he may regret but his weakness for Lynn overpowered his will to do what was right. Feeling the buildup, Drew prepared himself for what was about to happen. His body became cold and tensed; his eyes felt as if they were about to explode, he was losing control. It was about to happen; Drew could no longer control or prolong his oncoming orgasm. His eyes begin to watered from the pressure that was building inside of him. It was too late to reconsider his decision now, it was happening and as his thrusts went deeper inside of Lynn, so had his semen.

Chapter: 34

Excusing herself from the morning services, Karyme left for home. She could barely see the road from the tears that were falling from her eyes. The thought of Drew with Lynn was weighing heavy on her mind and she became sick from it. Before she could make it home, Karyme pulled over to the side of the road. She got out of her car and ran in front of it to throw up. Her sickness may have been mental but it transitioned to being physical. It was a crushing blow for her to have to accept the idea that Drew had gone back to Lynn. How could Drew allow Lynn back into his life after she deserted him doing his time of need? This wasn't the first time Drew had fallen prey to Lynn and if Karyme had to bet, it won't be the last. Lynn had the tendency of running away when things got tough and once the waters were calm; she returned to Drew's waiting arms as if nothing had ever happened. It shouldn't have been a surprise by what happened. She should have suspected Lynn would return after the charges were dropped against them and Drew had recovered. Karyme had overestimated Lynn by thinking she was out of the picture and for doing so, she was left with a broken heart. Gloria had forewarned her many times that Drew could never love anyone like her and as much as she hated to admit it, Gloria was correct.

Drew had once again passed her over but this time, he'd done so after she'd decided to give him her most precious jewel. It should have been enough to keep Drew forever but she'd underestimated Lynn's return. It's sad to think, Drew could be so clueless as to what was about to happen to him. He is under the assumption that he and Lynn have a future together but sooner or later, he was going to wake up to find her missing again. To say Karyme's goose was cooked was an understatement. In reality, there was nothing she could do to recover her losses. She'd given up her future by turning down the job offer of a lifetime. She even defied her mother's wishes to stay away from Drew and for it, she was left broken hearted. Karyme found herself stuck at Hillcrest Farms, having to share an office with the man that left her for his ex-girlfriend. What in God's name was she thinking? How could she believe she could maintain a relationship with a man she knew hadn't gotten over his ex-girlfriend?

Feeling she was about to throw up, Karyme rushed to the ditch line and throw up on the side of the road and threw up. Holding her stomach, Karyme laid across the hood of her car, allowing the warmth from its engine to soothe her upset stomach.

For over two hours, she'd held in her tears and now that she was alone, she could finally cry without anyone being around.

Driving upon the scene, Mason saw what he thought was Karyme's car stall on the side of the road. Getting out to investigate, Mason saw Karyme lying across the hood of her car. She hadn't noticed Mason behind her and continued crying out loudly. By leaning across the hood of her car, Karyme's dress was high above her hips, nearly exposing her buttocks.

"What a pretty brown ass." Mason thought to himself as he watched from a short distance. Building the nerves to move forward Mason made his way over to where Karyme was. "Are you ok?" Mason asked, touching the lower part of Karyme's back.

Feeling a hand on her back, Karyme jumped.

"Oh, I'm sorry if I scared you. Is anything wrong?" Mason asked.

"No, I'm fine," Karyme replied.

"You need any help?" Mason asked.

"No, I'm fine," Karyme repeated.

Realizing, she was alone and in the middle of nowhere with Mason, Karyme hastily returned to the safety of her car. She didn't want to have to answer any questions concerning her state of mind, especially from Mason.

Her dislike for him dated back to high school and though it was a kind gesture, by him to offer his assistance, Karyme wanted no part of it. Mason followed Karyme to her car, he couldn't resist from staring at her thighs and imagining what it would be like to lie between them. Mason had heard about her alleged relationship with Drew but after seeing her crying, he was sure, it must to have been true because from the way Karyme was crying, their fairy tale must have ended.

Chapter: 35

Drew's appearance in church left nearly the entire congregation in disbelief. Those who saw him entered, stared as he and Lynn were ushered to their seats. For weeks the congregation speculated the purity of Drew's relationship with Karyme but after seeing him arrive to church with an unknown beauty left astonished. Rumors had circulated that Drew association with Karyme went deeper than their supposed friendship but to see him in church with Lynn, left them to ponder if Drew's appearance with another woman was a hoax. Drew's involvement with a catholic girl hadn't gone over well with the majority of the church members, but seeing him with Lynn, gave them hope that Drew had come to his senses by choosing a good Southern Baptist girl. Most who knew the Harrison family believed their faith was too strong to mix with another religion. Some saw Drew's relationship with Karyme as a fluke or him being curious, while others questioned the morality of his character. As far as the congregation was concerned, Drew and Karyme were as different as day and night and the likelihood of them having a successful relationship was less than zero. Nancy was the first to argued that Karyme was the ideal girl for Drew. She refused to factor religion with her son's right to happiness. Though she lost her argument to convince the church members of Karyme's value to her son, Nancy continued to rally behind them. She respected Drew's friendship with Lynn but her wishes were that he maintained his relationship with the woman that loved him unconditionally. Regardless if the church agreed, or disagreed with Drew's decision to be with a Catholic girl, it was ultimately Drew's decision to make.

Gloria nearly jumped out of her seat after seeing Drew and Lynn ushered into church together. Seeing Drew bringing another woman in church was like a slap in her face. To make matters worse, Gloria's younger sister Kelly was quick to point out her mistake for letting Drew get away. Kelly quietly poked fun at her sister for having to sit and watch her ex-boyfriend sitting across from them, holding the hand of another woman while her atheist boyfriend was somewhere committing sins. Gloria was bewildered as to why the church usher chose to sit Drew and the "Rich Bitch" across from her. Having to see Drew holding Lynn's hand instantly caused Gloria to become angry. To salvage what was left of her pride, Gloria opened her purse and removed Mason's ring and placed it on her finger. It was foolish to think that Drew would even consider coming back to her, but Gloria never gave up hope. Seeing Drew with Lynn, reminded Gloria of how it was when they were together.

213

Leaving Drew was the worst decision she ever made. She had a good man but she didn't see the value of him, not until it was too late, and now, she was suffering from having to see the love of her life, holding the hand of another woman. God knows, by no means could she blame anyone but herself. She may have been a cheater, a liar, along with many other things but Gloria could honestly say, she never stopped loving Drew. If only she could get a final chance to prove her worthiness; she would undo all the bad things she ever did to Drew. Gloria continued to focus her attention on Drew. She reminisced about the good times they shared and though it was hard having to watch Drew with Lynn, she maintained her sanity. However, before church concluded, Gloria became fidgety and was unable to resist from staring at Lynn. She began questioning what Drew saw in Lynn. Lord knows, Lynn was as skinny as a rail and dressed as homely as Karyme but for some unexplained reason, Drew was attractive to that style of woman. In Gloria's opinion, there was nothing special about Lynn, other than she was rich and though she heard whisperings about how attractive Lynn was; she didn't agree. As far as she was concerned, Lynn was just another chick who was trying to impeded on what was once hers.

Seeing Gloria steadily staring at her, Lynn gave her a smirked and waved hello at her. Of course, Gloria didn't take too kindly to her actions. It was enough to warrant her to walk across the aisle, and slap the shit out of Lynn; not to mention that jack ass ex-boyfriend of hers, who chose to bring her to their church.

"The audacity of that motherfucker, for bringing that bitch to our church," Gloria mumbled to herself.

Feeling that Lynn was taunting her made it nearly impossible for Gloria to set idle. Drew and Lynn's presence was preventing her from concentrating on the service and Pistol and Mattie had taken noticed.

"That son-of-a-bitch," Gloria whispered under her breath. She was having a great morning before Drew fucked things up by bringing that bitch to church with him. Gloria tried focusing on the message but was unable to do so. She was flustered and unconsciously began tapping the heel of her shoes against the wooden floor of the church. Her act was distracting, causing Pistol to nudge her.

He wanted her to focus on the message the good Reverend was presenting and even though Gloria acknowledged him by stopping, she couldn't focus because her focus was on Drew and the bitch he was sitting with.

Immediately following the benediction, Drew and Lynn left the church quietly. They opted not to socialize with the congregation and stood outside by their car to wait for Nancy and Joanna. As they had done for years, the congregation gather in front of the church to discuss the day's sermon and today was no exception. Seeing that Nancy and Joanna were busy talking, Gloria emerged from the crowd to make her way over to where Drew and Lynn were standing. It wasn't surprising that she was dressed in a tight-fitting dress two sizes too small but Gloria felt the need to accentuate her coke bottle shape. It was fair to say her presence demanded attention and the church was no exception. Men, young and old alike, eagerly casted their eyes upon Gloria, as she walked by. To say Gloria wasn't a sight to behold would be a misstatement. She was beautiful to say the least and boy was she ever sexy. Gloria strut was like a model walking down the runway and as she made her way toward Drew and Lynn, Drew could feel his heart in his throat. He had a bad feeling that Gloria was up to no good but knew if she chose to act stupid, she wasn't going to like the results.

Seeing Drew's uncomfortable stance, Gloria chuckled to herself as she made her way up the small incline where Drew and Lynn were standing. Gloria saw what she believed was Drew salivating over her and it encouraged her to walk even sexier. As Gloria got closer, and got a better view of Lynn, she formed a quick opinion of her. Gloria understood why Drew was salivating over her as she walked toward him. Lynn looked to be no older than fifteen. She had a light covering of freckles scattered across her face. Not only that, Lynn was wearing one of Nancy's old dresses, giving her the appearance of an old woman. It was funny to think Drew left her for a half-breed, a mutt, someone who was born because of money and because of it, she was sure to leave Drew once she came to her senses. Seeing Lynn in such bad condition gave Gloria a sense of superiority. She was prepared to flaunt what she had to capture Drew's attention and she was going to do it in front of his precious Lynn.

"Hello Mr. Harris, and hello to you too," Gloria said, referring to Lynn.

215

"And hello to you," Lynn replied. Although they were on church ground, Lynn had no problem with dotting Gloria's eye if need be. Knowing what Lynn was capable of doing, Drew intervened.

"Gloria, I don't believe you have been formally introduced but this is my lady, Ms. Ashlynn Baldmont. Lynn, this is my ex, Gloria," Drew said.

"Your lady," Gloria questioned.

"That's right, his lady, soon will be his wife," Lynn replied. Lynn hadn't forgotten their blow up over the phone and was less than three seconds from showing her ass at church.

Gloria wanted to shake things up with Drew but her attempts failed. Seeing she hadn't made any waves, Gloria began talking about the service while flaunting her hands, hoping Drew would notice the engagement ring she was wearing. It was Gloria's hope that Drew would become jealous after seeing it was his grandmother's ring but Drew, never noticed it. Instead, Lynn was the first to react.

"Congratulations, how long have you been engaged?" Lynn asked.

"Since Friday night; matter of fact, it's your grandmother's ring Drew," Gloria responded with a smirk. She was anxious to know how Drew was going to respond but didn't get the reaction she was hoping to receive and became pissed. Drew hadn't responded the way she expected, he showed no emotion nor did he say anything and because of it, Gloria decided to throw Drew under the bus and did so by inquiring about Karyme.

"Where's your little sidekick that's been coming with you to church?" Gloria asked with a condescending sneer.

"Karyme decided to attend her church today?" Drew responded.

"I see why, you got your little girlfriend with you," Gloria countered.

Drew knew what Gloria was trying to do but he wasn't going to feed into it. Gloria had crossed the line, by infringing upon his relationship with Karyme, while being in the presence of Lynn. Yes, it was wrong the way he chose to handle the situation with Karyme but no gossiping Hoochie momma bitch was going to ruin his relationship with Lynn. As for Lynn, Gloria had answered what she suspected.

Drew was someway involved with Karyme but now wasn't the time to probe, she and Drew had just settled their differences and she wasn't going to ruin it. Maybe, in time Drew will confess what she suspected but that was for another day.

Chapter: 36

Now that her showdown with Gloria was over, Lynn had time to reflect on today's occurrence. As you may have guessed, Lynn was eager to bring up the topic of Karyme. She didn't hide her concerns regarding Drew's relationship with her, and was vocal about how she felt, but ultimately, Lynn knew, now wasn't the time to discuss it. Of course, Drew denied being physically involved with Karyme, and assured Lynn, she didn't have anything to worry about. To lessen the tension, Drew admitted his love for Karyme was nothing more than a sisterly love. Lynn wanted to believe Drew but it was hard to imagined not wanting a physical relationship with a woman so beautiful. Karyme was too beautiful not to be attracted to. She and Drew was spending long hours together, and as much as she didn't want to believe Gloria's accusations surrounding Drew's and Karyme relationship, it was hard not to. Lynn knew she was up against a fight to regain Drew's affections. Though affected by the thought Drew could love someone else, Lynn couldn't much blame him. She'd deserted him doing his times of need and even though it was by no fault of her own, she was old enough to have a voice of her own. Luckily, she'd been given another chance and there was no way she was going to blow it.

"Let's go to the lake," Lynn suggested.

Lynn had a plan to win back her man but she had little time to do so. Her father was due to arrive within the hour and she had no time to lose. Drew was quick to say yes. He took the ATV from the garage and the two made his way to the lake. Drew suspected Lynn wanted to spend time together before leaving but he had no idea that she wanted to make love again. Arriving at the lake, Lynn settled under the old magnolia tree for shade to sit and talk. They hadn't brought a blanket; however, the ground was soft and cool and they decided not to lay the blanket down.

"I wanted to spend a quiet moment with you before my father came," Lynn said. She knew she was going to be punished for pulling such a stunt but Lynn was prepared to accept her punishment. She wanted her father to know how much she loved Drew and what she was willing to do to be with him.

"How severe do you think your punishment is going to be?" Drew asked.

"I don't know nor do I care but if we were married, there'll be nothing they can do to us," Lynn responded.

Drew wasn't sure how to respond to Lynn's statement. Yes, he did ask to marry her once they returned back to the university from Oregon but things had change, he'd changed. He'd given his heart to another woman. Drew couldn't say if getting married was what he wanted. God knew he loved Lynn and he was willing to try to recapture what was lost but he didn't know if he could, now that he'd fallen in love with Karyme. Karyme was the woman he wanted to spend the rest of his life with but after today, he couldn't say for certain if Karyme wanted anything else to do with him.

"What do you think?" Lynn asked.

"About marriage?" Drew responded.

"Yeah," Lynn replied.

"I think it's a great idea, but let's wait to see how your parents are going to react," Drew responded. He hoped it was enough to deter Lynn from acting on impulse. She was riding high and had forgotten about what she was facing. Drew may have been put on the spot by Lynn but he wasn't going to disappoint her after the lengths she'd gone through to be with him. He was obligated to at least give them a chance to rekindle what they'd lost.

Overwhelmed with the idea of them possibly getting married soon, Lynn began kissing Drew. She guided him to the ground, and in doing so, they began undressing each other. It was by far the most passionate lovemaking Drew had ever made with anyone. Drew was on a mission to rekindle the love he once felt for Lynn and they'd gotten off to a blazing start. He owed Lynn that much after the sacrifices she'd made on his behalf. Once again, they threw caution to the wind by engaging in unprotective sex. They both knew the risk they were taking but neither of them gave it a second thought. Whether it was the best decision could be debated, but Drew didn't care about himself, his thoughts were about Lynn and what she wanted. Lynn on the other hand thought differently. It wasn't that she wanted to deliberately get pregnant to keep Drew. The truth was, they'd discussed marriage as well as starting a family. Her beliefs were, by giving Drew the family he wanted, he would make her his wife.

Chapter: 37

Gloria watched impatiently as Mason played a game of pool with one of the locals at Club Funky's. She hadn't been in the mood to be at Funky's or any place for that matter. Seeing the images of Drew being with Lynn continued to replay in her mind. It should have been a sign for her to finally moved on but it wasn't. Gloria wanted revenge, she wanted to get even with Drew as well as his "Rich Bitch". Gloria felt disrespected by Drew for bringing another woman to their church. It was hard having to see Drew with Lynn, not to mention the times he brought his little senorita to church with him, but it was nothing like having to see Lynn. The smirk Lynn had on her face was enough to warrant her a good old country ass kicking. In Gloria's closed little mind, she believed Drew had abused her. Not only had he abused her mind, he pretended to be in love with her, just to fuck her. Her desire to get even with Drew and Lynn had taken precedence over everything, including her relationship with Mason. Having to accept the idea of Drew not wanting to be with her was unacceptable for Gloria. She refused to believe Drew was in love with "The Rich Bitch" or his little "Wetback". Gloria believed Drew was only with Lynn because of his desire to be amongst the rich and powerful.

Lynn was his crutch for reaching the pinnacle that he so desperately sought after and after getting there, he was surely going to dump her in the trash where she belonged. It was crushing to know Drew was with the "Rich Bitch", but she found solace in knowing "The Wet Back" was discovered crying and puking her guts out after learning Drew had chosen his "Rich Bitch" over her. Unlike Karyme, Gloria hadn't shaded a fucking tear over Drew. She knew without a doubt, she was going to win Drew's affection when everything was over said and done. But for making her look like a damn fool in front of the church, Drew was going to have to pay. She wanted to bring Drew to his knees but didn't know what angle to take. Gloria continued to contemplate on how she was going to get even with Drew, as she watched Mason run the table of pool. Yes, she had no one to blame but herself for losing Drew, but that didn't stop her from blaming everyone else. She'd chosen to make the decision to be with Mason and now that she had, Gloria realized, she'd fucked up. Still, it hadn't given Drew the right to use her like an old pair of boots to walk in the mud. Yeah, he'd gotten over on her but for doing so, Drew had become enemy number one.

Gloria continued to think of ways to end Drew's relationship with Lynn as she watched Mason win game after game of pool. Her first thought was to tell Lynn she was still fucking Drew but she couldn't because word of their affair may get out and she didn't want to deal with Mason's jealous ass. Thinking extreme, Gloria entertained thoughts of seducing Drew to get pregnant. She knew by getting pregnant Drew would do the right thing and marry her. Drew may have been a motherfucker but he was a man of honor and integrity. Being a family man was all Drew ever wanted to be which convinced Gloria, he would undoubtably do the right thing and marry her to give his child a name. But what about Mason? How was he going to fit in her equation? Mason had been her lone supporter through her rough times and to throw him to the curve would be barbaric but there was no other way. Mason was about to be crushed by her actions, but as life go on and so would he.

"You ready to go?" Mason asked after finally losing a game.

Gloria's answered by saying yes. She couldn't wait to get the hell out of that shit hole. She was ready to go home and after deciding on how to get even with Drew, she was ready to put her plan in motion. But Mason threatened to derail her plan by suggesting that she spend the night with him. Deflecting his plan, Gloria expressed her desire to go home to rest. Her excuse was that she was tired and needed sleep because she was scheduled to work another 12-hour shift at the hospital the following morning. Gloria's excuse only increased Mason's effort to convince her to spend the night with him. He was persistent and was refusing to take no for an answer. He even informed Gloria that he would be the perfect gentleman, promising to resist any temptation of trying to seduce her but it wasn't enough for Gloria. She insisted on going home alone to complete the things she needed to do for her long shift the following morning. To get Mason off of her back Gloria assured him, she would give him plenty of quality time doing the upcoming week. It was only then Mason ceased his persuasiveness to convince Gloria about spending the night with him but in doing so, Mason sensed a changed in Gloria.

Since her medical conference, things had changed between them. Though Gloria would let him make love to her, she wouldn't allow him to hold her afterward. Mason began to believe that there was someone else. Who? Mason couldn't answer, but his suspicions surrounded Drew. Once home, Mason blew Gloria a kiss and waved goodbye as he waited for her to enter her house. After doing so, Mason slowly droves from Gloria's driveway home.

His drive home was less than a minute because Gloria lived just across from him, with an empty lot separating them. On his way home, Mason couldn't erase his suspicions that Gloria was planning to meet Drew. He'd hoped that he was over reacting but his suspicions were driving him crazy. He had to find out if his suspicions were correct. God forgive him for what he would do to the both of them if they were fucking behind his back. Mason parked his car behind his house. He looked across the path towards Gloria's house and got an idea to spy by way of the over grown lot that faced Gloria's house. It was unpopular but it was a decision he felt needed to follow. Mason was about to break his golden rule by going against his morals but he didn't feel any remorse about what he was about to do. Mason walked through the path that separated the two housing divisions and concealed himself within the confines of the wild shrubbery to get an unrestricted view of Gloria's house. He positioned himself between two wild bushes to get a clear view of the entire house to watch Gloria's every movement. He chuckled at the thought of himself hiding in the woods spying as if he was a policeman on surveillance. By no means did he want to be a cop or to have anything to do with one. He only wanted to find out what his girlfriend was doing behind his back, but why had he resulted on doing something so unlike him? Any other woman Mason wouldn't have given a damn about but Gloria wasn't just any other woman; she was about to become his wife. Gloria was the one-woman Mason had dreamed of having, since learning how to love. He couldn't bear the thought of losing her to Drew yet again or to any man for that matter. Mason was willing to fight to the death; if it meant keeping Gloria and if he had to face Drew, then, family or not, he was willing to fight til the death.

Inside the house, Gloria tried unsuccessfully to contact Drew but continued calling in spite of it. Desperately seeking the chance for the opportunity to vent her frustrations, Gloria continued calling, and after trying for more than an hour, she finally reached Drew on his cellular phone.

"Where the fuck you been? I've been trying to call you for over an hour." Gloria screamed; demanding an explanation.

Not wanting to alarm his mother who was sitting across from him on the front porch, Drew evasively tried to keep their conversation as basic as possible. He didn't want to implicate himself to his mother, that he was talking to Gloria. God knows, Gloria wasn't one of his mother's favorite people and by all accounts Nancy had reasons to despised her. Like most mother's, Nancy tolerated Gloria because of

Drew's love for her but to say that she wished Gloria would disappear from his life forever would be an understatement. Gloria's actions not only embarrassed Drew, it did so to their family. Her blatant disrespect to the Harrison name is what pushed Nancy over the edge. Nancy had always stayed clear of her children's affairs but she couldn't in good conscious allow Gloria to continue her wrath in destroying her family's good name. Once Drew's relationship with Gloria was declared over, Nancy forbade him from having any further association with her. She kept a close eye on him after their breakup and it wasn't until Drew showed interest in Karyme that Nancy became relaxed.

Seeing that Drew wasn't giving her the attention she was seeking, Gloria began screaming over the phone. To prevent his mother from hearing Gloria's voice, Drew tried silencing her by placing his hand over the phone. He waited as Gloria vented her frustration and after minutes of ranting and raving, Gloria finally lowered her voice and began speaking normally. Now that she'd gotten Drew's attention, it was Gloria's window of opportunity to cast her rod and reel Drew in but Drew was stalling; leaving her no other options but to lash out once more. Gloria didn't want to hear Drew's bogus excuses nor was she taking no for an answer. She was going to see Drew one way or the other, even if it meant driving to his house. By threatening to drive over, Drew quickly caved in to Gloria's demands. It was against his better judgement to meet with her but he was left without a choice. God knew what would happen if Gloria showed up at his house. Without a doubt his mother would go ballistic. So, Drew did the next best thing, he agreed to meet Gloria at Larry's restaurant.

Gloria quickly showered and changed into her black lace panties, and bra. She dressed in a short skimpy skirt, to give Drew easy access, in the event they have sex in the back of Drew's large station wagon. If their meeting went as she'd planned, Gloria was fucking Drew before the night was over. Before leaving, Gloria stood in front of her mirror to look at herself. She was satisfied with the way she was dressed, however, she contemplated how she was going to wear her hair and after trying different styles, she decided to wear it loose. It was an easy choice, especially after remembering Drew loved running his hands through her hair while making love to her. If her night went accordingly to plan, she was getting pregnant. To add fuel to the fire Gloria sprayed Drew's favorite perfume all over her body.

223

 Seeing she was running behind schedule, Gloria got her father's keys to his car and rushed out of the house to make the twenty-minute drive into town.

Hiding between the confines of some thick wild shrubby, Mason saw Gloria leaving the house and got into her father's car and drove off. He was sure she was going to see Drew and sprinted to his car to follow her. Speeding from his driveway; Mason tried catching up to the taillights of Gloria's car but lost sight of her. Guessing she was on her way to see Drew; Mason sped down the secondary road, towards the farm at a high rate of speed. His plans to ruin Gloria and Drew's reunion was all that he could think of and the thought of them being together had Mason furious. He could barely maintain control of his car at the high rate of the speed he was traveling. Just the thought of knowing Gloria was back with Drew was enough to make Mason want to confront the both of them with the shot gun he'd taken from Monkey Carson. Mason arrived at Drew's house but didn't see Gloria or Drew's car in the yard. Not seeing them left Mason with the idea they were probably cuddled up at a hotel in town making love and laughing about how stupid he must be, for thinking she was at home.

Believing Drew and Gloria were shacked up in some motel, Mason quickly made a U-turn and sped towards town in searched of them. He prayed he wouldn't find them parked at a motel because if he did, he was going to kill them both. Unfortunately for Drew and Gloria, Mason had brought more shot gun shells and was prepared to use them if need be. Mason drove through every hotel and motel lot in town, looking for any signs of Drew and Gloria but found nothing. Determined to find them, he continued his search; driving through town looking everywhere he thought they could be. Frustrated by not finding them, Mason droved recklessly through town; nearly causing several accidents in the process. His mission was to locate Drew and Gloria and he didn't give a damn how long it took. Acting on a hunch; Mason drove by the hospital and found Drew's car parked across from Gloria's in Larry's Restaurant parking lot. Mason slowly circled the restaurant looking to find Drew and Gloria. He spotted them sitting across from each other in a rear booth. They were talking, what about, he didn't know. Mason strategically positioned his car in a parking space to observe what was happening inside and though he was unable to decipher what their conversation was about, he suspected it was about them getting back together. Mason's first instinct was to bum rush the restaurant and bitch slap the of both of them but now wasn't the time.

He needed to know the truth about Gloria's relationship with Drew and to do so meant he had to wait it out.

Inside the restaurant, Drew tried to make sense of what was so urgent that Gloria needed to talk to him about. If he had to guess, he'll say, it had to do with Lynn. Nursing on a glass of tea, Drew listened as Gloria ranted about still being in love with him. It didn't matter that she was wearing Mason's ring, her goal was to get Drew to understand how important it was to her and what she was willing to do to get him back into her life. Gloria could best be described as a woman who wanted her cake and eat it too and though she was confused about a lot of things, loving Drew wasn't one of them. Gloria never stopped loving him but her attraction toward Mason was too strong for her to resist. More than anything, she was attracted to Mason's impulsiveness which kept her guessing. He generated the excitement she craved and the more he gave the more she wanted. There was no comparison when it came to having fun between Mason and Drew. Mason fed her cravings, while Drew was a total turn-off. To put it mildly, Drew was as boring as a lazy summer's afternoon. He didn't possess the pizzazz Mason had and to be fair to Gloria, she tried relaying her feelings to Drew but each time she addressed her concerns, Drew brushed them off as if what she was saying wasn't important. As time went on and Drew became more dedicated to his education and taking over his family's company, Gloria found herself turned off by him and more attracted to Mason.

In her opinion, Drew had skipped being a young adult and had become an old boring ass man who wanted to get married and have a house full of kids. Gloria couldn't say for certain, why she decided to accept Mason's ring when she wasn't fully all with wanting to marry him. However, without a doubt, Mason's devotion and financial support is what played a major part in her decision to leave Drew. Unfortunately for Mason, Gloria couldn't get over what she had in Drew. What she had was financial stability, something she could never have with Mason. Gloria's attraction to Drew had nothing to do with her love for him. Yes, she loved him and yes, she wanted to come back to him, but she was still hung up on Mason's unpredictability. You see, Mason was exciting and he gave Gloria the rush she wanted to have, but Drew was the man with the money, and the man that would give her the life she wanted.

Wishing he was anyplace other than sitting in front of Gloria, Drew sit quietly, blocking most of what Gloria was saying from his mind. He wasn't in the mood having to hear her bullshit and after years of walking around blinded by her charm, he had finally seen her for the lying conniving bitch she really was. It was no secret what Gloria was trying to do, she'd played those same games many times before, and like a fool, he would always fall for them, but not this time. This time Drew wasn't going to fall for the old okie doke, he wasn't falling into bed with Gloria. He was taking his ass home because he didn't need any more problems to deal with. He'd just screwed himself from having a life with the woman he truly loved and all because he couldn't say no to a piece of ass. As far as Drew was concerned, Gloria was old news. He had more important things on his plate, and Gloria wasn't one of them.

Seeing that Drew wasn't going to adhere to her attempts to seduce him, Gloria did what she had always done when things didn't go her way; she lashed out.

"And another thing Drew Harrison, why did you bring that Bitch to church with you? Why would you embarrass me like that? Gloria asked

Drew waited a few seconds before answering. He had his family's reputation to consider. The Good Lord knew he didn't want to provoke that crazy bitch, so he had to calculate what he was going to say before saying it. Drew's goal was to answer Gloria as clear and precise as he possibly could without inciting an argument or a physical altercation. Hoping to erase the embarrassment she faced earlier Drew answered by informing Gloria, he brought Lynn to church with him because he'd asked her to be his wife and wanted to formally introduce her to the congregation. Needless to say, Gloria wasn't receptive to his answer. Instead of getting the warm reception Drew and Lynn gave her when she announced her engagement to Mason, Drew got the total opposite.

"What! How in tarnation can you contemplate marrying someone you only known for a few months?" Gloria questioned.

"It's been a year," Drew responded.

Drew's response caught Gloria off guard and after taking a few seconds to comprehend what he said, Gloria's temper got the best of her.

226

"You motherfucker; you mean to tell me, all the time you were fucking me, you were fucking that bitch too?" Gloria said, raising her voice loud enough for the entire restaurant to hear.

"Gloria, lower your voice please," Drew instructed, hanging his head from embarrassment.

"So, what you're telling me is that I was only your fuck Ho? Is that's what you're saying? Is that what you're saying Drew? Answer me got dammit" Gloria screamed.

"Gloria please; you're embarrassing me, as well as yourself," Drew said in a low tone of voice. He didn't have to look around to know they had the attention of everyone inside the restaurant, the silence inside indicated it.

"I'm embarrassing you? Man, fuck you, and your bitch ass momma too." Gloria replied, before continuing to vent. "Just because your momma is the town mayor and you run a got damn million-dollar farm don't make you any better than us common people. That's right everybody; Mayor Harrison's son over here is nothing but a lying, cheating, piece of shit," Gloria said as her voice echoed through the restaurant.

Drew could do nothing but take the onslaught of insults that Gloria was throwing at him. He wasn't going to get into a shouting match with her, he had too much respect for his mother's position as mayor, as well as himself. Instead of creating a scene, Drew wanted to hear Gloria out but after realizing their conversation had gotten out of control, Drew began making his way to the exit door of the restaurant with Gloria fast on his heels, spewing obscenities.

"So, now that you're with the "Rich Bitch" I guess I'm yesterday's news huh?" Gloria asked. "Well fuck you nigger, and that raggedy ass car you drove up here in."

Gloria was harsh as she screamed out at Drew and physically pushing him from behind. Gloria was willing to do anything to incite Drew. She continued to badger him, hoping he would break and when that didn't work, Gloria grabbed hold of the back of Drew's shirt.

"Where the fuck you think you're going? I ain't finish with your bitch ass yet." Gloria screamed out.

Too embarrassed to walk with his head high Drew looked to the floor in an effort to hide his emotions. This was the last straw but he wasn't going to do anything that was going to come back to hunt his family or himself. Gloria refusal to allow Drew to leave had gotten out of control. She wanted to embarrass him and it was fair to say she had. Her antics nearly caused Mason to get out of his car to investigate what was happening but as hard as it was, Mason managed to stay in position to further monitor what was transpiring. His fiancé was having a showdown with her ex-boyfriend and though it was concerning, Mason took pride in seeing Gloria slang Drew around like a rag doll.

"So, it's like that?" Gloria asked. "You gonna turn into a pussy and run with your tail tucked between your legs."

For the first time since knowing Gloria, Drew wanted to slap her to sleep but he kept thinking of the consequences it would cause. There were a lot of people who would benefit in seeing him do something stupid to use against his mother in the upcoming election. So, without responding to Gloria, Drew simply walked away, leaving her sounding out obscenities towards him. There was nothing Drew could have said to get Gloria to understand they weren't going to work out. She was used to getting her way when it came to Drew but no more, those days were gone, Drew had retaken his life and learned a valuable lesson in the process. Never was he ever going to have any association with Gloria's crazy ass again. He had done the right thing by not feeding into Gloria's jealous rage. There was no doubt what took place at Larry's was going to be all over social media as well as on the front page of the Jefferson Free Press but Drew felt he would deal with it when the time came. In front of staff and patrons visiting the restaurant, Gloria had called him a cheater, a liar and a pussy, for refusing to fight like a man. In a way Gloria was right; he hadn't been a man when it came to facing her or Lynn for that matter. The fact remained; he should have severed ties with Gloria months ago but he was too much of a pussy whipped fool to let go the stick of burning dynamite he was holding. You see, Gloria was the envy of every woman in town and she was every man's fantasy. When it came to wanting to satisfy her partner Gloria aimed to please and did so every time they were together. But a funny thing happened, Drew realized sex wasn't what made him happy, he learned being in love was most important to him.

Drew walked away without looking back, leaving Gloria to stand alone.

Gloria had embarrassed him for the last time and he couldn't have felt more relieved knowing he had no reason to ever want to talk to her again. Taking a deep breath, Drew inhaled the sweet smells from the restaurant as he made his way to his car. It was over, after years of being blind, he'd finally saw the light.

Watching Drew get into his car and drive away left tears in Gloria's eyes. She'd fucked up by embarrassing him for perhaps the final time. It was over between them, Drew didn't want anything else to do with her, he'd made it clear that she was dead to him. Gone was her dream of becoming Ms. Gloria Harrison or giving him the baby, but perhaps what she would miss mostly was the lifestyle Drew was able to provide for her. Sure, she had Mason but she didn't love Mason the way she loved Drew and the probability of it ever happening was less than zero.

Gloria left the restaurant under the camouflaged of a sudden heavy downpour. Out of desperation she grabbed a menu from the front desk to covered her head as she made a mad dash to her car. Once inside, Gloria placed her face against the steering wheel to finish her cry before leaving. It was hard to imagine life without Drew. She had been Drew's girl since middle school, he was the first man she fell in love with and the first man to make love to her and now, the first man to say no to her. Tonight, may have been a disaster, but Gloria found herself in this position many times before and each time she had, she found a way to battle back into Drew's heart.

Still parked at the opposite end of the parking lot, Mason watched Gloria drive away. He wasn't sure what happened but he wasn't sold on the idea that Gloria wasn't having an affair with Drew. He'd seen her shake the shit out of Drew, and from the looks of it, Drew was steamed about getting embarrassed. Mason couldn't say but if he had to bet, he would bet it had to do with his engagement to Gloria. Mason followed Gloria from a distance, taking the interstate behind her. He entertained the thought of catching up to Drew to run off the road but changed his mind after realizing it was a stupid thing to do. God knew, Drew wasn't worth the money it would cost to repair his car or the rift it would bring between the families. Mason was going to have to find some other way to fuck Drew up for backstabbing him but for now, he was going to play the role of the unsuspected dumb ass, who was clueless to what was happening with his lady.

Once home, Mason contemplated calling one of his many side chicks as a payback to Gloria for lying to him. His body was burning with a desire to get even and he wanted to take out his frustration on someone but he thought better of his decision. Instead, Mason decided he would take it out of Gloria the next opportunity he got. If being a slut was what she wanted to be, he was going to treat her like one.

Mason was about to get undressed when he heard a knock on his front door. It was late and he couldn't imagine who it could be. Making his way to the door, Mason opened it and to his surprise, Gloria was standing in the rain, without an umbrella. She was dripping wet from head to toe and she wanted to come inside.

"May I come in?" Gloria asked.

Without uttering a word; Mason stepped aside, allowing her to enter.

Chapter: 38

Standing with her eyes closed, Gloria braced for the moment Drew burst through the front doors of the church to rescue her from having to marry Mason. She visualized Drew interrupting the service, pleading for her not to marry Mason because he loved her. Gloria visualizes Drew falling to one knee and asked her to marry him in front of God and everyone witnessing the ceremony but like most fantasies, this one wasn't coming true either. Drew wasn't going to burst through the doors to save her from a wedding she didn't want. He'd made it known that his heart belonged to someone else and she had no place in it. Gloria had failed her mission to make Drew hers and for doing so, she would have to pay for her mistakes for the rest of her life. By all accounts, Gloria had made a vital mistake in believing by wearing Mason's ring and setting a date to marry him, Drew would become jealous and from his jealousy, he would come running back to her. Like a damn fool, she placed all of her eggs in one basket and sadly, her gamble failed. Gloria miscalculated Drew's love for her by thinking it was strong enough to stop her from marrying Mason.

Opening her eyes, Gloria nervously listened as Reverend Hightower instructed her to repeat the words after him. In doing so, Gloria came to the realization that Drew wasn't going to interrupt her wedding; nor was he going to whisk her off into the land of enchantment. Gloria was actually getting married and whether she wanted to or not there wasn't a damn thing anyone could do to help her; she was on her own. The tears that fell from her eyes had nothing to do with her being overwhelmed by getting married, in actuality, her tears were that of regret. Gloria couldn't deny her feelings for Mason because he'd proven that he was willing to stand up and be the man she needed in her life but she didn't love him the way he needed to be loved. She only accepted his proposal after she'd lost Drew and was unable to lure him back into her grips. Gloria's well-calculated move somehow backfired, leading her to be in a marriage she didn't want. Sure, she could have said hell no, but saying hell no would make her the laughingstock of the town and Mason probably would get his revenge by beating the hell out of her. Gloria was doomed, she had no other choice but to marry Mason. Wiping her eyes, Gloria slowly repeated the words said by Reverend Hightower. This should have been the happiest day of her life but unfortunately, it was perhaps her worst and as Reverend Hightower pronounced them man and wife.

231

Gloria cringed as Mason gently cupped her face with both hands to kiss her. He had sealed the deal in making her his wife. They were officially, Mr. and Mrs. Mason Harrison Tyler.

An overwhelmed Mason jumped for joy as he and Gloria turned to face their guest. Mason had finally married the one woman he'd dreamed of having for so long but Gloria wasn't as jubilant. Her immature decision to entice Drew back into her life had failed miserably and by all accounts, she would have to live with it. Pistol, Mattie, and youngest teenaged daughter Kelly, stood with the small group of family and invited guests to applauded the newly wedded couple exited the church. Pistol hated the idea that Gloria had married Mason, not to mention the idea of having to attend a wedding he didn't agree with but he was force to do so by his wife, who wanted to show support. Having to hear Reverend Hightower pronounce Gloria and Mason husband and wife, nearly cut Pistol heart in two but he managed to get through it. He wasn't going to accept Mason as his son-in-law nor was he going to invite him to sit at his table for dinner. As far as he was concerned, Mason was nothing to him. Pistol believed Gloria had made a horrendous mistake that she would regret; his only hope was that Gloria would realize it sooner than later.

Mason didn't get the rice shower he was hoping to receive but he had gotten the woman he'd been dreaming about his entire life. As he and Gloria made their way outside the church, they were surrounded by plenty of cheers. Friends of the bride and groom were ecstatic at the idea they'd gotten married and even though the families of both children felt differently, they kept their feelings to themselves. Today, it was all about Mason and Gloria. It didn't matter their parents didn't approve of their marriage or were willing to take a bet on how long it would last. The most important thing was having to hide their frowns knowing in their hearts, their children's marriage wasn't going to last.

Mason and Gloria waved to the crowd from inside the limo as it pulled away. To those who were in attendance the couple's face resembled a perfect picture of happiness but inside, Gloria was sick to her stomach. She had to put on a show to convince Mason it was the happiest day of her life but in all actuality, Gloria was embarrassed having to stand in front of her friends and co-workers, while participating in a rotgut wedding any trailer park trash was capable of affording. For giving her such a cheap wedding, Gloria was hoping Mason had kept his promise to buy her the large craftsman style house, she'd been drooling over.

The house was located in the new sub-division that was less than a mile past the Harrison's estate. Gloria had driven through the neighborhood and found that the house she wanted was under contract. Seeing it under contract led her to believe, Mason had kept his word and purchased it for them. Anxious to know her wedding gift, Gloria asked for her wedding gift early. She was expecting Mason to hand her the keys to her new craftsman's home and she wanted them immediately but Mason's hesitation was persuading her, he hadn't kept his part of the bargain. Instead of giving Gloria the keys she wanted to her new house, Mason smiled and removed a bottle of champagne from the small refrigerator inside the limo to celebrate. Gloria didn't want to toast their damn wedding; she wanted the keys to her house and Mason was pussy footing around.

"I want to make a toast first," Mason said, holding the bottle of champagne. Gloria reminded him of her white gown and how she didn't want to spill champagne on herself. Opting for the white wine instead, Mason toasted to a life full of happiness and love forever. Gloria smiled and followed it with a kiss. It was hard to overlook that Mason was a good man and though she wished she hadn't agreed to marry him, she was willing to make the best of it.

Mason, could finally exhale knowing he'd married the woman of his dreams. However, even though Gloria was no longer on the auction block, it was his goal to continue protecting his investment. Seeing her with Drew at Larry's was a picture he couldn't erase from his mind. He didn't know who called the meeting or what went on between them but something alarming had occurred and if the rumors were correct, Gloria blasted Drew over something that went down earlier in the day. What actually caused the altercation was never revealed but whatever it was, pissed Gloria off enough to want to fight. As the limo continued its slow drive to the reception, Gloria pleaded for Mason to give her, her wedding gift. Though reluctant, Mason instructed the driver to make a right turn. He hated he was going to have to disappoint Gloria so soon after marrying her but she had put him on the spot. Gloria was excited at the idea that she was about to be given the keys to her newly built home. The idea of it was overwhelming enough that she nearly began crying. If Mason had indeed brought the house of her dreams, Gloria would be indebted to him forever. Mason had built a reputation for giving her everything she wanted and that's what attracted her to him.

Mason had a heart of gold when it came to her and he was willing to do anything to please her and even though she knew he couldn't afford to buy much, she was sure he'd made a way to get her the craftsman house.

Minutes before arriving at the subdivision, Mason decided to confess to Gloria about the house. He knew it was going to be a crushing blow to her but it was better to tell her now than her being shocked once the truth came out.

"Gloria, I need to tell you something," Mason gawked, as he saw the limo approaching the new sub-division.

"What is it?" Gloria asked.

"I couldn't get you the craftsman home you wanted," Mason admitted, as he searched for the perfect lie to tell.

"Why not, you worked a shit load of overtime for weeks. Why couldn't you get the house I wanted? You promise me you would do so," Gloria said.

"Somebody beat me to it," Mason responded. It was a lie but that's all Mason could think of at the time.

"So, which house did you buy for us? Was it the one beside it?" Gloria asked.

Mason didn't have the heart to again break Gloria's heart but he had to level with her. "Honey, the fact is that I couldn't get either house, the bank said I don't make enough money."

"Got dammit!" Gloria said to herself. "That motherfucker misled me into believing he brought me a fucking house when he hadn't."

Pissed beyond talking, Gloria shut down, she stared out the side window while refusing to acknowledge Mason. It all made sense now and if Mason thought she was going to live in his grandfather's infested mold and mildew shack, he had fallen off of his rocker and bumped his nappy ass head. Gloria had no intentions of living there, nor did she want to live with Ms. Dolly Mae. Either way, she was signing her death warrant. Gloria knew she couldn't bring Mason to live with her parents. So, where the hell were they going to live? God knows, her father would never approve of them staying under his roof. After considering her options, living with Ms. Dolly Mae seemed like the logical choice.

Ms. Dolly Mae was a very sweet woman but her obese size and poor hygiene were enough to make a buzzard puke. Gloria couldn't say if Ms. Dolly Mae wasn't washing her body but being fat and reeking of sour milk was more than she was willing to stand for, but regardless of how bad Ms. Dolly Mae's body odor may have been, it was still better than living in a mold-infested, rundown shack.

It was fair to say, Mason had failed her, when it came to keeping his promises. Not only did he give her a cheap ass marriage, but he also couldn't provide her with the house he'd promised. Mason undoubtedly had fucked up her life after tricking her into marrying his broke ass. Now, she was going to be the laughingstock of Jefferson County. She should have known something was about to come down the pike when Mason start talking about what he was going to do with his grandfather's property he'd inherited as a wedding gift. Gloria thought he was kidding when he announced he was quitting his job to become a dairy farmer; something he absolutely knew nothing about. Somewhere in the back of that confused little mind of his, Mason actually believed he could build a company to compete against Drew and the Hillcrest Cooperation. Needless to say, Mason failed to realize, he didn't have the finances or the education to compete against a well-established company like Hillcrest Farms, which had been in business for over thirty-plus years. Anyway, what bank in their right mind was going to give Mason's stupid ass a loan for millions of dollars, without any kind of strategic plan to present when applying? The Hillcrest Cooperation had grown immensely over the years and it wasn't the same company when Mason and Drew used to hang out as children. Several products were added to the company's brand, and with their new state-of-the-art processing plant set to open in a few weeks, the company was about to blow up. They'd launch their pork and poultry business, along with their organic fruits and vegetables to add to their already milk and cheese lines.

If what Drew had confided in her were facts, the company will have a much larger Human Resource Office, veterinarians on site, as well as quality control inspectors, and a cooperate lawyer. It was more than what Mason's dumb ass could ever imagine in a planning stage. Frankly speaking, it would be an impossible task for Mason to become a dairy farmer, no less a profitable one. If he attempted to press his luck, his dumb ass would be bankrupted within the first year. Although Gloria didn't give a shit about having to bust Mason's bubble, she did care about the property his dumb ass was about to piss away.

Now that they were married, she had a stake in the property, too, and with that being said, she had her future to look after. If she had anything to do with it, Mason was going to sell the property to the highest bidder, and to be honest, she didn't give a damn whom he sold it to, as long as it brought in a boatload of money.

"How in God's name was Mason going to run a freaking company when all he ever did was turn a damn stop-and-go sign for a road crew?" Gloria thought to herself as she poked fun at Mason and his employment.

It was hard having to hear the truth from his new wife, who's longtime relationship with Drew, classified her as being an expert with his family's business. But regardless of how Mason may have felt about the past, he couldn't erase the fact that Gloria was right by what she was telling him. It pissed him off having to hear the truth but he had to soldier up and come to grips with the fact that he could never measure up to Drew. Simply said, Drew was everything Mason wasn't and all that he inspired to be.

Unlike Mason, Drew was well educated and had been taught the business at an early age by his mother, who took over the company, after his father's death. Drew was far advanced at running circles around him if he chose to compete against them. Mason hated the idea he couldn't measure up to Drew. Drew's fucked up ways had buried him and left him feeling he was inferior to Drew.

As the car drove the property line on its way to Grandpa Harrison's old homestead, Mason couldn't help but reminisce about starting a company. He may not have the intellectual skills to know how to start a company but with hard work, he was sure he could build a company to rival Hillcrest Farms. Nancy was in the same predicament as he, when his uncle died, but she managed to turned Hillcrest into a successful company. However, there were questions surrounding how Nancy managed to keep Hillcrest Farms running, after it had been on the verge of bankruptcy for years. Rumors also stated, Nancy had borrowed her limit and couldn't secure another loan to keep the failing company afloat but overnight, something happened. She somehow managed to secure another loan and with it, turned Hillcrest Farms into a multi-million-dollar empire, and doing so less than ten years. Although widespread speculations had Nancy securing a bailout loan from the president of the First National Bank, in Jefferson because she slept with him a time or two, but that's neither here nor there.

Regardless of how she obtained the money, the fact remained, she and the Harrison children became the wealthiest family in the county.

Having seen the disappointment in Gloria's eyes was enough to make Mason want to do something to make her happy. Yes, he was guilty of lying to her because he was too ashamed to admit he didn't have the money or the credit to qualify for the loan he needed to buy a house. Mason knew he would have to do something if he was going to keep Gloria as his wife. He had been around her long enough to know Gloria's thought pattern and without a doubt, she would leave him to go back to Drew, if he didn't do something to rectify the problem. If only he could convince Gloria to take a walk with him inside the house, he could paint her a clearer picture of his plans to renovate the old house, but Gloria refused to get out of the car.

"Come on, let's go inside and I'll show you what I'm going to do." Mason boosted.

"No, I'm not ruining my $8,000 dollar gown to go inside some dirty ass old house to make you happy. Besides, I know every smelly little inch of its layout." Gloria responded.

It was true, Gloria did know the layout of the house. God knows, she'd frequent it many times with Drew, before going there with Mason. Seeing that Gloria was never going to stay in the house, Mason presented her with a more appealing solution. Aware of how badly the Harrisons were interested in acquiring the property. Mason suggested they sell it to them and build the house of her dreams. Mason didn't have to twist Gloria's arm to convince her to agree to sell, once mentioning he would build her the house of her dream, Gloria was ready to sell. Finally, Mason was thinking like a husband, instead of the damn fool he was.

Chapter: 39

Sitting on the front porch with his guitar, Drew tried playing but found it difficult to do so. His thoughts were of Karyme and how he was going to win back her heart. It had been weeks since Lynn's visit and Drew found himself regretting the route, he took with hiding the truth from her. Maybe, if he had done things differently, they would have been together today. But it was too late to play Monday morning quarterback, especially after he had fumbled the game away. Having time to overlook what happened, Drew continued to be confused about his feelings towards both women. He loved Lynn but questioned her loyalty when it came to fighting for their relationship. Karyme was as loyal as anyone could be, never once had she deserted him or their friendship. In Drew's opinion, Karyme was the ideal woman but like an ass, he chose to toss her aside and now, he found himself alone and wishing he'd done things differently. It was highly unlikely that he would ever get a second chance because Karyme now saw him as being a hypocrite, and to be frank, she was right. He had often confused love with lust and he was clueless about the meaning of love. It wasn't until he fell in love with Karyme that he knew what true love felt like but like an idiot, he let it fall through his hands. As they say, everything happens for a reason, and in this case, it was because of stupidity. Like the geniuses they were, the Boldmont's found a way to ruin his relationship with Lynn without having to order Lynn to do anything against her will. This time, her parents did so by appointing Lynn Chief-Operation Officer of Boldmont Enterprises. They knew what would bring a wedge between the two of them and by appointing Lynn to such a lucrative position, the Boldmont's were keeping her busy enough to neglect him. Thanks to Lynn's decision to taking online classes, along with being appointed to the Board of Directors, she had no time for him. Lynn was bitten by the cooperate world and nothing was more important than that. Lynn would call from time to time, to say hello, but that was as far as it went. Whenever Drew tried making some sort of plan to drive up to see her, Lynn would explain why they couldn't see each other for one reason or the other. Either there was homework she had to catch up on or she was behind on her work at the office. After a few weeks of excuses, it didn't take a rocket scientist to knew it was over between them. In other words, the Boldmont's had called checkmate and all Drew could do was conceded. It was no need to fight something that wasn't meant to be. Drew understood, his best option was to dust off his pride and chalk it up as a loss.

For the first time in years, Drew felt alone. It was tough not being able to call Karyme to talk and though she continued her job as co-president, she was rarely in the office. Karyme spent most of her time supporting the company by traveling the east coast, meeting with distributors who were interested in doing business with the Hillcrest Cooperation. But it hadn't stopped Drew from trying to repair the damage he'd caused. Needless to say, his efforts were for naught because Karyme wanted nothing to do with him. She refused to discuss anything outside of business but Drew wouldn't take no for an answer. Karyme meant too much to him to give up on her so easily. She'd been the only person outside his immediate family that understood him, and had stood by him doing the worse times in his life. Her loyalty was unlike any, and sadly, he not only destroyed her trust, he broke her heart. Drew's mistake was that he started an ill-advised relationship with her without completely resolving his situation with Lynn. It wasn't that he didn't love Karyme, because he had always adored her, she was the woman he never wanted to lose.

Seeing his mother returning home from Mason and Gloria's wedding reception, Drew wiped the tears from his eyes and waited for her to join him on the front porch. In doing so, Nancy had a look of disgust on her face. She had something she wanted to talk about and from the looks of it, she was anxious to do so immediately. Nancy's excitement to share what happened was well received by Drew. He needed to laugh to help ease the pain of his broken heart. Taking a seat on her porch swing, Nancy began by gossiping about the wedding and wedding reception. She laughed, as she told the story about Gloria's hesitation to repeat the words of the good Rev. Dr. Hightower. Not only that, Nancy swore, she saw Gloria cringed when Mason kissed her once they were pronounced man and wife.

"She actually cringed when Mason kissed her," Nancy said. "I don't know why Mason married that Polecat, because that wedding isn't going to last a farting spell."

"She never loved Mason, she only used him," Drew responded.

"Everybody knows, she only married him because you didn't want anything to do with her anymore," Nancy replied.

Nancy was right, Drew didn't want to have anything, except a friendship with Gloria, and if Nancy had her way, he wouldn't have that. Unbeknownst to Nancy, Gloria had come to see Drew at the office last night. She admitted to not wanting to marry Mason but she was being forced to do so by her mother.

Gloria's parents used most of their life savings to help give her a decent wedding and they didn't want to lose their money. Gloria also admitted that she was still in love with him and she always will be. Gloria understood it was over between them and had finally given up on the idea of them ever getting back together. In a way, Drew believed her, Gloria was sincere in what she was saying and though she didn't want to marry Mason, she knew it was in her best interest to do so. Gloria biggest downfall was her not knowing what she wanted out of life. Her problem consisted of her not being satisfied about what she had. In talking with Drew, Gloria admitted, she felt he wasn't adventurous enough. She craved excitement and Mason provided it for her. Gloria may have been labeled as the biggest slut in Jefferson County but she was actually a very good person. She just didn't know what she wanted out of life. Sadly, she chose to marry Mason, hoping it was what she needed to find true love.

Drew listened, as Nancy laughed as she told the story about what happened at the wedding reception.

"After witnessing what I thought was the worst wedding I'd ever attended; the reception was even worse. Who in God's name would have had a reception in their back yard doing the middle of autumn, without heated tents. Not only was it cold as ice outside, people started leaving because they ran out of food, but they had plenty of alcohol," Nancy said, before describing what happened to Reverend Hightower. "It was so cold the good Reverend Doctor kept drinking cups of hot spiced punch to keep warm without knowing the punch had been spiked by some imbecile. It didn't take long for the good Reverend doctor Hightower to passed out. Lord, have mercy, the man had to be carried inside the house to sleep it off. Then there were the skirmishes that broke out. Drunk men, women and children were all fighting. I left after that; Lord knows I didn't want to in the mist of that mess if something major had broken out."

On a lighter note, Nancy told the heartwarming story about Mason and how happy he was. It was a look of elation that she'd never seen in him before. But sadly, it probably was going to be the last time he would ever feel that way.

Some time in his immediate future, Gloria was going to pull the rug from under his feet and when she did, he was going to crash. Again, Drew agreed with his mother, he didn't know how long it was going to take before Gloria made her move, and leave Mason broken hearted.

However, if Gloria believed she was going to run over Mason, she had another thing coming, Mason had gotten what he wanted and sooner or later, he was going to show his spots. There was no way Mason was ever going to forgive her for sleeping with other men as he had. Mason would undoubtedly kill her if he ever found out she was sleeping around on him.

"Did you talk to Karyme today?" Nancy asked.

"No," Drew replied.

"Well, I talked to her at the reception and I can tell you this, she still loves you," Nancy acknowledged.

"Karyme won't have anything to do with me," Drew responded. His face showed signs of a broken man and even though Drew knew he sabotaged his own relationship with Karyme, it still hurt like hell.

"Have you heard from Lynn?" Nancy questioned.

"No, and I don't expect to hear from her either," Drew responded.

Drew didn't know whether to break down and cry or bust out in laughter. His life was at a standstill and he had no idea how to get it going.

"Mom, I messed up and it hurt like hell because I'm in love with Karyme and I don't know how to get her back," Drew confessed.

His mother had been right all along, Karyme was the woman he actually loved; he was just too thick headed to accept it. It's funny it had taken losing her for Drew to understand how important she was to him but it was too late, it was over between them.

Web of Deception Book 2   The Betrayal Continues   J.W. Hill

Chapter: 40

It had taken most of the day for Gloria to get a minute to herself, and she did she decided to call to check on Drew. It was going to be an awkward feeling talking to Drew after she'd just gotten married but that's exactly what Gloria was about to do. She wanted Drew to know that her heart still belonged to him and that she would be there for him, whenever he needed her. It was a strange pledge for a newly married woman to suggest but Gloria had heard the news about Drew's breakup with Lynn and wanted to put her bid in for whenever he was ready to start dating again, but before Gloria could dial Drew's number, she heard a knock on the bathroom door.

"I'm trying to use the bathroom," Gloria announced.

"Gloria, the photographer is ready to take the last set of pictures for the day," Mason said.

"I'll be there in a minute," Gloria responded.

Gloria shook her head out of frustration after acknowledging Mason. This was the first time she'd had a chance to be alone and damn if Mason had to ruined it. Frankly speaking, Mason had been a thorn in her ass the entire wedding and she was tire of it already. Gloria didn't know if she could handle Mason wanting to stick to her like glue but she promised herself she was going to give it her best effort. Instead of calling Drew, Gloria opted to send him a text instead. She waited a few minutes for Drew to respond and after not receiving an immediate text back, she left the bathroom to join Mason outside.

It had been a long day and though most of their invited guest had left. There were still a few stragglers who continued to party and was showing no signs of leaving but the D.J. was about to end the music real soon, and Gloria couldn't wait. Once the final pictures were taken, Gloria made her way through the small group of remaining guests to thank them for coming. She was exhausted and wasn't in the mood to mingle but kept a positive look to hide her true feelings. In a surprising turn of events, Gloria saw Karyme walking towards her car to leave. It was the perfect opportunity for Gloria to catch up with Karyme to probe her for information about Drew. Now that Drew and the" Rich Bitch" had broken up, had he started fucking the "Wetback"? These were two of the questions Gloria was dying to know.

Gloria couldn't say for certain but her instincts were telling her the little "Wetback" was probably the culprit that ended Drew's relationship with his little rich bitch. Lord knows, she'd interfered enough with her relationship with Drew when they were together.

Approaching Karyme, Gloria tried to put on her happy face. She wanted Karyme to think that today was the happiest day of her life. You see, Gloria had reason for wanting to give Karyme the impression that she was as happy as a kid at Christmas. It was because Gloria didn't want Karyme to know she was fishing for information on Drew's availability. What Gloria didn't know was Karyme wasn't buying her bullshit, she knew what Gloria was all about. The entire town knew, Gloria wasn't in love with Mason and only married him because Drew didn't want no parts of her slutty ass, but Karyme decided to play her game anyway.

"Hey, Karyme, wait up," Gloria asked while making her way over to where Karyme was. "Hey, I wanted to thank you for coming. I know we hadn't gotten along over the years but it meant a lot to me that you came."

Karyme smiled, "Thank you, for inviting me."

"Maybe this is a step in the right direction for us to become better friends," Gloria added.

"Maybe," Karyme replied.

"What happened to Drew, I thought he was coming with you? Gloria asked, hoping it was enough to get a response from Karyme to build off of.

"He was coming but you know Drew, business comes first. Oh! I nearly forgot, he wanted to give you this, and to congratulate you and Mason for him," Karyme responded while reaching inside her car's glove compartment to remove an envelope, containing card and passed it to Gloria. "And this is from me," Karyme said, giving Gloria a second envelope.

"Thank you so much, and could you thank Drew for me please?" Gloria asked. "I mean, I'm going to send you all thank you cards but I want Drew to know how much his gift means to me. Gloria knew an envelope containing a card meant only one thing, money, and she couldn't wait to open it to see how much it was.

The truth was that Drew hadn't sent a thing; Karyme had taken it upon herself to give the married couple a gift in Drew's name. After speaking to Drew's mother, Karyme learned Drew hadn't sent the happy couple anything, so, after leaving the wedding Karyme drove to her bank and withdrew a thousand dollars for Drew. She then stopped by the Family Dollar Store and brought a cheap card and scribbled Drew's name in it, before placing the money inside and sealing it. Karyme knew Gloria wasn't going to read the card, and assumed Gloria was only going to open the card and take the money without noticing the signature on it. Giving Gloria and Mason a wedding gift was her parting gift to the Polecat for electing to go forward with her life, without having to depend on Drew for anything else.

"Can I ask you a question, without you getting upset? Gloria asked.

"Depending on what it is," Karyme responded.

"Are you and Drew, a couple? I mean, you don't have to answer if you don't want to, I just thought that being he and that girl from Maryland had broken up, the two of you would be on hot and heavy." Gloria asked.

Karyme had no idea what Gloria was referring to. As far as she knew, Drew and Lynn were still together but then again, she hadn't spoken to Drew since Lynn's visit, but if they had broken up, she didn't know anything about it.

"No, we're not getting it on hot, and I don't know if Drew and Lynn have broken up," Karyme replied.

Gloria should have felt embarrassed by her aggressive questioning towards Karyme regarding Drew's relationship with Lynn but like always, Gloria was Gloria and she didn't give a damn what anyone thought as long as she got what she wanted. Sadly, Gloria had made it obvious that she was still in love with Drew. It was not only sad for Gloria, it was all too sad for Mason, who loved that idiot with all of his life. Getting tired by Gloria's questions, Karyme said her goodbyes, before getting into her car to drive away.

Chapter: 41

With their honeymoon to Daytona Beach coming to an end, Mason and Gloria prepared to make their way home to jump start their future together as a married couple. Mason understood in order to have a successful future with Gloria, he first had to sell his grandfather's farm and for Gloria, it couldn't happen fast enough. It was during their honeymoon that Gloria persuaded Mason to reached out to Nancy and present her with a proposal to buy their property. It wasn't a hard decision for the Nancy and Drew to make. The mere idea of acquiring what should have been theirs from the beginning was an easy decision to make and they quickly jump at the chance to purchase it. Although Mason was all in for a quick sale, he wanted a fair offer in return and the Harrison's were all too happy to accommodate his needs. Mason went as far as hiring a surveyor the following morning after an oral agreement was reached over the phone. It was funny to think Mason didn't give a second thought about selling his grandfather's farm to Nancy and the Hillcrest Cooperation. If you asked Mason if he had an emotional attachment to grandfather's estate, he would be quick to say "Hell No", his grandfather's estate didn't mean jack shit to him, nor did he cared about who land the deal. As quiet as it was kept, Mason didn't exactly like his grandfather. He often would say, "Fuck granddaddy and his five hundred acres of land." It was without question that Mason resented his grandfather because of his favorability towards Drew. Drew was without a doubt their grandparent's favorite and they never tried hiding the fact. Drew was the chosen one, the male selected to carry on the Harrison name and no matter how hard Mason tried to win their grandfather's acceptance, he could never do so. As for Drew, being the chosen one meant he was in line to inherit the Harrison legacy but before the old geezer could ratify his will, he died. Lucky for them, Dolly Mae stumbled upon the copy and got rid of it before anyone knew about it. It was a good move on their part, so good, Mason could now get the things he wanted for his wife.

Some would argue that Dolly Mae stole the property from Nancy and robbed Drew of what should have been rightfully his from the beginning but Mason would beg the differ. Mason would argue that Andrew Jr. died before his grandfather, which vacated the property back to his mother.

This meant he was next in line to inherit the property and he could sell it to whomever he wanted to and by sheer coincidence, Nancy and the Hillcrest Organization had the money to keep it in the family. The sale of the property meant; Mason could provide his beautiful wife with everything she wanted. But Mason worried that his mother wouldn't accept his decision to sell the farm. It was her gift to him to live on but he didn't give a damn about living on a farm; no, farm life wasn't for him. Thanks to the Harrisons' greed for land, they were about to make him a very well-off man.

Mason was two hours from home when he received a call from Nancy and Drew and what they said nearly made him lose control of his car. The Hillcrest Cooperation was calling to officially make an offer for his property. Never in his wildest dreams had Mason imagined his property was valued so high. He was flabbergasted at Nancy's offer of $1.5 million dollars. The thought of being offered that amount of money for a rundown old farm with a few barns and couple of lakes was enough to cause Mason to pull over on the side of the road. The offer was so impressive, Mason nearly said yes before Nancy could finish her sentence. Agreeing meant he and Gloria were instant millionaires and the thought of it nearly brought tears to his eyes. Without becoming too hasty, Mason informed Nancy they could meet once he returned home. Mason explained, he would have to discuss the pending deal with his mother before agreeing, but was sure the four of them could come to some kind of an agreement. In ending his conference with Nancy and Drew, Mason placed his head against his stirring wheel. He couldn't believe the offer that he was presented with. If everything went accordingly to planned, he would be in position to live a lifestyle he had only dream about.

"Mason, what's wrong?" Gloria asked.

"You won't believe what those motherfuckers just offered for the property?" Mason replied.

"What! some bullshit money?" Gloria asked.

"You just ain't gonna believe it," Mason said in disbelief.

"What? tell me," Gloria asked.

"One and a half million dollars," Mason replied.

Gloria wasn't sure she'd heard Mason correctly and asked him to repeat himself. Like Mason, she nearly had a conniption on the side of the road. Gloria began picturing the life she was going to have, right from the start, starting with building the largest house in the county. For now, her worries were over and she had her lucky stars to thank for going through with the wedding with Mason.

Mason and Gloria continued their trip home after celebrating the news, and then it happened. Greed began wigging its ugly little way into Gloria's head. She had the bright idea to put the property on the market for a free for all with the winner being the highest bidder. Personally, Mason didn't like the idea and told Gloria as much but Gloria insisted it was the way to go. She explained, if the Harrison offered $1.5 million dollars, then the property must be worth more. The only family that was capable of generating that much capital was the Kerrigan's and Abernathy families. Mason didn't like the idea of selling his property outside of the family but he couldn't deny Gloria didn't have a point. He had his family to look after and he needed to take the best deal he could get.

With less than ten miles away from home, Mason remained on his high. He glanced over at Gloria as she slept peacefully and thought to himself how lucky he was to have a woman such as her. Mason didn't know what the future held for them but knew he was going to give it his all because for the first time in his life, he was about to have stability and he owed it all to his wife. Gloria had given him the push he needed to overcome his fears of becoming a man. She had shown him the life he'd been missing and for that he was forever grateful. As Mason overlooked his life, he couldn't believe how it trended in the right direction after being in limbo for more than twenty-two years. Two years ago, no one could have told him that he'll be the one marrying one of the most beautiful women in Jefferson County or become a millionaire in the same year. After being labeled the black sheep of the family, this was his opportunity to show all of his doubters what he was capable of doing with his life. Mason's comparison to Drew caused him to resented Drew for years and though he still had problems with wanting to maintain a friendship with Drew, at least he could make direct eye contact with Drew, without having to look away. In a way, Mason wanted to think he was better than Drew but deep down inside he knew the truth. It was true he'd stolen Gloria away from Drew, but in the opinions of many, stealing Gloria hadn't measure up to the accomplishments Drew had achieved.

For Mason, it had, all the accolades Drew accomplished in his lifetime, didn't mean dilly squat to him. As far as he was concerned, he'd gotten everything he wanted in life and that was Gloria becoming his wife and having the finances to take care of her.

After hours of driving, the newly married couple arrived home to a small family parade. Gloria's mother and sister was present, along with Dolly Mae to welcome the newlywed's home. It was a bitter sweet moment for Gloria because she was hoping her father would be there. Unfortunately, Pistol was overly disappointed and refused to accepted the idea that Gloria had married Mason but on the bright side, at least her mother and sister were there to help celebrate their homecoming. Mason unpacked his small Mustang with mostly Gloria's bags and carried them to their room. Entering, he saw that his mother had decorated his room with a new queen size bed and matching comforter and linings. The room was fit for a king and his queen and Mason couldn't have been happier. Things were finally looking up; Dolly Mae had accepted his marriage and he was about to become a rich motherfucker.

Chapter: 42

Karyme's day was full of surprises as well as disappointments. Against her better judgement, she accepted an invitation to meet Lynn for lunch and a day of shopping. Karyme was astonished by the idea of being invited into Lynn's world and didn't hesitate to accept. She wanted to learn more about the woman Drew was so fascinated with. The plan was to meet at the DC/Maryland National Harbor at noon, from there, they were to have lunch, followed by a day of shopping and girl talk. It was something Karyme had always wanted to do with a friend but she had neither a friend nor the money to spend. After years of fantasizing, Karyme was finally in a position to splurge. Not in the sense of spending thousands upon thousands of dollars but a few hundred before seeing a giant reduction in her bank account. It was funny to think Karyme was spending the day with the woman that stole the love of her life from her but she was doing just that. Strangely enough, Karyme didn't blame Lynn for what happened between her and Drew, Karyme believed, Drew made his choice and after weeks of sobbing, she finally made peace with it. It was hard having to avoid Drew, especially after Gloria reminded her of Drew's plan to marry Lynn. Karyme remembered how Gloria couldn't wait to tell her the news and how she gloated when telling it. Gloria even made a big deal out of describing the ring Drew was supposedly designing for Lynn. It was a hard pill to swallow but Karyme dealt with the pain and accepted her faith that Drew wasn't going to be a part of her life. Only her mother knew what she went through. Sophia was there to comfort her each night while literally rocking her to sleep. Now, she was about to spend the day with the woman that stole her future.

Karyme arrived minutes before noon and found Lynn waiting in front of the Tanger Outlets parking lot. After greeting each other cordially, the ladies made their way inside. Their first order of business was to have lunch and Karyme couldn't wait. Like Lynn, she hadn't eaten breakfast and was starving. It was fair to say, Karyme wasn't looking forward to discussing Lynn and Drew's wedding plans. She didn't know how she was going to react if Lynn began discussing her upcoming marriage to Drew. Chances were, she was going to have to pretend to be happy and assist Lynn with anything she needed. As Drew's friend, it was her responsibility to support them, even if she didn't agree. Lord knows it was going to be a difficult thing to accept but Karyme signed up for it by accepting Lynn's invitation.

After deciding on fried crab cake sandwiches, the ladies began talking for the first time since meeting at the plant. While talking, Karyme understood why Drew was so attached to Lynn, because Lynn not only was a beautiful woman; she possessed a personality to match. It was like night and day between Lynn and Gloria. Lynn was someone you could easily become friends with, but as for Gloria, well, Gloria was from a different breed, a breed in which Karyme wanted no part of. It wasn't until the middle of lunch when Karyme learned the reason Lynn invited her to meet, and it had nothing to do with her wedding plans. Lynn explained, after many nights of pondering which direction, she wanted to go, Lynn decided to officially end her relationship with Drew. Lynn explained, she struggled for weeks upon which direction she wanted to take, but after careful consideration, she ultimately decided, it was in the best interest of both she and Drew to end things peacefully. Lynn's decision came as a shock to Karyme. The news of Lynn's intentions hit her like a ton of bricks, and she couldn't help but think of Drew and what it would do to him. What was so disturbing to Karyme, was the fact that she predicted Lynn would desert Drew once things became troublesome. Karyme felt a great sense of sadness for Drew because he didn't deserve what Lynn was about to do to him. Drew was a loving person who was willing to give his all to anyone in need, but sadly for him, his choice in women always seem to come back to bite him in the ass.

"I don't understand you; you say you love Drew but you're breaking things off with him. Why?" Karyme questioned.

"I do love Drew, and I want more than anything for him to be happy, but Drew could never be happy with me," Lynn responded.

"But why, why break the Drew's heart? He's giving up everything to make you happy," Karyme asked.

"Maybe, that's the problem," Lynn answered.

Lynn's mind was made, she was walking away from her relationship with Drew and she was asking that Karyme be there for him to help ease his pain. Lynn's request was unusual to say the least, so much so, it was almost insulting. Karyme could have interpreted Lynn's dismissal of Drew as picking up what was left of her trash, but Karyme believed Lynn had enough respect for Drew as well as their relationship to think of him in that manner. Lynn wanted Karyme to be there to comfort Drew. She didn't want him to have to suffer because of her.

It was silly to think Karyme wouldn't be there for Drew after years of being the best of friends. It was hard trying to solve the riddles Lynn was presenting. One minute, she loved Drew and wished things could work out for them, and the next, she was walking away for one reason or the other. Regardless of how Karyme may have felt about the way Lynn was ending things with Drew, she wasn't going to stand by and allow her to lead Drew astray; without doing anything about it. Karyme was going to be the shoulder Drew needed but that was as far as it was going. There was no way she was entertaining the thought of getting back with Drew, especially knowing that Lynn was still in love with him. You see, with Drew, Lynn had the tendency of changing her mind like the weather and Karyme didn't want to revisit the pain she suffered weeks ago.

Karyme found herself wondering, why had Lynn changed her mind after planning her future with Drew. Drew was every girl's dream, and the ideal guy to take home to meet your family. Karyme had to know what was going on with Lynn, and her reasons for wanting to separate from Drew.

"I'm sorry, but I don't like the way you're treating Drew. He loves you, and for you to keep breaking his heart is wrong," Karyme said. Karyme was voicing her opinion while trying to protect Drew's heart from being crushed. Lynn wasn't being fair to him, especially after he was preparing to forgo his dreams of running his family's company to be with her. Lynn was acting like a spoiled little rich girl who was undecided on what she wanted in her life.

"I know what you must be thinking, but I'm not ending things with Drew because I don't love him," Lynn answered.

Lynn's lack of a clear explanation was becoming frustrating. It wasn't what she was saying, it was more of what she wasn't saying. Lynn's aloof behavior was enough for Karyme to scream but it had to be a reason for her reluctance to come forth as to why she was ending things with Drew. Karyme felt something heavy was about to come down the pike and had to know what it was. Drew's livelihood was at stake and though they weren't on good terms, Karyme's love for him was far greater than her displeasure of him.

"I don't get it, is it because your family is against your relationship with Drew?" Karyme asked.

"Yes, and no," Lynn replied. "Yes, my family is against Drew and me getting married, but only because they feel that I'm too young, and I agree with them.

"Then why couldn't you have told Drew the truth when he asked you to marry him," Karyme asked.

"He didn't ask me, I asked him to marry me," Lynn responded.

"I don't believe you; it's more than what you're telling me. I know you love Drew; you have to, because no one would have gone through what you went through to be with him. Something happened, what? Karyme asked.

Lynn nearly broke and because of it, she decided to level with Karyme as to why, it wasn't conducive to try to have a future with a man that wasn't in love with her.

"I want a future with Drew, I want him to love me, as much as I love him, but it'll never happen," Lynn said.

"Why?" Karyme asked.

"Because he's in love with you, and I know, you're still in love with him," Lynn said.

Though Karyme tried hiding her feelings, her face told a different story, Lynn was right, she was in love with Drew. It was no need to deny the obvious, Lynn was aware of what may have happened in her absence. It was the reason she invited Karyme to spend the day with her. She wanted to talk about Karyme's relationship with Drew and how far it had gone. You see, Lynn was looking for someone who would look after Drew now that she had accepted the responsibilities of taking on the reigns as Operation Manager for Boldmont Enterprises. Lynn wanted to make sure Drew was in good hands of someone who loved him and that he could love. It was funny to think, she wasn't the selfish type who was only thinking of herself.

Especially knowing there were predators out there like Gloria who was waiting for the chance to inject her poison into Drew again. Karyme was exactly who Lynn was looking to give Drew the love he deserved. There was no doubt that Karyme was in love with Drew, she'd exhibited it doing her last visit. to see Drew. Lynn saw many signs that Drew and Karyme were involved but chose to ignore because she was overly anxious to rekindle her relationship with Drew. She remembered Karyme's reaction when first meeting her outside the plant.

She saw that Karyme had been crying; then there was the bruise on Drew's cheek. When inquiring about it, Drew played it off by saying he and Karyme had a disagreement regarding a decision he made, but refused to elaborate on it. Drew hadn't been forthcoming about wanting to marry her. All that bullshit about promising to love her and forever being faithful was nothing but a bucket of hogwash. In actuality, Drew had moved on with his life and had done so with his beautiful Latina best friend. What should have been grounds to hate Drew for being the lying SOB he was, wasn't. Lynn had no grounds to hate Drew, or compare him to Marshall for that matter. The truth was, Lynn hadn't been accessible to Drew doing his time of need. Instead of standing by him, she'd crumbled from the pressure her parents applied on her and left Drew stranded.

What made things worse was the mere fact that she hadn't been indispensable to Drew's needs. Instead of concentrating on the bad things Drew had done, Lynn chose to concentrate on the good things about Drew. If the truth be told, Drew could best be described as being amazing. He was there when she needed him most. He was the friend that refused to say no to refusing his help. Lynn credited Drew for giving her a new outlook on life, one which she'd never believed would never come again. Drew not only taught her how to love and trust again, he gave her a reason to live. He showed her how it felt to be loved and what it felt like to give love. Drew's unselfish ways often placed her in front of his own wants and needs. No, Drew couldn't be blamed for falling for Karyme; he deserved to be loved, something she was only gave on a part-time basis. Lynn could only blame herself for placing Drew in that position, after deserting him time after time. The fact that Drew was willing to forgo his happiness with Karyme to make her happy, spoke of his character. It was impressive to know he was willing to throw away everything he'd built with Karyme to make her happy.

Karyme apologized for her role in interfering with Lynn's relationship with Drew. Karyme clarified; it wasn't her intention to allow her emotions to act out in her decision to become involved with Drew. Karyme went on to explained, she thought things were over between she and Drew but admitted, she had been in love with him since childhood. In a lot of ways, Lynn couldn't blame Karyme or Drew for what happened between them. What happened between her and Drew was natural and unpreventable.

Lynn could only blame herself for not being there when Drew needed her most, and now that Drew was happy with someone else, who loved him unconditionally, Lynn was willing to embrace Karyme, by giving her blessing. It was a bitter sweet moment but Lynn did what she felt was the right thing to do. After giving Karyme her blessing, Lynn promised to never impede upon their affair ever again. It was tough having to give up on the man she was in love with but Lynn did just that. She understood her shaky ride with Drew was over, but in her time of being with Drew, he'd taught her so much and she was forever in his debt.

After a day of shopping, the women embraced and said their good-byes. Lynn was relived knowing she'd done the right thing for herself and for Karyme. Lynn arrived home late in the evening. As always, Sophia was waiting up for her. Sophia had no idea where Karyme had gone and frankly, she didn't question her because Sophia knew without a shadow of doubt, Karyme wasn't with Drew. Finally, after weeks of suffering, Karyme seemed to be moving on with her life. Within the past few days Karyme seemed happier and more relaxed now that she wasn't with Drew.

There was even a rumor that she was spotted out to dinner having dinner with Joshua McInnis. Joshua McInnis was the son of no other than Franklin McInnis. The McInnis' were a prominent family that lived outside of the county. They owned First Savings and Loan Bank in town, which the Harrison's were associated with. Sophia was hoping the rumors were true about Karyme and Joshua because if it turned out to be true, it meant she was over Drew for good.

Chapter: 43

Dressed in her nightie, Lynn sat on her bathroom toilet and prayed for a negative result from her pregnancy test. She wanted to kick herself for her ill-advised decision to have unprotected sex with Drew. Things had changed, she'd made the decision to move on after realizing Drew was in love with Karyme. It was only fair for her to allow Drew to be happy because he made her happy and gave her the will to love again. He even was willing to forgo being with the woman he was in love with to make her happy. It was now her turn to give Drew the happiness he deserved. Drew needed her support and she was willing to give it to him without animosity. She loved Drew with every inch of her heart but her first love was the family's business and she was on path to achieve that dream. It was a dream Lynn was about to live but only if her pregnancy test was negative. Lynn recognized the possibility of being pregnant was probable and it scared her shitless. She had all the symptoms, starting with missing her period, tender and swollen breasts, increased urination, nausea, fatigue and perhaps the most important symptom, morning sickness. Certain smells would cause her to run to the bathroom to throw up and it left her frantic by the thought of shaming her parents yet again. Being pregnant out of wedlock was far worse than having to be admitted in a mental facility after suffering a mental breakdown. How could she have been so thoughtless and inconsiderate to intentionally try to get pregnant. Drew didn't want to have unprotective sex but she forced him into having it. Again, she was selfish by wanting to get back at her parents for what they'd done to her but now, she was left wishing she had done things differently. If the test came back positive, not only would she ruin her own future but that of Drew's as well. The mere thought of being on track to achieve her dream to be CEO of Boldmont Enterprises was exhilarating in itself but now her uncalculated mistake could surface and ruin everything she was about to receive. Also weighing on Lynn's mind was Drew and what it was going to do to him and his family. She'd walked away from their relationship to allow him to be with Karyme and now, she was possibly pregnant with his baby. So many thoughts were running unrestricted through Lynn's mind and without answers she had no idea what to do if it was determined she was indeed pregnant. Standing, Lynn cut the bathroom light on to see the results. After doing so, she fell to her knees. The test showed a positive result, she was pregnant with Drew's child.

Chapter: 44

Furious after her argument with Mason, Dolly Mae stormed outside to her car to leave for work. She was disgusted by Mason's decision not to share their agreed-upon amount from the sale of the farm. Looking to place blame on someone other than her son, Dolly Mae chose to accuse Gloria of convincing Mason to renege on his promise. What other explanation could there be as to why Mason changed his mind so quickly? It had been less than eight hours since they'd last talked, and within that time, Mason was singing a different tune.

"What the hell happened after I went to sleep?" Dolly Mae said to herself. What made Mason change his mind so quickly? Dolly Mae couldn't say for certain, but it had Gloria's name written all over it. There couldn't be any other reason. Once again, that high-yellow bitch had gotten into Mason's head. Tomorrow, one point five million dollars was going into Mason's bank account, and thanks to that yellow bitch, Mason was only giving her a lousy, one hundred thousand dollars. Nancy had forewarned her how manipulating Gloria was and the dangerous games she would play to get what she wanted. It had been less than two weeks since she and Mason were married, and Gloria had already convinced him to sell his grandfather's property, along with keeping the half-million dollars he'd promised her. If Mason didn't wake up and smell the coffee soon, Gloria would undoubtedly spend every cent of money he has. Dolly Mae was now regretting her decision to give Mason her father's estate as a wedding gift, but it was too late to second guess herself now. Her only hope is that he would come to his senses before it's too late.

****

The excitement of being married, continued to run rapidly through Mason's veins. Still in the state of disbelief, he stared at his new wife and wondered, if he had died and gone to heaven. Having Gloria lying next to him was an overwhelming feeling but to knew she was going to be there with him for the rest of their lives, nearly brought him to tears. So many years he'd fantasized about Gloria becoming his wife, but never in his wildest dreams did he ever believed, it would come true. Now that Gloria was his wife, it was his duty to protect her from the evil forces that surrounded her. It was no secret that Drew posed the biggest threat to his marriage. The influence Drew had over Gloria was legendary, surpassing anything he could imagine.

Drew's influence on Gloria had Mason on edge. He'd fought tooth and nail to make his dream come true and now that it had, Mason wasn't going to allow Drew to worm his way back into Gloria's life. Gloria denied having any romantic feelings towards Drew, and though her denials gave him some relief, Mason's intuition told him differently. The sheer terror that Drew could destroy his dreams caused Mason to sweat profusely as he set in bed with Gloria.

"Are you ok?" Gloria asked.

"Yeah, why you asked?" Mason replied.

"You're sweating like crazy," Gloria responded.

Mason laughed, and joked that it was she who was causing him to sweat because she was his everything, his dream come true. In reality, Mason thrived on the feelings Gloria gave him and seeing her dressed in her nightie, while lying next to him, caused a tingling sensation inside of him, unlike never before. It was like seeing Gloria for the first time and seeing her left Mason more love-struck than ever. Gloria was his model, his movie star, and the angel he'd prayed for his entire life. Not only was Gloria breathtakingly beautiful, she was his. In Gloria, Mason found his purpose in life, his purposed was to love her, and to be the best husband he could be.

Seeing how beautiful Gloria was, Mason found himself wanting to make love to her, but it was going to be an impossible task to convince her to put away the pamphlets, she was studying so carefully. The pamphlets contained the floor plans to the house Gloria was looking to build and the likelihood of her putting them down to make love to him was less than zero. Gloria's mind was totally focused on building the perfect home, and thanks to him; nothing was going to deter her interest. Gloria wanted the largest house in the county, and she was only months away from it happening. Building her dream home meant having the status she wanted. Having the largest mansion in Jefferson County was Gloria's way of sending notice to everyone that she didn't need to marry a Harrison to have everything she wanted. Once again, Mason had provided her with the things she wanted in life, and like before, he had been the key to her success, but sadly, she still wasn't happy. It's hard to believe that Mason was in position to give her everything her heart desired, and she still wasn't satisfied. The lifelines Mason extended Gloria would never go unnoticed but it wasn't enough to fully commit her to the fruits of his love.

Seeing that Gloria was on track to far exceed their agreed upon budget set for their house, Mason opted not to intervene. He was afraid to say no to anything Gloria wanted because he knew she would rebel against him and he didn't want that to happen. However, Mason's concerns heightened after learning Gloria wanted to build their new house across the lake from where Drew was rumored to be renovating their grandfather's old house. Mason hated the idea that Gloria wanted to be so close to Drew and when he asked why? Her response was that she wanted to rub salt in Drew's wounds by having the most expensive house in the county. Indeed, what Gloria was saying didn't make sense because Drew didn't own a house and it was only rumored that he was going to renovate their grandfather's old house. For Mason, having the largest house in the county didn't mean dilly squat, his goal was to keep his wife happy and if building her the most expensive house in the county was the key to that happiest, then he was willing to go with her plans.

Chapter: 45

To Drew's surprise, Karyme returned to work early the following morning. It was fair to say, Karyme was Godsent and seeing her face was the boost Drew needed to push him over the edge. Like hundreds of times before, Karyme was there when he needed her most and today was no exception. But perhaps what was most shocking was the mood Karyme was in. Not only was she as gorgeous as she'd always been but she possessed a smile that was second to none. It was the first time since their relationship abruptly ended that Karyme had come to the office on a weekend. It was as if she knew he needed her. Late last night, Drew received a phone call from Lynn, officially ending their relationship. It was a relationship he suspected had ended weeks ago and though the novelty of it had worn off, it was gut-wrenching nonetheless. It seemed awkward hearing what he already knew from Lynn and though her call was unexpected, Drew didn't get the butterflies he was accustomed to receiving when hearing Lynn's voice. However, it left Drew with an empty feeling inside because he chose to give their relationship another chance, hoping the magic would return, and when it didn't, Drew's pain began because he'd gambled on his true love for Karyme and lost. Losing Karyme was the hardest thing he'd ever had to deal with and he was still struggling with not having her in his corner. Not only had he lost the lady of his life, he'd lost his best friend, but seeing Karyme entering the office could be best described as being remarkable. Drew hadn't seen her in weeks and the sight of her nearly brought tears from his eyes.

"Good morning," Karyme said as she entered the office. She made her way past Drew to sit at her desk. "Wow, it's been a while, since I sat here" Karyme said, looking down at her freshly polished desk.

"Yes, it has, far too long," Drew admitted.

"Miss me huh?" Karyme asked.

"More than you can imagine," Drew answered. He was hoping he hadn't jumped the gun by reading more into what Karyme said but he was so excited to see her. Like Karyme, Drew was ready to lay down an olive branch and re-establish the closeness they once shared. All Drew could think of was how much he'd missed Karyme. Welcoming her home was all he wanted to do but in doing so, his best course of action was to take things slow.

God knows, Drew wanted to rush over to Karyme and squeeze her senseless but he needed to take baby steps toward regaining his footing. Whether he acknowledged it or not, Drew was skating on thin ice and he didn't want to fall into a body of water without first learning how to swim. It was imperative that he regained Karyme's trust but until he could, Drew had to be careful and follow Karyme's lead. This was his chance to get back the girl he adored from a young age and Drew was determined not to do anything to ruin that chance.

Feeling remorseful for what he'd done to Karyme, Drew felt the need to ask for forgiveness for hurting her. Drew was uncertain if this was the right time to talk about what happened between them but now more than ever, he wanted to come clean. What was so comical was the fact that Drew had no idea Karyme already knew the truth. Lynn had told her the entire story of what happened between them.

"Karyme, I'm so sorry for what I did to you. You have to believe me when I say, I never intentionally meant to hurt you. The truth is, I'd gotten over my head and I didn't know how to handle what was happening." Drew teared up some and his voice cracked. He was willing to give any and everything to make things right but to do so, he felt he needed to come clean. Without holding anything back, Drew told the complete story of what happened. He even admitted being intimate with Lynn doing her visit but left out some of the details that could have buried him. Karyme listened to Drew as he spilled his heart out to her. Drew was being honest for the first time and Karyme applauded him for doing so. but it didn't give him the pass he was expecting to receive. Sure, Karyme was willing to forgive Drew and would have done so whether he was honest or not because she loved him that much.

Karyme also had been briefed by Lynn about their sexual encounter and was adamant Drew only made love to her because she forced herself on him. It was Lynn's belief that Drew wasn't attracted to her anymore because he was in love with Karyme. It was a belief Karyme had taken to heart and after understanding the dilemma Drew must have been in, she found it easier to forgive him. Perhaps from instincts, Karyme pushed her chair from behind her desk and walk over to where Drew was sitting. She set on the edge of Drew's desk and wrapped her arms around Drew's neck. Gently, Karyme placed her forehead against Drew's and stared into stared into eyes. She wanted him to see how sincere she was in what she was about to say.

"You're the best friend I've ever had and I love you unconditionally." That was all Karyme needed to say for Drew to lose his composure. Within seconds, he was crying like a baby. "I forgive you," Karyme confessed, as she held Drew close to her bosom. It was hard to understand why Karyme chose to forgive him after he showed little to no respect to their relationship. Drew's callous behavior nearly destroyed Karyme. Never would he ever again, make a decision so inconsiderate. Drew had learned his lesson, and lying would never be a part of his life again. After nearly a month, Karyme had chosen to forgive Drew. Without calculating his next move, Drew instinctively began kissing Karyme without resistance. They were on track to start anew and Drew couldn't have been happier. He swore to never hurt Karyme again. From this day forward, Drew was going to follow his heart, instead of his mind. Holding Karyme, Drew contemplated asking about the rumors spreading across town, regarding her relationship with Joshua McInnis. According to the rumors, Karyme was deeply involved with Joshua. Some said she had been introduced and accepted by the McInnis family. Some even went as far as saying, Karyme was about to resign her position at Hillcrest to accept a more lucrative position at First Savings and Loan Bank. Before Drew could go forward with his quest to reunite with Karyme, he needed to know the truth.

"Sweetie, I have a question I need to ask you," Drew said.

"What is it?" Karyme asked.

"Rumors has it that you're dating Joshua McInnis and you guys are heavily involved," Drew said.

"I've gone out to dinner with Josh a couple of times but it's nothing serious, we're only friends" Karyme responded.

Drew was cognizant of the quote; "We're only friends," bullshit. Lord knows he heard it a million times with Gloria but this seemed different. He could see in Karyme's eyes the love she had for him. Maybe, it was the way she held him or the way she kissed him that convinced him she was for real. It felt like the first time they discovered love. Hearing that Karyme wasn't serious with Joshua gave Drew the hope he needed to feel about his chances to resume his relationship with her. As Drew held Karyme in his arms, it felt like a dream. He remembered the old saying that "God works in mysterious ways."

It was a statement his grandparents would always say when unexpected things happened. Lord knows, his grandparents were right. It is true, God does works in mysterious ways and Drew couldn't praise him enough.

In the days that followed, emotions began heating up between Drew and Karyme. Sophia saw what was happening and did her best to intervene but her best efforts weren't good enough. Karyme was in love and this time nothing was going to stop her from getting what she wanted. Though she and Drew agreed to keep things slow, they couldn't follow the path they'd carved for themselves. The pressure of wanting to be together increased tremendously as their desire to have each other began heating up. By weeks end, Karyme and Drew initiated a decision to take their relationship to the next level. Drew and Karyme made a decision that would even cause their parents to raise an eyebrow. They made reservation to spend the weekend together in a cozy one-bedroom cabin in the Shenandoah National Park. Though Karyme was excited about spending the weekend with Drew, she was scared to death to tell her mother. Karyme knew what Sophia's reaction was going to be and she would have rather taken an ass whipping with three braided switches than tell her mother. Though Karyme promised Drew she would inform Sophia about their plans, she hadn't as of yet. She knew Sophia was going to blow her top when she learned about their plan.

No one could imagine the pressure Karyme was under but she'd told Drew she had talked to her mother and she was fine with it. Now, they were literary minutes before they were scheduled to leave and Karyme hadn't spoken to her mother. She looked across her desk to see the clock was nearing 11 am. Her knees began to shake as she reached for her purse to leave for the day. Karyme's plans were to drive by the Harrison estate to pick up her mother before driving into town to shop for some last-minute items. Today was Sophia's short day and Karyme was hoping she could ride into town with her. On their drive into town, Karyme's plan was to discuss the matter. She knew it wouldn't go over well with Sophia but Karyme's back was against the wall, she had no other choice but to tell her mother and hope for the best. Driving to pick up her mother, Karyme continued to rehearse what she was going to say but once seeing Sophia come out of the house, Karyme's mind went completely blank. "Lord, help me please," Karyme said to herself as she watched Sophia secure the front door of the Harrison Estate and began making her way toward the car.

"Hi baby girl," Sophia said, opening the door to the car. Sophia was in a good mood and looking forward to a long weekend. Monday was Presidents Day, which meant she was off until Tuesday morning. It wasn't that her work was hard because with Joanna off at college and Drew only home to sleep, the only work Sophia had to do was minor dusting and maybe having to vacuum twice weekly. Things were a far cry from the way it used to be when the kids were small.

"Are you off for the day?" Sophia asked.

"Yes ma'am, I was hoping you would ride with me into town," Karyme asked.

"I would love to," Sophia responded.

After learning that Karyme wasn't returning to work and was riding into town, Sophia decided to go with her. On their way into town, Sophia began making weekend plans that included Karyme. Sophia's suggestion caught Lynn off guard. She hated to have to disappoint her mother but Karyme knew what she needed to do and even though she knew it was going to upset her mother, Karyme had to admit her plans. Temporarily closing her eyes, Karyme said a quick prayer, before admitting her plans.

"Mama, about this weekend, I'm not going to be here," Karyme whispered while turning onto the main road.

"Where are you going?" Sophia responded.

Karyme nearly froze but knew it was now or never. She knew how her mother would react to her decision to go away for the weekend with Drew, she just didn't know the severity of it.

"You have plans for all three days?" Sophia asked.

"Yes, Ma'ma," Karyme answered. "I'm going out of town with Drew for the weekend," Karyme reluctantly admitted. Karyme was shaking like a leaf as she made her confession. She was uncertain if Sophia understood that her trip was a romantic getaway rather than a work-related one but soon realized she hadn't.

"I hope you're sleeping on different floors," Sophia stated, while under the impression it was a business trip.

"Ma'ma, this isn't a business trip, Drew and I rented a cabin and are spending the weekend together at the Shenandoah National Park." Karyme said. She attempted to read Sophia's thoughts but never got the chance because Sophia exploded like a ton of explosive.

"Oh, diablos no," Sophia screamed. "No te crie para ser la puta de nadie." Sophia said in Spanish which translated in English as meaning; "I didn't raise you to be no man's slut." Whenever Sophia became upset at Karyme, she would always revert to speaking in Spanish and today was just an example. Sophia demanded that Karyme turn the car around to take her home. Sophia refused to go shopping with Karyme after learning her intentions.

She couldn't believe Karyme could involve herself again with Drew after being nearly destroyed by him only weeks ago. Karyme tried explaining the situation but Sophia refused to hear what she had to say. Sophia warned Karyme that under no circumstances should she ever go away with a man she wasn't married to no matter how deep in love she thought she was with him. Realizing it wouldn't be a good idea to continue her drive into town, Karyme turned the car around and headed home to take her mother. As for her going into town to shop, Karyme planned to do just that once taking her mother home. On the way home Sophia continued ranting and raving about the sacrifices she made for Karyme to have a better life than she and Karyme was ruining it by running after a man who was only using her. "He's still in love with his college sweetheart," Sophia screamed out. She couldn't believe the ill-advised decision Karyme was about to make. Once Sophia was finished speaking negatively about Drew's intentions of Karyme, she asked the dreaded question.

"Are you still a virgin?" Sophia asked, fearing Karyme had lost her virginity to Drew. Waiting for Karyme's answer, Sophia prepared herself to hear the worst. Karyme's first thought was to lie to prevent hurting her mother but she couldn't, she respected Sophia too much to result to lying to her. Though hesitating, Karyme admitted she had lost her virginity and it had been to Drew. Karyme explained, she had done so because she and Drew was in love and she strongly believed he was going to be the man she married. Of course, Sophia didn't take the news well and began crying. Her daughter had made the biggest mistake of her life by trusting a man who hadn't fully given in to the idea that his relationship with his college girlfriend was over. Not wanting to hear any more of what Karyme had to say, Sophia got out of the car and rushed inside of the house.

Karyme followed but at a slower pace. She wanted to console her mother, but Sophia was too upset to talk civilly. Believing their conversation was over, Karyme went to her room to room to begin packing for her weekend away with Drew.

While in her room sitting on her bed, Sophia struggled with Karyme's decision to go away with Drew. She didn't want Karyme to follow her in footsteps by getting pregnant by a man who claimed to love her, only to learned he had lied and wanted no parts of her or her baby. With that weighing heavy on her mind, Sophia left her room enroute to have it out with Karyme. Seeing that Karyme was wrapped in a towel and about to get into the shower, Sophia had her to sit on her bed. Speaking in Spanish, Sophia laid her demands on the table. To save her daughter from destroying her life, Sophia felt the need to be stern to give Karyme the shock she felt she needed.

"Call Drew right now and tell him you're not going with him. Not only that, I want you to end all association with him," Sophia demanded.

Although Karyme wasn't caught by surprised, she wasn't willing to listen to what her mother had to say. Her mind was made to spend the weekend with Drew and nothing Sophia could say was going to change her mind.

"I no longer want you to work for the Harrison Cooperation. You're going to quit your job there," Sophia demanded.

"Ma'ma, I'm twenty-one, and you don't have to make decisions for me anymore," Karyme said convincingly.

Karyme's response was more than what Sophia wanted to hear. For the first time in her life, Karyme wasn't going to allow her mother to dictate her nor was she going to stop seeing Drew or quit her job. Frankly, Karyme felt she was old enough to make her own decisions without having her mother to do so for her and as far as she was concerned, her mind was made and there was nothing Sophia could say or do to persuade her change it. On one hand, it wasn't surprising that Karyme was refusing to obey her mother's demands. She was in love with Drew and after discussing their plans, they were ready to go forward with their future.

Seeing that she couldn't change Karyme's mind, Sophia's next move was to do something so drastic, Karyme wouldn't have any choice but to change her mind.

Sophia believed, if Karyme was old enough to make her own decisions, she was old enough to live on her own. Feeling strong in her beliefs, Sophia announced her decision without factoring in the consequences. Of course, she had no plans of kicking Karyme out of her house, but hoped it was enough to scare Karyme straight, but Sophia's plan backfired.

Shocked that her mother had asked her to leave, Karyme showered, got dressed and packed a small bag and left, before Sophia got the chance to apologize. Driving away from the house, Karyme began to cry, she couldn't believe what had happened. Never in her wildest dream would she had imagined her mother would kick her out of the house because of a disagreement but that was exactly what happened.

Sophia watched from her living room window as Karyme drove away. She suspected Karyme would return once she cooled down and would apologize for the way talked to her. Like any other misunderstanding, Sophia believed they would work it out between themselves once cooler heads prevail. In a lot of ways, Karyme was correct by saying she was old enough to make her own decisions. Sophia became so focused on Drew, she failed to realize she was fifteen when she became pregnant. Karyme was not only six years older than her mother; she was thirty years more mature than she was when she was her mother's age. Maybe Sophia was wrong to assume Karyme was making a mistake by choosing to be with Drew. Over the years, she had seen the two of them together and saw how well they'd bonded. All and all, Drew was a good guy and he'd always looked after Karyme, Sophia just couldn't understand how they could become lovers after being best friends for so long.

Hearing the doorbell, Drew answered it and found Karyme in tears. He didn't have to guess why she was crying; he knew Sophia had thrown down the gauntlet. What Drew didn't know was that Sophia had ordered Karyme to leave because she refused to stop seeing him. Seeing that Karyme was a total wreck, Drew wrapped his arms around her to calm her. He then led her into the house to the family room, where he had her sit. To help calm Karyme's nerves, Drew poured Karyme a glass of brandy. Anxious to know why she was crying; Drew asked Karyme what happened. He was shocked to learn Sophia had taken such a drastic stance to block Karyme from seeing him. Once calming Karyme, Drew exited the room for more than three minutes. Once returning, he grabbed hold of Karyme's hand and led her upstairs to his bedroom.

It had been years since Karyme had been to Drew's room and just as Lynn had described, Drew's room could match any five-star hotel but what stood out mostly about his room was the essence of Moroccan Amber. The scent was so intoxicating, Karyme found herself wanting to make love to Drew before they left for the mountains. But Drew didn't have making love on his mind, he had something more important, something that was about to change Karyme's life forever. He led Karyme to his closet and opened it. Inside was a closet full of suits and in every color with boxes of shoes stacked to match each suit.

"Choose a suit," Drew asked

"Why do you want me to choose a suit? Karyme asked.

"Because it's going to be the suit I wear for our wedding today," Drew answered.

"Huh?" Karyme said in disbelief.

Unable to comprehend what Drew was saying, Karyme asked him to repeat himself. Drew followed by dropping to one knee and officially asked Karyme to marry him. Karyme's dream was about to come true, the man she loved with all of her heart and soul had asked her to marry him. Yes," Karyme shouted out, before placing her hands over her mouth. She had just said yes to become Mrs. Andrew Christopher Harrison. Drew didn't have a ring on hand but used his college class ring as a substitute until they could purchase their wedding rings for the ceremony. Drew explained, before going to the jewelry store to buy their rings, they first had to go to the Circuit Court to obtain their license. After getting their license and their rings, they were going to city hall, where his mother was waiting to marry them. Karyme couldn't have been more excited and though it wasn't the marriage she envisioned; she was marrying the man she loved. Still, there was an empty spot in Karyme's heart because her mother wouldn't be there to see the happiest day of her life.

"Drew, I want to invite my mom," Karyme said, hoping Drew would agree and to her surprise, he was on board. He even agreed to go home with her to ask for Sophia's blessing. Karyme selected Drew's blue double-breasted suit to get married in. She didn't know exactly what she had to be married in but was sure she had a dress to match.

The couple left the house to meet with Sophia. Neither, Drew or Karyme knew how Sophia would react to the news, but knew, Sophia needed to know. Entering into the driveway, Karyme turned off her engine and waited for Drew to arrive. Once Drew arrived, the two of them made their way to the house. Using her key, Karyme and Drew nervously entered the house. Standing by the front door, Karyme called out for Sophia. She didn't know what to expect but prayed her mother would accept the idea of them being married. Coming from her bedroom, Sophia faced the couple. From the look in her eyes, Sophia had been crying and after seeing Karyme, she instantly became apologetic for her earlier blowup. It didn't matter that Drew was there to see her apologize, Sophia's thoughts were on getting her daughter to come back home. In other words, Sophia was asking for forgiveness for the immature way she handled Karyme's decision to spend the weekend with Drew. Karyme too apologized for what she felt was disrespectful. Karyme emphasized how important it was to have Drew in her life and how she was looking forward to sharing her life with him. Never before had Karyme went against her mother's wishes and she wanted Sophia to understand that she was capable of making her own decisions whether they were right or wrong. Drew followed by adding how much he loved Karyme. He promised to forever love, honor and support Karyme for the rest of their lives. His statement left Sophia with an ambiguous look on her face. She was uncertain what Drew was trying to say but was sure it was more important than a planned weekend trip to the mountains.

"Ma'ma, Drew and I have something to tell you," Karyme said. She didn't know how her mother would react to the news and listened as Drew went forward with it.

"Miss Sophia, I know you don't approve of Karyme and I going on a weekend trip together and I understand. I too would have concerns, if I was a parent. But Karyme and I aren't going to the mountains as a single couple, we're going as husband and wife," Drew explained.

"What are you saying? Sophia asked.

"Ma'ma, Drew and I are getting married today, and it would mean the world to us, if you could bless us, by being there," Karyme asked.

The news was not only shocking, it left Sophia undecided on if she could agree with her daughter having a shot gun wedding. Her first thought was that Karyme was pregnant but remembered Karyme had her menstrual cycle less than a week ago.

She didn't know what to make of it and said nothing. Her dreams were that Karyme would have a real wedding, not some ceremony at the justice of the peace, but the fact remained, Drew was about to make her baby girl the happiest woman in the world.

"I promise you Ms. Sophia, I will give Karyme the wedding of her dreams and you can help with the planning the moment we get back, if you like," Drew said, hoping it was enough to convince Sophia to attend their wedding.

"Ma'ma, it's what the both of us want. Please say you would come," Karyme asked.

"I don't understand the hurry but it's not for me to understand. I will support the two of you, and give you my blessing," Sophia responded. "Oh my God, my baby is getting married today," Sophia said. Whether she wanted to or not, Sophia rushed to shower and get dress. Her daughter was getting married and she was going to be there to support her.

Chapter: 46

Constance was on her way downstairs when she stopped at Lynn's door to listen to what she thought was her vomiting. It was late-autumn and it was flu season. Maybe, Lynn had contacted a virus but Constance's thoughts weren't in line with that of Lynn having a virus but the possibility of her being pregnant. It had been a little over a month since she stole out of the house to visit Drew. To be sure she heard Lynn vomiting, Constance opened Lynn's bedroom door and walked inside her room. Once inside, Constance could hear Lynn's shower running and assumed she was in the shower. Constance's motherly instincts were advising her to investigate her daughter's apparent sickness further but as a parent, she wanted to give Lynn the privacy she deserved. Lynn hadn't been herself lately and the likely cause was Drew but to Constance's knowledge, Lynn hadn't made any attempts to see him. Thank God, Lynn had seen the light and had enough sense to cleanse herself of that farm boy, but in doing so, she was becoming more reclusive each day. Something was wrong, what, Constance wasn't sure but her suspicions were causing her to become more attentive to Lynn's movements.

Lynn joined her parents' downstairs for breakfast but was able only to eat a slice of toast before having to excuse herself. The smell of the scrambled eggs and bacon began to get the best of Lynn causing her to nearly threw up at the table. Lynn blamed her illness on the raw oysters she'd eaten at a seafood bar the previous night but Constance wasn't buying her story. Lynn could tell her mother was seemingly reading her mind and suspected it was more to her condition, then she was sharing. Excusing herself from the table, Lynn ran upstairs to her bathroom. She barely made it before releasing what contents were left in her stomach. Lynn was having doubts about surviving her morning sickness and believed she would have to do better if she was to conceal her pregnancy. She hadn't altogether decided on what she was going to do but found herself leaning towards having her baby. Whether she would keep it or not, depended on what her parents had to say. Lynn didn't want to be another rich girl whose parents sent them away to stay with relatives or an extended stay in Europe until the baby was born, then force her to give it up for adoption. Not wanting to go that route, Lynn considered aborting her baby before having to give it up for adoption. She couldn't live with herself, knowing her baby was growing up someplace other than with her.

Riding into work with her parents, Lynn's line of thinking remained on her pregnancy and what to do about it. Becoming a mother dominated her thoughts and she was remained undecided on what to do. Deep down inside, Lynn wanted to have the baby but having it meant having to inform Drew and informing Drew meant going back on her word to Karyme. Although the idea of having a family was appealing, Lynn had a lot to consider. She knew there was no way Drew would allow her to raise their child alone and wouldn't hesitate to marry her, but her gut instinct was telling her; Drew didn't love her enough to give her the love and commitment she needed. Maybe in time, Drew would fall back in love with her but she couldn't risk being hurt again. Having the baby to trap Drew was something she never wanted to do, but seemingly she ended up doing just that. Yes, she made a mistake in her decision to intentionally get pregnant but that was before she realized Drew had fallen in love with Karyme.

Setting at her desk, Lynn found herself holding and caressing her stomach. She was intrigued at the idea of becoming a mother and though she remained undecided on what to do, she realized she had to inform Drew about her pregnancy. After all, he was the father, and telling him was the right thing to do. With that in mind, Lynn reluctantly called Drew. She prayed that he was available to talk but his phone went straight to voicemail. It was unusual for Drew not to answer because he always had his phone with him. Perhaps he was in a meeting but then again, it was possible he didn't want to talk to her. Whatever the reason, Lynn knew she had to keep trying until she reached him. Desperate to speak to someone, Lynn chose to call her sister. Confiding in Ashley wasn't something Lynn was accustomed to doing but her mind was running rapidly and she needed to talk to someone she felt she could trust.

Lynn trusted her therapist and considered her but felt having the support of her sister was more important. Lucky for Lynn, Ashley didn't have class but she was busy being made love to by the new man in her life who was in a doggy-style position. Seeing the call coming from her family's office, Ashley abruptly ended her morning sexual encounter to take the call. As you may have imagined, Ashley's new love interest wasn't happy with her decision to stop, and out of frustration, he got out of bed and rush to the bathroom.

"Hello," Ashley answered.

"Hey, sis, you got a minute?" Lynn asked.

"Sure, what's up?" Ashley asked.

"I need to talk to you about something important. Are you alone?" Lynn asked.

"Yeah, why? What's wrong?" Ashley asked again, detecting anxiety in Lynn's voice. "Don't tell me, you and Drew are trying to make it work again?"

Before telling her story, Lynn asked Ashley to hear her out before judging her. Holding back her tears, Lynn began explaining to Ashley that she'd slept with Drew without using protection, and now she was pregnant. In her confession, Lynn admitted to sleeping with Drew with the intention of getting pregnant and now that she was, she was regretting doing so. Lynn went on to state, she hadn't factored in all the dynamics that came without using protection, and after doing so, she realized, she'd made perhaps the worst mistake of her life. Needing guidance on what to do, Lynn asked Ashley for help. Although Lynn was uncertain of how she wanted to handle the situation, she was quick to eliminate the topic of discussing an abortion, not until all of her options were exhausted. Lynn admitted she intentionally tried getting pregnant with the hope of getting their parent's blessings to marry Drew but that was before she was promoted. After her promotion, Lynn realized she wanted to delicate her life to the family's business and didn't want the responsibility of becoming a wife but most importantly, she didn't want to become a mother. Stunned, by what she was hearing, Ashley asked Lynn, if she was going to tell Drew about the pregnancy. Lynn hesitated, before admitting to be on the fence about it. To hear Lynn had gone and gotten herself pregnant was not only shocking but downright unbelievable. Though Lynn was accustomed to screwing up, never in Ashley's wildest dreams, would she have imagined; "Little Miss Goody Two Shoes" would have deliberately gone out and done something so stupid. Lynn's screw-up was the motivation Ashley needed to take full advantage of Lynn's fuck up. Lord knows she didn't have to backstab Lynn because Miss Goody Two Shoes" had cut her own jugular after being hand pick to take over the family's company. Though ecstatic, Ashley couldn't help but feel compassion for her sister. Instead of celebrating, Ashley held her emotions inside, at least until they finished their conversation. Lynn's fuck up not only provided Ashley with the advantage she needed to become Boldmont Enterprises' new head person, but she could also become their father's favorite. However, Ashley couldn't overlook Lynn's ability to land on her feet. For years, Lynn had shown signs of being irresponsible and each time, she landed on her feet as if she was a cat.

What was so mind-boggling was the number of times that Lynn fucked up, not to mention her well-publicized visits to the "Nut House" and after all of that, she still was given the key to the President's office. So, why in God's name would she deliberately sabotage her chances by getting pregnant? Who in their right mind would do such a thing? The only answer Ashley could produce was that Lynn wasn't interested in the company as much as she was with finding true love. In all fairness, Lynn was as shrewd as they came when it came to business. She knew the company better than most of the executives working for it and that's because she was taught by the best, who molded her in his image. Everything was given to Lynn, even though she didn't deserve it. Ashley felt she should have been the one to succeed her father once he retires. She made the better grades and was on schedule to graduate next year. Lynn on the other hand was a college dropout who was taking online classes. To say that Lynn chose to throw away the gift their father bestowed upon them was an understatement but then again, Lynn was familiar with screwing up. No one with a sane mind would piss away the opportunity to head a multi-million-dollar company before they become twenty-one.

Lynn's quest to live a fairytale lifestyle had finally come around to bite her in the ass, and deservedly so. But this time, she had committed the most serious of all blunders and once the news broke, she was going to pay dearly. It was unimaginable to think their parents were going to approve of her having a baby out of wedlock and to hear Lynn break down in tears over the phone only substantiated what Ashley already knew.

Throughout their childhood, Lynn had been labeled the good twin, the twin that always listened and obey their parents' wishes. Ashley believed, once the news hits the fan that the golden child slipped up and got herself pregnant, all hell was going to break loose, causing their father to reverse his decision to appoint her CEO of the company. Maybe now, their father will finally see Lynn for the fuck up she really is.

The sisters talked for more than an hour while trying to decide upon an acceptable solution. As much as Ashley didn't want to help Lynn, she ultimately felt compelled to do so. Unfortunately for Lynn, a suitable solution wasn't reached. Lynn was adamant she didn't want to explore the idea of aborting her baby but to be frank, she had no other options but to terminate her pregnancy. Lynn went forth with the idea to inform Drew about her pregnancy even after Ashley strongly advised her against it.

273

Ashley knew, if Drew learned about the pregnancy, he would want to do the right thing and marry Lynn but then again, Drew marrying Lynn could be a good thing. To assure her victory in their father's eyes, Ashley needed Lynn's blunder to come to light. She was unsure how to make it happen without getting her hands dirty, so Ashley suggested Lynn discuss the matter with their mother. Ashley argued, by telling Drew before speaking to their parents could complicate things even more. What Ashley said made sense but talking to their mother about being pregnant out of wedlock wasn't going to be an easy thing to do. Constance train of thought was one way and one way only. Regardless, something had to be done, whether it was telling Drew or her mother first, because time was of the essence. Lynn ended her conversation with Ashley more confused than before. She hadn't considered her parents when she made the decision to get pregnant. Lynn not only screwed up her life, she'd also done so to everyone who cared about her. By becoming pregnant, Lynn most likely lost the chance to run Boldmont Enterprises but as she thought about it, she realized, running the company wasn't as important as her becoming a mother. She wanted more than anything to keep her word and allow Drew and Karyme to be happy but Drew had a right to know he was about to become a father.

Sitting at her desk, Lynn began questioning herself if aborting her pregnancy was the right thing to do. She was afraid to raise a child as a single mother and though Drew wouldn't hesitate to marry her, Lynn knew he wasn't in love with her. Her decision not to fight for Drew may have been the second worst decision she'd ever made but it was the right decision. No matter how immature her decision was to get pregnant, she never thought the consequences would be so extreme. Whether to have her baby was by far the most important decision Lynn would ever have to make. To keep her child meant she would need all the support she could muster. Lynn knew Ashley's support wasn't going to come without a price. By supporting her, Ashley would most likely assume a more lucrative position, before taking over the company. Their father's health was declining rapidly and he wanted her to take over but there was about to be a shake-up not only in the family but in the business.

Less than thirty minutes before the board was to meet, Lynn rushed outside to a nearby food cart to purchase a chicken salad sandwich. Having been sick this morning and not eating anything, Lynn was starving.

She purchased chicken salad combo, a bag of chips, and a ginger ale, before rushing back to her office to eat lunch, but only got as far as the secretary's desk, before being overcome by the aroma of her food. Feeling a sudden urge to barf, Lynn dropped her lunch in the secretary's trash can and rushed into the nearby lady's room. Constance, who had just gotten off the phone with Ashley saw what had happened and followed Lynn into the lady's room. Entering, Constance stood quietly outside the stall, listening to Lynn threw up. Her hunch had been correct, Lynn was pregnant and after speaking to Ashley, Constance was now certain. Having no idea her mother was standing outside the stall, Lynn exited and was startled to see Constance waiting on her. Constance's blank stare nearly caused Lynn to panic.

Lynn tried maintaining a cool demeanor but she'd been caught with her hands in the cookie jar and even though she continued to blame her illness on the seafood she ate the night before, Constance knew the truth.

"How far along are you?" Constance asked.

Without denying or confirming her mother's accusations, Lynn walked past Constance to rinse her mouth in the sink. Constance followed Lynn and hovered over her as she rinsed out her mouth. Constance began pressuring Lynn to admit what she already knew but Lynn stuck to her story. Knowing the truth, Constance desperately tried to contain her anger, she could feel herself losing her patience and begged Lynn to admit the truth. Still, Lynn stuck to her story. Owning up to what she had done wasn't something Lynn was prepared to do, at least not at work. Lynn felt her confession should be at home in privacy but Constance didn't see it that way, she wanted to hear the truth immediately. After not getting the answers, she was seeking, Constance took matters into her own hands. In a blind rage, she grabbed hold of Lynn's collar and shove her against the mirror on the wall.

"How fucking far along are you?" Constance demanded with a raspy voice.

Lynn was shocked at the stance her mother had taken. Constance actions had placed fear in Lynn, leaving her too afraid to move a muscle.

"You stupid little girl, why are you determined to screw up your life?" Constance screamed, pressing her forehead tightly against Lynn's. "Why can't you be like Ashley?"

Her mother was right, why couldn't she be like Ashley. Ashley didn't care about love or anyone for that matter, Ashley was a narcissist who only looked out for herself. That in itself was more than she could ever want in life. Lynn couldn't see herself living the life Ashley was currently living. Lynn wanted to feel love and to give love. She didn't want to sleep around to fulfill her sexual needs.

After not getting the answers, she wanted to hear, Constance took a more drastic matter by placing her arm across Lynn's chest, securing her tighter to the mirror. She wanted Lynn to understand how serious of a mistake she'd made and how detrimental it was to get a handle on it before it was too late. Lynn remained restrained against the mirror without knowing what to do. She tried breaking free of her mother's grip but couldn't; Constance's leverage was too great and as Constance continued to demand the truth, she used a more forceful tone of voice.

Realizing she couldn't hide her secret anymore, Lynn collapsed. It was over, her ordeal of hiding the evitable had ended. Sobbing uncontrollably, Lynn substantiated what her mother already knew, she was carrying Drew's child.

"How far along are you?" Constance asked again.

"I don't know," Lynn responded.

"You don't know? When was your last period?" Constance asked.

"Four weeks ago," Lynn answered.

"Good, we still have time," Constance replied.

Constance was relieved to learn Lynn hadn't bypassed her term for an abortion. Furthermore, she was ecstatic to learn Lynn hadn't divulged her pregnancy to Drew. Constance's plan was to eliminate the problem before it was too late and even though she was disappointed Lynn was considering keeping the baby, she was confident she could convince Lynn to change her mind.

Wiping Lynn's tears, Constance embraced her; to show support. Constance didn't have much time if she was going to work her magic to convince Lynn to abort her baby but like most mothers, Constance had a few tricks up her sleeve. She understood before making any serious moves, she first had to regain Lynn's trust.

She'd made a mistake by forcing her to drop the charges on Marshall and Mia and she nearly paid for it. For months Constance was force to treaded on thin ice until Lynn found it in her heart to forgive her. Now, Constance again, found herself in a similar situation but unlike the last time, she wasn't going to force Lynn to do anything she wasn't prepared to do. The only problem Constance faced was having to prepare Lynn for what was best. As a precautionary measure, Constance suggested that Lynn contact a Planned Parenthood counselor to set up an appointment. Constance explained, it wasn't to convince her to abort her baby but to talk with a counselor to discuss her options. Lynn listened to what her mother had to say. She agreed that talking to the counselor could present more options for her and decided to make the appointment. Once Lynn agreed to speak with a counselor, Constance began to relax, knowing her problem was half over. She was on track to solve Lynn's problem, whether Lynn wanted to or not but Constance understood Lynn wasn't going to change her mind overnight. She would have to immediately begin working on her before further damage was done to their family's reputation. By pushing Lynn to have an abortion, Constance didn't think about the consequences she'll have to face when she met God but felt the sacrifice was worth the penalty.

Meeting God was the last thing Constance worried about. It was the embarrassment that Lynn would bring to their family that topped her agenda. Constance's desire to keep the impression of their perfect family was her biggest concern and she was willing to do anything to protect it. The mere fact that Lynn was only nineteen was more than enough for her to want to cover up Lynn's pregnancy. She and Harry had worked diligently to build their reputation to become socialites within their community and now, their hard work was in jeopardy of being destroyed by their hot-in-the-ass daughter who couldn't keep her legs closed. Feeling the need to give Lynn the support she needed, Constance escorted her back to her office. She had Lynn lie on the couch and even placed a pillow under her head and feet to make her comfortable. Constance was determined to keep Lynn's condition under the radar. She instructed Lynn rest and promised to cover for her at the meeting. Leaving Lynn's office, Constance felt confident she had made enough of an impression on Lynn that she would agree to an abortion without as much of an argument. All it would take was for her to have patience and things would work out the way she wanted it.

Relieved her secretes was out, Lynn closed her eyes and begin to visualize having a family with Drew. She rubbed her stomach and smiled as she imagined Drew's reactions after learning he was about to become a father. Being a husband and a father was all Drew had talked about and it was about to happen. However, Lynn remained concern about Drew's feelings for Karyme. Though he never acknowledged his true feelings, Lynn felt his love for Karyme was more than he was willing to admit. Perhaps being pregnant was precisely what they needed to reignite the fire between them. Sure, some would say this was a fool's way of thinking and in most cases, it was but not in this case. Drew was different; he wanted a family more than anything and Lynn was willing to give him exactly what he wanted. Before drifting off to sleep, Lynn continued to consider her options and the best route to take. She revisited the idea of telling Drew and though it may not have been her best option, it was the right thing to do. So many lives would be affective if she chose to tell Drew but if she followed her mother's suggestion, Lynn would have to abandon any idea of having the family Drew wanted. Lynn had a decision to make and only days to make it. As hard as it was Lynn had to make the best decision that would benefit everyone involved.

Constance returned to Lynn's office directly after the board meeting. As promised, she'd covered for Lynn by saying she was still suffering from a mild case of food poisoning. To ease Lynn's upset stomach, Constance arrived with a hot cup of mint tea and saltine crackers. She watched Lynn sip her tea before revisiting the subject of finalizing her plans to make an appointment to speak with a counselor at a nearby planned parenthood clinic. Constance assured Lynn it was her decision to make but stressed how important it was to make a decision before it was too late.

"You're about to become the face of this company, don't sabotage this opportunity." Constance said, hoping it was enough to convince Lynn it was the best thing to do. After listening to what her mother had to say, Lynn reluctantly agreed.

Chapter: 47

Karyme had overslept for the first time since becoming interim president of Hillcrest Farms and was running late picking up her mother for work. Before she reached the door the doorbell rang. Opening it, Karyme was surprised to see Gloria standing with a look of shock on her face. It was obvious the reason she showed up unexpectedly but Karyme didn't have time for Gloria's games this morning, she needed to pick up her mother, who was waiting for her.

"Oh Karyme, you scared me. Why are you answering doors so early in the morning, I thought you didn't start work until eight," Gloria said jokingly. It was all she could say before having to pick her lip off the ground. The rumors were true, Drew had married his little burrito. Somehow Karyme had tricked him and maneuvered herself from the outhouse to the big house.

"That fucking bitch," Gloria said to herself before noticing how small the diamonds were in Karyme's rings. Karyme's rings were no comparison to the four carats she was wearing on her finger. Mason had made up for his earlier flop and though she didn't have the wedding she wanted, at least she had a wedding. Karyme on the other hand didn't because Drew was a cheap ass. Not only had he gotten Karyme rings from the cracker jack box, he married his little Latina princess in the front of a justice of the peace. What a fucked-up way to get married but on second thought, the little "Wetback" didn't deserve a wedding.

"Gloria, what do you want, because I'm running late," Karyme asked.

"No good morning, how are you this morning Gloria, nothing but what do I want? Hum, I see you're becoming snooty already," Gloria responded.

"I'm really running late, what can I do to help you?" Karyme asked.

"First of all, I want to congratulate you and Drew and secondly, Mason asked me to come by and invite the two of you to join us for dinner at Castello's tonight," Gloria said. "We thought it is the least we could do being you didn't have a real wedding. That sounds like Drew, always taking the cheap way out."

"Gloria, please, don't do this," Karyme asked.

"Ok, ok, I apologize but will you call me and let me know? Gloria asked.

"Sure," Karyme responded as she hurried past Gloria to her car.

Gloria followed closely behind as Karyme reached the main road. Gloria who was driving Mason's car to work, found it hard to believe that Drew had actually married their maid's daughter. It had only been a few weeks ago when he was boosting about a huge wedding, he and the "Rich Bitch" were planning, but in a turn of events, he'd married the little "Wetback," instead. How in the hell did that little sneaky bitch wiggled her way into Drew's life and bed? Karyme's marriage to Drew was frustrating for Gloria to understand because she was hoping to have another chance to be with Drew.

Throughout her shift, Gloria thoughts were only of Drew and his marriage to Karyme. It was hard for her to believe not only that Drew had gotten married but he'd married Karyme. The only reason Gloria could think as to why Drew's sudden marriage to Drew occurred was because she was pregnant. She had forewarned Drew to never sleep with Karyme because she would start spitting out babies like watermelon seeds but like the trusting idiot Drew was, he chose not to listen and now he was stuck with her for life.

"How could Drew allowed this to happen?" Gloria said to herself. It broke her heart knowing Drew's ring was on Karyme's finger instead of hers. It didn't matter that she was married, in her mind Drew was the only man she could ever love.

Once completing her pass on, Gloria left the hospital in route to pick up Mason from work. Thank God, she only had to work an eight-hour shift today because since learning the truth about Drew and Karyme, she wanted to go home and go directly to bed. Mentally, Gloria was drained and after a calling Drew for more than twenty times unsuccessfully, she didn't want to have to hear anything negative Mason had to say.

Arriving at Mason's job site, Gloria instantly became pissed when learning Mason had to work overtime. It was frustrating having to wait for him to finish working, especially after she had finished a long shift. The bottom line was they needed another vehicle, and as soon as Mason got into the car, she was going to suggest it. As Gloria sat impatiently, her frustration continued to build. Several men continued to gawk at her while trying to engage in conversation. Finally, after what seem like forever, Mason arrived.

"Hey baby, pop the trunk," Mason asked. He removed his work boots and placed them in the trunk before changing into a pair of sneakers. Getting inside the car, Mason wasn't at all filthy but reeked of asphalt. Gloria made it obvious she hated the idea of having one car between them and suggested Mason buy her a car. It was a request Mason was willing to fulfill and suggested they stop by the dealership before going home.

Three hours later, Gloria signed the last of the paperwork and was given the keys to her dream car. She left the dealership driving her brand-new orange 2023 Chevrolet Corvette Z-06. Gloria was as beautiful as the car she was driving and as she drove off the lot, all eyes were on her. Before leaving the dealership, Gloria asked Mason if she could go show off her car to some of her friends before coming home, and like the hen-pecked fool he was, Mason agreed. Sadly, Gloria had no intentions of seeing her friends, her intention was to go to see Drew at his office. She knew Karyme was probably going to there but she didn't give a damn, her mission was to find out why he married Karyme.

Gloria arrived at Drew's office approximately twenty minutes later. She saw Drew's old woody station wagon still parked in the parking lot but didn't see Karyme's old jalopy. Parking, Gloria made her way to the office and found the outside door unlocked. Entering, she followed the hallway that led to Drew's office. Turning the corner, Gloria saw a light on and knew Drew was most likely alone. She saw him sitting at his desk but didn't see any signs of Karyme. Standing outside of Drew's office, Gloria announced herself.

"Well, if it ain't the married man," Gloria said, entering the office.

Looking up to see Gloria, Drew nearly jumped out of his skin. It wasn't that he was afraid to be in the same room with her but her unpredictable ways scared him, and knew in all probability, Gloria was up to no good.

"Gloria, what brings you by?" Drew asked.

"I have a bone to pick with you. You didn't invite me to your wedding, I had to find out from the town's gossip. I at least sent you an invitation," Gloria said.

"Karyme and I decided to have a small wedding with only our parents present," Drew responded.

281

"Hum, did you place a bag of shit in the corner to keep the flies off Karyme?" Gloria joked.

"Gloria, I'm not in the mood for your antics today. Karyme is my wife and you will respect her or get the hell out of my building," Drew demanded. Drew had come to Karyme's defense, and why shouldn't he, Karyme was his wife and Gloria was going to treat her with respect.

"I apologize for that insensitive statement, I shouldn't have said that," Gloria replied.

Seeing that Drew was pissed, Gloria decided to change the subject. Yes, she was jealous of Karyme and because Drew had married her. Gloria resented the fact that Karyme was highly intelligent and had accomplished everything she sat her mind to do. In a lot of ways, she wished she was Karyme.

"Why didn't you return my calls? I tried calling you all day," Gloria said. "You have no idea how frustrating that can be."

"I've been busy," Drew said, before stopping Gloria short of sitting on his desk. "Don't sit on my desk, take a seat in the chair."

"Are you afraid that your little senorita will see me sitting on her desk? Look at me, I'm wearing only hospital scrubs.

"It doesn't matter what you're wearing, you're not going to sit on my desk. I'm a married man and I'm going to respect my wife." Drew said. Drew was right, he was a married man and he had taken a vow to love, respect and honor his marriage. Before sitting, Gloria leaned over Drew's desk and kissed Drew on the cheek. "Congratulations," she said before sitting in one of two chairs positioned in front of his desk.

"Where's the wife?" Gloria asked.

"At her mothers, she should be back any minute now," Drew answered.

Short on time Gloria quickly began questioning Drew. Her first questioned pertained to his premature breakup with Lynn. Though it was none of her business, Drew was more than happy to tell the story of him realizing the moment he knew he was in love with Karyme.

The strangest part of Drew's story involved the amount of the years he proclaimed to have been in love with Karyme. Two of those years were when they were together; Drew had given her an engagement ring. Drew's confession had thrown Gloria for a loop. They were supposed to have been planning their marriage but unbeknownst to her Drew was in love with his little "Wetback." Drew's admission had Gloria wanting to slap his face. She even attempted to stand but thought better of it. Still, Drew's admission had Gloria feeling sick to her stomach, knowing she'd been played. Seconds later Gloria heard what she thought was footsteps walking toward Drew's office. Her first thought was to get out of her chair and lay across Drew's desk spread eagle but the scrubs she was wearing was too tight. Drew had played her for the last time, it was time to get her get back, the only problem was she didn't know how.

"Hey Sweetie, sorry it took me so long, I had to talk to mom about something," Karyme said before realizing Gloria was sitting at Drew's desk. Karyme walked behind Drew's desk and kissed him. Turning to Gloria, Karyme spoke. "Hi Gloria, what are you doing here?"

 Many thoughts of a comeback flashed through Gloria's mind, but she chose not to respond. Gloria turned her head to block out the sight of having to see Karyme kiss Drew. Karyme had married the man she was supposed to marry and for doing so, Gloria became more than determined to belittle Drew.

"Actually, I came by to show you guys my new car I got today," Gloria said.

"I saw it on my way inside, congratulation," Karyme responded.

"It was a gift from my husband," Gloria boosted.

"It's a beautiful car," Karyme replied.

 "What is it?" Drew asked.

"A 2023 corvette Z06," Gloria said proudly.

"Wow, that must have cost a penny?" Drew responded.

"Try $190K, you know me, when I do something, I do it big," Gloria bragged. "Come on, let's go take a walk around,"

Standing from behind his desk, Drew and Karyme followed Gloria from the office outside. Seeing Gloria's overpriced toy wasn't something Karyme was interested in; she took a step back to allow Drew to take a walk around. Karyme watched Gloria as she stared at Drew. Karyme suspected that Gloria wanted to be alone with Drew and she wasn't going to allow it. It was time for Gloria to stop chasing after Drew, and if Gloria continued, she was going to have to have a talk with her. Karyme watched Drew's excitement as he inspected all the gadgets inside the Gloria's car.

"So, Karyme, tell me, how does it feel being Mrs. Andrew Harrison? Gloria asked.

"I'm Mrs. Karyme Renee' Harrison, I married Drew because I love him, not because of who he is," Karyme responded impolitely. She felt she needed to inform Gloria of who she was and that she didn't need Drew or the Harrison name to be somebody. Gloria could only nod her head in approval. Karyme had gotten one up on her but Gloria was planning to come back to with a stunner to shut Karyme's fucking mouth.

"Being you're married now, why don't you get Drew to replace that piece of shit Yugo you're driving? And while he's at it, get him to replace that fifty-year-old station wagon he's driving," Gloria laughed. Yall need to live like the millionaires you are."

"We don't need to show we're millionaires and to correct you, my car is a Hyundai Accent," Karyme responded.

"They're the same," Gloria responded.

Gloria was beginning to irritate Karyme and as much as Karyme hated to interrupt Drew with his fascination of Gloria's car, it was time to go. Karyme had heard enough of Gloria's antics and her gloating about all the new things she had and was getting.

"Is Drew going to build you a house or are you staying in the house with his mother and sister?" Gloria mocked. She knew the answer to her question, she just wanted Karyme to acknowledge the momma's boy was never going to leave the nest.

"No, we're going to reside at Hillcrest Manor," Karyme replied.

"Huh, wow, that's a bummer," Gloria responded in disbelief.

Karyme's patience had worn out completely. She couldn't take anymore of Gloria's antics and decided to leave by announcing to Drew that she was returning to the office to lock up for the night. It was her way of getting away from Gloria but Gloria wasn't finish with her, she had one more question to ask.

"Before you go, can I ask you one last question without you becoming offensive?" Gloria asked.

"Depends on what it is," Karyme replied.

"Are you pregnant?" Gloria asked.

"What kind of question is that?" Karyme responded.

"I mean, you know, you and Drew got married, just like that," Gloria said, snapping her fingers to indicate the timing it took them to married.

"Oh, so you think Drew only married me because I was pregnant. Well let me enlightened you Gloria, I'm not pregnant and to answer your question, Drew married me because he loves me, and I love him. So, get it through that thick ass head of yours, that Drew didn't ask me to marry him because I was pregnant but because he loved me. Me, Gloria, not you, not Lynn, but me. You got that "Miss Prissy," Karyme said with an angry stare.

 Without responding, Gloria turned and walked away. She realized she was seconds from getting her ass steamed rolled across the parking lot, and quickly made a b-line to her car to leave. Karyme promised herself to never allow Gloria to get away with insulting her ever again. For years, she'd been the victim from Gloria's bullying, but no more; from now on, Karyme was going to stand her ground, even if it meant having to kick Gloria's ass.

Chapter: 48

Karyme arrived at her mother's house shortly after work. There she met her mother with the idea they were spending some mother, daughter time together. was the happiest Sophia had ever seen her daughter and she had Drew to thank for it. Things had gotten better now that she and Drew were happily married and Sophia was resting better because of it. Today's meeting had nothing to do with Drew or the Harrison family but Karyme's family. It was time to level with Karyme and where she came from and who was her family. As a child, Sophia had a good family and a good upbringing. It wasn't until she committed the biggest sin of getting pregnant that ruined the future she was hoping to have. Because of her mistake, Sophia chose to run away, instead of facing what was ahead of her. Today, she was going to tell Karyme the story of her life and what happened to cause her to turn her back on her family.

For this occasion, Sophia chose to sit and talk in the living room in her small double wide trailer. Instantly, Karyme sensed something was wrong. Because Sophia once discussed she and Drew moving in with her, Karyme first thought was that her mother was lonely and wanted them to move in with her.

"Ma'ma, is everything ok?" Karyme asked.

Sophia smiled, and chalked it up as being tired but Karyme knew differently. She joined Sophia at the table and grabbed hold of her hand. From the look on her face, Karyme believed her mother was about to reveal something heavy on her. Gone were thoughts of her wanting her to move back home, Karyme was thinking it was more of a medical problem but Sophia looked healthy and showed no signs of being sick. Maybe, she wanted to move back in the Harrison's mansion and live like they once had. Karyme was sure Nancy and Drew wouldn't object.

"Ma'ma, what's wrong?" Karyme asked with a concern look on her face. She waited nervously for Sophia to respond.

"There's an urgent matter I need to talk to you about," Sophia insisted. Using her hand to cup Karyme's face, Sophia spoke. "Princesa, I see how happy you and Drew are and it makes me feels really good to see my only child with the love of her life. But I asked you to come over for another reason. I need to tell you something I should have told you years ago.

You have a right to know who you are and where you came from and I'm going to try to fill in some of the blanks for you," Sophia said.

"What is it Ma'ma?" Karyme asked nervously.

"It's about your pa'pa," Sophia responded.

"My papa, what about him?" Karyme asked.

"He wasn't killed in an automobile accident," Sophia said.

"But why would you say he had?" Karyme asked.

Karyme was clueless about what she was about to hear but believed her mother had a good reason for hiding the truth from her. Sophia gave Karyme time to get comfortable before beginning her story. She forewarned Karyme, what she was about to tell her could change the way she thought about her but Sophia reminded Karyme that she was a vulnerable teenage girl who got tied up in something she knew nothing about. For years, Karyme wondered what type of man her father was and after years of wondering, she was about to find out. The only thing Karyme knew about him was that he was in the navy and that he was black. For most of her life, Karyme thought her mother ran away from home because she had fallen in love and got pregnant by a black man and she was about to learn if her theory was true. Sophia began her story when she was fifteen and how she was forced to grow up after spending the summer with her oldest sister Maria. For the first time ever, Karyme learned she had three uncles, Jose, Fernando, and Antonio along with her aunt Maria.

It was exciting to know she had a family with names and she had a million questions to ask but first, she needed to find out about her father. Sophia opened up by talking about her sister Maria and how close they were.

"Maria was fifteen years older than I but you wouldn't have known it by the way we were always together. I remember the day Maria decided to enlist in the navy, I never dreamed she would ever leave me. Maria was not only my sister; she was also my best friend and her leaving nearly devastated me. Nearly ten years passed before Maria came home, and when she did, she brought home a husband and two children. Maria's surprise husband and family nearly caused Papa to lose his mind. Papa argued that she should have at least called and told them about it.

Maria had married a fellow navel petty officer named Phillip Todd. Phillip was a handsome man; he was short but built like Drew. He'd gotten out of the navy and was expected to get a job on base. Phillip seemed really nice but Papa couldn't stand him and never gave him a chance. Papa was tough on him because he didn't trust him, and after three days, Maria and Phillip packed up and left for Washington State but before she left, Maria promised that I could come to visit for the summer if Papa allowed it. I hated to see Maria go but being stationed in the states for the first time in ten years, meant I could go visit her and I did, after some serious pleading to papa. Mama convinced him to allow me to go and even though he didn't want me to. I remembered seeing papa cry for the first time when they put me on the plane. I didn't know why, but maybe he knew it was going be the last time he saw me."

"Do you know if they are still alive?" Karyme asked.
"No," Sophia responded.

Over the years Sophia contemplated calling home but relented at the last minute. She was ashamed and wasn't ready to face the actions of what she did. Sophia went on to tell the story of how she and Maria resumed spending time together doing her stay. Doing this time, Sophia explained she'd grown even closer to her sister as well as her children. As far as Phillip was concerned, he worked mostly but found time to spend with them on the weekends. Things changed when Maria got orders to leave for a two-month training exercise in Hawaii. Sophia was left in charge of taking care of the house while she was gone and Sophia did what was expected of her. She kept the house the way she was expected to do. The children were in bed by 8:00 and Phillip's dinner was always on the stove when he got home.

"Things changed after Maria got orders for ten weeks of training in Hawaii. I considered leaving but Maria insisted I stay to help her family until she returned. Her leave was to end a week before school started and Maria promised if I stayed, she'll buy all of my school clothes and supplies. After hearing what she was going to do for me, I couldn't refuse. The first week went about as well as it could go. I had the house clean, the children fed, bath and in bed by eight o'clock. Phillip's dinner was warmed in the oven when he came home. Most nights, he came home late after being out drinking with his friends, which was good for me because I had time to be by myself. It wasn't long before Phillip began making passes at me. I thought it was because of his drinking but he kept doing it even when he was sober.

It wasn't hard to figure out what he wanted but he was my sister's husband, he wasn't supposed to be acting like that toward me. I kept rejecting his passes and told him to stop but he never did. So, I tried avoiding him. I'll be in bed when he got home, hoping it was enough to avoid him but I was helpless to him. He started coming into my room at nights and before long I was powerless to his advancements. I tried fighting him off but it was useless, he was too strong. It was the first time he had his way with me and after that night, he was visiting me every night. He told me he loved me and he wanted to marry me. I was only fifteen, but I should have known better. I really believed Phillip loved me and within three weeks after my sister had left, I'd fallen in love with him and moved into my sister's bedroom with him. Phillip told me once I turned eighteen, he was going to divorce Maria and was going to marry me and we were going to start a family of our own. Like a fool I believed him; I may have been fifteen but I knew what I was doing was wrong. Still, I continued doing it and for some reason, I couldn't stop."

After hearing what her mother endured, Karyme didn't have to ask who her father was it was obvious, she was conceived by her uncle. The son-of-a-bitch had taken advantage of a naïve, fifteen-year-old girl. Seeing how upset her mother was Karyme had heard enough to know who she was and what happened that caused her mother to flee but Sophia wasn't finished.

She needed to tell the entire story for Karyme to know what she endured to ensure that Karyme achieve the goals she set for her. Sophia wanted Karyme to know what role her father played in her decision to run away from her family. By becoming pregnant by Phillip, Sophia not only brought embarrassment upon herself, she had done so to her family but perhaps her greatest sin was that she had not only fallen in love with her sister's husband and was carrying his child. Karyme watched a teary-eyed Sophia choke on her words as she revealed what happened after she told Phillip about being pregnant.

"Finding out I was pregnant was one of the happiest days in my life. I'd brought a home pregnancy test from a downtown drug store and it had come back positive. I was naïve to think Phillip was going to share my enthusiasm but I did.

I was so excited to tell him we were having a baby together and to convince him that we should start our family early but it didn't take long to realize Phillip didn't share my enthusiasm, but even then, I thought after thinking about it, he would change his mind. God, I was so stupid to believe Phillip was going to leave Maria for me but boy did he give me a dose of reality. First, he accused me of trying to trap him, then he followed with a demand that I get an abortion before Maria returned. When I refused, he packed all of my clothes in a trash bag and threw them outside, along with me. What was so damning was him admitting his true intentions. He said he never intended to leave Maria. He said Maria was his meal ticket and he wouldn't dream of leaving her for some young and dumb teenaged slut. He said he bet his friends he would pop my cherry and after doing so, he didn't want to have anything else to do with me. What that being said, I was crushed, I couldn't believe Phillip was doing this to me but in reality, I had done it to myself. I got so mad at him, I threatened to tell Maria about us but he said she wouldn't believe me. He boosted that Maria would never leave him, no matter what he did. He said she loved him and she would never leave him. After throwing me out, Phillip threw sixty-dollars at me and slammed the door in my face. Scare, ashamed, and guilt-ridden, I took the money and brought a bus ticket to Las Vegas to start a new life."

"Why didn't you abort me?" Karyme asked.

"Because I fell in love with you the moment, I learned I was carrying you inside of me," Sophia responded. "The only thing I've regretted was becoming involved with my sister's husband but not for one second have I ever regretted having you," Sophia said, as she wiped the hair from Karyme's face. Sophia kissed Karyme's forehead. "Having you was my greatest accomplishment and I thank God every day for blessing me with you."

It was at that moment, Karyme and Sophia embraced. They cried on each other's shoulders, knowing they couldn't have made it without each other. The truth of what happened was more than either of them could stand and for a split-second Sophia decided to stop talking but felt it was too important for Karyme not to know what happened to her. Before going further, Sophia waited to gather her thoughts and after doing so, she resumed her story. She talked about how she survived the streets without having anyone to depend on. Though Sophia wanted to call her parents to ask if she could come home, she knew she couldn't.

It was no way her father was going to allow her to keep her baby and she couldn't give it away for adoption or abort it. Unable to stay at the shelter for fear of being reported as a runaway, Sophia slept anywhere she felt was safe. She slept mostly doing the day and stayed awake throughout the night. Having no money, she was forced to eat out of trash cans and accepted bag lunches in the park that was provided by the neighborhood churches. Though scared and lonely, Sophia refused to give up on life. To survive, she maintained a level head and lived with the idea that bad luck won't last forever. Sophia knew eventually her misfortunes would change if she continued to hold on to her faith. But as time continued, her misfortunes continued to get worse. Still, she refused to give up. She couldn't quit on life, she had to make it on her own.

Entering her eighth month of pregnancy, Sophia told how she stumbled upon a free clinic and decided to enter to seek medical attention. Telling her story, she was placed in the Covenant House where she stayed until Karyme was born. From there she was reassigned to a shelter for women and children. Doing the day she went to school, while Karyme was taken care of by the daycare center. By the age of eighteen, Sophia went on to say how she got a job at a factory and save enough money to get her first apartment, just outside of town.

Sophia said she stayed there until work became slow and her job ended. Karyme was ten then, and from there, she made the decision to travel east with hopes of finding work. Sophia said she took the last of her money and brought two bus tickets that got them to the Jefferson County Bus Station. It was at the town's diner that they came into contact with the Harrison's and the rest was history.

"It was hard and though there were times I didn't think we were going to make it; I couldn't quit. You were my responsibility and the only reason I fought so hard to live. I would trade my life for you at any second," Sophia said convincingly.

Sophia didn't have to say anything more for Karyme to be any prouder of her. She had accomplished more than anyone her age could have in her position. Sophia was a fifteen-year-old child when she was raped by her brother-in-law and became pregnant. How could a man kick out a fifteen-year-old child that was living in a foreign place, throwing her sixty-dollars, like she was some street whore and forgetting about her? Phillip was no father she wanted meet and as far as she was concerned, the dreams she once had of him were wasted dreams.

As for her mother, Karyme couldn't have been prouder of her. It's true what they say, "God won't put any more on you, then you can bear." It was because of Sophia's determination that Karyme was here today and Karyme strongly believed she owed her mother much gratitude, not only for protecting her with her life, but loving her enough to willfully accept the challenges life bestowed upon you.

Chapter: 49

The sound from the alarm clock alerted Lynn it was time to get up. It had been the second consecutive night in which she hadn't slept and the bags under her eyes substantiated it. Today was going to be the longest day of her young life and she wasn't looking forward to facing it. The thought of having to abort her unborn child was haunting and it was leading her to entertain other ideas. The problem she faced with having a baby out of wedlock was that it would expose her family to public ridicule and that was something Constance wasn't going to allow. For Constance, it was all about looking good to her circle of friends and nothing else mattered. She hadn't considered the degree of mental complications she was subjecting Lynn to nor did she care. Constance was well aware of Lynn's stance on abortion but needless to say, she refused to entertain Lynn's opinion. As for Lynn, though she was against what her mother was pushing her to do, she knew disappointing her was far worse. Still, the thought of taking the life of a helpless infant to gain favor with her parents wasn't a decision Lynn was willing to consider. There had to be another solution and Lynn was all in at finding it.

Lynn sat on the edge of her bed with her fingers interlocked over the crown of her head while trying to brainstorm a solution to her problem. Although she was afraid to stand up to her mother, Lynn ultimately knew, the only way to get what she wanted was to fight for what she believed in. But to be frank, Lynn wasn't equipped to stand up to her mother's bullying. Lynn quickly melted at the first sign of trouble and Constance knew it. Lynn's timid behavior was the key to Constance's success when it came to pushing her agenda upon her. Constance had drawn the life she wanted for her daughter and it was safe to say, having a baby wasn't a part of it. By allowing Constance to dictate her life, Lynn was robbing Drew of the family he wanted and the child she wanted to give him. Lynn's problem was that it was no way Constance would relent to her decision to have Drew's baby because she was only nineteen and Constance looked at her as being a baby herself. In a way, Constance was right with her analysis, mentally, Lynn hadn't matured enough to care for a baby. She had her entire life to live and Constance didn't want her to throw it away by having a baby.

Getting out of bed Lynn made her way to the shower. She held on to the hope of maintaining the courage to stand up to her mother but doubted if she could.

What Constance wanted her to do was against God's wishes, as well as hers but even going against God's wishes wasn't enough for Constance to change her mind. Constance's take on Lynn's situation was based on her own wants and needs. Constance believed aborting Lynn's fetus was for the betterment of their family as well as Lynn's future. Lynn was her father's choice to be his successor once he retired but if she chose not to eliminate her mistake, chances of her becoming CEO of Boldmont Enterprises would diminish tremendously. Running the company had always been Harry's dream for Lynn but if she chose not to have the abortion, her father's high expectations of her would surely change for the worse. By no means was Lynn irresponsible; her only blunder was her weakness for love. In reality, she strongly believed Drew was the right person to give her the love she was seeking but her unsettling behavior had pushed him into another woman's arms. Feeling time was of the essence, Lynn broke her promise to Karyme and called Drew. Her decision would undoubtedly put her at odds with Lynn. However, Drew needed to know the stake of his baby's faith. Lynn was uncertain as to how she was going to tell Drew or how he was going to accept the news but she was confident the two of them could work things out once the truth was revealed.

Lynn's heart rate increased as Drew's cellular phone began ringing but to her disappointment, Drew's phone went straight to his voicemail. Uncomfortable with leaving a message of such importance, Lynn decided instead, to leave a message for him to contact her immediately. She had less than five-hours before she was schedule to be at the planned parenthood building for her procedure and time was quickly ticking away. Desperate to talk to Drew, Lynn did the unthinkable by calling the office. She knew in all likelihood Karyme was going to answer the phone but chose to weigh her options. It took only three rings before her call was answered.

"HillCrest Farms Incorporation, Karyme Rios-Gonzalez speaking. How may I be of assistance?" Karyme asked.

"Oh, shit," Lynn said to herself. What was she thinking about calling the office? Hell, what was she going to say? Should she pretend it was the wrong number and hang up or be woman enough to asked for Drew? Lynn knew time was running short and she had no other choice but to ask to speak to Drew.

"Good morning, Karyme, this is Lynn, how are you?" Lynn asked.

"I was doing great until you called," Karyme answered. "You gave your word; you would stay out of Drew's life for good. You said you was going to give Drew and I a chance to make things work?"

Lynn felt Karyme's pain and disappointment but her desperate attempt to speak to Drew outweighed her promise to Karyme. Lynn apologized for reneging on her word and explained how crucial it was to speak to Drew. Lynn tried assuring Karyme her desire wasn't to come back into Drew's life but to discuss an issue she wasn't at liberty to say to her. Unfortunately, Lynn's past overzealous behavior was more than enough to cause Karyme's concern. Lynn was like a rotating door when it came to Drew's heart; and once she entered it, she would stay a few days before breaking things off; leaving her to help pick up the pieces of Drew's broken heart to mend. Karyme's quest to protect Drew from being hurt again, sent her into action. She was honest with her intentions not to inform Drew. Lynn needed to talk to him. Karyme's explanation was simple and as Drew's wife, it was her responsibility to protect her interest. Though it was easier to tell Lynn, she and Drew were married, Karyme chose not to do so. She was aware of what the shock of learning that she and Drew were married could do to Lynn's mental status and how it could affect her relationship with Drew. Karyme couldn't risk sabotaging her future with Drew after waiting so long to get the opportunity to become his wife. The only decision was to refuse to relay Lynn's message. Listening to Lynn's desperate pleas to talk to Drew, caused Karyme to become suspicious. Something more was going on and for her piece of mind, Karyme needed to know.

Sadly, for Lynn, reaching out for Drew, whenever she needed him was over, Drew was a married man and his obligation was to his wife. However, though reluctant; Lynn agreed to give Drew, Lynn's message. It was hard not knowing what was so important Lynn urgently needed to talk to Drew about but Karyme didn't want to seem jealous. She wanted to give Lynn the impression that she and Drew was in a good place and in a lot of ways they were. Though their marriage was new, Karyme couldn't have been happier. She was living her dream and didn't feel Lynn could come between them again. Ending her conversation with Lynn on a good note, Karyme promised to give Drew, Lynn's message. Karyme remained apprehensive about Lynn's intentions but felt complete trust in her ability to maintain her marriage.

Riding into work with her mother, Lynn spoke very little, leading Constance to suspect she was having second thoughts.

Lynn's face not only displayed her lack of sleep but the fear of what she was facing. Sensing Lynn was close to changing her mind, Constance felt the needed to do something extreme. She wanted to keep Lynn focused on eliminating her pregnancy by being proactive. Constance wanted to eradicate any potential risk that could come back to bite them in the ass. As a mother, Constance had failed Lynn miserably with the situation regarding Marshall but she wasn't doing it this time. This time, Constance promised herself she was going to be the mother she should have been doing Lynn's rape scandal. Constance couldn't deny, by eliminating Lynn's problem she was protecting her future as well as their family's legacy. But to do so, she needed to be sure that Lynn erased all traces of Drew from her life, including his bastard child. It wasn't going to be an easy task to accomplish but it wasn't going to be difficult one either. Constance's first plan of action was to help Lynn deal with her conscious. If she was successful at doing so, it was a sure bet, they could get through the rest.

"We're going to get through this together," Constance said; assuring Lynn she was going to be by her side throughout her ordeal. Although Constance tried assuring Lynn that everything was going to go as planned, it wasn't convincing enough. The more Lynn thought about aborting her baby, the harder her decision was becoming. Lynn had become intrigued by the thought of becoming a mother and found herself fantasizing about sharing a life with Drew.

Now at the office, Lynn spent the early part of the morning with her door closed. She needed time to be alone to decide the path of action she was going to take. From her office window, she stared across the harbor; as she reminisced about when her life was simpler. Falling in love with Drew was the best thing she'd ever done. It was the first time she'd ever felt love, but most importantly, she knew, without a shadow of a doubt, that Drew's love for her was true. Drew, by all accounts, was the greatest love of her life, and though she was reminded by Karyme how she chose to leave him, Lynn was confident the baby she was carrying would bring them back together. Being with Drew was like a scene from a romance novel. His love was unlike any she'd ever known and the more she thought about him, the more she wanted to make it work between them.

Lynn understood the consequences she was going to face if she chose to have her baby instead of aborting it. She would lose any chance of ever running Boldmont Enterprises but she began questioning herself if running the family's company was more important than becoming a mother and a wife. By prematurely choosing to end her relationship with Drew, Lynn was uncertain if they could regain the steam they'd generated. She'd chosen Boldmont Enterprises over Drew and the love they shared for each other. She'd made perhaps, the biggest mistake of her young life. Now, she was considering changing her mind to go back to the man she loved more than anything. But the problem she was facing now was if Drew was willing to accept her back into his life this time.

Seeing the clock approaching ten, Lynn knew she had less than an hour before she was leaving for the clinic. Frantically, Lynn called Nancy hoping she knew Drew's whereabouts but Nancy's cellular phone went to her voicemail. Lynn followed by calling Nancy's office phone but her secretary answered and informed her, Nancy was in an important meeting. Desperate, Lynn called Drew's house landline but Sophia was unaware of where he could be. Frustrated, Lynn fought to keep her emotions intact. She needed to talk to someone but didn't know who to turn to. Thinking outside the box, she found solace in hearing the voice of her therapist. They talked less than ten minutes before Lynn abruptly ended their conversation. She felt no ill will towards her therapist but her mission was to find Drew before it was too late. She had less than an hour to reach Drew and was worried she wasn't going to reach him in time. Lynn knew she couldn't panic nor could she give up her quest to find Drew. Though it was unusual for Drew not to answer his phone, Lynn refused to believe he was avoiding her. Someone or something was stopping her from speaking to him and she was praying it wasn't Karyme. Against her better judgment, Lynn decided to call Drew at his office again, but before doing so, she thought about the hurt she was going to bring to Karyme. Ultimately, Lynn understood that speaking to Drew was far more important than hurting Karyme's little feelings. She had a baby to protect and in order to protect it, she had to get verification from Drew on what to do. Preparing herself for another showdown with Karyme, Lynn dialed the office. This time, the secretary answered. She stated that Drew hadn't arrived at the office, and before Lynn could ask when she was expecting him, her call was transferred to Karyme's office.

Hearing Karyme's voice sent chills down Lynn's spine. Lynn was sure Karyme was going to put two and two together and realize what was going on but at the time frame she was facing, she was willing to risk being exposed. Lynn knew, if she wanted to maintain her secret, she had to keep her emotions intact. Before Karyme could speak, Lynn apologized for disturbing her again, but stated she needed her help with tracking Drew's whereabouts. Lynn explained, how imperative it was for her to speak to Drew before eleven o'clock, but emphasized her speaking to Drew had nothing to do with wanting to reconnect with him. Needless to say, Karyme wasn't convinced by the shield Lynn was trying to build. Something of the utmost importance was happening, and it had nothing to do with their upcoming case against the city of Eugene and University Police Departments. Lynn's desperate attempts to reach Drew went deeper then what she was admitting. Something else was going on and Karyme wanted to get to the bottom of it. There was only one reason why Lynn needed to contact Drew before 11:00 am.

"Oh my God, you're pregnant," Karyme screamed, nearly dropping the phone.

There was immediate silence on Lynn's end of the line, and her reaction alone gave Karyme the answer she was dreading. Lynn was pregnant with Drew's baby and she was calling to notify him of it.

"You are pregnant, aren't you?" Karyme asked again.

Lynn continued to be silent, before suddenly erupting into tears. She didn't have to admit she was pregnant her tears verified Karyme's suspicions. It was a shocking blow to Karyme, one that nearly knocked her out of her chair. How was she going to accept Drew being the father of another woman's child, while married to her? Again, Drew had damaged their relationship by getting Lynn pregnant. Though she credited Lynn for staying away and giving them time to jell, she condemned her for intentionally interfering with their marriage before it had the chance to start. The news was far worse than Karyme could have ever imagined but she tried handling it like the lady she was. What was so bizarre, Karyme felt sympathy for Lynn after hearing her cry over the phone and chose to console her. Maybe it was the sound of uncertainty in Lynn's tears that compelled Karyme to reach out to her, but even so, Karyme couldn't overlook the pressure of Lynn's baby could do to their marriage.

Lynn admitted, she felt alone and was being pressured by her mother to abort her baby for the sake of the family.

It was hard not to feel sympathy for Lynn and without good conscious, Karyme couldn't turn her back on her. Karyme wanted to help Lynn and if it meant having to walk away from her marriage to Drew, then she was willing to do so. Lynn pregnancy had placed her in a precarious situation. Lynn was alone without the support of anyone, Karyme believed it was up to her and Drew to make things easier for Lynn. Karyme had no idea where Drew was but assured Lynn, she was going to do her damndest to help find him. Karyme shared Drew's message, stating he had a special meeting this morning regarding his future but didn't say anymore. Like Lynn, Karyme was left in the dark as to where Drew was and like Lynn, she was very concerned. Once the call was over, Karyme placed her hands over her face and began to cry. She was in disbelief and felt her marriage to Drew was in serious jeopardy. She couldn't compete with a baby, nor did she want to. Lynn's baby needed a father, and having to live with the pain of not knowing who her father was until recently was too much to bear.

At exactly ten o'clock, Constance entered Lynn's office. It was time to leave for the clinic and though Lynn didn't want to go, she didn't want to fight with her mother. Instead, she began stalling by pretending to tie up loose ends. Lynn began by passing Constance her edited copy of the monthly report to check for mistakes, hoping it was enough to buy her some time but Constance wasn't interested in reading Lynn's report, she was eager to leave for the clinic. For Constance, it was imperative that they left early, so she could find street parking before the lunch crowd arrived. It wasn't that the clinic didn't provide parking because they did for all of their patients; the truth was that Constance didn't want to be seen parking in the lot or be seen entering the front entrance of the clinic. Her plans were to find street parking that was at least two to three blocks away from the clinic and enter through the rear of the building unseen. Seeing that her mother wasn't interested in reading her monthly report, Lynn reached for her purse to leave. She followed Constance down the hallway to the elevator. Inside, Lynn remained quiet, reserving time to reflect upon her thoughts. Getting out of the elevator, the women exited through the second-floor double doors that led to the parking lot where Constance's SUV was parked. Clutching her phone, Lynn prayed that Drew would call before it was too late. They were less than fifteen minutes away from the clinic and the thought of having to abort her baby without Drew's input was weighing heavy on her mind.

On the way to the clinic, Lynn contemplated different ways of how she was going to tell her mother she had changed her mind but was too afraid to stand up to her, fearing the backlash it would come from it. So, like the good daughter she'd always been, Lynn said nothing and allowed Constance to go forward with her plan. Lynn wished; her parents would have given Drew a chance to prove himself before casting him aside. If only they had given Drew an opportunity, they would have understood why she loved him so much. But now, it seemed to be too late, and unfortunately for her parents, they would never see the type of man Drew is.

With less than a five-minute ride from the clinic, Lynn again stared at her phone. Her eyes began tearing, as her prayers for Drew to call increased, and with each second that passed, threatened the life of their unborn baby. Lynn's only hope rested on the hands of Karyme to find Drew. Though skeptical, Lynn wanted to believe Karyme would keep her word and find Drew, but wouldn't blame her if she chose not to. Like her; Karyme was deeply in love with Drew and like Karyme, Lynn wanted a future with him.

It felt like a million years ago when she was the center of Drew's life but like a fool, she didn't appreciate the man Drew was. Instead of loving and appreciating what Drew brought to her life, Lynn pushed him into Karyme's arms. Now, she was alone, wishing she'd done things differently. How could she not realize Drew meant more to her than heading her father's company? Drew had proven his love and had done so by forgiving her for all the hurt and pain she brought into his life and she still refused to appreciate him for the man he was. Though mature for her age, Lynn was immature regarding love and relationships. Some of her immaturity came from being inexperienced at love but most of it resulted from allowing her parents to control her life. When it came to doing things her way, Lynn didn't have the courage to make decisions without having an input from her parents. Unlike Ashley, Lynn wasn't headstrong; she cared about what her parents thought of her. Ashley on the other hand didn't give a damn what anyone thought of her. She did what she wanted to do, and didn't care if anyone approved it or not. But if she chose to follow Ashley lead, the magnitude from the consequences she would receive would forever haunt her.

Locating parking a block away, Constance grabbed hold of Lynn's hand and led her across the street. She sensed that Lynn was getting cold feet and wanted to get into the clinic before she changed her mind. Crossing the parking lot, Constance and

Lynn headed toward the rear entrance of the building. Constance felt a hint of resistance from Lynn once making their way to the rear entrance's door but whether Lynn was having second thoughts or not, she was having the abortion. Lynn silently cried inside as she held her stomach with her free hand. She knew, within the hour, the life that is growing inside of her would no longer exist. Lynn remained uncertain how she was going to stop her mother's mission to end her pregnancy but knew she had to do something immediately if she was going to keep her baby. Standing at the rear door of the clinic, Lynn prayed as passionately as she knew how. She pleaded to God, asking him for forgiveness, and pleaded for him to give her the strength to stand up to her mother. As they waited for the door to be opened, Lynn's whimpering transformed into an all-out cry. Tears fell uncontrollably from her eyes as her knees buckled, and she fell to the ground. Crying out to her mother, Lynn confessed her desire not to abort her baby. Needless to say, Constance ignored her and demanded that she stand up from the pavement. Still in tears, Lynn pleaded for her mother to allow her to keep her baby but Constance was quick to silence her. There was no way she was going to allow Lynn to bring shame to their family again.

"You brought this on yourself, young lady. Now get up, so we can take care of your fuck up." Constance grabbed hold of Lynn's outstretched hand and assisted her to her feet. She escorted Lynn inside the building and was relieved she had done so without being noticed. To further conceal her identity, Constance sat behind a potted tree in the rear of the waiting room and watched anxiously as Lynn registered for the procedure. If things go as planned, within the hour, their problem was going to be eliminated. Lynn remained quiet after registering. She sat across from her mother, who refused to sit beside her. Lynn had given up hope of Drew calling and was settling on the idea that aborting her baby was going to happen.

In the meantime, Karyme was still on the phone trying to locate Drew when he unexpectedly walked into her office. He was upbeat and excited to give Karyme his good news. After having paid a visit to his lawyer, Drew was thrilled to announce the city of Eugene and the University Police Departments had decided to settle his case against them rather than allow it to play out in court. Drew announced they were about to receive a combined sum of twelve million dollars in punitive and civil damages. He rushed behind Karyme's desk, lifted her in his arms, and spun her around.

"I love you, my wife," Drew said, kissing Karyme as he placed her on the floor.

Breaking Drew's grip, Karyme created enough space between them for Drew to listen to the news she had to tell him. Karyme had no idea how she was going to break the news but knew time was of the essence. Standing at arm's length, Karyme's behavior alerted Drew that something was wrong.

"What's wrong? Drew asked.

"I tried calling you all morning. Why didn't you answer?" Karyme asked.

"I'm sorry, I was in a meeting with my lawyer, I had my phone on mute," Drew responded. "What's wrong?" Drew asked again, seeing that something was troubling Karyme.

"Drew, we have a big problem," Karyme responded.

"What?" Drew questioned.

"I don't know how to tell you this, but," Karyme replied, pausing in the middle of what she was trying to say while holding her throat.

"Baby, what's wrong? Drew asked again, nervously.

Nearly breaking down, Lynn fought through her tears and informed Drew it was imperative that he call Lynn. She wasn't certain how he was going to react to the news but knew their marriage would change forever when she did. "It's Lynn, she's been trying to reach you all morning. She needs you to call her immediately."

"No, my life is with you now, I'm finally happy and I don't need any more of her drama," Drew responded.

For the first time, he was in a good place without drama. He loved being married to Karyme and wanted nothing to interfere with it, but Karyme was persistence with him contacting Lynn but why?

"You have to call her before it's too late," Karyme screamed out.

Karyme didn't know what else she could do to convince Drew to call Lynn without telling him why. She picked up her office landline and passed it to Drew, selecting the redial button to call Lynn's cellular phone.

"What's going on?" Drew questioned as Lynn's phone ranged.

"You have to stop Lynn before she aborts your baby," Karyme blurted out.

Chapter: 50

Lynn heaved a sigh of relief after it was announced her doctor was running behind schedule. It was a sign she had been waiting for. The announcement that the doctor was going to be late had given her the hope she so desperately needed; her odds had improved that Drew would call in time it was too late. Waiting impatiently for Drew's call had Lynn sitting on pins and needles. She continued to contemplate how she was going to tell her mother; she'd changed her mind about having the abortion. Lynn didn't know what angle to approach her mother or if she had the strength to stand firm once challenged, but she knew she had to do something. She wanted to believe she had the courage to stand up for her belief but in all honesty, she didn't. Lynn feared the repercussion Constance would impose if she disobeyed her wishes. If only she had the courage Ashley had, things would be different. There was no doubt what Ashley would do if she was in her situation. Ashley would put her fears behind her and face her opposition bravely. Mentally, Ashley was as strong-willed as they came and was willing to fight her opposition until she got what she wanted, but sadly, Lynn wasn't Ashley; she didn't possess Ashley's lion heart or her killer instincts but it wasn't going to stop her from trying. Lynn wanted the courage Ashley possessed, but to get it, she had to overcome the fears of what her mother could do to her. Somehow, Lynn had to make things work in her favor, and to do so, she had to stand up to the Queen Bitch. It was all about fighting for what was right. The time had come, for Lynn to be her own woman, a woman capable of fighting for what she believed in, and whatever the consequences, she had to be willing to accept it.

Taking the first of two deep breaths, Lynn expressed her desire to keep her baby. She began by suggesting how marrying Drew would solve their problem. It was the solution people had done for years. But as you may have imagined, Constance didn't agree with Lynn's suggestion and let it be known to the entire waiting area who could hear their conversation. Having had enough, Lynn did the unthinkable and began to resist her mother's hold on her.

"Mom, I've had just about enough of you telling me what the fuck to do," Lynn said, as she stood to leave. "I'm tired of you dictating my life.

"What did you say to me?" Constance reacted in disbelief.

"I'm done with you telling me what to do. I'm keeping my baby," Lynn responded with a stone face.

Since falling in love with the idea of being a mother, Lynn was unable to think of anything else. For the first time in her life, she was willing to stand up and fight for what she wanted and felt good. But by no means was Constance going to lay down to Lynn's wants. Instead, Constance doubled down on the pressure she was applying, which resulted in Lynn firmly securing her feet in the sand. In an element of surprise, Constance grabbed hold of the sleeve of Lynn's blouse and forced her to sit beside her.

"Sit your little ass down," Constance demanded. "Who the fuck do you think you're talking to, young lady?" Constance questioned while gritting her teeth. She placed her forehead against Lynn's and whispered aggressively to her. "Please don't make me show my ass in here."

"Mom, I'm not having an abortion, at least until I can talk with Drew," Lynn said. Though her voice cracked from fear, Lynn continued to stand her ground.

"The hell you're aren't," Constance responded in a forceful tone. "There's no way, I'm going to allow you to have that bastard child or marry that farm boy."

With the both of them at a standstill, Lynn suggested they go outside to a more private setting but Constance wasn't having it; she knew by going outside, Lynn would refuse to return inside the clinic. Constance needed to reevaluate the situation to regain control of her weak-minded daughter and started by releasing her hold on Lynn's blouse.

"I don't want to show my ass in here, but if you make me, I will," Constance threatened. She was surprised that Lynn was defying her wishes and though she couldn't force Lynn to have an abortion, she could amp up her phycological game.

"This is going to break your father's heart when he finds out you're pregnant. You know how weak his heart is and God only knows what it's going to do to him. And to think he was about to appoint you, Chief Executive Officer next year." Constance said, hoping it was enough to scramble Lynn's mind.

Taken by surprise, Lynn sat quietly, trying to comprehend what her mother had said.

She couldn't believe her father had plans to promote her a year earlier than expective. If what her mother was saying was true, she was going to be CEO in a year. With this new information, Lynn was considering the idea of going forward with her initial plans to abort her baby.

"Mom, all I'm asking, is that you allow me to talk to Drew before I do something I may regret," Lynn asked. She knew it wasn't something her mother wanted to hear but Lynn showed compassion in her request. It wasn't that she'd taken abortion off the table, she only wanted to talk to Drew to see if being a husband and a father was something he was interested in being. Like everything else, Constance had gotten into Lynn's head, confusing her enough to reconsider her stance on having her baby. The pressure of putting her career over her love for Drew and their unborn child not only brought Lynn to tears, but it was also enough to persuade her to follow the nurse to the examination room. Lynn wanted her mother to understand how unfair it was for her to terminate her pregnancy without first discussing it with Drew, but Lynn failed to convince her. Though Lynn found the strength to stand up to Constance, she lost her battle to protect her most cherished gift. Following the nurse to the examination room, Lynn began undressing to change into the sterile gown. Lynn knew what she was doing was wrong, but she felt the need to please her mother. Disappointing her parents was the worst thing she could ever do, but if pleasing them meant having to give up on her dream of becoming a mother and a wife, then so be it.

Dressed and sitting on the examination table, Lynn waited for the doctor to arrive. A million thoughts entered her mind but what mostly stood out to Lynn were thoughts of her baby and the future she could have as a mother and wife. Thoughts of Drew increased after thinking about how he was going to react if she chose to abort their child without involving him in her decision. Lynn's thoughts, suddenly brought on an all-out panic attack causing her to leave the examination room. Dressed in only her gown while carrying her personals in a bag, Lynn returned to the waiting room in search of Constance. It was time to leave and Lynn wasn't taking no for an answer. She wasn't going to have the abortion, at least until she talked to Drew and she didn't give a damn how her mother felt about it. Hearing Lynn's frantic calls, Constance returned from the break room to find Lynn running through the waiting room partially naked. Constance quickly embraced Lynn and tried escorting her back to her room but Lynn refused to go.

Lynn cried out about her desire not to have the procedure without first talking to Drew. Constance knew if the abortion wasn't done now the likelihood of it ever happening was great. She grabbed hold of Lynn's arm and tried escorting her back to the examining room but Lynn was fighting her tooth and nail. Lynn's determination to leave the clinic brought out every ounce of strength Constance could generate to keep her there. Lynn was winning the battle of attrition as Constance found herself becoming weaker. She had to think quickly if she was going to get Lynn to stay, and though Constance hated to have to use her ace card, she felt she had no other choice.

"Lynn, please listen to what I have to say, before we go rushing off," Constance asked before releasing her grip of Lynn's arm. "There's something I think you should know."

"What Mother, what is so important you have to tell me?" Lynn asked.

"It's about Drew," Constance replied.

"What about Drew?" Lynn asked.

"There's no other way to tell you this, but Drew's been two-timing you," Constance said.

"Mom, I don't want to hear that bullcrap," Lynn spouted out. "Drew has been the one man that has stood by me thick and thin. It was me who pushed Drew away, not Drew choosing to be with someone else," Lynn said.

"Ooh baby, I wish Drew loved you like you deserve to be loved but believe me, it's not true," Constance responded with sympathy. "I hate so much to tell you this but Drew's been carrying on an affair with your sister."

"I can't believe you, there's no low you would go to convince me to have this abortion, is it Mom?" Lynn said.

"No honey, it's true; Ashley told me. That's why I didn't want you and Drew to be together. Can't you see, he's no good for you.?" Constance said.

Hearing her phone ringing and seeing it was from Karyme's office, Lynn quickly answered, "Hello."

307

"Lynn, I just got your message. I hope I'm not too late." Drew asked, nervously.

Not sure how to respond; Lynn paused. "I haven't had the abortion, if that's what you mean," Lynn said.

"Thank God," Drew said, releasing a sigh of relief. "Don't do anything until I get there. I'm leaving now," Drew announced.

Anxious to know the truth about Drew's affair with Ashley, Lynn closed her eyes, and blurted out the question she was dying to know.

"Why couldn't you have told me, you've been sleeping with Ashley?" Lynn asked unsuspectedly to Drew.

Floored by Lynn's question, Drew struggled to think of the right thing to say and began stuttering while searching for the words to come to mind. It was all Lynn needed to substantiate her mother's story. Drew wasn't the man she thought, he was no better than the Marshall. Lynn doubled over after feeling as if she was shot in the gut. The pain was so excruciating, Lynn's only reaction was to cry. Her knees buckled and she fell limp into her seat and dropped her phone on the floor. Once again, Ashley had deceived her by sleeping with a man she'd fallen in love with, but what hurt most was the idea that Drew withheld information so crucial from her. How could he be sleeping with her sister and telling her he loved her? Pulling herself together, Lynn picked her phone to say her final farewell. She wished Drew well and asked that he never contact her again. Whether she meant it remained to be seen, but for now, it was over between them. Lynn demanded that Drew not drive up because she was terminating the pregnancy. Lynn wanted nothing tying them together and no matter how hard Drew pleaded for her not to abort his child, Lynn refused to listen.

"Lynn, please, don't do something out of spite. What happened with Ashley and I was before you and me," Drew tried explaining but it was too late, Lynn didn't want to hear what he had to say. But it didn't stop Drew from trying his damndest to convince Lynn not to do anything she would regret but Lynn made it clear that she didn't want anything to do with him or their baby. Ending her conversation with Drew, Lynn speed-dialed Ashley and waited anxiously for her to answer. Lynn returned to the examining room to change back into her street clothes as her mother followed her.

Her abortion wasn't going to take place today but it was going to take place nonetheless. Today, she had a bigger fish to fry and that fish was Ashley.

Witnessing what she believed was the beginning of a meltdown, Constance positioned herself at the door, still hoping to convince Lynn to stay, but it was obvious Lynn didn't want to hear what she had to say. Lynn was fed up with her mother's bullshit as well as the rest of her family. She was tired of being the pawn in their games, and though Constance tried reiterating how important it was for Lynn to terminate her pregnancy before leaving the clinic, Lynn refused to listen to the point she was trying to make.

"Mother, I don't have anything else to say to you. You knew about Drew and Ashley and you never said a word until now and why? Why Mom?

I can answer that, it's because you would do anything to get me to have an abortion, so I wouldn't ruin your reputation amongst the socialites. You deliberately kept the truth from me, until it was beneficial to you." Lynn explained.

"That's not true, I was only looking out for you. I don't want you to be like one of those hood girls who have babies for every man they sleep with, you're better than that. I want what's best for you," Constance responded.

Fully dressed, Lynn left the clinic with Constance following close behind her. Constance hadn't anticipated this side of Lynn and though she was overjoyed Lynn had washed her hands of Drew, there was still the matter of getting rid of the mistake she was carrying inside of her. Constance's second worry was what Lynn was going to do to her sister when they met. Lynn had already broken Ashley's nose once and only God knew what she was going to do to Ashley this time around. Perhaps, what Constance feared more than anything was Lynn's mental stability. She didn't want this to be the cause of Lynn having another mental breakdown but if it happened, she wanted to be nearby to recognize it before it spun out of control. Constance worried about Lynn but she was more concerned about her husband's health once learning the truth. Harry hadn't been in the best of spirits for the past few days and she didn't want him to have to find out about the mess she'd created by opening Pandora's Box regarding his daughters.

Unable to reach Ashley in the clinic, Lynn wasted no time calling her again once reaching the parking lot. Lucky for Lynn, she caught Ashley between classes and wasted no time getting to the point.

"Hello little sister, what's up?" Ashley asked. Ashley was in a good mood after receiving her test scores from one of her business classes. Not only that, she was in the presence of her new boyfriend and was anxious to introduce him to Lynn, but unfortunately, she never got the chance. Before she could tell Lynn about him, she was bombarded with the question pertaining to her sleeping with Drew. The question caught Ashley totally by surprise, and like Drew, she stumbled over her words to explain. Ashley admitted they'd slept together, but stated it was before Drew's commitment to her. Ashley explained, what happened between her and Drew happened a long time ago. She had moved on since then; to someone she cared about a lot. But how had Lynn found out about her affair with Drew?

"Oh my God," Ashley said to herself after realizing their mother had spilled the beans. "It's not what you think. What happened, happen a long time ago," Ashley tried explaining in code. She didn't want her new boyfriend to hear what she was discussing with Lynn and attempted to conceal their conversation by covering her phone but couldn't muff the sounds of Lynn's screams.

"You must get a kick out of fucking my boyfriends. You even slept with Marshall, not that I give a damn, even though it hurt to know you were a better fuck than I?" Lynn acknowledged.

"That happened after you broke up with him," Ashley admitted.

"Oh my God, shut up with the excuses. I hope your new boyfriend doesn't find out that you're nothing but a got damn slut," Lynn screamed.

Perhaps the worst sound Ashley was force to listen to, was having to hear her sister crying over the phone. She hated to have hurt Lynn but her jealousy of her was too overpowering to resist. Ashley wanted to explain but Lynn refused to listen. She didn't want to hear any more of what Ashley had to say. She'd gotten the answers she needed and didn't want to talk anymore. Ashley and Drew were guilty as charged and she was through with both of them. Now knowing the truth, it should have been easy for Lynn to shun the both of them but doing so presented a problem. For one, she was carrying Drew's baby and she was still in love with him.

As for Ashley, it hadn't been her first rodeo, she had ridden every stallion Lynn was ever attractive to. Ashley had done so with her high school crushes, the first man she'd ever slept with and now Drew. But why had Ashley been so deceptive when it came to her and the men she loved? Lynn didn't have the answers but knew, it was morally wrong and downright disrespectful. How could she had been so naïve not to see what was going on under her eyes?

Maybe she knew the truth and didn't want to admit it to herself but it all made sense now. For months, Lynn pondered why Ashley seemed to have Drew wrapped around her finger. Whatever she suggested, Drew was quick to please her, whether he agreed with it or not; and then there were Ashley's greetings. She would always kiss Drew on his lips whenever they met. What should have been the obvious, Lynn chose to overlook and for doing so, her heart was left shattered.

Frustrated, Lynn abruptly ended her phone call with Ashley only to be faced with a return call from Drew. Refusing to take his call, Lynn dropped her phone in a trash can as she walked past it. She needed to be alone to think and decided what her next form of action was going to be. Leaving the clinic parking lot, Lynn made her way across the street with Constance following in hot pursuit. Stopping short of the city sidewalk, Lynn turned in frustration to face her mother. Keeping her feelings to herself, Lynn requested to be left alone. She wanted to absorb the shock she'd just encountered but needless to say, Constance refused to give her the time she was requesting. Instead, Constance went forth with her effort to convince Lynn to return to the clinic for her scheduled procedure. Disappointed that her mother would suggest such a thing after giving her the worse news of her life, Lynn looked at her mother in disgust before turning to walk away. Sensing Lynn was about to do something impulsive, Constance continued to follow her. The faster Lynn walked; the more difficult it became for Constance to keep up with her. With Constance in close pursuit, Lynn made a mad dash across the street in an effort to lose Constance in the lunch crowd but it was all for nought, because Constance remained hot on her trail. Lynn's inability to lose her mother prompted her to start running. She could barely see from the tears that were running down her face but Lynn wanted to be alone to gather her thoughts. She managed to temporarily lose Constance after blending in the lunch crowd but it hadn't hindered Constance from searching through the crowd until she found her.

311

It was urgent that Constance caught up with Lynn to prevent her from committing a spur of the moment decision she would regret for the rest of her life. Approaching the corner of the street, Constance forced her way through the crowd and got within arms-reach of Lynn. Seeing her mother hand about to grab hold of her, Lynn tried making a daring escape across the street but Constance was able to grab hold of her arm.

"Lynn, wait, let's talk about this," Constance pleaded.

Though pleading to talk, Lynn had heard enough. There weren't going to be anymore talking, Lynn was done. She wanted to get away to be alone but her mother was refusing to allow her to do so. Constance had a firm grip on Lynn's arm as Lynn tried everything in her power to break free. In an effort to break free, Lynn forcefully pulled away from her mother and in doing so, she lost her balance and stumbled from the sidewalk into on-coming traffic. Seeing what was about to happen, Constance screamed in horror as she saw Lynn staggering out into oncoming traffic. Trying to beat the light, the cars were speeding and couldn't stop. They made an effort to avoid striking Lynn but sadly, one car couldn't. The impact of Lynn striking its windshield, helicoptering Lynn into the air, over oncoming traffic, onto a parked car, before falling violently onto the sidewalk; striking her head on the curve.

Shocked by the horrendous act that transpired in front of her, Constance ran across the street to where Lynn was lying. Fortunately for Constance traffic had stopped, giving her clearance to reach Lynn. The sight of seeing Lynn's unconscious bloody body lying helpless in the street caused Constance to nearly passed out. Lynn was dying and there wasn't anything Constance could do to save her. Constance screamed for help as the medical staff from the clinic quickly arrived on scene to administer medical assistance. Everyone on scene was doing everything in their power to help save Lynn's life but she continued to be unresponsive. For the first time in her life, Constance felt helpless. Her baby girl was dying in front of her and there wasn't a damn thing she could do about it. Falling to her knees, Constance began praying to God, pleading for him to spare her daughter's life. It was because of her, Lynn lay dying on the street and to save her, Constance began bargaining with God. She asked to trade her life for Lynn's.

THE END